OXFORD LIBRARY OF
AFRICAN LITERATURE

General Editors

E. E. EVANS-PRITCHARD
G. LIENHARDT
W. H. WHITELEY

Oxford Library of African Literature

A SELECTION OF AFRICAN PROSE
I. Traditional Oral Texts
II. Written Prose
Compiled by W. H. WHITELEY
(*Two volumes*)

THE HEROIC RECITATIONS OF THE BAHIMA OF ANKOLE
By H. F. MORRIS

SOMALI POETRY
An Introduction
By B. W. ANDRZEJEWSKI *and* I. M. LEWIS

PRAISE-POEMS OF TSWANA CHIEFS
Translated and edited with an Introduction and Notes
by I. SCHAPERA

THE GLORIOUS VICTORIES OF 'ĀMDA ṢEYON, KING OF ETHIOPIA
together with THE HISTORY OF THE EMPEROR AND CEÔN OTHERWISE CALLED GÂBRA MAZCÂL BY PERO PAEZ
Translated and edited by G. W. HUNTINGFORD

THE CONTENT AND FORM OF YORUBA IJALA
By S. A. BABALỌLA

A SELECTION OF HAUSA STORIES
Compiled and translated
by H. A. S. JOHNSTON

AKAMBA STORIES
By JOHN S. MBITI

LIMBA STORIES AND STORY-TELLING

RUTH FINNEGAN

WIPF & STOCK · Eugene, Oregon

Wipf and Stock Publishers
199 W 8th Ave, Suite 3
Eugene, OR 97401

Limba Stories and Story-Telling
By Finnegan, Ruth

ISBN 13: 978-1-5326-4505-1
Publication date 12/5/2017
Previously published by Oxford University Press, 1967

PREFACE

ONE of the characteristics of Limba society is that it possesses a literature, albeit only an unwritten one. In long-drawn-out evening sessions stories are told with vivid gesture and dramatic effect and admired or echoed by enthusiastic listeners, riddles are propounded, and narratives interlaced with songs. In the business of the day too a literary flavour is often apparent: proverbs and parables sometimes embellish the speech of the more eloquent elders, a story may be used to make a point in some legal discussion, and special occasions for elaborate oratory are recognized and exploited. To a superficial observer the Limba might seem to be mainly preoccupied with the care of their upland rice farms or, the day's work over, with noisy carousals over their palm wine; but in fact much of their life is permeated by what is in its own way a literature.

This volume is devoted to certain aspects and examples of this Limba oral literature, and primarily to their stories. These stories are treated as a form of literature in its own right, worthy of study in literary terms. In the past it could be assumed without question that, in the case of non-literate African societies, it was not feasible to speak of their having a 'literature' at all; this arose partly from a narrow and strictly etymological definition of the term 'literature', and partly from the particular theoretical interests of those British social anthropologists who tended for a time to hold a monopoly in the study of such peoples. Consonant with these interests examples of what were classed as 'folktales' or 'myths' could either be ignored or else approached primarily in terms of some other aspect of the society—often its structure, values, or stability. But by now this point no longer needs to be lengthily argued. The increasing interest in African verbal art in its own right and the scope of the present 'Library of African Literature' speak for themselves. We no longer need to try to account for African stories, songs, or poetry in terms, as it were, of external causes, but can assume at the outset that it is suitable to regard them as a form of literature.

Limba stories, then, fall within the sphere of Limba literature. But, it must be stressed, they are not only literature, they are also *oral* literature. This simple but crucial characteristic implies peculiar interests and problems of its own; and it is this which dictates much of the discussion in the introductory chapters of this volume.

At the very outset this oral nature of Limba literature immediately raises the question of which parts of Limba speech, or of Limba formal speech, are to be included or excluded in a study of their literature. This sort of problem may, indeed, be involved in an analysis of many types of literature; but in the case of an unwritten literature it is raised in a particularly acute form. Among the Limba there are many formal linguistic usages which are thought of as attractive in themselves and suited to occasions. A certain formality of language is associated with speeches in law cases and the rhetorical harangues required at important funeral ceremonies. Many of the dramatic devices used by story-tellers to enhance the effect of their narrations are also employed, up to a point, in some vivid account of a recent event or a histrionic argument between two individuals. Prayers, invocations, and songs all have their required diction and form, related in various ways to those of the stories and the process of story-telling. In the case of an oral literature, therefore, it may be impossible to draw a clear-cut line between what could be classed as 'literature', and the formal, and in a sense literary, elements in other speech. In practice this volume deals with those forms which the Limba include under their term *mbɔrɔ*, a word which refers primarily to stories but also sometimes covers what we would more normally call riddles, proverbs, or, occasionally, historical narratives. Songs also frequently occur in the body of a story and the words of such songs are therefore included; I was not, however, able to make any systematic treatment of songs as a whole, and this account therefore deals only with Limba prose literature and not with their poetry. The stories presented here, then, have been singled out as representing Limba oral literature according to a rather arbitrary classification. However, it is a convenient and a real category. Limba stories are by any standards a type of 'oral literature' and the theoretical problems involved need not cause any difficulty provided it is remembered that here it is even less possible than with a written literature to draw any theoretical and final distinction between forms of linguistic expression; nor, indeed, is it possible to have a really complete view of Limba 'literature' without some consideration of style, rhetoric, and form in other contexts than those of the stories treated here.

A more significant consequence, perhaps, of the oral nature of Limba literature is the extent to which this form of art is fundamentally dependent on the actual delivery and the occasion on which it is narrated. This is an essential part of the artistry of Limba literature. Each narration is a performance in its own right and depends for its effect not only on the excellence of the narrator's composition but equally on the details of his performance—on the style of delivery, the gestures, the songs interspersed in the narration, and, not least, on the active participation of the audience. The living artistry and subtlety of Limba story-telling and hence of Limba stories are almost wholly lost when they are regarded as fixed texts on a page for a reader's eye.

It is for this reason in particular that I have given a long account of the details of oral delivery and stylistic devices in Limba story-telling.

This is not included just for pedantic or antiquarian motives; the reason is simply that without a knowledge of this essential aspect of Limba literature it is impossible to appreciate the complexity, or, indeed, the nature, of this form of art. From one point of view, perhaps, these Limba stories about people or animals are only simple ones; to some, indeed, the written translations here may seem to represent only a rather crude form of art; the stories are relatively short, uncomplicated, and lacking in certain of the characteristics of a sustained piece of written literature; furthermore several of the plots are not by any means unique to the Limba but also occur in examples of oral as well as written literature elsewhere. But when one also takes into account the artistry of the actual narration of these tales and the way in which an individual narrator makes, on each occasion, his own contribution to the traditional forms, then something of the truly *Limba* nature of these stories, and their complexity, begins to emerge. To grasp their literary impact one must go beyond the actual texts to the whole dramatic process of story-telling which gives them so much of their meaning and subtlety.

A related feature of this oral literature is the shifting and unfixed nature of the stories. There is no 'received' or correct text of any traditional story. Limba story-telling is a living art and the traditional themes and motifs find their realization in the actual performance, embellished on each separate occasion with differing dramatic devices, emphases, and wording, or with episodes or references peculiar to the occasion. Even the 'same' story told by the same story-teller may vary from narration to narration, in wording as well as enactment. Thus each performance has its unique qualities, and this facet too of Limba oral literature must be understood for a full appreciation of its nature.

Owing to the dependence of Limba stories on the particular occasion of their narration, the part taken by the story-teller is of central importance. It is he who orders and shapes the themes into a single story and, if he is a skilled story-teller, gives it effectiveness by his delivery and enactment of the plot. He unites in himself the roles of both composer and performer and it is his contribution in both these spheres that is crucial to the success or failure of any story. Thus this aspect also of Limba oral literature—the part of the story-teller—must be discussed.

Besides these consequences which follow from the oral nature of Limba literature, a further point of presentation is raised by the unfamiliarity, to an English reader, of the subjects and background of the stories. A full understanding of the point and nuances of Limba literature obviously also depends on a knowledge of the nature of Limba society—their occupations and preoccupations, their day-to-day life, the cycle of their year, their political or religious presuppositions. Only a brief indication of some of this background can be given in this volume. But it must be remembered that much of the impact of Limba literature, in the context in which it is actually delivered, depends on an implicit knowledge of this background, of the ways people are perceived to behave or intend, of the kinds of actions the Limba consider amusing or touching or tragic, and the sorts of events thought likely—or even wildly unlikely—to befall an individual.

Little has previously been published about the Limba, and what few comments have appeared in print have sometimes given a totally false picture.[1] This volume deals only with one aspect of their culture, their oral literature. Nevertheless it is a significant part of the whole of Limba life; for their experience of the human and the physical world round them is represented and mediated through their literature, the stories translated and commented on in this volume.

As well as giving some account of the culture of a little-known people, this volume may also be of interest in a wider context. The detailed discussion of composition and performance among a people who in one sense have not a particularly striking or complicated literature and yet can use it as a vehicle of subtle and dramatic expression, may be illuminating or stimulating for the study of others and perhaps serve to remove some possible misconceptions about the nature and artistry of oral literature.

[1] For example the extreme and much-quoted assertion of Sayers in 1927 that 'Limba is a very fourth-rate language in which, so far as my experience goes, it is almost impossible to get any fine shades of meaning expressed . . .': E. F. Sayers in *Sierra Leone Studies* (old series), 10, 1927, p. 113.

ACKNOWLEDGEMENTS

DURING the research for this volume I was dependent on the help of many people, both in the field and while writing, and without their kindness I would have found the task impossible. First I must thank those who made the fieldwork possible by financing my two visits. A grant from the Colonial Social Science Research Council[1] (C.D.W. Scheme R.1212) supported me during the early part of my first visit in 1961, and this was supplemented by a generous grant from the Horniman Fund. My second visit was made possible by the kind award by Somerville College, Oxford, of the Alice Horsman Travelling Fellowship. To these three sources I wish to make most grateful and sincere acknowledgement. I also wish to thank the Warden and Fellows of Nuffield College, Oxford, for the award of a studentship which enabled me to write up the results of this field research in 1962–3.

I spent a year in 1961 and about two months in 1963–4 working in Limba country, mainly in the eastern half. During this time I received much kindness and hospitality from many people in the area and elsewhere in Sierra Leone which made my stay a pleasant and a worth-while one. The administrative officers in the north were both generous and informative and I owe them special thanks; I would like to express particular gratitude to Mr. and Mrs. G. R. B. Blake, Mr. L. Flower, and Lieut.-Commander P. J. Eckford for the great kindness and forbearance they showed me. I would also like to thank the many members of the American Wesleyan Mission who helped me, particularly the Rev. and Mrs. Wolsey; and Mr. and Mrs. A. Wanstall, Mr. D. F. Finnegan, and other members of 'Delco', the Sierra Leone Development Company. The Principal and staff of the University College of Sierra Leone at Fourah Bay also showed me great kindness; I am particularly grateful to Mr. and Mrs. K. Dalton and Miss A. Spackman for their hospitality; above all I would like to thank Dr. and Mrs. H. Turner for the way they welcomed and introduced me to Sierra Leone—without them my stay would have been very much less pleasant. I was also fortunate in having interesting discussions while in Sierra Leone with Dr. and Mrs. D. Dalby, Dr. and Mrs. P. Kup, Dr. J. Dawson, and Dr. D. P. Gamble. But my greatest gratitude for help during my period of fieldwork is to the many Limba who made my stay fruitful and possible; to the chiefs in whose chiefdoms I was welcomed to stay (particularly the late Alimami Pompoli II of Bumban, Alimami Salifu of

[1] This body has now been abolished and its interests transferred to the Ministry of Overseas Development.

Kakarima, Alimami Gbawuru II of Kabala, and Alimami Seku II of Kamabai); to those of every village and age who taught and helped me; to my assistant Suri Kamara whose support and help were invaluable; and, above all, to the story-tellers who told both the stories in this volume and many others.

For academic help and stimulus my greatest debt is to my teacher Prof. E. E. Evans-Pritchard; only he can know the immense amount I owe to his advice, criticism, and support. I am also grateful for teaching or discussion to Prof. J. Berry, who first started me on the path to learn Limba; to Dr. Godfrey Lienhardt and other members of the Oxford Institute of Social Anthropology; to Professor Wilfred Whiteley; to Mr. Thomas Kargbo; and to my husband, Dr. David Murray, who has helped in ways too numerous to mention both in the writing of this volume and during my second visit to Limba country in 1963. Finally, I would like to thank my parents for the many ways in which, perhaps unknown to themselves, they have contributed to this volume; it is to them that I would wish to dedicate it.

R. F.

September 1964

CONTENTS

PART I

LIMBA LIFE AND STORY-TELLING

1

THE LIMBA

I. INTRODUCTORY

THE Limba are rice farmers living in the hilly savannah country of northern Sierra Leone. There are probably a little under 200,000 of them in this area; in addition, some thousands have gone, temporarily or permanently, to Freetown and other of the larger towns of Sierra Leone, or have travelled south to tap and sell palm wine to the local people. In Limba country to the north, modern communications and Western education have been more recent developments than in the south; there are relatively few Western-educated Limba, and, more than many of the peoples of Sierra Leone, the Limba have a reputation for retaining much of their traditional custom and culture, a culture of which the oral literature is an important part.

The seven chiefdoms into which the Limba are at present[1] divided extend over roughly 1,900 square miles. However, around and among these Limba chiefdoms dwell many other peoples with whom the Limba come in contact. Their closest neighbours are the Temne in the south, Koranko in the east, and Susu in the west; and the Limba have much in common with these neighbouring peoples. Throughout much of this century, there has also been an influx from the north of Fulas and Mandingoes, whose way of life is distinct from that of the Limba; they keep herds of cattle, build up great wealth as traders, and have won a reputation for their learned practice of Islam. The Limba, keeping to their indigenous custom of rice farming with little division of labour and little or no Koranic learning, contrast themselves constantly with these foreign peoples among them; they have yet been greatly influenced by them and there are relatively frequent references to them in Limba oral literature.

There is no record of when the Limba first came to this area of Sierra Leone, but it is likely to have been several centuries ago.[2] Towards the middle of the last century they seem to have been divided roughly into three main spheres of influence, ruled over by the chiefs of Bumban in

[1] Unless otherwise indicated descriptions apply to conditions in 1961.

[2] A. d'Almada marks them on his map in roughly their present area, next to the 'Temenes' (Temne), *Tratado breve dos Rios de Guiné*, 1594.

the east, Bafodea in the north, and Tonko Limba in the west. This situation was upset first by the bloody incursions of Samory (or Samodu) with his armed Sofa horsemen in the 1880's and then, more permanently, by the British Declaration of a Protectorate over the area in 1896. At first the Protectorate was only lightly administered, especially in the remoter north; but this development still resulted in many changes. The early large chiefdoms were split into smaller units, roads were gradually built, missions settled, and a few schools opened. With the consequent demand for labour in the Freetown area and the desire to obtain cash, young men went down country to look for work and wages. Today there is constant coming and going between the north and the south and people travel daily through Limba country, and elsewhere, in the great passenger lorries that drive along the laterite roads. Yet in spite of such changes it would not be true to say that Limba interest in story-telling has vanished. On the contrary, new themes and new interests are added to the old as returned migrants or city men introduce their new interests to the traditional themes told and embroidered in the up-country Limba areas.

The Limba speak a 'West Atlantic' language, one of the *Kissi-Landoma* sub-group.[1] There are several different dialects and a man from the far north finds difficulty at first in understanding one of the southern Limba dialects. Nevertheless, in spite of the differences—which the Limba delight in discussing—they are agreed that 'the Limba language is one; the Limba people are one'.

2. LIMBA VILLAGES

Beside the winding laterite roads or the narrow bush paths that run through Limba country in northern Sierra Leone are grouped compact clusters of thatched huts or 'pan'-roofed houses. It is in these villages that Limba social life is centred, and from these that they go out to make their rice farms on the sides of the hills around them. The villages are the most common settings for the various stories told by the men as they sit relaxed by their huts in the late evenings, and it is therefore important to understand something of their appearance and significance.

Some of them are perched high on the tops of hills, often surrounded by a thick growth of great cotton trees, a relic of the defences necessary during the unsettled times in the far north during the last century. These villages are reached by steep winding paths up which both visitors and residents returning home from their farms in the evenings must labour to reach the settled community at the top, and up which the women travel many times daily with their water containers balanced on their heads. Other villages, often with larger houses, markets, and stores, lie on the two main roads that branch up to the north through Limba

[1] Westermann and Bryan, *Languages of West Africa*, pp. 12–13.

country and along which many passenger lorries travel each day. Yet others are approached by narrow paths leading through the bush or by rough earth tracks cleared by the local people in the hope that motor vehicles may at last enter their settlements. All the villages are separated from each other by tracts of bush—in the south open savannah forest and farm bush, cultivated or fallow, and in the sparsely populated north by grassland or scrub interspersed with farms.

The size and appearance of Limba villages vary considerably. Kabala, for example, the largest of Limba settlements, with a population of several thousands, is the headquarters of the most northerly of the administrative districts of Sierra Leone, Koinadugu. It is a flourishing and busy town set among hills, originally inhabited by the local Limba and their neighbours the Koranko, but now also crammed with visiting or settled traders, mainly Fulas and Mandingoes, and containing representatives of practically all the fifteen or so linguistic groups of Sierra Leone. There is a large and crowded market surrounded by Lebanese shops and some concrete houses; interspersed among these more solid buildings and towards the outskirts of the town are many square 'pan'-roofed houses built of mud blocks, thatched houses, or round huts of mud and wood. On one side of the town are grouped the administrative buildings, with offices, a prison, and a hospital. On another lies the compound of the Limba Paramount Chief of the area, made up of the households of his relations and close followers, with their families. This compound is the focus for most of the Limba political or religious activity in the town; people continually come to discuss or negotiate with the chief, sacrifices are performed in the open space between the houses, and in the evenings stories may be told.

But most Limba settlements are on a smaller scale than Kabala. Those on the main road, especially Paramount Chiefs' towns, are the nearest in size to Kabala, and often have several large and impressive houses, stores, and a large proportion of 'pan' compared to thatched roofs. Such villages or towns may have about 80–100 houses. Most villages are smaller than this, often with 20–50 houses or huts, those in the more densely populated south of Limba country tending to be larger. The more remote and poorer the village, the greater the number of round thatched huts. A headman or wealthy elder will always try to build himself a square 'pan'-roofed house, usually with money brought or sent back by relatives who have gone down country for paid work; the number of such houses seems constantly to be increasing. But there are still very many villages which basically conform to the traditional pattern—made up of round thatched huts, each with a common central room and smaller private rooms to the side. The houses are normally inhabited by one large family—a man with several wives and children, and perhaps his old mother and some younger brothers with their wives; and the village is often divided into three or four compounds consisting of a ring of houses facing on to a central circular space, each compound inhabited mainly by those connected by kinship.

In both the small village and the large town it is in these open circular spaces or compounds that much of Limba life is conducted. Rice is laid out there to dry on huge mats, dances are performed, sacrifices and rituals carried out, and the dead buried. Between the compounds there are often high fences of cane grass which dwarf the children as they run between them. In the centre of the village is usually built the hut of the chief or headman who 'owns' the settlement, a member of the ruling family whose ancestors first, it is said, cut down the bush to make a village in that spot. In his shaded veranda people gather morning and evening to bring greetings, exchange news and views, and hear the elders argue cases. Not far from the village is the watering-place where people go to bathe and the women walk daily to wash the clothes and fetch water; and just by the entrance to the village is the smith's open hut, the focus for much of the men's secret ritual. A few fruit trees and bushes can be seen scattered among the huts, and often there are tall poles bearing a white flag erected on some ceremonial occasion, and a single large tree said to have been planted as a 'sacrifice' by the first founder of the village.

Although Limba villages vary in size and appearance in different parts of the country, they are in many ways alike in what they mean to those who live there and in the activities carried on within them. Each is called by the Limba word *mɛti*, a village (or town); a human being, *wɔ mɛti*, is literally 'one of a village'. The village is regarded as the central community, and those who live for a time in the small settlements or hamlets of two or three huts very near the farms are obliged to come to the village proper for all important occasions. Within the village there is economic co-operation, especially at the busy times of the farming year. It also forms a political unit under its own chief or headman and is represented by its spokesman at larger gatherings. Sacrifices are made on behalf of the village and those who are at the farms come there for all major rituals like the initiation of their children. When adults die they must be brought to the village for burial.

Whatever the scale or location of a village, much the same characteristic activities are pursued there. Groups of men can be seen gathered on the verandas of houses, especially those of the chief or leading elders, taking part in the typical Limba activity of formal speech-making—perhaps a dispute is being settled and the contenders reconciled, perhaps some negotiation is being conducted, contract solemnly ratified, or announcement formally made. The smith's hut at the edge of most Limba villages is another centre of activity in the busy farming season as the smiths and young men sharpen their hoes and matchets for the following day's work. The men spend their leisure standing at their upright looms in mid-compound weaving long strips of cotton cloth, twining huge baskets for rice, or building or rethatching their houses in the dry season. Morning and evening they go to their palm trees for wine, and sit with their companions in special clearings in the bush, drinking and talking together; some wine is brought back to the village as a gift to a wife's people or to the chief, and the drink goes the rounds among the company. The women seem always busy, yet proceed with an air of leisure and humour. They are continually spreading out the rice to dry in the sun, then pounding it with wooden pestles and cooking it in great iron pots over open wood fires at the backs of the houses. They look after their children, carry firewood and water, or, when they have time, sit to spin the local cotton, sing to their children, or dance with their friends. On the low front wall of the hut wares are laid out for sale by the women; trade is conducted on a larger scale in the few big markets in the towns, and the women can make much money over the months as they sell their oranges, cassava, or tobacco 'by penny, penny, penny'.

From these villages, both men and women go out to tend the upland rice farms on the hillsides. At some seasons of the year the village seems deserted, for the work in the farms demands all the available people. The houses stand empty with only the hens and goats running through the compounds and an occasional woman or old man sitting by. But at other times, and during the evenings, the village is full of life and noise, with people exchanging news, stopping to gossip, calling their children, eating, or joining in formal speaking, dancing, or singing.

The Limba village, then, wherever situated, is the main centre for most purposes in life—economic, political, social, and religious. Those who go down country to seek work often continue to look to their own villages and even when they do not return still send back money and gifts, or welcome and help visitors from their homes. The village is the focus of social activity and it is not surprising that so often in Limba stories it forms the context of the action, and a familiar and evocative setting can thus be pictured by the listeners as the backcloth of the plot.

3. RICE FARMING

The main occupation and preoccupation of the Limba is their rice farming. The cultivation and consumption of rice is a matter of significance not only in everyday life but also in their literature. Almost all Limba are in fact rice farmers, in this contrasting with the cattle-keeping and trading Fula or Mandingo in the same area; even those who have other sources of wealth as smith, diviner, or even chief, still normally control and work their own rice farms. Though there are also important secondary crops such as 'millet',[1] swamp rice and cassava, dry upland

[1] *Digitaria exilis.*

rice is the staple and the Limba regard themselves primarily as rice-producing people. The growing and eating of rice is, in Limba eyes, one of the main characteristics which differentiate them from the other peoples with whom they have come in contact.

The division and organization of the Limba year centre round the rice-farming cycle. This year begins in March with a sacrifice to the dead ancestors and the clearing of the bush left fallow for several years; this is soon followed by the burning and reburning of the felled bush. The next phase is the busiest time of the whole year: this is the sowing and hoeing in of the new seed, when the young men and boys form co-operative companies, hoeing in haste to finish the work before the heavy rains begin. After this come the long months while the rice is growing and the women go to weed the luxuriant growth in the farms, forming companies of their own to finish the work quickly, accompanied by song, drum, and dance; then follow several weeks during which the children must guard the ripening crop by chasing off the marauding animals and birds. At last, about October, the crop is ripe for harvesting. The families reap and eat the grown rice, and a great dance is held as the men thrash the gathered grain. Then comes the time of rest and rejoicing when people eat their fill of rice and have leisure to travel, marry, and perform ceremonies. Thus each year proceeds through its various phases of work—clearing, burning, hoeing, weeding, chasing, and harvesting—and the due rituals and ceremonies are co-ordinated with the progress of the year and of the rice.

Rice farming for the Limba is more than a merely economic or chronological matter. Each agricultural phase has its own associations of co-operation between friend and kin, and the characteristic songs, speeches, drums, and dances that accompany it. Farming is regarded as a matter of excitement and value in itself as well as a necessity and labour, and people of all ages speak with enthusiasm and interest about the growing of the rice, recounting the dances and songs that accompany rice farming or describing in conversation or story the various phases of the farming year in a way full of meaningful and fascinating associations for the Limba who hear them. People sing in the farms, even when they are alone, because 'we are happy there. There is our work. That is *our* books, our food.' In several of the stories rice farming is shown to be the destiny of the Limba given them by Kanu (God) in contrast to the books and money given to the white men, or the Koranic knowledge of the Fulas. The story in which the giving of rice to the Limba is depicted, *Kanu gave food*, was narrated in a tone of drama, almost miracle, as the various phases of the rice-growing year were described, one after the other—the way the set operations were performed, the sun and rain came out at the right seasons, the rice grew seeds and became ripe; 'and when they had finished harvesting it was much more than what they had sowed'.

Rice is also regarded as the main food. Though other foods have their importance, specially in the period just before the rice harvest, rice is always assumed to be the preferred and most honourable food of all. Even in the wet season, for instance, when others are having to make do with millet, the local chief tries to keep a store of rice to give publicly to visitors; he would be ashamed to offer them only millet. The Limba regard the eating of rice as one of the characteristics of a human being, and in their literature the inhumanity of a monster is emphasized by his refusal to eat rice.

The actual eating of rice also has its own customs. Men, women, and children usually eat in separate groups, but handfuls of food from the common dish may be given as a sign of honour or affection to someone outside the circle. Great emotional significance also attaches to the 'scrapings' of the pot; this part belongs by right to the woman or girl who has cooked and she can give it as a special gift to whoever she pleases—perhaps her favourite child, a close friend, or a lover. Thus in the story of *The hunter and the three twins*, a real impact can be achieved by the mere mention that the mother in her joy and affection gave her returned husband and children not only their expected shares of cooked food but all the extra scrapings as well; and the various circumstances and associations of eating form a constant and popular theme in Limba oral literature.

Rice, then, whether raw or cooked, is an object of constant interest. When, as so often in the stories, references are made to the cultivation, preparing, cooking, or eating of rice, the meaning is far more rich and full of overtones to a Limba than would be possible with any foreign reader. Manifold associations are evoked—of song and dance in the farms, drumming, co-operation, the preparation of food by the women, the customs associated with eating, and, finally, the sight of the rice gradually coming up in the fields, becoming brilliant green in the rain, developing seeds, and growing ripe and yellow for harvest. The constant references to rice farming in Limba stories do more than merely set the scene or give a chronological framework; they add an extra dimension of meaning and vividness to the whole narrative.

4. CHIEFS

Among the Limba the principle of chiefship is of the greatest significance and most Limba would find it difficult to conceive of social life at all in its absence. The central point of each Limba village, to which a stranger is always first directed, is the house of the local chief, however slight his authority may be. He himself looks to the larger sub-chiefs who control the area in which his village lies, and they in turn are bound to the Paramount Chief of the whole area by whose authority all those in his chiefdom carry on their daily lives or hold their respective positions. Though in fact Limba Paramount Chiefs rule over no great area—the biggest of the seven Limba chiefdoms is only 372 square miles in all—the institution of chiefship is an important one to the Limba. In their oral literature too chiefship is a frequent subject, and in many stories winning the chiefship is the conclusion and climax.

However, the actual position of chiefs is not so simple. There are several grades of chiefs, and their duties, aims, and organization have undergone various changes over the last century, not least with the British declaration of the Protectorate in 1896. The present position is that each of the seven Limba chiefdoms is ruled over by a Paramount Chief elected from the hereditary ruling family of the area. He is helped by a Tribal Authority composed of village heads and local elders, a Speaker, sub-chiefs, and a President of the official chiefdom court. He is recognized by the Sierra Leone Government and is responsible for such matters as the collection of local taxes. Below him are six to eight sub-chiefs who have authority over the various 'sections' of the chiefdom, and below this again are the heads of villages. Strictly only the Paramount Chief of a chiefdom should be called a 'chief' (*gbaku*), and it is he who represents the ideal chiefship of which the Limba primarily think. But to a lesser degree all those with authority also partake of the virtues and functions of the paradigm—sub-chiefs, heads of villages, even wealthy elders who undertake some of the functions of a chief; and the usual word for chief is sometimes, in a secondary sense, attached to such people. Thus all Limba society is composed of grades of individuals, each with authority on the model of a chief, each, even down to the head of a family group, acting as the centre of his own particular unit, all holding their authority 'by grace of the chief' who owns the whole.

The nature of Limba chiefship and of people's views about it, both now and viewed historically, may emerge best through a brief description of three Limba chiefs. These include two contemporary chiefs and one historical figure, Suluku.

Suluku of Bumban is one of the most famous chiefs in Limba history and tradition. He held power in the late nineteenth century over one of the three main spheres of influence into which Limba country was then divided. Various stories are recounted both of his great and warlike power, and of the way in which he held his country in peace and 'spoke' between his people. He ruled from his centre in Bumban, a plain between two great rocky hills which guard the entrance to the valley where his descendants still live.

His power and position as one of the leading chiefs in northern Sierra Leone, in control of one of the most important towns on the trade route to the north, is well attested in written as well as oral sources, for he was visited and mentioned by European travellers and administrators.

Governor Sir Charles King-Harman, for example, reports that in 1901 he went to Bumban 'to see the old chief Suluku, one of the most powerful and influential chiefs in the Protectorate. . . . Suluku gave me a cordial reception and came to visit me in great state, gorgeously apparelled and escorted by sub-chiefs, headmen, and two of his wives, who assiduously fanned him or wiped off the perspiration as it appeared on his face and neck. . . . In reply to a casual reference to the hut-tax Suluku poohpoohed the idea of any trouble in the matter. "I am Suluku" was sufficient to indicate his authority and position in the matter.'[1]

Limba traditions also speak frequently of Suluku's great authority. It is said that he had one hundred wives and many slaves and cattle, and that people from all over the north of Sierra Leone used to come to Bumban to 'greet him', have their cases settled by him, and bring gifts of rice and wine. He in his turn received them and gave them presents to take home. Many magic powers are attributed to him. He could, it is narrated, transform himself into some other shape in order to travel round and survey his chiefdom, and is sometimes said to have been the son of the powerful spirit Kumba who helped him to gain and keep his position. Stories are told about the way in which he defended the Limba from the invading and marauding Sofa horsemen in the 1880's, and his descendants in the modern Biriwa still speak with pride and drama of his great deeds and the awe in which he was regarded by all surrounding peoples.

Suluku is thus one of the most famous characters in Limba history. Those directly connected with him pass on the actual traditions they heard from their fathers about his deeds. To those in the remoter villages he is a more mythical figure and many wonderful stories of his magical powers are still told and retold in various forms, narrated with awe and admiration. He has come to represent the ideal of the power to which a Limba chief could attain, winning respect not only from the Limba but from European visitors as well.

Unlike the great Suluku, and yet sharing in some of his ascribed attributes, is a more modern chief, Alimami Salifu of Kakarima in Kasonko, in the centre of Limba country. His tiny chiefdom has recently been amalgamated with another, but he still acts and considers himself as a Paramount Chief, a position he was elected to in 1945. In appearance he could be said to typify the characteristic Limba picture of a traditional chief—a long flowing robe of strong native cloth, open leather sandals, an indigo turban wound round his head, leather amulet on his chest, and metal charms on wrists and ankles. Like any Limba elder he visits his farm to help and direct the work there and view the progress of the rice. He also makes more formal expeditions accompanied by his followers, one of them always carrying the chief's drum; he travels through his

[1] King-Harman, *Visits to the Protectorate*, p. 8.

chiefdom and round the area of which his little chiefdom now forms part, to be present at the larger gatherings—initiations in the various villages, 'memorial' rites for dead chiefs or important elders, or ceremonies at the central town where the new Paramount Chief lives. But most of his time is spent in his own village dealing with lengthy cases, negotiations, and speech-making. Morning and evening people crowd into his veranda and long speeches are made. These are, at the conclusion, summed up by Alimami Salifu who speaks with rhetorical emphasis, often striding about the floor, throwing back the long sleeves of his gown as he gestures to emphasize a point or using the abrupt alternation of shouting and near whisper to create a dramatic effect. On other occasions he receives strangers who have come to visit him bringing news or merely in greeting; again long speeches of welcome and compliment are delivered, gifts are ceremonially exchanged, and perhaps sacrifices jointly made. When a large village ceremony or sacrifice is due it is he who supervises the arrangements, often providing a beast from his own small herd of cattle, and, in return, ceremonially receiving contributions from the visitors and residents. He knows the traditions of the early days, and passes these on with authority to the young men of his own household.

He is ready to use what real powers he possesses, so that people are sometimes afraid to make open complaint against him; he is also ambitious for his village, struggling, for example, to have a motor road built up the steep slopes of the hill on which Kakarima is perched. Yet even those who sometimes secretly murmur about his power still assume that without him to speak for them or remember and recount to them the wisdom of 'the old people', their social life and activity could not continue as at present. From the point of view of the inhabitants he is an essential focus for the life of the village and the chiefdom.

The same is true of Alimami Seku II, the chief recently[1] elected over the chiefdom of Biriwa. He lives in Kamabai, the village on the modern main road which has now assumed dominance over nearby Bumban, the historic home of Suluku. Alimami Seku belongs to a collateral branch of Suluku's family, and, according to Limba custom, was chosen from among those in the ruling family eligible to succeed the last chief of Biriwa. Unlike the majority of Limba in his chiefdom, and, indeed, most of his close followers, he is a Muslim. This accords with the increasing interest in Islam among many of the chiefs in northern Sierra Leone, and also forms for him a valuable link with the Muslim Mandingoes now widely settled in the Biriwa chiefdom. He is younger than many Limba chiefs, and takes great interest in such matters as a piped water supply, control of palm-wine selling and drinking, and the order and cleanliness of Kamabai which is now one of the more flourishing

[1] Late 1963.

Limba towns; he also has relatively frequent contact with the District Officer and other Government officials. Having spent some time in the diamond area in the south he is popular with the young men who travel to or have returned from there. At the same time he knows how to please the elders by his courtesy and ability to speak, and by his respect for the old people and old traditions. His adherence to Islam has not prevented him from carrying out lavish sacrifices for the peace and unity of his chiefdom according to the traditional ceremonies. Since his accession, in accordance with Limba custom, he has been brought many gifts by those living in the various sections and villages of the chiefdom, and he has therefore joined in the requisite performance of the long speeches of acknowledgement and thanks that must accompany these. Over the months of his rule Alimami Seku has slaughtered many cattle, especially at the Christmas festivities when many people crowded into Kamabai, and has given great feasts for the local and visiting people. Thus he has quickly gained a reputation both for kindness and generosity, and also for his rhetorical ability; he has the power to speak with great drama and effectiveness, and embroiders his speech with proverb and story.

In these three examples can be seen something of the general functions of Limba chiefs, and the Limba view of these. The central responsibility of any chief is to 'speak'—that is to arbitrate between people, reconcile contenders and decide cases, and make formal speeches of many kinds. Formal cases have now, by law, been transferred to a recognized chiefdom court under a court president, but chiefs still widely continue the older traditions of speaking among people. The ability to 'speak' well is continually given as an essential quality of anyone with authority, especially a chief; without a chief, it is often said, there would be fighting and quarrelling everywhere; and, in practice, chiefs do seem to spend much of their time in formal speaking with and between their people.

A chief is also expected to be generous and hospitable. This can be seen both in everyday practice and in some of the literature—in the story, for example, of Kanu giving the chiefship to the one man who was willing to entertain him. A chief receives many gifts of produce and money from people locally, and, if a Paramount Chief, nowadays a substantial salary as well. In theory—and largely in practice—much of this is then redistributed among the people in occasional gifts, help to those in special difficulties, conspicuous hospitality to strangers, and lavish contributions on such important occasions as initiations, sacrifices, or funerals. In addition, a chief should know everything of importance that is going on in his chiefdom. He must be told of all major events such as festivals, big sacrifices, violent quarrels, or deaths, and, when appropriate, should send a gift or message or be present himself.

People are continually coming in to the chief's house to bring him news or just to greet him, and he is as continually sending back messages of instruction, condolence, or greeting, or replying in formal speeches to those who approach him. He 'owns' his whole chiefdom and thus must know it, and has general responsibility and authority over it, symbolized by his possession of the chiefly drum.

Thus a Limba chief—whether an important Paramount Chief or a mere local headman—spends much of his time speaking with people, settling cases, and receiving reports. Unlike traditional chiefs in some other parts of Sierra Leone, Limba chiefs are accessible and close to the people; in spite of the typical regalia and chiefly dignity, they are not essentially different or removed from others, or separated from them by a hierarchy of officials. Nevertheless, in Limba eyes, their society could not function without a chief at the centre—a recognized centre for settlement of disputes, reconciliation of interests, and redistribution of both knowledge and economic goods. And it is 'by grace of the chief'—a common phrase—that men act and hold their positions.

That chiefs here, as elsewhere, sometimes abuse their position or use force against the less powerful is, of course, true. Indeed, provided the chief concerned is an historical one or living at some distance from the speaker, it is implied that there is something admirable in a chief who, like Suluku, had and used great powers. But in the present, kindness, wisdom, and oratorical ability are explicitly expected of the chiefs. Although, clearly, not all of them always act up to these ideals, nevertheless the Limba picture of the ideal qualities of a chief is one that in many ways is true to the facts; without the presence of chiefs as in some sense a focus for social action, Limba society could not function as it now does, and their society and their view of their own actions would perforce be different.

Chiefs and chiefship are, as already mentioned, common topics in the stories. The experience which contemporary Limba have of the nature and ideals of chiefship naturally gives meaning to their literature. However, it should be made clear that the picture of chiefs presented in the stories often does not correspond to the facts of Limba society today. In Limba as in other literature poetic licence and exaggeration is one among several devices for enhancing a story. To describe a chief as having huge possessions of gold or unlimited power, perhaps to kill all strangers who fail a certain test, is a recognizable and an attractive exaggeration of certain aspects of chiefship which are known on a moderate scale to all Limba. Another factor may be the tendency to archaize. Though Limba chiefs have probably in fact never possessed all the powers and unparalleled riches attributed to them in story, it does seem probable that some of the nineteenth-century chiefs, such as Suluku, were both more warlike and ruled over wider areas than the present-day chiefs. Though there have been many detailed changes in their position, these are not often reflected in the literature. There are few or no references in the stories to Speaker, President, Section Chief, tax, police, or District Commissioner, and it is the native and traditional followers and functions of the chief that are stressed rather than modern administrative offices or officials. Governmental signs of power are not, in most stories about chiefs, mentioned so much as the traditional symbols of authority, such as the chief's drum, his chair, head-dress, long gown, and, sometimes, whip; it is these which are most commonly spoken of as being given to the new chief in the stories.

The exaggerated picture of a chief, then, reflects the common tendency in the stories to exaggerate riches and numbers. In this case it serves to enhance one of the common images—the traditional chief, secure in his power and wealth, untouched, apparently, by the modern innovations of elections, taxes, or government administration. It is for this happy position of chiefship that the heroes of stories are so often pictured as striving.

5. MARRIAGE AND THE FAMILY

Marriage is an important topic in Limba conversation and literature. For a young man the marriage to his first wife marks a major step forward in his social and economic status within the village, comparable in importance only to his initiation into manhood; now for the first time he is in a position to cultivate a private strip of farm for his own use and that of his family, and to have legitimate children of his own to work for and honour him. The men therefore await marriage with great expectancy, all the more so as, especially in the case of a first marriage, the arrangements are hard, expensive, and protracted. Corresponding to this, the theme of the difficulties of wooing and marrying a wife is very common, and without some knowledge of the background the effectiveness of this theme might not be fully apparent.

The marriage negotiations are long and involved. Girls are often betrothed in childhood, so a young man may have to wait many years for the wife that is promised to him. He may see her gradually growing up over long years—first learning to walk and talk a little, being weaned, growing bigger month after month, beginning to take pleasure in the gifts of clothes or ornaments brought to her, and then, at last, the great occasion when, between about twelve and fifteen years old, she is initiated into womanhood in the *bondo* society, and she and the other new initiates are brought out of their month's seclusion in the bush and lined up, oiled and adorned, on mats in the village compound. This ceremony is one of the main occasions of the year and is often referred to in the stories; the future husbands dance ecstatically, wild with joy that their wives are at last women and will soon be given to them. Soon afterwards the husband will pay over the main bulk of the bride-wealth he must give her parents, in addition to the many gifts and services he has provided for them over the earlier years and the constant, and sometimes wearing, deference he has had to show them. His wife is then at last given to him—an occasion for rejoicing in real life, a sign of triumphant success in the conclusion of a story. This whole process of wooing a wife is one of the most crucial in any man's career and it is not surprising that the stories should contain so many references to it, references which are found effective and pointed by the Limba audiences to whom these stories are addressed.

The men wish, if possible, to have many wives, though in practice this is usually only achieved by chiefs or village elders. The reasons the Limba give for their ambitions in marriage are quite simple—'rice and people'. These two go together: if they have many wives, and thus children and dependants, they will be in a position to make a larger farm and produce more rice; and rice in its turn brings the possibility of wooing yet more wives and attracting other people by lavish hospitality and show.

Since rice and children are the central concerns of marriage many of the duties of husband and wife hinge on these two aspects. Each has a part to play in the cycle of rice farming—the husband must clear the bush and hoe in the seed, the wife is in charge of the weeding, and both join in the final harvesting. The relations of husband and wife are often represented in terms of their sharing of rice. A man who suspects his wife of unfaithfulness sometimes says that what she has done is to blow on the sauce to separate off the poor part for her husband and keep the rich sauce underneath for her secret lover; and when a man complains of his wife in a hearing before the chief and elders he may speak, with great dramatic fervour, of the way in which *his* rice was secretly given away to another man—'she went and gave the rice to him; and he went off, *fuuu*, right off with the rice!' The other main interest of marriage is children, and much turns on this aspect. Children are an essential part of a successful marriage, for not only is a prosperous farm likely to result from their co-operative labour, but after the father's death, he, with the other ancestors, will be remembered in prayer and sacrifice. Special rituals are performed so that a wife may bear many children, and wives are intimately concerned with the rights of their own children as against those of their co-wives. It is over children that friction often arises in Limba marriage—the husband may be accused of showing favouritism among the children, or co-wives may quarrel bitterly on this score, often through jealousy that one has more or healthier children than another.

Though marriage is assumed to be a necessary aim for both men and women, and people continually speak of the mutual and very real interdependence of husband and wife, the Limba also at times see marriage as involving conflict. Many of the cases that are heard at small local courts before chief and elders are concerned with quarrels between husband and wife or with the more drastic cases where a wife has left her husband for another man and a refund of the bridewealth is therefore being demanded. Relations between husband and wife are a frequent object of direct or allusive comment in Limba oral literature; many of the stories about the greedy anti-social spider and his wife Kayi treat of this topic, the spider constantly trying to get the better of his wife.

Corresponding to this realization of the potential frictions involved in marriage, Limba men have a somewhat ambivalent attitude to their wives and to women in general. It is assumed on the one hand that one of the most important things for any man to win is a wife and that without her help he cannot achieve his aims of wealth or honour. Yet at the same time the men are continually speaking of how bad and troublesome wives are. They complain—sometimes, it seems, with some justification—that 'as soon as you shut your eyes, they are out of the house after another man; you can't trust them at all'. Limba women, though they are in theory subject to their husbands and generally considered inferior to men, are nevertheless in many ways independent. In the remoter areas they spend much of their time farming their own plots of land on which their husbands may help but the produce of which is owned by the women. In the villages on the main roads the women have specially good opportunities to earn large amounts by marketing and sometimes have a larger cash income than their husbands. They also frequently go off to visit their parents, before whom their husbands are always in a position of inferiority, and to attend meetings of their own *bondo* society, strictly closed to men. Besides this there is always the possibility that a woman may decide to leave her husband for another man, and although there are various pressures put on a woman to prevent this, they are not always effective and the husband may be helpless. Unlike a mother or even to some extent a sister, wives are not permanently bound to a man; they are unrelated, untrustworthy, and always liable to go off.

The view of women as independent or treacherous in their role as wives is also common in story-telling, an activity which is almost exclusively a masculine one. The wife who tricks her husband for love of another man is one of the conventional motifs in Limba literature. Sara, for example, is promised the chiefship by Kanu but, because his wife betrays the secret to her lover, nearly fails to gain it; finally, however, the virtuous husband triumphs and is declared the rightful chief. Such references to the behaviour of wives have a real point for the

Limba who hear or tell the stories. Wives are sometimes the expected aim and support of any man, and yet, very frequently, evil and treacherous as well.

Other relationships within the family are also of great importance. They affect both individuals and the general structure of a village as a whole, since families form the basic units for economic co-operation and ownership. A father, for example, is a very significant figure. He holds authority over his household where he has an analogous position to that of a chief in a wider community. His children and other dependants help in the farm under his directions, and even if they go away to earn money elsewhere they often send him back contributions. The father also receives the main bulk of the money and goods paid over in bridewealth at the marriage of his daughter. Even when his sons marry he still has a certain amount of jurisdiction over them and until they have several children or wives they often remain in the same house under his authority. A father is often depicted as a rather remote and even stern figure, specially towards his sons, but it is accepted that ultimately he has the responsibility for his children and, as depicted in an extreme form in *Parents are best*, they turn to him for help and support. Parents-in-law are also important figures and, especially a wife's mother, must be regarded with great respect. A man should bring them gifts and show them great deference since they have given him that greatest of all gifts, a wife. This is conventionally a relationship of formality rather than affection and as such is a common motif in Limba literature. In complete contrast to this is the Limba picture of a mother. A man always speaks of his mother with the greatest sentiment, pointing to the many years she cared and suffered for him, and her unending love for him. A mother is pictured as a model of unselfishness, consideration, and affection, and the one person among all others that her children can depend on completely; this is strengthened by the way a mother in practice supports her children against others and, when her husband dies, may choose to stay on in the home of one of her sons as his 'old mother who makes the house sweet'. In return, children normally treat their mother with affection and care for her in old age. Because of this, the tragedy in certain stories about a mother betraying her child, as in *The story of Deremu*, is all the more effective.

In these and many other ways the relationships connected with household, marriage, and family are of concern to the Limba in the daily organization of their lives. Only some of these have been discussed here. But perhaps enough has been said to illustrate how such relationships may also be a matter for comment and interpretation in the stories, and how some knowledge of the Limba experience in these contexts is necessary to grasp the effective significance of certain episodes and allusions in their literature.

6. RELIGION

Finally, some account must be given of Limba religious beliefs and practice. Like many other West African peoples, the Limba assume the existence of a single High God, and at the same time lay great stress on the power of the dead, their ancestors. These beliefs are not contradicted by the long influence of Islam in this part of Sierra Leone, nor by the more recent Christian missions, effective though these have been in certain limited areas. It is true that the spread of Islam seems to have been increasing rapidly over the last few decades, and in the west and far north of Limba country there are now many Muslims; elsewhere, too, many Limba chiefs and elders are attracted to the practice of a religion associated in their eyes with dignity, prestige, and close links with the many wealthy Mandingoes now settled in their chiefdoms. However, the Limba in general are not considered prominent or influential as Muslims —this they tend to leave to the Islamic Fula and Mandingo among them —and in the eastern portion of Limba country at least, where almost all the present stories were collected, the direct influence of Islam is by no means great. Most Limba here quite explicitly state that they are not Muslims and, though they have a certain detached admiration for the rites and knowledge of Islam, they prefer in practice to concern themselves with traditional Limba rituals of sacrifice and prayer to Kanu and the dead.

The Limba attribute the ultimate causation of everything to the being they refer to as Kanu.[1] Kanu is always conceived of as remote, inaccessible to human beings, and uncomprehended by them. He lives far off in the sky surveying the doings of human beings on the earth below him. It is of no interest to humans to try to speculate upon his nature or intentions for, beside Kanu, they are powerless and can do little or nothing to know or to influence him. Yet it is he in Limba belief who is ultimately responsible for everything that happens on earth. His name is often to be heard on Limba lips, especially in situations of unexpected joy or great sorrow. It is he who is considered the ultimate cause behind a man's fortune or misfortune in life, of death, of the number of children born in a household, of the successful election of one man to chiefship and the failure of another, and of all the events and even existence of the world. Though the Limba naturally also concern themselves with what they judge the proximate causes of events, for these, unlike Kanu, they can hope to affect by their own direct actions, they are clear that, in the last analysis, 'everything is [caused by] Kanu', man lives and exists 'by grace of Kanu' (*thɔkɔ ba Kanu*).

It will be clear that this accepted picture of Kanu as a remote being,

[1] Or Kanu Masala. In the west of Limba country he is often called just Masala, in the east Kanu, and sometimes in the extreme north Allah.

at once all-powerful and unknowable, is not in accord with the way in which he is represented in Limba oral literature. Kanu frequently appears as one among other characters in a story, and his actions and intentions are directly portrayed by the narrator. He plays different parts in the various plots in which he appears—in one a kindly father, another a seeker for palm wine, yet another a kind of chief in a magical land beneath the waters or above the sky. These stories are not regarded by the Limba as myths, which could give them real information about the nature and acts of Kanu, but just as stories like any others. Kanu is often shown as acting in a quite uncharacteristic way, and the very unusualness of his actions makes the stories particularly effective with a Limba audience.

The second essential aspect of Limba religion is reverence for the dead. References to the dead are most infrequent in Limba literature; yet in everyday life they are of central importance. Sacrifices and prayers are made specifically to 'call the dead', the traditional ways are 'what we found from the ancient people' (the dead), and men speak of their ancestors as being near them, caring for them, and accessible to their prayers. They are pictured as being in the village in contrast to Kanu who is far away in the sky and inaccessible.

The dead are 'the old people', those who have passed through the various stages of life, to reach respected elderhood and finally the most honoured status of all, among the community of the dead. They are invoked and sacrificed to by their children, and regarded not as a remote class of separate supernatural beings, but as close to their descendants, concerned for them as a father cares for his children, and in many ways sharing their essential humanity. 'The dead are Limba', they say, 'they are us'; and 'they bore us and taught us, for they are the old old people who were in the light [i.e. alive] in the old days.'

Unlike Kanu, then, the dead are conceived as being accessible to human beings. A dead father, for example, is said sometimes to come to his son in a dream, or a drummer or singer in the fields may attribute his skill to direct inspiration from the dead. There are also ceremonial occasions at which divination is performed and the answer is interpreted as having been made by the dead, signifying their wishes or acceptance to the living. The most important of the ways in which living and dead come into communication is through a sacrifice (*saraka*). This may take one of many different forms, but the paradigm is the slaughter of a beast after an invocation over it by the eldest men as they stretch out their hands to the animal and call on the dead by name, praying for peace and 'cool hearts'. After the animal has been killed, the meat is divided among those present, with due portions given to those representing other villages, and the vultures which come are seen as a sign that the dead have accepted their prayer. Such sacrifices take place at many levels. They may be for one household only, the owner giving what offering he can afford (usually rice-flour or a hen) and calling on the common dead that unite the members of the house; for a compound; a village; or a whole chiefdom when the famous ancestors of all the leading villages throughout the land are called on by the gathered elders. Thus in ever-widening circles the various sacrifices bring together those who are linked in a common ancestry and hold their present status 'by grace of the dead, the old people'.

The exact relations between Kanu and the dead are not clearly defined. In a sacrifice Kanu is often called on as well as the dead, and some Limba, when the question is raised, tentatively suggest that perhaps the dead convey the requests of the living to Kanu in somewhat the same way as a father intercedes for his children with a dominant chief. But this is a matter which is obscure to the Limba themselves, and though they agree that the dead are clearly closer and more pliable than Kanu, their precise relationship is not one about which they are normally concerned.

It can now be seen why it is that 'the dead' do not normally appear in Limba stories. They cannot be represented as a separate category of beings with special supernatural characteristics of their own juxtaposed to humans, for in Limba eyes the dead are merely human beings who were once alive and now are dead and buried, basically resembling their children who are now on earth. From this point of view it might be said that *all* the characters in the stories are 'the dead' in that the stories are set in the past and their characters are thus by now among 'the old people'. Possessing essentially human qualities as they do, there is no point in introducing the dead into the stories as a special category. For in spite of the important part played in Limba life by prayers and sacrifices to the dead, they are at root not special separate beings at all, but the human beings of the old days—'they are us'.

Kanu and the dead form the main subjects of Limba religious interest and practice. However, a third category of beings must be mentioned briefly. These are the 'spirits' of various kinds who appear so frequently in Limba stories, and about whose wonderful exploits many tales are told, mainly by the children, to more or less credulous listeners.

These spirits differ from both Kanu and the dead in that they are conceived of as essentially capricious and undependable. They are not thought of as having relations among themselves nor as existing in a separate world of their own, but are basically individualistic beings. Unlike the dead, they are non-human—indeed they are sometimes spoken of as 'animals'—and live 'in the bush', unattached to the settled community of the village. Throughout Limba country one can hear the names of a great number of these spirits (the children particularly can give long lists of the local ones), but with the exception of a few famous ones, well known by reputation to all Limba, there seems to be an infinite number of both named and nameless spirits which have only a very local recognition, and that sometimes only among one section of the community. One or two in an area may be given formal offerings and associated with the well-being of a village or particular ruling line, but in general spirits are thought not only to be individualistic in themselves but also only to come into contact with single individual human beings who cultivate them.

An individual is said to 'take' a spirit by seeing it one day in the bush—a possibility open only to those individuals born with 'double eyes' or special 'clear' spiritual vision (*kele*); then, if the spirit likes him, he makes an agreement with it. The spirit undertakes to help the man gain his desires—perhaps to win the chiefship, to become rich and respected and have many wives, or to become an expert dancer, drummer, or diviner. In return the man is said to pay respect to the spirit and, usually secretly, to give it offerings. Sometimes the spirit, if it is a 'bad' one, later demands a price for its help, often the life of one of the man's relatives, and if he refuses to pay this he is likely to die himself; but he has meantime been able to excel in his chosen field and become an object of admiration to his friends.

It is often in these terms therefore that the Limba account for outstanding success or unusual ability; the man has taken a spirit to help him. According to the same idea many Limba suggest that some Europeans too must have spirits who help them—how else could they produce money or invent their effective and mysterious machinery? But, like most other people who have taken spirits, the Limba add, they will never publicly admit to this.

Spirits then, individualistic beings who are not given communal recognition but are of interest only as and when they are thought to make contact with certain chosen individuals, are particularly suitable characters to appear in Limba stories. 'A spirit', as a supernatural being who may encounter the hero and undertake to help or harm him, can be effectively introduced into a story by a narrator just as he wishes, in much the same way as 'a fairy' is brought into European tales. The stock associations of an undependable and potentially cruel yet powerful being will already be grasped by the audience, but it is open to the storyteller to treat the subject in detail as he likes.

In terms of these beings—Kanu, the dead ancestors, and, in a rather more marginal way, the spirits of the wild bush—the Limba explain and interpret the world around them and the place of humans in society; and these interpretations, though not by any means identical with the representations in Limba literature, yet have a real and meaningful connexion with them.

There still remains one aspect to consider here. This may perhaps be described as the way in which the Limba treat the problem of evil. Clearly they accept that people fall short of ideals and there are many ways in which men and women err. With many of these—open quarrelling, fighting, theft, adultery, acting in a selfish and self-willed way—there are public and recognized ways of dealing. This is one of the main functions of all those with chiefly authority—to deal with the cases of such offenders and, where it is possible, to persuade them with winning speeches to become reconciled or atone for their misdeeds. Other ways in which men sin are hidden. One such offence, of great moment to the Limba, is that of *yaŋfa*, 'slander'. There is no exact translation into English, but the word suggests acting unfairly, showing secret favouritism, making trouble for another, and, most often, speaking evil of a man behind his back but smiling to his face: 'eating with you, finding out your secrets and then going to tell them to others'. In everyday life there is no set way in which to seek out those who malign you in this way; but in the stories there are many examples in which a man 'slandering' another is depicted as in the end falling a victim to the very 'slander' he himself began.

But the most feared way in which people are thought to sin against others is through the secret malice hidden in their hearts. Like many other African peoples, the Limba believe that certain men and women have the power to injure their fellows through the mystical means of witchcraft. A witch is thought to go out secretly at night to hurt those of whom he is jealous, and, by his witchcraft, can cause death or illness by mystically 'eating the "heart" '—the life—of his enemy. The belief in witchcraft is important in day-to-day Limba life, and, after a death, divination is normally made to discover if it was due to a witch; if so, there are set means by which the one considered responsible can be sought out and punished, or a similar attempt in the future frustrated. The Limba consider witchcraft as a peculiarly dreadful crime, in that it is, in the normal way, impossible to detect; a man may smile and laugh with you by day, and greet you well, concealing the jealousy of his heart; but at night he goes out to try and kill you by his witchcraft. This theme also comes in the literature; even one's nearest and dearest may secretly be trying to bewitch you, as with the boy's own family in *A story of witches*. In *The story of Deremu* there is the even more tragic case where a mother uses what is regarded as a form of witchcraft—giving him to a spirit to kill—against her own son.

It is from all these evils that the Limba strive to be guarded when they pray to Kanu and the dead for peace or a 'cool spirit' (*thɛbina lima*). Though there are various recognized ways of trying to combat these evil tendencies severally, ultimately, the Limba believe, protection from them is only possible 'by grace of Kanu and the dead', those to whom they make the due prayer and sacrifices in the open compounds of their villages and thus keep people's hearts 'cool' and well disposed to one another.

In these ways the Limba represent to themselves the world around them and the nature of human action and personality. The actual social and individual experience of the Limba is connected with the presentation of human action and experience in their literature, and both influences and is influenced by what we might call their literary experience. There is no single directly functional connexion that can be demarcated between the life and literature of the Limba; but without knowing something of the one it is impossible fully to appreciate the other.

2

LIMBA ORAL LITERATURE AND THE MEANING OF 'STORY' (*MBƆRƆ*)

TO understand Limba literature one must also know something of their culture—the various modes of artistic expression, the place of oral literature in this, and the idea of *mbɔrɔ*, the Limba word usually translated as 'story'. The most significant literary forms are the narrative stories, and these, the main subject of this volume, must be discussed in some detail; as will be shown, they are in some ways closely related to the specialized Limba arts of dancing and singing. Other forms of *mbɔrɔ* such as proverbial sayings, riddles, and analogies must also be described briefly, for through these it is perhaps possible to gain further insight into the general Limba concept of *mbɔrɔ*.

I. LIMBA ARTISTIC EXPRESSION

Story, song, and dance are of daily importance in Limba life. All such artistic expression and inspiration, whether of singers, story-tellers, dancers, or drummers, is thought to come from essentially the same source—the dead, the 'old people' (*bebɔrɔ be*). In the Limba view this inheritance includes within its range such apparently diverse elements as, for example, the rhetorical and winning force inherent in the words of a speaker in a formal law case, the songs sung by a story-teller in the course of his narration, the persuasive and formal prayer to the dead for peace and health, the weeding songs of the drummer in the fields as he calls to the women to show their speed and skill, or a song of thanks spontaneously sung and danced by an old woman when she sees an honoured visitor approaching. Language, song, and rhythmic movement form one complex of artistic expression, and one in which, diffident though they are in a European context, the Limba are convinced of their own competence, wit, and profound wisdom, of 'the sense we found from our old people'.

Within this general cultural inheritance—sometimes referred to as 'Limba things' or 'Limba times' (*malimba ma*)—it is possible to distinguish different aspects of artistic expression. These are primarily drumming, dancing, singing, and the telling of stories.[1]

[1] Visual art is of relatively minor importance among the Limba, and is not considered here.

Drumming is a much-practised activity. Everyone can drum a bit and is ready to do this on any occasion. It also has a specialist aspect, and many occasions have their own special kinds of drums and drumming; this is almost all done by men, and in the case of certain drums there are widely recognized experts who receive honour and gifts for the exercise of their skills. Much the same applies to dancing, which also has its own specialists who perform on certain prescribed occasions. These dancers are not professionals, for they all rely primarily on rice farming for subsistence and dance only in their free time; but they are considered to be experts who deserve honour and reward, and they are often so famous for many miles around that they are specially invited to come and dance at important ceremonies in and beyond their chiefdom. In addition to such experts there are also many forms of dancing in which all Limba are more or less competent. Besides named dances which are performed on ceremonial occasions, dance and rhythmic movement run all through Limba work and leisure. People are likely to break into the step of a dance on any occasion, sometimes apparently quite unconsciously, and even the day-to-day farm work often recalls the rhythm and movement of dances, specially when the work is organized to the accompaniment of drum and song. Sometimes the dancer or drummer sings by himself, and is echoed by the spectators, sometimes it is primarily the whole group which sings as it circles round the central performers. Singing is closely associated with dancing, so that whenever anyone sings at all, in a sense he necessarily half dances as part of his song, even if only by small movements of his head or hands. Songs are most typically led by a soloist, usually the dancer, drummer, or story-teller, and are then taken up in chorus by all those who are watching, working, dancing, or listening. But up to a point everyone is able and ready to sing, so that singing is constantly occurring in an informal way in all aspects of Limba life; people are always liable to break into snatches of song—out of spontaneous happiness, to lull a child, or, specially by women, to express respect or thanks to someone. Singing thus resembles dancing in that each has both a stylized form mastered only by experts and also a general aspect, as a form of artistic expression which can be, and is, exercised by all members of the society.

Even a slight acquaintance with Limba singing, drumming, and dancing reveals something of the complexity of these modes of artistic expression. In a discussion of Limba literature, therefore, it is important to realize that the stories make up in fact only one facet of Limba culture. Indeed in the sphere of music and dance the Limba both use a more specialized and differentiated vocabulary and lay more explicit emphasis on expert skill than they do in respect of the stories. In the case of the Limba, therefore (and, indeed, possibly for many other West African peoples), it would be quite wrong to assume that spoken art is the chief medium of artistic expression. European scholars tend to describe literature because it is relatively easier for a foreigner to write about than music or dancing. But it must be remembered that Limba stories, however important, are not necessarily what they themselves would wish to present as the most important aspect of their artistic culture.

Nor can their story-telling be altogether divorced from the other aspects of artistic expression; my discussion of it in this chapter therefore in some respects isolates it from its true context. In the actual performance of the stories, for example, songs often form part of the narration, and in practice it may often be those expert in the musical skills who also tend to be the best story-tellers. The various aspects all belong to an integrated culture which is held to be both infinitely old, since inherited from the ancestors, and re-enacted through the skill and memory of each individual performer.

Finally, this brief reference to Limba music and dance illustrates the way in which in these spheres too artistic expression is not primarily a matter of private enjoyment or emotion, but a dramatic activity into which individual performer and audience join in a manner very similar to the dramatic activity of both telling and listening to the stories.

Within this whole complex of their cultural inheritance, the Limba distinguish as a special class that of the 'story' or 'parable' (*mbɔrɔ*, pl. *mbɔrɔiŋ* or, more common, *thabɔrɔ*). The most common application of the word *mbɔrɔ* is to a story, in the sense of the narrative tales which form the majority of the texts translated here. It can also mean a proverb, a parable, a wise or imaginative saying, an elaborate metaphor, a riddle, or an analogy; the plural form, *thabɔrɔ*, also sometimes refers to an historical narrative. The wide range of meanings of *mbɔrɔ* is summarized by Clarke[1] as covering 'adage, fable, legend, parable, proverb, riddle, story, tale, anecdote'. This general concept and its various applications are discussed later in this chapter.

The Limba themselves are quite conscious that these 'stories' form an important and definable part of their cultural heritage, and one of which they are proud. In the field I found that while they were sometimes puzzled by the purpose of my investigation of, for example, religious or social customs, they at once appreciated the point of questions about their literature. So once the first few texts had been recorded, the flow of offers to tell more stories was at times almost too great to be coped with. In one sense, I had no choice *but* to collect them. Once stories began to be told people were prepared to continue almost indefinitely. Admittedly, they said, I would never master all the stories, for their numbers are often represented as infinite—'even if you stayed for three years and heard several stories each night we would not have

[1] Limba–English Dictionary, 1929, p. 40.

reached the end'—but unless I was willing to record stories I was, they implied, insincere in my claim to wish to know Limba culture.

2. TYPES AND CLASSIFICATION OF STORIES

Within the broad class of 'story' (*mbɔrɔ*) the Limba themselves do not make any further clear division. In most dialects[1] the same term is used to cover a wide range of formulations, from 'folktales' in the accepted sense of the word to shorter forms such as riddles and proverbs, as well as what we would normally call historical accounts. None of these classes are strictly differentiated by the Limba.

The primary and most common application of the term *mbɔrɔ* is to stories such as those which make up the bulk of Part II—tales about Kanu, about twins, about individual human heroes, and about animals, mainly the spider.[2] Though these stories shade into other formulations to be discussed later, they can from our point of view be broadly distinguished as a class on their own and are treated independently in the present section. In Limba terms, however, one cannot draw up any definitive typology either between these stories and the shorter forms, or among the stories proper themselves.

In speaking of these stories proper one obvious classification to adopt might be that in terms of the chief characters of a story, and this, in fact, is a division I have roughly followed for convenience of presentation. Some stories are about people; some about Kanu and origins; and some about animals. This division however should not be understood as an attempt at a scientific typology in either Limba or theoretical terms. The amount of overlap is too great for any strict differentiation in this way, for many stories include references to several of these three classes of characters at once. The story of *Koto and Yemi*, for instance, speaks of the origin of the differences between white men and black and brings in Kanu as one of the characters; yet the plot and tone is almost exactly the same as in another story of two twins with the same names which clearly falls among the stories about people since episodes about Kanu and origins are not included (*Two twins*). In *The story of Bayo* the actors include animals, a human child, and a spirit, and the tale ends with an explanation of the present relations between humans and animals. The same applies to *The dog and the wheel* which speaks of Kanu, a white man, and several animals. In many cases therefore it is

[1] Certainly in Biriwa and Yaka, the two dialects I knew best. I am told that in Tonko Limba riddles are referred to as *ŋalɔŋkande* (lit. 'tying each other') and 'proverbs' as *thaiŋ*. The special term *gbaŋki* is sometimes used to refer to the telling of a story which includes singing.

[2] In the discussion here and elsewhere the specific examples cited are mainly from the stories translated in Part II, but general points are also based on my knowledge of many other stories I heard or recorded during my two visits.

almost impossible to decide in which group to present any given story, for either the characters overlap or a very similar story reappears with a more or less identical plot but different actors. The divisions I have made therefore have been purely for convenience and not for the sake of postulating any theoretical typology.

Other possible classifications also seem unsuitable here. One obvious dichotomy, for instance, might seem to be that suggested by Berry in his discussion of West African prose narratives; he speaks of 'fictional' and 'non-fictional' narrative, the latter 'regarded in context as true' and covering not only legends and chronicles but also 'myths, chiefly stories of the deities and the origins of natural phenomena'.[1] But this does not wholly fit the detailed Limba situation. Historical accounts, it is true, can be distinguished from other narratives in that the occasion and purpose seem to be different (though there may be similarities in other respects). But if, with Berry, we interpret 'myths' as 'chiefly about the deities',[2] the difficulty of separating them off clearly from other stories is, as already mentioned, a serious one, for characters of all kinds, including Kanu and spirits, may come into the same story. Similarly the criterion of being regarded as 'true' is not an easy one to apply. Certainly historical narratives do seem to be 'regarded as true' in a way, say, humorous animal tales are not; but whether and how far some of the stories which refer to Kanu or origins are regarded as 'true' in a similar sense is not at all clear. There are, for example, several different tales about the origin of death or of palm wine, and those who knew more than one version did not seem to be embarrassed by their apparent contradiction; these, as well as other apparently very different tales, were 'good stories' and at the same time often expressed something 'true' (*thia*) about the world or 'us Limba people'.

Equally difficult to apply to the Limba material would be a differentiation in terms of general purpose or point. Again historical narratives form a case of their own, but when this criterion is applied to the corpus of stories as a whole the distinctions break down. On the face of it, to settle whether a story is intended to be basically an explanatory or aetiological tale, a dilemma, or a moralizing story might seem, on the basis of the form of the story, to be very easy; stories do often end up with explanation, question, or moral and this kind of classification might seem a straightforward one. However, when many stories have been recorded it is clear that the moral or explanation is in a sense often not an integral feature of the story at all, but merely one of several stylistic devices to bring it to a fitting conclusion. Thus with the very similar tales of *The man killed for a banana* and *The man killed for a spinach leaf*, which, as far as plot goes, are merely versions of the 'same' story, one ends with a moral,

[1] Berry, *Spoken Art in West Africa*, p. 6.

[2] There are few or no Limba stories about 'the origins of natural phenomena'.

the other with an ascription of origin; and many other examples of this kind of combination of similarity and difference could be cited. Which kind of ending is adopted in the case of a particular narration seems to depend on the story-teller or the occasion rather than to be a defining mark of a special fixed type of story. Similarly with dilemmas: in some plots certainly a concluding dilemma seems an essential feature;[1] but in many others whether or not a dilemma is stated seems to be a matter of choice for the teller rather than an inherent characteristic of the story itself. In two very similar stories, *Three twins and an elephant* and another tale incorporating the same plot, a dilemma was never stated at all in the second version even though it had seemed an integral part of the first. In several other stories, such as *Two friends* or *Sara miser and Sara scrounger*, a dilemma could perfectly well have been added as an explicit question for the audience (in fact I think I heard this done in one story about *Two friends*), but in the narrations I recorded they are left implicit and not stated. Another difficulty is that if the addition of an explicit dilemma was made a significant diagnostic feature, this would lead to the classing together of stories that were otherwise very different indeed. The narrations, for example, of *The story of Kubasi* and *Four wives* each ended with a question about who should inherit the chiefship; but these stories, long and elaborate, bear little relation to such brief forms as *A dilemma about three smokers* and it would be misleading to class them together.

Rather more illuminating might be an analysis of the purpose of a particular narration taking into account the circumstances in which it was told. Stories are occasionally told during the day when they are introduced into a formal case before the chief or a group of elders. A story is told to 'give someone sense' (*thi funuŋ*), showing him in a parable either that he had acted wrongly himself or that he, and others, should try to act in a certain way in the future. Instead of telling the offender directly and immediately where he had gone wrong a good speaker should 'go round long in parables' first (*a silɔkɔ haaŋ ka thabɔrɔ tha*) and in this way find his way more surely to the man's heart. It is only very rarely that long or at all elaborate narratives are told in such circumstances; only a man who is 'very very able' (*wo bafunuŋ wo gbaŋ gbaŋ*) can do this. More often only an analogy, a metaphor, or, at most a very brief episode is brought in, and such cases shade into the 'proverbs' and analogies to be discussed later. There are occasional cases of longer stories. One was by a chief who had been brought a new wife; in his speech of thanks he told a story with the plot of *Marriage and a bush cow's milk* which, I was told, was to exemplify to his new wife and all the other women present that obedience to one's husband is the essence of marriage.

[1] e.g. *A dilemma about three smokers* and various stories based on the plot about the pregnant woman and the bones.

However, the distinction between such stories told during the day and those enacted in evening story-telling is not in fact very far-reaching. Not only is the same term (*mbɔrɔ* and *thabɔrɔ*) used for the story in each case, but much the same story may be told in both of the situations described, by day on a formal and serious occasion, at night for enjoyment. I was told several versions of the chief's tale about the wife and the bush cow's milk as a tale just like any other. Naturally the tone of the different narrations varied according to the occasion, as it always does in Limba stories; but there was no clear difference that could not be equally paralleled by similar differences among stories told only in the more typical evening narrations.[1] It would also be wrong to assume that a story told with a purpose is not also told and listened to for its own sake; or that the evening stories do not also include some element of seriousness or relation to a particular audience or individual. There is not, then, an absolute distinction between the two types of narration. In any case, stories told on formal occasions with a primarily moral purpose are rare and do not form a good basis for any general classification of Limba literature.

The difficulty encountered in drawing up any exact typology in terms of purpose or any other element has in fact a real and positive relevance for the understanding of the nature of Limba stories. It inevitably brings to the fore one of the most striking characteristics of Limba stories—their 'unfixed' and fluid nature, the sense in which the exact form of a story is not laid down once and for all but varies more or less according to the individual teller, the audience, and the occasion. There is no one prototype or 'correct' form which could be regarded as the unit for classification. To ask, as have some folklorists in the past, for a definitive typology would be to blur this essential feature of the tales. Certainly many of them may end with a moral, an explanation, or a problem; but these are not so completely fixed that they cannot be varied in a given narration. It would be truer to say that all stories, to a greater or a lesser degree according to circumstances, can contain some or all of several elements—moralizing and generalization; explanation; comparison, whether implicit or stated as an explicit dilemma; and, finally, an intention to amuse and entertain by an interesting plot, a shocking episode or character, and a vivid style and delivery.

Though not positing any strict classification within Limba literature, I shall, for convenience, discuss the stories under the subject headings suggested above. I shall first describe certain aspects of stories about, respectively, people, Kanu, and animals; and later consider briefly other forms which can be more clearly separated off, yet in the Limba terminology are also classed as *mbɔrɔ*—historical narratives and shorter formulations such as proverbs, riddles, and analogies. In this way some idea can be given of the wide range of application of the term *mbɔrɔ*.

[1] Described below pp. 64–66.

(a) *Stories about people*

On the whole, stories primarily about people seem to be the most popular and often the most elaborate. The longest tales I was told tended to be mainly about human characters, and it is possible that in this kind of story there is the greatest scope for innovation and variation by individual story-tellers. However, it is not easy to come to any clear conclusion in this matter, since, as already mentioned, this group of stories shades into the others: tales with different characters may share the same plot, there may or may not be encounters with supernatural beings, and morals, dilemmas, or explanations of origins are freely added as endings.

There are a few stock heroes and heroines. The most common is a man called Sara. It was he, for example, who was taught by Kanu to tap palm wine, who rescued his elder sister from the monster she had married, who tricked his brother-in-law and became chief. However, it would be misleading to speak of these tales about Sara as forming a 'cycle' in the sense of being concerned with the adventures of some definite mythical hero thought of as possessing a continuous existence and individuality from story to story. That this is not so is clear when the various adventures and roles are compared—in one story Sara is greedy and stupid and dies from his own obstinacy (*Sara and the guinea fowl*), in another his goodness and hospitality win him chiefship from Kanu, in a third he is a poor man who gains chiefship by his cunning. The point is made explicit by the occurrence of a story which speaks of *two* Saras—*Sara miser and Sara scrounger*. These stories, then, cannot be regarded as a 'cycle' of tales about a single character. The significance of the name Sara becomes clearer when it is realized that Sara is the name the Limba say should be given to an eldest son; in the north it is even sometimes used as the general noun to refer to an eldest son. 'Sara', then, might be described as a stock name given to a Limba man or the stock human being to whom adventures may befall in stories—a kind of representative of humanity.

The other commonly named heroes are three 'twins' of whom the 'eldest' is Tungkangbali, 'daring things', the next Palongbali,[1] 'fearing things', and the 'youngest' variously named Yisinua, Yisahosaho, or Wunekeria. These stories are all marked by their light-hearted tone and rather far-fetched and shocking character; they are always greatly enjoyed by the listeners. Tungkangbali is conventionally represented as headstrong, irresponsible, and ungrateful, while his two brothers try to restrain him.

There are few other stock names in the stories. Sira often appears as a girl's name, Sara's counterpart. In several of the longer stories, the

[1] In some dialects called Tungkangbei and Palongbei (or Payongbei).

narrator gives a hero some name such as Deremu, Kubasi, or Bayo, but these names do not recur in other stories. Occasionally a character may only be given a name in passing at a late stage of the story.[1] The only other common names in the stories are those of twins who, in story as in life, often have their own special names, particularly Koto and Yemi; other names for twins are Siema, Luseni, and Saio(ng).

Other Limba stories are about unnamed characters, and commonly begin with such phrases as 'a man came out', 'a man married a wife', 'three children were born'. However, even within this anonymity there are some stock characters.

One of the most common figures is that of the hunter. Hunters are, after chiefs and smiths, among the most important people in a Limba village. They train for many years with a master hunter to learn not only the technique of tracking and shooting, but the secret leaves and medicines by which they can succeed and also gain the protection of the hunter's spirit. Special powers are commonly attributed to a hunter, and he, alone of human beings, is imagined to be confident and experienced even alone in the bush at night. The several stories about hunters, therefore, are about a figure who is in any case an important and slightly mysterious one among the Limba.

Twins are frequently the central characters. They too are commonly believed to possess special powers, for they are 'clear-eyed' or able to see spirits and witches, and thus are said often to become famous as great hunters, diviners, or witch-catchers. They are therefore especially suitable protagonists in stories about some fantastic or far-fetched topic—the twins, for instance, who revived their long-dead father or the twin who visited a world below to bring back a wife for his brother. The number of 'twins' in a story is very commonly three. This accords with the Limba view that the child following twins, usually called Saiong, is himself a kind of twin; they are thus three in all. The number also gives them an additionally mysterious and impressive character. Most twins in story, with the exception of Tungkangbali and his brothers, are represented as acting together and helping each other.

Other stock figures also occur such as the motherless and helpless orphan, the childless mother who wishes to conceive, or the 'moriman', or skilled Muslim, whom a hero consults for divination or magical help. However, very often the subject of the tale is identified merely as 'a man', 'a woman', 'a child', or 'a chief' and referred to merely in these terms throughout the story, in the same way as the animal characters discussed later.

Stories about people therefore could be said to fall into several very rough groups—stories about Sara (and Sira), about the irresponsible Tungkangbali and his brothers, about twins, hunters, and anonymous

[1] e.g. in *Wooing Sira*.

characters. These various groups of stories too may possibly differ among themselves in their potentialities for elaboration and expansion. But such distinctions are very rough ones, and each group shades imperceptibly into the others.

(*b*) *Stories about Kanu and origins*

Kanu figures in several stories, many of them also about origins. The Limba concept of Kanu has already been discussed. Although he lives far away in the sky, in many of the stories he is pictured as coming down to earth, often to institute the present customs or facts of Limba society, or as being approachable in his own dwelling by those who have the cunning to seek him there. That is, Kanu's character in the stories is the opposite of his usual everyday one. All these stories are set in the past, a past that is now no longer repeated, and part of their effectiveness as stories in the Limba context lies in their complete contrast with the normally assumed inaccessibility of Kanu.

Stories about 'God' or far-off origins are commonly referred to as 'myths'. Certainly as far as subject-matter alone is concerned this is an appropriate term for these Limba tales. It is, however, a term which I avoid here, as many of the other characteristics commonly implied by the word 'myth' are absent in the case of the Limba tales. It may remove some possible misconceptions about the nature of the Limba stories about Kanu if I briefly discuss the senses in which 'myth' would be a misleading term for them.

In the first place, as already mentioned, the Limba themselves do not make any clear differentiation between these stories and others; nor is it altogether easy to force such a distinction on them from the outside. Stories in which all the emphasis is on the interest or excitement of the plot may end up with some tacked-on ascription of origin without this being at all an important part of the story as a whole: it is difficult, for example, to assert that the story of *The man killed for a banana* or *Two women* should be classed with origin stories, even though one ends with a (fanciful) explanation of the origin of women chiefs, the other with an account of the origin of certain kinds of death and barrenness. Certain stories in which Kanu appears are in fact little concerned with Kanu as such and speak rather of the animal and human actors involved in the action.[1] In the sense, then, of being obviously distinct from other tales, the Limba stories of Kanu and origins are not 'myth'.

Furthermore the term 'myth' often seems to carry the connotation, perhaps because of our familiarity with Greek and Roman mythology, of an accepted and more or less systematic body of knowledge about religious topics or deities, known either to everyone or to recognized

[1] e.g. *The dog and the wheel.*

experts. In this sense at least, the Limba tales cannot be accorded the title of 'myths' for they do not form part of any systematic theology, philosophy, or mythology. Some of the tales contradict others; thus there are several accounts, some much the same, others very different, of the origin of death, of the first discovery of palm wine, of the reason for the differences between black and white men, of the spider's presence in people's houses, and of the institution of rice farming by Kanu. Those who knew of both accounts did not seem to be worried by this diversity, or wish to discuss which was the true one. Nor were such stories well known throughout Limba country or produced as relevant or significant evidence to describe the acts or nature of Kanu. The story of the separation of Kanu from men (*Kanu and the python*) might seem to be the obvious foundation for any systematic account of Limba religion —yet it did not seem to be widely known or of any *particular* interest to the listeners on the occasion I heard it told; it was merely one good story among several. Also there seems to be no accepted picture of the nature or acts of Kanu as we might perhaps assume if we were to class the stories as 'myths'. Sometimes Kanu is presented as like a chief or a kindly father, as, for instance, in the stories which describe how he came down to institute chiefship or rice farming; sometimes like a stern but just judge; sometimes like a poor man who goes round begging for wine; in yet other stories he seems to be merely one character like any other, necessary for the action of the plot; he differs from any other chief, say, only in living in a strange world under a pool or above the sky. In one story there are even two Kanus introduced into the action as 'Kanu above' and 'Kanu below'—an idea that does not fit with the usual Limba concept of Kanu but is yet suitable for the plot of this particular story. The stories, then, are not interpreted as sacred tales giving systematic and accepted information about the nature or actions of Kanu, or as describing once and for all the first origins of the natural world or of Limba society.

These stories about Kanu and origins are not, it seems, taken particularly seriously by the Limba in so far as they are concerned with these subjects. Certainly some are serious in tone—specially those to do with death and rice farming. But here, it would appear, it is not the introduction of the character of Kanu that causes the difference in tone, but the serious nature of the other topics—death, agriculture—with which the narrator is concerned in the story. There are many other stories which are as light-hearted as any among Limba tales, and yet include Kanu among their *dramatis personae*. *The girl taken by Kanu* is an obvious example, or the second version of *Kanu gives chiefship*, which was told in a high-spirited way to an amused audience. Stories about Kanu, then, differ among themselves just as do stories about any other characters. From the point of view of tone there is no one category of stories which could be distinguished as 'myths' because taken seriously in a sense that others are not.

Furthermore Limba stories about Kanu are not told on prescribed occasions, nor do they seem to serve any special function in the society that is not equally served by stories on other topics. They are not associated with a ritual, endowed with any especially deep 'meaning', nor repeated identically in different tellings. It would then be an artificial division to separate them off sharply from the rest of Limba oral literature as a class of their own, whether under the dignified term of 'myth' or any other.[1]

There is perhaps one sense in which stories which introduce Kanu are rather different in degree from other Limba stories. This is in their particularly effective force as a commentary on the nature of the world or human action. To relate some institution to its origin or to Kanu is to comment on some special characteristic of it that the story-teller may want to bring out, or to praise some particular element as having been given and approved by Kanu. Thus chiefship, in one version, is said to have been instituted by Kanu after he had gone round in the guise of a poor and unattractive beggar asking for hospitality; this brings out the point that chiefs should be kind to strangers and poor people, for this was the reason and occasion, in this story, for chiefship being given by Kanu. Similarly the various stories of Kanu and rice farming point not so much to certain actions by Kanu in the past as to the present situation, the way in which the farming cycle fits with the climatic year and both is and has been the right and honourable destiny of the Limba people.

There are few or no stories about the origins of natural phenomena. This in itself is significant, for what is often being described in the stories about Kanu and about origins is not primarily some postulated historical event in the past, but a comment or detached generalization about the relations and purposes of present human society. The stories do not provide an explanation of causes in the past, but an explication of the present occupations and preoccupations of mankind.

In this sense, therefore, some (not all) of the stories about Kanu differ from other stories in providing an opportunity for the narrator, if he wishes, to lay more stress on the element of explication or commentary in a wider context. However, in this they differ only in degree from other stories, for this is an element more or less inherent in most Limba literature, either in the form of an explicit moral or generalization added to the end of a tale, or indirectly implied in the tale through the actions and situations described there. The interests and relations of social life are imaged in the stories about people and about animals as well as in those about Kanu.

[1] In certain other African oral literatures, however, such a distinction does seem a valid one.

(c) Stories about animals

The stories about animals are liable to be rather shorter than tales about people, and—contrary to what is sometimes popularly supposed of West African 'folktales'—are not in fact the most common type of story. They are marked by rather more humour and, sometimes, obscenity, and perhaps exhibit slightly more stress on parallel structure than in some of the more elaborately constructed tales about human beings. But these stories too cannot be clearly separated off from others, for the subject-matter and *dramatis personae* of the various groups overlap, as do the stock endings which occur in every type of story.

The most common character in these tales is the spider (*wosi*). He is most frequently represented as stupid, gluttonous, selfish, and irresponsible, consistently outdone by his wife Kayi who is both bigger and cleverer than he, but whom he continues to try to outwit. The relations between him and his wife represent everything that is wrong and upside down—the spider acts in an anti-social and unfitting way in trying to trick his wife of her food, in telling lies about her, in insulting his mother-in-law, and turns out to be weaker and more foolish than his own wife. Occasionally he is represented as a cunning trickster getting the better of bigger animals like the elephant or the leopard, but this picture of the spider is less common. Listeners often find the spider stories especially comic and they are told in a vivid and uninhibited way by the narrators. The spider is never represented as a creator or 'culture hero'[1] in Limba literature, but appears as a conventionally amusing figure.

A few other animals are also introduced with stock characteristics. The antelope,[2] for example, is represented as small, shy, but very clever, able to escape even the lion, the leopard, and the greedy spider, using his wits to save himself and not injure others. The goat too is clever, and outwits bigger and stronger animals, but is pictured as more egoistic and deceitful than the retiring antelope. The leopard is dangerous, unscrupulous, and full of deceit, but liable to be outdone in the end. The small squirrel is also clever and comes to the help of his bigger brother. These characters are well-known ones, and spoken of in other contexts as well as that of story-telling.

Rather different is the picture of the finch (probably a species of fire finch) who very often appears in the stories in the role of a diviner. One of the chief characters, human or animal, goes to him to consult him about the future, and the finch throws the stones he was left by his father, utters his special cry of *se se*, *se se*, and gives an answer in much the same manner as the diviners known in real life. The finch in this role

[1] As he is among some other West African peoples, for example the Ashanti *Anansi* and perhaps the *Pa Nes* of the Temne neighbours of the Limba.

[2] A small animal, probably the royal antelope or water chevrotain, often contrasted with the bigger, duller deer.

is never the protagonist of a story, merely a secondary character essential to advance the plot.

Dogs also appear fairly commonly. They differ from other animals in that they are closely attached to human beings, specially hunters, and are not one of the 'animals in the bush' who form the subject of most animal stories. Dogs are usually introduced as a foil to human action rather than as actors on their own account.

The effectiveness of many of these animal stories when told depends very much on the audience's knowledge of the behaviour or appearance of the animals concerned. Thus, for example, the shyness and caution known to be characteristic of the antelope makes its triumph over the spider or leopard all the more telling; the spotted skin of the leopard is the amusing pivot of the plot in the story of *The goat, the leopard, and the lion*; and the point of the joke in *The monkey and the chameleon* is that it was so very extra clever of the monkey to accuse the chameleon of having stolen the wine because the Limba commonly say of a drunk man that 'his eyes turn round'—and, as all Limba know, the chameleon's eyes do, literally, seem to turn round. The stories are made even more effective by the mimicry of a clever narrator.

Many of the animal stories end with the statement of a moral or with the account of the origin of some characteristic or habit of a bird or animal, or of the present distribution of animals, some in the bush, some in the village. But these conclusions, as with similar endings in stories about people, often do not seem to be taken over-seriously as an integral part of the story. Often the emphasis seems to be rather on some general attribute of the species or on the way in which their actions illustrate some situation or tendency than on any serious concentration on the moral or origin.

In presenting these animal tales I have not, as is often done with African folktales, used capital letters in translating their names into English. To say, for example, not 'the leopard' and 'a leopard' but 'Leopard' or 'Mr. Leopard' would, in the case of the Limba, be misleading. With the doubtful exception of the spider stories, the animals referred to do not seem to have any separate existence as individuals, so to speak, over and above their appearance in each particular story. In addition the typical introductory phrases, such as 'a lion came out' or 'a chimpanzee once reared a goat', etc., are, in Limba, stylistically reminiscent of the similar formulations in stories about people, where to use a proper name would also be unsuitable; one is not, for example, tempted to write in English 'Woman was once married' or 'Hunter came out'. Both here and in the animal stories the general term ('a hunter', 'the leopard' rather than 'Hunter' or 'Leopard') is preferable. This is specially evident in the clear cases where more than one individual is concerned—e.g. in 'two pythons caught a deer'. Finally the motive which may have led many translators to use terms for animals as if they were proper names does not seem quite to apply to the Limba situation. Presumably the point that the translators wished to bring out by their use of capital letters was that the animal stories are not just pointless or sentimental fantasies about animals told for their own sake, but in a sense abstractions or generalizations, so that what is being spoken of is not just any elephant but the *type* or *idea* of elephant—Elephant. In Limba animal stories, however, if any abstraction is being made it seems to be not of the animal but of a certain situation, so that it is the implication for human society that is exemplified by some story ostensibly about animals.

In the course of this discussion of certain characteristics of various groups of Limba stories I have laid more stress on what they are *not* than on what they are—tales about Kanu are not 'myths'; animal tales are not about Mr. Elephant; the stories cannot be strictly divided by subject or purpose. This, however, has been necessary. Much has been written or implied about African folktales that, when applied to the Limba at least, would be totally misleading; thus it is essential to clear away certain misconceptions before the tales can even be allowed to speak for themselves. It is perhaps only in the stories about people that the literary aspect is at once evident to an English reader—perhaps paradoxically owing to the happy chance that fewer of such stories happen to have been recorded from Africa and that therefore less speculative and confusing commentary has been introduced. In the stories about people at least it is clear that it would be artificial to assert that they are, for example, primarily to do with the utilitarian statement of morals or the validation or stabilizing of social structure (an approach which has seemed attractive to some of those who have discussed tales about animals or 'God'). They are self-evidently akin to our own literature and need not be subjected to any far-fetched interpretation to make them intelligible. I suggest that once certain confusing preconceptions are removed the other groups of stories, those about Kanu and about animals, can be seen to be of fundamentally the same nature as those about people, and to fall equally within the category of Limba literature.

3. OTHER FORMS OF *MBƆRƆ*

The Limba word *mbɔrɔ* has a wider range of application than the English 'story'. So far only the stories proper have been discussed—tales about people, Kanu, and animals—and these indeed seem to be the most common or even the primary applications of the Limba term *mbɔrɔ*; in fact in one dialect (Tonko) *mbɔrɔ* seems to bear only this limited meaning, and other forms are distinguished in terminology.[1]

[1] See above, p. 28.

However, in most dialects of Limba there are also secondary applications of the word *mbɔrɔ*. These cover historical narratives, riddles, proverbs, analogies, and even certain figures of speech.

(*a*) *Historical narratives*

Historical narratives are both like and unlike the kinds of stories discussed so far. How far they resemble them varies to some extent with the purpose and content of the particular narration. The similarity in tone, style, and effect to the other tales is most marked in the occasional narratives about the famous and wonderful chiefs of the past, which often recall stories about more fictional heroes. The renowned Suluku of Bumban, it will be remembered, is described as possessing many magical powers, and such marvellous stories tend to cluster round the names of famous historical or far-off chiefs and to be related by ordinary people with something of the same kind of tone and effect as the more common stories about people, Kanu, or animals. The actual members of the chiefly houses hand down the traditional genealogies and histories with more seriousness, tending to avoid tales of the marvellous, though they are not averse to a dramatic representation of their ancestors' great deeds. For them, the history is related not just for its intrinsic interest, wisdom, or enjoyment, but also so that the members of the chiefly house will know how to make good their claims to birth and dignity when the time comes for them to contend for chiefship.

Such historical narratives are often referred to by a periphrasis like 'speaking about the old days' or 'about the old people', but sometimes the same term is used as for 'stories'—*thabɔrɔ*, the plural form of *mbɔrɔ*. The delivery differs from the stories proper in that there are no songs, and it is sometimes rather more serious in tone; but it may also portray amusing or exciting incidents or details and include many of the characteristics of style and delivery so evident in the stories,[1] such as dramatic dialogue, imitation, swift narrative, and vehement diction. The topics and treatment also tend to be different from those in the stories, and historical narratives do not usually conclude with any of the stock endings for stories—morals, dilemmas, attributions of origin, and so on.

Historical narratives thus have much in common with the stories proper, and are sometimes referred to by the same term; but they also fall into rather a separate category in treatment, form, delivery and, very often, purpose.

(*b*) *Shorter formulations—riddles, 'proverbs', analogies, etc.*

Mbɔrɔ and *thabɔrɔ* also sometimes refer to many briefer forms which might seem at first sight to belong to a quite different category; riddles,

[1] See below, pp. 77 ff.

proverbs, morals, a witty or imaginative saying, an elaborate metaphor, or an analogy.

Riddles are often asked among children. Simple examples are: 'I have tied water into a parcel', to which the reply is 'Orange'; or 'What child is older than its father?', where the answer is 'A wicker fish-trap' because the end called the *hatoŋ* (lit. child) is woven before the rest of the trap, so that the 'child' is thus 'older'. A rather different type in which what is suggested by some *sound* must be identified is, for example, '*Gbekeŋ gbakaŋ*—the axe comes out of the tree'; the point here is that the first two words are expected to suggest the sound made by an axe chopping a tree. Sometimes the riddles are more elaborate, as in the series which open with the stock phrase 'the children of the old man', or 'the children of my father'; these 'children' have then to be identified through some resemblance or analogy implied in the original statement. An example of this type runs: 'A story (or riddle—*mbɔrɔ*) for you. The children of my father once went on a journey. They went far, the two of them. When they were coming back, you could not count them—hundreds, hundreds, hundreds, thirty of them. It is finished.' The answer is 'groundnuts', because when someone puts the two parts of a nut in his mouth and chews, the pieces become too many to be counted.

Such riddles obviously bear some similarity to stories in form, beginning with what is a frequent opening in stories ('a story for you') and the term for 'once' (*nde*), ending with one of the stock verbal conclusions, 'it is finished'.[1] They are also akin to stories ending with a dilemma, and I have sometimes, when asking for a further example of a riddle, been told a dilemma story instead. Of the riddles, one could sum up by saying that some analogy of sound, nature, or situation is usually suggested which must then be correctly identified by the listener.[2]

The term *mbɔrɔ* is also sometimes applied to formulations of the kind we might perhaps term 'proverbs' or pithy sayings. 'The female hen shall not crow in Biriwa' is one example of this kind of saying which is well known in the Biriwa chiefdom. In it the Limba are asserting that they will never allow the Mandingo strangers to win Paramount Chiefship there as they had been trying to do; for, it is implied, though many Mandingoes have settled in Biriwa and taken Limba wives, and thus are now related to the Limba ruling house through the female line, authority belongs of right to the Limba who have inherited it through their fathers. Another such saying runs: 'You want a big thing—like an ant-heap getting a felt hat. It did not go to Freetown.' The reference here is to the black ant-heap, shaped rather like an umbrella so that it can be imaginatively seen as having a hat on its head; this recalls the fact that when a Limba makes an expedition down-country to Freetown, if he

[1] On these forms in stories see below, p. 87.

[2] For other examples of riddles see Part II.

prospers there he always tries to buy certain objects to display his wealth when he reaches home again, including, very commonly, a broad-brimmed felt hat. The meaning of the saying is that there are some people who are ambitious to get fine clothes and possessions as a sign of wealth and experience; but this may be at bottom only empty show; they are no more than an ant-heap which seems to be wearing a felt hat, the mark of the travelled man, and yet has in fact never moved at all!

Such sayings are frequently used in the context of persuasion. When a case is being heard by a chief or elder someone may plead for the offender, saying, for example: 'Do not blame the chimpanzee for his ugliness.' The purpose of this is, by analogy, to make the general point that however bad a child may be it is not right to go to extremes in scolding or punishing him, just as to go on complaining about the notorious ugliness of the chimpanzee is both useless and unreasonable. By means of the particular analogy a general truth is being put forward implicitly, and the actual occasion and fault put in a wider context and perspective. Similarly a brief form of words, referred to as *mbɔrɔ*, may be used to make a point tersely and allusively in the course of some argument. Thus, for example, when a chief's emissary to a memorial ritual was, as he considered, insulted by one of the visitors, he replied briefly, smiling and full of relaxed humour: he had once heard, he said, of a man who pointed rudely at a dead man's face, but found that in return the corpse bit him. This was a *mbɔrɔ* through which the visitor was to be recalled to his senses by the implication that it is dangerous to offend even an apparently helpless person, for you cannot tell the consequences; but at the same time it avoided any open quarrel or overt rebuke. Another example is that of a woman being told by the elders that she is like a *kuwɔ* tree, a tree which grows only near water. The oblique suggestion is that she is only willing to live with a rich man, not with a poor or 'dry' husband. The elders are speaking allusively, 'going round in parables' (*silɔkɔ ka thabɔrɔ*) as they consider she will be more likely to listen than if they are merely angry and direct with her.

It seems that such sayings among the Limba have mainly a local and limited currency and are not known in common to all Limba or cited widely with an identical grammatical form in each case. In both these ways they seem to differ from what we generally term proverbs, which have a very widely accepted currency in a prescribed form. How exactly such Limba sayings arise is not quite clear. But it is probable that many originate from some analogical and witty allusive form of words used by someone in a speech or public occasion, which is then taken up by those who heard it and thus gains wider currency for a time. Thus the saying about the hen not crowing in Biriwa was, I was told, first used in a speech by one of the Limba elders on an occasion in the

1950's when the Mandingoes were considering putting up a candidate for the chiefship election; it was used as an oblique and tactful warning to them to withdraw. In various forms[1] this allusion is now a common one among the Limba in Biriwa. Among the several English proverbs that I tried to translate into Limba one in particular, that about the pot calling the kettle black, was found appealing and was taken up by one man to be used, in his own words, as an effective *mbɔrɔ* in a Limba context. Thus, both in the lack of a precisely prescribed verbal form and, possibly, in the way new forms are introduced, these 'proverbs' are in certain respects very similar to the stories proper discussed later.

This similarity is even more evident in the way that such 'proverbs' shade into forms which could be referred to as parables or even stories. Occasionally the moral or generalizing element in some allusive comment is so drawn out that it more or less absorbs the whole statement and it is not really clear whether we should count it as an expanded proverb, a moralizing analogy, or a story. A few stories, perhaps especially those by elders who are accustomed to moralize and reconcile people by their speeches, seem to consist almost as much of didactic generalizing as of narrative. This was noticeable, for example, in the stories by Bubu Dema; his telling of *Kanu and the star*[2] did not involve a very clear plot or lengthy narration, yet the main point of the 'story' as far as the teller was concerned was conveyed unmistakably—the generalization, expressed first by analogy and then directly, that it is futile and ridiculous to try by human means to struggle against one's destiny, the innate qualities or weaknesses with which Kanu has endowed one. In this case the 'story' was in many ways very similar to Limba forms which might be described as a kind of 'proverb'. Another example, but one in which the 'story' aspect was dominant, was that of *Marriage and a bush cow's milk*. This was told, as mentioned earlier, by a chief as a public admonition to the wives present at the time. In Limba such expanded morals, parables, and stories are all equally referred to as *mbɔrɔ* and the different forms seem to shade into each other.

Besides this overlap with stories or parables, these 'proverbs' at the other extreme also shade into mere figures of speech or brief analogies, all these being included within the range of *mbɔrɔ*. Informal analogies are common in arguments, oratory, or joking, and are a form of speech which is admired.

Analogies are particularly effective in speeches, often used in the form of a rhetorical question. Thus, for instance, an old village headman was, early in 1961, objecting to the idea of Independence as he then understood it: the white men had pity for them, he said, but if they were left to themselves 'that is like a child trying to walk for itself before it is able and falling down and hurting itself—and is that good?'

[1] See the forms given in Part II, p. 337.

[2] See Part II, pp. 286–7.

Metaphors are also used to make effective and decorative points in speaking. A man may speak of change—the leaves on a tree blown by the wind; of the chief's word as a heavy sledge-hammer (*humɛkɛ*) which overbears the ordinary light hammer (*huthoda*) of other people; or make an allusion to the positions of chief, sub-chiefs, and people by speaking of a house: the roof is the highest of all and has most respect, but the upright poles too are essential to support the roof, and even the ground must be there too—'look at the ground, you cannot do anything without that'.

Analogies are also frequently introduced to convey to a listener some point that seems to be obscure to him. This was especially so in my case. Limba of every kind continually tried to elucidate unfamiliar customs or concepts for me by trying imaginatively to posit some situation they thought I *would* be familiar with, and then arguing by analogy from that. Thus, to give one simple example, a Limba hunter who had also travelled widely was once trying to convey to me how the Limba think of the 'heart' (*huthukuma*): drawing on his own experience, experience which he knew I shared, he spoke of a lorry: 'The lorry is always there,' he said, 'but without its driver it cannot go or move in the right direction, can it? Well, the heart is like the driver. Without it a person can do nothing.' People often tried to explain through the conventional analogy of a 'book', something accepted to be one of the distinguishing possessions of white men. It was constantly being put to me that 'farming is *our* book' i.e. that to the Limba farming is as economically and affectively important as they suppose reading to be to the Europeans. 'Our hoes are our books', they often say, or 'when *we* hear something, we put it in our hearts; our hearts are our books'. By such analogies with books, several points are conveyed simultaneously. First, this implicitly recalls the stories[1] about the destiny of the Limba—hoeing or farming—as against the Europeans with their books. Secondly there is the two-fold implication both that Europeans are superior in that they are able to write, a quality constantly associated by the Limba with European wealth and mechanical efficiency, *and* at the same time that the Limba too have a system of memory and tradition which is, in its way, comparable to the European and, likewise, not to be despised. This kind of analogy therefore, like many of the stories, can also be used as a vehicle for some generalization or detached comment, and may merge into what might in English be called a proverb or moral. Overtly directed to convey some special point to a listener by comparing it to something else which is well known to him, it may also have many implicit associations and overtones of wider comment.

This Limba propensity to use analogy or conscious metaphor in argument and speech-making can now be further exploited by the more

[1] e.g. *White and black brothers.*

skilled among the candidates in the modern context of election to chiefship. Each candidate is normally allocated a symbol by the government officer in charge and a picture of this is put on his respective ballot box, while he holds an identical picture in his hand so that his supporters will know into which box to put their votes. The candidates brandish their symbols and often use them to draw morals and persuade the people to vote for them. In one chiefdom election I witnessed, the candidate who had as his symbol a picture of a 'cutlass' (one of the most common farming implements), displayed it vociferously to the crowd with

> Here is the cutlass; we use it to clear the bush, to do our hard work, to keep going. Here is the cutlass—hard work. If you don't work hard, you won't get anything, you won't get anything good . . . here is the cutlass.

The holder of a house as symbol used it subtly against this junior contender by implying without openly stating that perhaps that man, with his cutlass and the impetuosity of youth, would keep them too hard at work:

> See the house. When many people go to the farm, when they come back in the evening after their hard work, they rest. The house holds them and keeps them well.

A third candidate who had a lamp as symbol spoke more quietly:

> Please support me, me with the lamp. I took the lamp because my father, the last chief, was very kind to you all. His kindness spread all round like a lamp. If I gain the chiefship I will help my people to get light; let them remember my father's goodness.

Sometimes an analogy or 'parable', as *mbɔrɔ* and *thabɔrɔ* are sometimes translated by literate Limba, is purposely used as a kind of joke, specially popular and amusing when, as often, some of the participants have been drinking. One exchange, for instance, referred to as *thabɔrɔ*, was with a man who was drinking the potent locally distilled spirit. He joked with great mock solemnity that the bottle in his hand was not, of course, of spirit but of paraffin; he was forced to drink it, he said, because he had to have light; and inside his stomach there was a little light, complete with lamp and wick and everything; so he just *had* to sit there all evening, alas, drinking his bottle of paraffin to feed his lamp. All this was uttered with a dead serious expression while, as he had intended, the whole group round him were helpless with laughter.

Such verbal joking and analogies shade into a kind of minor verbal play or punning, and the way Limba sometimes tease a companion by pretending to take some figurative expression literally or in a sense in which it was clearly not intended. People may, for example, consciously play with the ambiguities of such words as the verb 'to eat' (*thɔŋ*) which can be used to mean either ordinary physical eating, or the spiritual consuming by a witch or spirit, or the spending or wasting of goods, specially money; thus a child who came to her grandfather to say shyly that she had 'eaten' the penny he had given her, provided an occasion for a long joke, enjoyed by all the adults, about how ludicrous it was to hear anyone claiming to have actually 'eaten' a hard metal coin. Such minor punning may seem far from the more elaborate analogies, stories, and parables described earlier. But it serves as yet another illustration of the part played in Limba communication by such elements as metaphor, analogy, and figurative expression.

In this section the many different forms of *mbɔrɔ* and their uses have been described. It can perhaps be said that it is this aspect of analogical and figurative expression that gives a certain unity to the wide range of application of the Limba term, a term which means not only story and sometimes (in the plural) historical narrative, but also such apparently diverse things as parable, riddle, proverb, analogy, or metaphor.

4. THE CONCEPT OF *MBƆRƆ*

The word *mbɔrɔ* in Limba, therefore, is used in a very wide sense; and a *mbɔrɔ* may, on different occasions, be used for varying purposes—for amusement, description, generalization, tactful means of persuasion or advice, dramatic and artistic expression related to song and dance; or for many or all of these at once. Yet in one sense the concept of *mbɔrɔ* is an integrated one. I will therefore conclude this section by pointing briefly to the two main strands which, it seems to me, run through most of the applications of the term *mbɔrɔ*. These are, first, the connexion with age and tradition, and, secondly, the idea of analogical expression which has been the main theme in the preceding discussion.

In the first place the word *mbɔrɔ* seems to be connected with the root *bɔrɔ*, old. *Mabɔrɔ ma* are the 'old times' or 'ancient ways', *bebɔrɔ be* the 'old people', usually referring to the dead ancestors, and *bɔrɔ* commonly occurs in various grammatical forms as the ordinary adjective meaning 'old'. *Mbɔrɔ ki* might then be translated literally as 'something old', with its plurals *mbɔrɔiŋ ki* and the more common *thabɔrɔ tha* meaning 'old things' or, specially the latter form, 'old sayings' or 'old words'.[1]

Moreover, whatever the linguistic facts about the derivation of the word *mbɔrɔ*, the concept does seem to be closely associated in Limba eyes with the idea of age and tradition. As was evident in the earlier discussion of religion, the Limba are very conscious of the wisdom and

[1] The prefix n/m/ŋ is typical of the *ki* class of nouns, e.g. *ntha ki*, thing; *tha-* is the typical plural prefix of the *hu* class into which fall most terms to do with words and speaking.

presence of 'the old people', the dead who are buried in the village where their descendants now live, and who know everything that happens to their children now in the world. This respect for the authority and wisdom of the dead is consistent with the emphasis the Limba lay on the basically traditional and enduring nature of *mbɔrɔ*,[1] in spite of its differing expression through individual story-tellers, and with the value they attach to their traditional stories and sayings. One reason, I was told, why people sometimes introduce parables into speeches or persuasion is that in this way you can 'bring in another's wisdom' as well as your own, and so bring to your words the stamp of authority. It was from the old people, it is constantly being stressed, that they first learnt their traditional culture which they now keep 'in their hearts' to 'bring out' on a particular occasion; and included in this traditional and authorized culture are the stories which 'we heard from the old people'.

The second main connotation of *mbɔrɔ*, apparent in at least the majority of the many usages of the term, is that of a comment or reflection in analogical terms. This is naturally especially clear when *mbɔrɔ* is used to mean metaphor, parable, and analogy; but even when it means the more straightforward stories, it seems to suggest this aspect.

Thus it is tempting to interpret the Limba view of 'stories' in general as involving a kind of indirect and analogical comment on the world—not a direct allegory or moral, but the drawing of a wider implication from some particular event or fact. In the case of 'proverbs' and even riddles the use of analogy to illuminate a general truth is quite clear. The same is true of a Limba 'parable', or cross between proverb and story. The case of historical narratives may seem rather different, as to some extent it is. Here too, however, some people evidently realize that in speaking, for instance, of the early founders of certain villages or their actions in the past something is also being said about the present relationships of their descendants. Analogical comment is quite explicit in some stories. As we shall see in the following chapter, the ending of many stories includes reference to some moral or generalization connected with the subject matter. Here a general comment is being introduced, an analogy with the events depicted in the story. Other stories, though not bringing in direct analogy, can also be interpreted as containing a kind of general comment in analogical terms on the ways of the world. It is this aspect which makes every *mbɔrɔ*, whatever its subject-matter, in a sense 'true' (*thia*)—a Limba term also used for assenting to someone's advice, exhortations or reflective generalizations. This is of course not the only theme in the stories; but it can be said that one aspect is a representation of something general implied through the

[1] This is discussed further in connexion with the genesis of stories, chapter 5.

account of particular events in a story. In this way a *mbɔrɔ* from the Limba point of view implies a kind of complex representation of life and action in analogical terms removed from the present situation, most often through the narration of particular actions represented as happening long ago or in a far-off place or by agents in the guise of animals.

3

TOPICS AND TREATMENT IN THE STORIES

So far I have discussed the various groups of Limba stories, roughly differentiated by their main characters, and the nature of the Limba *mbɔrɔ* in general. I now want to leave the shorter secondary forms of *mbɔrɔ*, and discuss some general points that apply to the stories proper, whatever their central characters; in particular to consider their main topics and how these are treated by the story-tellers.

I. THE SETTING AND GENERAL TREATMENT

Limba stories are not composed on the grand scale. That is, they do not treat such subjects as wars, sieges, great historical changes, or long-drawn-out and sustained events. On the whole the tales themselves are relatively short and simple, and the action is also usually presented as fairly brief. Since the stories vary so much among themselves, there are some partial exceptions to this, mainly in stories about people, such as *The man killed for a banana* or *Parents are closest*, in which the narrative may be thought of as covering the events of several years; but on the whole even this is unusual. In a few stories the narrator speaks of simultaneous events in two different places as when, for instance, in *The story of Deremu*, he switches from the mother up-country to her son in Freetown and back again; and in *Sira and the monster* the girl's brother at home is pictured as beginning to worry about his sister who has just been described as the prisoner of the monster far away. But again this is not very common and occurs only in the most elaborate stories.

Most frequently, perhaps specially in the rather shorter animal tales, the plot is simple in that there is little switch of scene throughout and we simply follow the successive actions of the protagonists. In all stories it is common for the action to take place in a series of parallel episodes so that even where there is change of scene this is not in terms of a 'flash-back' from one place or event to another unrelated one, but a following up of the hero as he travels in successive moves from one place to another.[1] This is what Kanu does, for example, as he looks in settlement

[1] See remarks on parallel structure in the following chapter, pp. 88 ff.

after settlement for a wise man (*Kanu gives chiefship*), or the girl who goes from chief to chief to search out her father's murderer in *The man killed for a banana*. From this point of view, Limba stories are uncomplex.

The geographical setting is that best known to the Limba themselves. The action is usually based in, or moves between, the central village where the chief or elders live, the farm, the farm settlement, and the path between these points; the various chiefdoms between which people can travel; and the bush, with its clearings for palm wine tapping and farming as well as its depths where animals and spirits live. There are also occasional references to Freetown (*Kakampi*) as the place where young men go away for work and money, and to the far-away mysterious country of England.

A kind of other-world is also sometimes introduced into the action. This may be entered through a deep pool into which the hero dives, as in the country found by one twin in *Koto and Yemi*. At other times it is located in the sky where, for example, the various animals go to find *The girl taken by Kanu*, in a cave entered through a series of doors as in *The hunter with three dogs*, or completely unlocalized as with the magic world in which *The orphan child* finds himself. These worlds are intentionally presented as fantastic. They are not seriously believed to exist by narrator or audience, but are suitable settings for far-fetched events in story. However, even these magical places are in fact represented as having very much the familiar background—that of village, farm, and bush. Although they may be referred to as 'a new world' they very often have a chief, houses, entertainment, formal speaking, and all the other social relations to be expected in a normal Limba context.

Sometimes the geographical setting is explicitly related to that around the audience by the common device of comparing places in the story to actual villages or chiefdoms. 'As far away as Kabala' is a fairly common form, or 'as from here to where the roads meet'. Sometimes actual names of people are introduced: 'He went as if to Sabena here' comes in one story, referring to a sub-chief in the narrator's village, and in another the heroine is pictured as travelling round chiefdoms in and near Limba country by the teller specifying the names of actual villages and chiefs—'She came as if to Bumban, to Pompoli' (*The man killed for a banana*). In this way the action is the more vividly set within the geographical context closely known to the audience and they can more clearly picture the various moves of the journey or the sort of distances envisaged. Here again the setting is basically that of village, bush, and farm, the context within which Limba social and economic life is carried on.

In the stories as a whole it is true to say that the supernatural element is not the dominant one. Certain stories, as already mentioned, take place in a far-off magical world, and certain kinds of fantastic exaggeration are common. A chief is pictured as having vast amounts of gold, possessions, and magic, magical acts and transformations sometimes take place, a human is able to understand the language of animals, or a boy enters into a farming company with the animals of the bush. Encounters with various supernatural agencies are also included—with Kanu in the old days, or, more often, with one of the spirits of the bush, with a 'monster' (a kind of spirit) or a 'great witch'. But the central characters are nearly always humans, or animals acting like humans; they are never supernatural beings acting and reacting among themselves. Even where the action is, as often, removed from direct reality by the common device of setting it in the past, in a far-off land, or in the guise of animal characters, the basic situation depicted is fundamentally a human one, belonging primarily to this world and not to any other grand heroic, supernatural or mythical stage.

2. THE TREATMENT OF CHARACTERS

The stories are in the main about individuals. They are not concerned with large-scale actions in which the long-term concerted acts and plans of many people must be depicted. The only partial exception to this is in the few stories in which twins are represented as acting jointly to achieve a common purpose, or in the series of successive and co-operative acts taken by those who go to retrieve a girl from the sky. But even in these cases the stress is not on the plan and execution viewed as a whole, but on the sequence of actions by individuals in a series of parallel episodes; each individual is pictured as coming forward in turn saying 'my time has come now', performing his part, and then giving way to the next character. The stories, then, are primarily about individuals and have a very simple structure.

The main characters that appear in the stories have already been described. They are either humans, named or unnamed, animals, or supernatural beings of various kinds—Kanu, spirits, a 'monster'. In a sense, there is little individual characterization. The hero is often just described as 'a man', 'an orphan', 'a chief', and some stock image of these figures seems to be evoked rather than a distinct individual personality. Even in the case of the named heroes—Deremu, Bayo, Kubasi, Sara—there is more emphasis on the part they take in the action of the story than on, say, their individual attributes or dispositions. The actors are presented from the outside, so to speak, rather than looked at in terms of their individual experiences or inner feelings—a side of experience for which there is in fact only a limited vocabulary in Limba. Some characters of course are introduced only in a secondary role, to serve the exigencies of the plot, and in these cases one would not expect any very vivid characterization; but even the leading characters may often seem rather shadowy if regarded as individuals.[1]

In the words of the stories, therefore, there seems to be little characterization. But it must also be remembered that each story was delivered to be seen and heard as a performance, rather than composed to be read from a written page. The impression given by the actual narration of a story may be very different from that given to a reader, for the characterization is then often seen to be vivid.

This applies particularly in the case of animals. Their way of speaking is portrayed by tone and expression, their action half-imitated—the shy perceptive way in which the antelope peeps round and sums up the situation, the blustering tones of the spider, the little light bat swinging patiently to and fro in his hammock smoking his little pipe; the helpless way in which the tricked leopard lies under the tree self-centredly imploring for help and making fine, shallow promises; the ludicrous picture of the gluttonous and stupid spider being dragged along behind the pot of rice he has tried to keep for himself, obvious prisoner to his own greed but even then trying to salve his dignity by pretending to walk or implausibly claiming that he was bringing the rice on purpose. In the portrayal of such episodes there is vivid and individual characterization in each particular performance.

The same tendency is also sometimes evident in stories not primarily about animals. A sympathetic and fatherly character was clearly attributed to Kanu in both *Kanu gave food to the Limba* and the later parts of *The stomach is chief of the body*, by the strikingly gentle and kindly tone in which he was made by the respective narrators to utter his directions to the other characters. Again, in *The story of Bayo*, the despair and lack of confidence of the rather humble and self-effacing child, who was apparently fated to be destroyed by the powerful animals he had become entangled with, was indicated throughout the story by the narrator's effective manner; it was particularly evident in the way in which Bayo did not at first dare to reveal himself to the monster—a common motif, used here particularly effectively—and then finally did so by saying 'Me' in so quiet and timid a tone that the audience could scarcely catch it. Sira's extreme vehemence in all she did was also drawn vividly in the story of *Sira and the monster*, first by the breathless and uncontrolled way in which she was presented as bursting forth when she saw her chosen suitor gleaming in the distance, and then by her final outburst where she threw herself at her brother's feet to thank him for delivering her.

Among the Limba, then, it is part of a good story-teller's art to give drama and vividness to the characters which in a written version may

[1] Apart possibly from the irresponsible boy Tungkangbali and perhaps some of the standardized characters attributed to animals, e.g. the spider or the antelope.

often appear lifeless. It is for this reason among others that any systematic account of *oral* literature—certainly that of the Limba—should include some description of its style, delivery, and technique, for without this the effect, even the nature, of the oral literature in question is obscured.

3. THE TOPICS OF THE STORIES

So much for the setting of the stories in time and space, and the characterization conveyed by many story-tellers. We can now briefly discuss or recapitulate the more common topics of the stories and the sorts of conclusions which are accepted as pleasing or suitable.

Perhaps the most common situation described or alluded to is that of marriage, or of love. This topic comes into stories of all kinds, whether about humans, animals, or origins. In these tales about diverse aspects of love or marriage, it would not be true to say that any one unified view was being presented. There are particular morals in particular stories, various facets are emphasized from time to time, and there are implicit comments on the kinds of ways people are known at times to behave, the sorts of things that are liable to happen or that might happen if customs were otherwise. But no one lesson or picture is being drawn. Wives (or potential wives) may be portrayed in one story as virtuous, perhaps willing even to suffer death, loss, or bereavement for their husbands, as in *Four wives* or *The story of Kubasi*; in another as bad, ready to betray a husband's closest secret or chance of real success to their lovers (*Sara, the spirit, and the palm tree*; *Kanu gives chiefship*). Just as in Limba experience and philosophy women are known to be faithful or unfaithful, imagined to be loyal or disloyal, thought of in their different roles of mothers, wives, lovers, sisters, according to the point of view of the individual at the time—so too in the stories there may be stock situations or characters, but these are open to a corresponding variety of treatment and emphasis. A girl may be pictured as innocent and attractive, with lovely clothes and beads, a young girl's breasts, fresh from initiation—'like the dew' as it is said in one riddle, or, in a story, 'standing there in her blackness with only her beads round her loins'—and yet the apparent sweetness and innocence may only disguise the fact that she is secretly plotting her husband's or lover's death (as in *The man killed for a spinach leaf*, and *The story of the great witch*). One girl may be pictured as obstinate and resistant to her parents' wishes for her marriage, thus leading either to her father's loss, as in *The story of a millionaire*, or to her own misery and repentance, as with the girl deceived by a spirit in *Sira and the monster*. Or the situation may be reversed so that it is the man, not the girl, that is misled by a spirit, seemingly a loving wife, whom he follows to her home where he nearly perishes: 'Ah,' he says when he knows the truth, 'it was love that put me here. If it had not been for that I would not have come here' (*The hunter with three dogs*). Sometimes the earlier situation is portrayed from the opposite point of view again and a girl's betrayal of father or chief or child may be pictured as praiseworthy, leading to the triumph of the hero whom she loves and for whom she sacrifices every other tie: 'I love you beginning from the world here as far as the place of death. So let us go together you and I' (*Story of Kubasi*).

Alternatively, the situation of love can be used to amuse. Thus the actions of *The woman with four lovers* are portrayed as ridiculous by the narrator's showing them in their over-numerous succession; or an intentionally ludicrous effect is created by the way in which the normal sweet talk between two lovers was interrupted by—of all things—the excrement the girl had tried to leave behind her in the forest; it rose up demanding to join in 'your talking that you are talking . . . both of us are to embrace the girl' (*The forbidden forest*).

Thus love, within or without marriage, may be pictured from many different points of view: as something dangerous and untrustworthy leading to death or loss; as sacrificial and able to save a man's life; as exciting and pleasurable as in the humorous description of the origin of sex (*The beginning of marriage*) or as something potentially laughable and far-fetched as in the series of formalities performed by *The woman with four lovers*.

Marriage itself is portrayed in various lights, with, at times, its potential paradoxes made plain. It is normally, for example, assumed in the stories that, as in real life, men must work to win a wife. This is sometimes portrayed in an exaggerated or even fantastic form. Perhaps the hero must greet a mother-in-law continuously through the whole course of the day, risk death or blindness to help a friend get a wife, climb up a pumpkin that reaches to the sky, or perform near-impossible tasks like clearing a huge farm in a single night or picking up basketfuls of minute millet seeds in the dark; and stories often end with the hero's success in acquiring a wife—'the wife was given' is always a suitable conclusion. And yet, after all, the opposite point is made in one story, perhaps one wife is *not* really worth risking death for; as the hunter's dog said 'Are there no other wives in the world? Are there no other wives? If it happens that [the hunter] goes hunting and kills meat will he not sell it and look for another wife? Will he die for this one wife?' (*The story of a hunter*).

Marriage is assumed to be a man's aim. And yet, as is shown in several stories, marriage too has its drawbacks. The strife and competition between husband and wife are depicted especially in the quarrels of the spider and his wife Kayi. He acts in a way that it is known a husband never should do (but sometimes perhaps actually does, or wishes to, act), and tries to trick his wife or get more food than is due to him;

while she, as a wife should never be (but sometimes, as even men occasionally admit, really is), turns out to be stronger and cleverer than her husband and outwits or surpasses him. There are many other possible difficulties in marriage. Sometimes there are no children and, as in life, the couple must sacrifice and seek help to obtain them; or the most loved wife may not conceive—'I and my husband have travelled much', says one woman, 'but we have not yet got children' (*Two women*); or even if she succeeds in bearing and rearing a child he may still die young. If there *are* children the co-wives may quarrel jealously over them, even, in one story, to the length of murder (*Jealous mothers*), or support their own children against the others (*Four wives*). Many wives and many children are what every man, in story and in life, most desires. Yet this too may have its bad side—'quarrelling will not end. One wife to one husband—they will not quarrel. But two people, three people—they will not love each other. For having children—when they have children in the marriage they will disagree' (*Jealous mothers*). Again, if there are several wives the tension among them may lead to one wife insisting on her exact cold justice, as illustrated in its extreme form by the one who demanded back her bead—the precise bead, no more and no less—swallowed by her co-wife's child (*Two co-wives*).

All these many points of view on marriage and love must of course be seen in the context of Limba marriage and the Limba view of women described earlier; only then can the associations and effectiveness of, for example, the infidelity of a wife or the labours of wooing be fully intelligible in the sense they would be to a Limba listener. In the whole context well known to both narrator and audience all these comments on the behaviour of men and women can be effective and meaningful, whether wry, ironic, perceptive or plain ridiculing. One of the significant points about such comments is their diversity—in marriage and love there are many diverse situations and aspects which can be depicted in the stories. It would be a mistake to suggest that the stories express some clear-cut message on the subject, as a foreigner who had encountered only two or three might at first be led to assume. Rather—once given the social background and common experience of the teller and listener—they can be seen to be full of varied comments, insights, or amused and far-fetched generalization on the kinds of ways in which people actually behave or would like to behave.

Much the same point applies to other common topics in Limba story. Many stories are about, or refer to, various types of family relationships other than those of marriage. *Parents are closest* makes the comment, in this case explicitly, that whatever a man has done, only his parents will stand by him through thick and thin, and others stay only in time of success: 'Fortune is not like the time of difficulty . . . the parent accepted for he bore him, everyone else refused. That is it.'[1] Other stories touch on similar relationships, though often without asserting such an emphatic generalization. The relations of mother and child are often illustrated. The close tie known to exist between mother and daughter is, in varying ways, important to the plots of *The man killed for a spinach leaf* where the daughter is brought up to the sound of her widowed mother's lullaby, and in *The story of a great witch* where the mother tries to stop her daughter's marriage—'for a long time they had quarrelled, the girl and the mother'. The very close affective bond that exists both in ideal and in practice between mother and child can thus be exploited, not only in stories that stress a mother's care for her son, as in *The story of an orphan* where she rises from the grave in answer to her need, but also in the stories where the opposite side is shown—a mother portrayed as going to the extreme and shocking lengths of plotting against her own child (*The story of Deremu*; *A story of witches*).

The position and fortunes of an orphan are a popular theme in story. His lot is one that is expected to elicit pity, so that his triumphs, whether in recalling his mother or in gaining chiefdom and riches, have a particular meaning through their paradoxical nature—that a child beginning from such well-known disadvantages should yet achieve success (for example in *The story of an orphan*; *The orphan and the goats*). Another theme is of the help given by a child or younger brother. This gains part of its point from the usual assumption in almost all social situations that age denotes authority and leadership. Yet in several stories, paradoxically and effectively, it is the young brother following far off, spurned by his elders, who in the end saves them by his cleverness or insight (*Three men, a boy, and a cow*; *The girl and the spirit*).

Relations within a family are thus frequent topics in the stories and plots are sometimes brought to a quiet end by the hero's returning home and giving an account of his actions ('announcing' them) to his mother or father. But there is no one rule for how these relations turn out in story, and though the topic is obviously a meaningful and important one, no single image of family life is being presented to the exclusion of others.

Another very common theme has to do with *yaŋfa*,[2] 'slander', or secret and often malicious gossiping. This is a frequent motif in the stories that end with an explicitly stated moral. Sometimes a character is depicted as motivated only by the desire to injure another, as the 'trouble-maker' (*bayaŋfa*) who told malicious lies to the chief to hurt *The boy that talked with animals*; but, in the end, 'you see now—the trouble-maker was killed by his own trouble-making' (*yaŋfa*). This kind of situation,

[1] Contrast this with *Kubasi* and *Four wives* where the parents, unlike the girl, will not risk death for their son.

[2] On *yaŋfa*, see above, p. 23.

however, in which a character's bad intentions are stressed from the outset is not very common; in fact Limba stories seldom contain a clearly designated human villain. More often the act of tale-bearing is presented as a necessary turning-point of the plot by which one character learns another's secret. The act itself is in the first place introduced as an apparently perfectly reasonable gesture of help to someone who is being deceived by another. Thus the hawk is helped by the hen against the finch who had deceitfully promised to repay a debt when 'he grew big—but he does not grow, that is his size' (*The finch's loan*); similarly the hawk is told how to recover his own money from the sun who so constantly frightens him off by his heat (*The sun, the hawk, and the hen*). Yet in each case this apparently helpful act is classed as *yaŋfa* and explicitly deplored.

The expression of this moral about *yaŋfa* is a standard ending to a story. Indeed this stock conclusion occasionally seems to be added on to a story which, on the face of it, might not necessarily have been expected to give rise to it at all; in the tale of *The spider, the elephant, and the hippopotamus*, another narrator might well have been content with a different ending, perhaps describing merely the origin of the spider's presence in people's houses, or his clever power in outdoing the other two; but on the particular occasion on which I recorded it the narrator was an old man particularly fond of adding morals, and so he brought his narration to an end by emphasizing that this was a case of *yaŋfa*: 'So you see, someone who is good at talking behind people's backs destroys people . . . so too with a Limba [human] who has nothing in the village himself—he makes two people fight.' The effects of tale-bearing, then, form a potential theme in plot and moralizing, but are brought into different stories in various ways—sometimes as the central interest of a tale, sometimes as a neat and satisfying moral conclusion.

Friendship and co-operation—or their absence—form another common topic. This is treated most obviously in the well-known plot about two friends, each willing to sacrifice himself for the other, to the extent of giving up his sight or a first-born child. A series of parallel episodes in which one after another of a group of people or animals performs 'his part' is also fairly common, often ending with a dilemma about which individual had contributed most (*The girl taken by Kanu*; *Three twins woo one girl*, etc.). Sometimes, on the other hand, companions are depicted as specifically *not* helping each other. This seems to be particularly common in the standard situation of travelling, a time when an individual is specially dependent on his companion. Injuring someone in this situation is often censured in the stories—'so do not act badly to your travelling companion'—and the one who begins the injury is commonly shown as being paid back in the end. There are many stories which open with two individuals, usually animals, 'going on a journey';

they describe the interested trickery of the one, then the final triumphant revenge of the other. The chameleon, for example, was accused of theft by the monkey at the beginning of the journey, but by the end he had in his turn invented a similar plausible lie against the monkey so that 'they beat the monkey till his tail fell out' (*The monkey and the chameleon*).

Competition and failure in due co-operation are also portrayed in other contexts, especially that of the formation of a co-operative 'company' (*kunɛ*). Here too the one who begins is conventionally the one to suffer in the end. Thus the greed of the animals who formed a 'farming' company with the child Bayo, hoping to eat him, was frustrated in the end by Bayo's triumph (*The story of Bayo*). A similar theme of revenge also sometimes occurs, in a more complicated way, in a longer and more elaborate story such as *The man killed for a banana*. Most often, however, it is introduced in a simple parallelism where a 'company' of ill deeds is embarked on by one character, then equally matched by the other. This is the theme of the typical 'company' between the monkey and the fish; the monkey said that the fish must sit on a chair to eat the rice—the fish could not, 'he has no bottom, when he tried to sit on the chair it was slippery'; but then the fish said the monkey was only to eat if his hands were clean—he scrubbed and scrubbed his black hand but 'it did not come clean—the blood came out' (*The monkey and the catfish*). Such stories commonly end up with the success of the one first injured, and this, sometimes with the addition of a moral stating that one should not try to take advantage of another, is a stock ending for such a tale. However, wanton injury does not in all cases necessarily lead to the punishment of the culprit. Tungkangbei is depicted as acting irresponsibly and anti-socially throughout; yet in the end he is rewarded and even praised (*Tungkangbei, Palongbei, and Yisinua*). Similarly the selfish spider is often frustrated, but once at least he gets away with his aggressiveness by his lies and hypocrisy towards the leopard (*The spider and the leopard*). Friendship and co-operation are generally approved in the context of Limba society and are often praised or exemplified in the stories, just as selfish injury and lack of co-operation are often blamed. But this is not explicitly and necessarily stated in every single story that refers to these common themes, and success as well as unselfishness may be highlighted.

As mentioned earlier chiefship is another important subject in Limba stories as it is in real life. There is no one way of representing a chief in the stories. He may appear as a judge, or as a kindly and sympathetic father; more often he is presented as powerful and wealthy (as in, for example, *Sara and the greedy chief*). Many different aspects of chiefship are brought out. Sometimes chiefs are presented as concerned with their duties to the poor and orphaned, and exhibit wisdom and hospitality as in one version of *Kanu gives chiefship*; sometimes they lose their tempers over something trivial, notably in *The man killed for a spinach leaf*; sometimes they are harsh and oppressive, as with *The cruel chief* and others. The struggle for power is another common theme, represented in the popular setting of a race for chiefship among various animals, or in a contest between individuals in cunning or wisdom: one of the standard endings is when the hero wins or inherits the chiefship. The various possibilities in chiefship, of which the Limba have had experience in both stories and reality are used in the narration of many and diverse tales.

Rice and food frequently appear in stories. Sometimes they provide not so much the subject-matter as the setting and background. As described earlier, the rice-farming cycle can provide the chronological framework within which a series of actions takes place, covering the typical farming operations well known to every Limba. The various stages are often gone through—clearing, hoeing, chasing, reaping, then the drying, pounding, and cooking of the food as in the stories of *Koto and Yemi*, *Kanu gave food to the Limba*, *The boy that talked with animals*, and very many others. Sometimes a struggle for food provides the central episode of a story, particularly in the tales about the spider and his wife. An ending in reconciliation is often pictured in terms of eating: 'they sat there and they ate' (*The spider tries to cheat his wife*), a satisfying ending with all the overtones to eating as one of the central themes of Limba marriage. The opposite ending for a story or section of a story may be the protagonist's hunger, an indication of failure and distress, which is often the spider's lot. Competition for food also enters into the many tales about rivalry and revenge, where, for example, one travelling companion cheats the other of his due share of the food, or where the various stages of a 'company' are marked by some or all of the participants eating together before the next stage of the story.

Eating is also a topic which may be presented as something amusing in itself. The competition in eating, for example, between the goat with its delicate sideways nibbling at the grass, and the elephant's huge consumption, was considered very amusing, specially the final trick by which the goat frightened away the elephant (*The elephant and the goat compete in eating*). In stories about the spider his stupid gluttony is a stock cause for amusement, and even the mere vehement assertion that 'he *ate*' is usually enough to raise a laugh. The fantastic lengths to which—it is humorously suggested—some people may go in their desire for rice is illustrated in an extreme form in the amusing story of *Sara miser and Sara scrounger*, where the avarice of the one led him actually to pretend to die and be buried to stop his friend sharing his rice, and the greed of the other made him persist in staying by the rice even through the supposed death and funeral of his friend. Greed for meat is found a specially funny topic. Even the mere word which refers to this (*thebede*) can produce laughter, and various stories about this proceed through a series of ludicrous actions perpetrated by characters trembling with excitement and stupidity at the thought of the meat—but always ending up without it. Perhaps the most popular theme of all is that of the woman so intent on her meat that she ignored the pains of childbirth, and her toothless new-born child who devoured the remaining bones by himself! In many stories, therefore, a reference to some aspect of eating—whether food, cooking, or hunger—is considered a sufficient and pleasing theme and conclusion.

Cunning is another common subject in the stories. The most frequent word, *hugbanaŋ*, means not only cunning, but also special powers, irresponsibility, and the capacity for extreme and far-fetched actions. It is asked, for example, who was the greatest in 'cunning' of the three twins who, respectively, shot an elephant when still four days' journey away, skinned it all with a finger nail, or packed it into the body of an insect (*Three twins and an elephant*); or of the three twins who tracked, reassembled, and revived their long-dead father, and their mother who cooked every piece of food for them in a minute pot and then served it separately—which was 'the most cunning' (*The hunter and the three twins*). Such stories about cunning or other similarly far-fetched actions commonly end with an explicit or implicit problem about which character was the most surprising (e.g. *The woman with four lovers*; *Three twins woo one girl*). Sometimes various clever tricks are shown by which the hero finally succeeds in winning chiefship. The most common motif here is for the hero, who has been shut up in a bag and is going to be thrown into the river, to cajole someone else into taking his place, only to return himself in triumph. The stories in which this kind of cunning is displayed are usually markedly humorous and light-hearted, and are frequently about twins, specially the trio made up of Tungkangbali and his brothers.

Other kinds of cleverness are also depicted—the clever wiles of the spider against the leopard, the timid intelligence of the antelope, or the ingenious reversals in some of the stories about competition and revenge (*The monkey and the chameleon*, etc.). Here too the actual trick is appreciated and its final triumph considered as a suitable and enjoyable climax. But this kind of cleverness is not felt to have the extreme humour associated with the amazing *hugbanaŋ* of the more far-fetched stories.

Some element of amusement, or at least entertainment, is present in various degrees in practically all Limba stories. But some topics are thought to be particularly funny. The effect depends partly, of course, on the style of wording and delivery by the narrator,[1] but certain subjects are found amusing just in themselves and recur in many stories. One is that of greed, especially, as already mentioned, greed for meat, of

[1] See the discussion in the following chapter.

hunger, and of gluttonous eating. Another cause for amusement is the act of beating or being beaten as described in story. One of the highlights, for example, in the tale about the fight between *The spider and the chimpanzee* was the way in which the spider was knocked down and defeated. In this case a story which in itself might seem to be of little interest can give the greatest delight to a group of listeners through the narrator's vigorous imitation of the blows given by both sides and the vehemence of his description. Extremes of astonishment in the characters are also found amusing, specially if enacted by a clever narrator, like the amazement shown by the people when Sara was thought to have killed his own mother (*Sara and the greedy chief*). Excretion is another topic which, in a story, can be thought very funny. Several of the stories about the irresponsible spider include this, and people tend to burst into delighted laughter at these points. If sex is brought into the stories, it does not seem in itself to arouse either amusement or interest; though there are many stories about love, licit or illicit, the humour and point lie primarily in the characterization or situation—such as the woman who painstakingly went through all the formalities of cooking for and greeting as many as four lovers one after the other (*The woman with four lovers*), or the brilliant way in which the adulterous goat escaped from the deceived husband and turned the tables on his informer (*The goat, the leopard, and the lion*).

Sometimes the amusing impact of the story for the listeners turns not on conventionally amusing topics—greed, beatings, astonishment, excretion—but on some incongruity or paradox in the situation. A hunter, for example, is shown dancing the famous hunter's dance which is performed only over some great killing—and over what? Merely a bush that waved in the wind (*The hunter and the bush*).[1] A man is called to be the chief mourner for the one he himself had secretly killed (*A clever husband*); and the dog and the cat, who are known to fight whenever they meet, are in one story depicted as lovers who jointly deceive the woman's husband before they are turned into their present shapes in one version of *Kanu gives chiefship*. Amusement may therefore in varying ways be produced by many different devices and topics—by the technique of the story-teller's style and delivery discussed in the next chapter, by the conventionally popular topics of beating, excretion, and, most of all, eating, and by some unexpected or paradoxical situation.

The final standard topic or theme is the rather different one of Kanu. This has already been mentioned earlier. Here the relevant point is to repeat that though Kanu comes into stories of many different kinds and subjects, his introduction into a narrative can be used to express some explicit commentary on the world, on the ways in which things happen, or people behave. White and black men, for example, are different and

[1] A story not included here.

yet somehow fundamentally the same and their different destinies and the aptitudes given by Kanu are accounted for in several stories, yet 'we are full brothers' (*Koto and Yemi*). In various ways, the world is full of paradox: the toad betrayed us and brought us death while the snake loved us, yet 'the one who loved us then, well, when we meet him now, we kill him. We do not kill the toad. Well, Kanu looks at us for that' (*The toad did not love us*); and—a common Limba sentiment—a man may work hard and deserve well, yet if Kanu has not given him aptitude and success his toil is useless (*Kanu and the star*; *Kanu scatters his children*). In such stories or parables, a kind of generalizing commentary on the world can be effectively expressed or made quite explicit in the conclusion.

4. CONCLUSION

This long discussion of conventional topics, favourite themes, and standard conclusions has been introduced not only to clarify certain general tendencies in stories, but also to illustrate further one important point already briefly referred to. This is that no *one* moral is being put forward, explicitly or implicitly, in the stories as a whole, nor is it possible to draw up any simple 'philosophy of life' from the stories. Even the very popular and common topics such as marriage, family relations, or chiefship are not treated from just one point of view. Many different insights and comments are brought in at various times. There are, it is true, certain basic presuppositions which one must recognize to understand the meaning of the stories in context—the common acceptance of certain institutions to do with marriage, farming, chiefship, and religion, all subjects discussed in an earlier chapter. One can also note the existence of certain literary conventions about the kinds of figure that can be introduced (the poor orphan, the gluttonous spider, the deceitful wife, etc.), the most likely topics for entertainment (food, beating, excretion, paradox, extreme actions and situations), or the most acceptable conclusions (eating, hunger, being given a wife, returning home, succeeding against another, winning chiefship, or the formal statement of a moral, dilemma, origin, or generalization). But, as we have seen, within this accepted framework there are many and diverse possibilities.

It would thus be misleading to say of Limba tales that there is any *one* message or purpose conveyed in the stories, or that each story must somehow have some fixed and definitive lesson which it is primarily intended to communicate. It is true that several stories do end with an explicitly stated moral. But, as already pointed out, even in these cases, the moral is not always an essential element of the story but is often tacked on as a kind of afterthought or neat conclusion and sometimes omitted altogether in otherwise very similar stories. Furthermore an explicit moral is only one kind of conclusion among several possible ones.[1] One aspect of story-telling is certainly a serious one; but stories are also, most definitely, for laughter and sociability as well. And the serious aim that may, in differing degrees, sometimes underlie the telling of a story is not a directly utilitarian one. People's wisdom and experience are passed on, certainly, and this is occasionally explicitly recognized by reflective Limba as one of the values of the stories. But this transmission takes place in a subtle way, not in terms of a simplicist moral or function; people's joint and individual experience is conveyed and reconveyed and reformulated through the complex medium of the stories. Therefore to pick on the moral element alone and assert that it is the central and significant point of the stories would, in the case of Limba tales, be a vastly over-simplified and distorted view.

Yet it would be equally misleading to assert that the stories are told 'merely for amusement', or that they could therefore be assumed to be irrelevant in any systematic understanding of a people's life and outlook. Entertainment is certainly an important element. But so are other aspects—the comments, insights, or amused and ironic remarks about certain situations, real or imaginary, that are so evident in Limba stories. These aspects are also a real part of their whole view of the world, and clearly relevant for any rounded understanding of, say, their general outlook on marriage, chiefship, or personal relations. In the stories something 'true' (*thia*) is being expressed, often in analogical terms, and the wisdom and experience common to one group or individual passed on in various forms to others, there to be reformed and, in turn, retold.

It is not necessary, then, to be forced here into either of the extreme positions often implied in remarks about African folktales—that is, that they are either ultimately utilitarian, with some clear social function or message, or else that they are mere amusing by-play and so, however intrinsically charming, irrelevant in any serious study of the society. Rather we can consider Limba stories as possessing much the same characteristics as our own literature. They have no one simple message—there is, after all, no reason to assume that the Limba, any more than we ourselves, see life as a simple matter. The stories are a complex medium through which comments can be variously expressed or implied. Indeed once we know something of Limba social and artistic conventions, it becomes natural to accept Limba stories as a form of literature in their own right, designed, in varying degrees, to achieve many of the purposes traditionally associated with literature—and, in their own context, to reveal something of the universal through the mask of the particular.

[1] In the stories included here, under a quarter actually end with the statement of an explicit moral.

4

STORY-TELLING

So far Limba stories have been discussed primarily as literature. But if the stories are a form of literature, they are also, it must be remembered, *oral* literature. Since performance as well as literary composition is an essential part of the art, one must also analyse the style and techniques of story-telling, the dramatic presentation, the occasion, and the audience, in a way that is not necessary in the case of written literature. To ignore these aspects in a discussion of oral literature would be to give an incomplete and misleading picture of its impact in its original context, in and for which it is composed.

I. OCCASIONS OF STORY-TELLING[1]

Limba stories are most frequently told in the evenings, after the sun has set. There is not an explicit rule that stories should not be told in the daylight hours, but in practice people are then normally occupied, specially at certain points in the farming year, and at these times it would be considered unsuitable to spend time during the day in story-telling. But, specially in the relative leisure of the long dry season, there are frequent light-hearted gatherings when stories are exchanged after dark in the home village when the day's work is finished. The most popular time is at full moon when people go to bed late, but at other times too stories are told either under the stars, or, since people like to see as well as hear the narrator, by the light of a paraffin lamp or blazing fire.

The most typical occasions are when people are sitting around together soon after nightfall, relaxed and full fed after the regular evening meal, perhaps with a cup of palm wine going to each of the men in turn. They may sit awhile chatting with, perhaps, some of the younger people breaking into intermittent snatches of song or dance and someone desultorily beating at a drum; if there is a moon the children may be running around, dancing or chasing each other. Then one child may begin to tease a friend by asking him a riddle (*mbɔrɔ*). This may be taken up by one of the older people, and then stories proper begin to be told, often starting with the shorter and simpler ones, then gradually moving on to the long elaborate ones, which may have songs and chorus led by

[1] I here refer only to the stories proper. Some remarks about the occasions for other shorter formulations are included in chapter 2, pp. 40–46.

the teller and echoed by his listeners. On another occasion one man, stimulated by some event or discussion or chance comment, or perhaps from nothing but high spirits or relaxed pleasure at the end of the day, may begin 'A story for you'—one of the stock openings; then people murmur and fall silent as he starts on his narrative, while the word goes round the village that so-and-so is telling a story and the people gradually gather to listen. The group increases as more people, men, women, and children, come to join it and listen attentively or join in the song and responses in reply to the teller.

When one story has finished and the teller has formally brought his narration to a close, another man often comes forward to follow up the last tale with one of his own. 'He takes it up', as one Limba put it, 'and shows his friend the wisdom he has in his heart, taking his share in the telling.' Once the session has really got going, there is even some competition in the telling and people may have to vie with each other for a hearing. If an outstanding narrator is there he may tell several stories on end, but normally people speak in turn while the rest of the group listens and assesses the narration. Even children make an attempt to tell a story, encouraged by their elders who are interested to hear what they can do. But it is mostly those generally recognized as good story-tellers that monopolize the session. Those who are very specially skilled and confident stand or move about in the centre of the group and lead the singing conspicuously, half-dancing as they move, and go in for long and elaborate tales; most people are more modest and sit as they tell their story, watched as well as listened to by the group round them. Sometimes a fierce competition develops between two friends, each determined to have the last word and win greater acclaim than the other; as soon as one has finished the other comes in with 'but *I* am not through yet'—and the contest continues until at last people are too sleepy to listen and begin to slip away to bed.

Such story-telling sessions do not take place on set occasions but arise spontaneously from the informal groups gathered together in leisure in the evenings. The form of art is a conventional one, it is true, but it is not expressed in formal set situations. Occasionally when someone known to be a specially good story-teller comes to the village people guess that he is likely to be easily persuaded to speak and gather hopefully in the evening, perhaps even giving him small gifts afterwards in thanks. But normally the gathering does not have even this degree of formality. People contrast the story-teller's art, one not involving special preparations or gifts, with the more specialized one of the drummer or famous singer. The story-telling session could be regarded in a sense as a kind of 'act of sociability'[1] rather than an organized artistic ceremony.

It is in this way, then, that stories are told and changed and exchanged

[1] As Malinowski phrases it, *Myth in Primitive Psychology*, p. 36.

all over Limba country. They are told after sunset in the farm settlements for amusement or distraction by those who spend long hours in the farm away from the village, either on the open platforms where the children scare the birds from the growing rice or under the scanty shelter of the rough farm huts. They are told in the main villages where most people return after the day's work or travel. In the larger towns on the main roads the old people speak with regret of how there are no longer such frequent and large gatherings as in their young days; yet even there people still exchange stories in the evenings, or take the opportunity of introducing a new story they have heard down-country or from a passing traveller. There, as elsewhere, there is still the occasional introduction of a story into a formal admonition or law case during the day, ostensibly to bring 'wisdom' to those present or make an effective point,[1] in practice often enjoyed for its own sake. Even in Freetown Limba living there sometimes gather together to hear and tell stories, perhaps bringing in Krio words or phrases, perhaps mainly in Limba, in much the same way as those in the rural areas from which they originally come. But the most typical occasions are still those in the home villages in the north where numbers of people are gathered together and can sit outside in the compound, with perhaps twenty or thirty people, or even more, listening to a series of stories over many hours often late into the night. Story-telling, it is stressed, is a public and not a private activity, and through these public occasions the tales are not only jointly enjoyed and performed but also 'bring wisdom' to the members of the group and publicly carry the story forward so that others too may know it.

2. THE AUDIENCE

The nature of the audiences for the stories has already been implied in the discussion of the occasions for them and for the other forms of *mbɔrɔ*. They vary somewhat according to circumstances. Riddles are told by one child to another, perhaps in pairs, perhaps in larger groups, and are often the preliminary to longer narratives. 'Proverbs', analogies, and parables are often used in small informal groups or, occasionally, introduced into a formal speech, perhaps one of those made in the course of a law case in an official chiefdom court, to an audience of perhaps thirty or forty men, or even as many as a hundred or more. But the most typical situation is the one just described where the wine circulates among a group sitting outside at night, perhaps at first six or eight of the younger men, later attracting a larger audience of their friends, of the elders, and of women and children.

This audience is very much a part of the whole situation and activity of story-telling; in this it resembles the related activities of speech-

[1] See above, pp. 30–31.

making, dancing, and singing. If there are women present, their conventional contribution is to clap at certain points during the story and at the end, showing honour to the speaker; this is also sometimes done by the younger boys, especially to accompany a song. All present react immediately to dramatic points, jokes, funny words, exaggerations, or mimicry, and there are always likely to be murmurs of agreement or sympathy, the taking up and repetition of such phrases in the story as the conventional interchange of greetings, exclamations of surprise or horror, and loud laughter, specially in the more far-fetched or indecent stories when even the narrator may hardly be able to control his mirth. Such participation by the listeners occurs on all occasions when a story is told—from the standard village situation to the less usual one of a Limba pastor preaching to a Limba congregation in Freetown.

The narration of a particular story may, as I have said, arise out of some event or common discussion so that in this way the listeners are already directly concerned in the subject of the story. Sometimes a direct point is made to or about one of the audience, as in *The story of palm wine* when the narrator, speaking of the origin of palm wine, addresses his remark directly to Semanka, the youth among his listeners most famous for his insatiable desire for wine. On some occasions a story is made more effective by bringing in some oblique and unstated reference to the actions or situation of one of the listeners; the reference is not made directly and he cannot thus object or take offence, but the listeners may recognize the resemblance between the acts of, say, one of the animal characters and one of themselves. In this way the audience is itself closely involved in the narration. They also often participate personally after the story has ended, in the sense of discussing what has been said, impressing any moral that has been included on each other, re-enacting the highlights, humming the song, or entering into light-hearted controversy about some problem posed at the end.

Besides this general participation by listeners, there are two special ways in which members of the audience formally take part in the story-telling.

The narrator sometimes chooses a special friend and designates him as the 'answerer' (*bame*), to 'reply' (*me*) to the narration. In *Sira and the monster*, for example, Karanke opened the story by calling on his younger cousin Konia, a close friend of his: 'Well, cousin Konia, well, listen to me carefully, you hear? I am going to tell Yenkeni [R. F.] a story.... But reply to me (*be ma meyɛ*) won't you? By grace of all who are sitting here.'

Once appointed, this 'answerer' must then interject phrases like 'yes' (*ndo*), 'mmmm', 'fancy that' (*woi*), 'really!' (*ee*) at appropriate moments, and react quickly with laughter, exaggerated amusement, or dismay at the events related in the story. He often repeats the important points or proper names of the characters in an undertone to emphasize them, or interpolates clarifying words such as the name of the character speaking or acting at the time, specially if the audience seems at all confused, with reiterations of key phrases at dramatic moments, brief questions when the point is a little obscure, or prompting if the teller appears to hesitate for a name or sequence. This formal practice of 'replying' often gives an extra impression of speed and intensity to the telling of a story, and, though by no means universal, is one way in which a member of the audience can formally take part in the actual narration.

The second and more common type of formalized participation is when all, or nearly all, of the group of listeners takes up the chorus of a song. The narrator sings the first line, which is then repeated or added to by the rest; sometimes they merely fill in the chorus, sometimes they take up the song completely while the story-teller gets his breath and lets them sing alone for a few moments before finally breaking in on the song in a raised voice to continue his narrative. At times these songs may possibly be standard ones, well known to all his listeners; more often they seem to be introduced and first sung by the teller alone until grasped and tentatively repeated by his listeners. In *Sira and the monster*, for example, the narrator half-chanted the song of the dogs as they ran, 'you are called, you are called', and then interjected the sung word *sɔyɔŋ*, which represents the sound of the dogs' leaping and jumping as they ran. This sequence was repeated eight times, and after the first two times, the audience grasped the improvisation and sang *sɔyɔŋ* while the narrator continued with 'we are called, we are called'. In another example, *Sara and the guinea fowl*, the teller sang the beginning of the bird's song about its name, interrupting himself for an instant to encourage his audience to join in—'answer!'; then all repeatedly sang in chorus the bird's reply to the question 'Tambarenke, Tambarenke' while the narrator rhythmically put in the higher notes which asked the bird 'what is your name?'; the song was then repeated by him and his audience at intervals throughout the rest of the story.

This practice of 'replying' (*me*) by which the audience is said to assist the speaker is one that is adopted by the Limba in many other contexts also. *Me* is used of the required reply of greeting to greeting, and of the formal admission of guilt or liability, a necessary stage in certain law cases. It also refers to the actions of the listeners when someone is making a formal speech; they should not interrupt the flow of his presentation but should 'reply' to his argument, perhaps by echoing his words or answering his rhetorical questions, perhaps by only a grunt or murmur at suitable intervals; in this way they are thought to play the important part of supporting or noting his main points as they are made. 'Replying' in song is also an important practice, applied in particular to the way in which the women as a group reply in chorus to the song of a soloist, and in this way take an essential part in the whole activity.

In the light of these other contexts the significance of 'replying' in story becomes clearer. Those who 'reply' are, in general, looked on as taking only a secondary part; but at the same time they make an essential contribution to the activity as a whole. 'Replying' to a story has similar implications. If one friend has been specially chosen to reply to the teller, he is therefore in the position of showing him respect, recognition, and the ready support of one who is both intelligently listening and acknowledging the other's right to lead. Similarly all those who reply to the story-teller, either in the generalized sense of merely reacting to his narration, or the specific singing in chorus in answer to his solo, are felt both to give their support to his telling of the story, and, as well, to make an essential contribution to it. Not infrequently the narrator recognizes this; as he ends his story he expresses gratitude to those who have listened or replied to him; he thanks both his special 'answerer', if he has one, and also all those who have been present and taken part, concluding, for example, 'by grace of you all who are present here. That is it. It is finished.'

It is clear, then, from an examination of the concept of 'replying' and its connexion with the actual behaviour of an audience, how far the situation of story-telling among the Limba is thought of as a kind of joint activity by both speaker and listeners, the one leading, the others replying and supporting. This contribution by the listening group is a necessary part of the drama of story-telling, one which must be understood in order to grasp the nature of the Limba stories themselves; this is all the more important to recognize when, as here, the stories can only appear bare on a cold page without the constant warm interplay between speaker and listener which is so central to the actual Limba situation.

3. THE STORY-TELLER

The Limba have no special word which means an expert story-teller. Stories can be and are told by anyone of whatever age or status, and, unlike the more specialized skills of drumming or dancing, without payment, special training, or inheritance from another. However, as described later, some individuals come to be recognized in practice as more experienced or skilful than others in narrating stories or leading the accompanying songs.

In general women do not often tell stories. This may be, in part, related to the fact that the men, though they work very hard at times, generally enjoy a more complete leisure at certain seasons and at the end of the day, whereas women are always occupied with cooking, cleaning, or tending children. The men usually sit around more in groups, and make more of a formality of speaking or handing out the palm wine. At another level, it is understood that it is a specifically masculine quality to be able to 'speak' well and thus make effective use of rhetoric, parable, or illustration, whereas a woman is expected to sit and listen, clap to show her respect and appreciation, or join in the chorus of the songs. However, women do know the stories and sometimes tell them, though in fact most of the stories I heard told by women were in a relatively unusual context—by the wife of a wealthy and literate Paramount Chief, and by a free-lance woman trader in the biggest of the Limba towns.

Apart from this qualification everyone is potentially able to tell stories, with various degrees of skill. Even children can tell them, partly because they are interested in riddles (also *mbɔrɔ*) and these shade into dilemmas and other stories. The stories told by children tend to be more sketchy and less complex, sometimes emphasizing the basic plot or the joke or just one incident, rather than the dramatic and vivacious effects stressed by a more experienced narrator or the moral or explanatory aspects sometimes favoured by the older men. But every Limba of whatever age would be expected to have some acquaintance with the traditional stories, and some capacity to tell them. Fanka Konteh, for example, who told many of the stories I recorded, would probably not be considered by most Limba as a particularly skilled story-teller; yet he was able to tell stories night after night, which were approved both by other members of his village and further afield.

That some individuals are more skilled is quickly obvious to a visitor, and at times clearly recognized by the Limba themselves by referring to someone's intelligence or ability (*funuŋ*) in story-telling in such approving phrases as '*he* knows how to utter stories' (*wundɛ a thɔ fuŋuna* (*mbɔrɔiŋ*), or 'so-and-so knows how to speak' (*wa na thɔ gboŋkila*). But they do not have a specialist vocabulary to describe this art.

This skill seems to be partly a question of memory and organization—of remembering the possible plots or topics, presenting them consistently, and attaching a suitable conclusion. Some people cannot cope so well with this and get muddled; they may drift unintentionally from one episode to another, mistakenly transpose two incidents in their excitement, thus confusing the listeners, or tack on an apparently inappropriate ending. However, those admired by the Limba generally do seem to impose a firm structure on both plot and the moral, problem, or explanation, etc. with which a tale may end, though this is not an aspect of story-telling which the Limba themselves are articulate in analysing.

A more important aspect in which some people are, in this case quite explicitly, thought to excel is that of the *manner* of their narration. This is discussed more fully below in terms of the 'style' and 'genesis' of the stories, but briefly includes both the narrator's capacity to embroider the skeleton theme of his plot with subsidiary details, pieces of vivid description and songs, and also the actual skill of his delivery—his gestures and mimicry of people or animals, his use of dramatic repetition and characterization, the variations in speed and tone, his vocabulary, and his skill in singing and persuading his listeners to join. Vividness and drama in the actual telling is something that excites Limba, and it is this that they praise in a story-teller more often than the content or structure of the specific story he has chosen to relate. Many of the tales told by Dauda Konteh, for example, had a minimal plot, but because of the vehemence of his enactment and his skill as a singer and leader of choruses, he was a popular and admired story-teller.

In view of the close association between story and music described in an earlier chapter, it is not surprising that those who are in practice recognized to be good story-tellers are also often skilled in singing, drumming, or dancing. This may be partly because those with the artistry and experience to lead in music are also likely to be able to master the delivery or the singing in a story and have the memory and sensitivity also necessary in spoken art. It is also possible that those who are known to be expert in the specialized forms of drumming or singing and thus much admired in Limba society, tend in practice to be more confident than others both in their ability to perform before an audience and in their general mastery of the culture of the old people, a culture which includes, among other things, the stories.

Instead of generalizing further on the character of 'the story-teller', for which there is no specialized word or role in Limba, I shall describe three of the story-tellers I encountered during my stay, who, among them, told many of the stories in Part II.

The first two are Niaka and Karanke Dema. Both belonged to Kakarima, a village with about 300 inhabitants under Alimami Salifu, the chief described earlier. Niaka Dema was a brother of this chief, though many years his junior. As is now not uncommon among the younger men, he had spent some years down country where he had learnt a certain amount of Krio and worked in one of the shops in Freetown[1] in order to earn money towards the bridewealth he would have to pay for his wife. Once he had succeeded in this and so was able to marry, he seemed to settle down with complete content to the life and culture of his home village; this is what he had aspired to all along, he said: to have a wife, children, and farm of his own, and so be able to 'keep up his father's compound' in his own home. He with his wife and three children shared a house just behind the chief's with his older brother, though Niaka probably hoped, as do most Limba, that one day he would acquire many wives and children and have a household and 'many people' of his own.

[1] A shop run by Indians, an experience he made use of in his story *Kanu scatters his children.*

Besides the main work common to almost all Limba—rice farming—Niaka had special skills practised by some only of his contemporaries—weaving cloth and making the large baskets for storing rice. But his special fame lay in his drumming. He was a 'master' in the art of playing the *kusuŋ* drum, and was known for this even beyond the boundaries of his own sub-chiefdom. In this part of Limba country at least, the long *kusuŋ* is thought to be superior to all other types of drum, and, correspondingly, very difficult to play well. Niaka had spent many years as an apprentice before mastering the art of beating this drum and singing the songs that go with it. He was perfectly aware of the respect (and presents) he might receive when, for example, he was begged to play for some important farming 'company', or for the great gathering at the boys' initiation dances when a *kusuŋ* player is obligatory and he might earn as much as £2 during a single night in continual small presents from the onlookers. He was proud, as befitted his skill, and so it was only for important occasions and when the sky was clear that he consented to play: 'by now I am skilled beyond all the other drummers. I am the master for anyone who wants to learn, I alone.'

The second of the two story-tellers from Kakarima was Karanke Dema, the junior smith. He had never been outside Limba country, and spoke no other language besides Limba. Though a member of the ruling clan, Dema, he had no close relatives alive apart from his mother of whom he was exceedingly fond. His father had died when he was still a small child, so he had then (rather unusually) attached himself to his mother's brother, Dokita, a senior smith. But Dokita too soon died, so that Karanke was once again thrown on his own; indeed it says much for his skill and ability that Karanke in fact held a rather respected position in the main village instead of living and working at one of the inferior farm settlements, for the loss of a father is a serious social and economic disability; it was for this reason that Karanke, though about thirty-five or forty years of age, had as yet no wife and thus was junior to such married men as Niaka. Karanke had finally attached himself to the senior smith then in the village, the chief's brother, and this man was teaching him smithcraft and spoke of one day giving him a wife.

In training to be a smith, Karanke had chosen the most difficult career open to a Limba, and, after chiefship, the most honoured. A smith has to labour as hard as anyone else on his own rice farm, and, in addition, hammer and work the heavy iron when others are resting. But he learns the skills of a smith, and the power to make invocations, to cleanse people who have trespassed, to take a leading part in the men's secret dances, and to recognize the ritual leaves for the traditional purifying medicines. In that he was a smith, therefore, Karanke could command general respect. He was also himself perfectly aware, though with full personal modesty, of his special access to the esoteric rituals and crafts of the honoured smith's art.

He was also rather admired for his technical skill in other respects and, in particular, for his artistry in music and dance. Among most of his contemporaries in the village, he was outstanding with his hands—he was a fast weaver, a maker of large baskets, carver of wooden mortars and drums, sewer of native cloth, and a strong worker on the farm. On many occasions people hoe or thrash on the farm with movements which implicitly or explicitly recall the steps of a dance; with Karanke this was especially marked, for he was at all times full of the rhythm of music and movement. In the evenings when work was over he used to come with his own plucking instrument,[1] singing and half-dancing, while the children ran alongside dancing delightedly, shouting 'Karanke is come, Karanke is come.' He was also one of the two best players in the chiefdom of the *ŋkali* drum, and the year when I knew him he had just for the first time been begged by the women to be the singer and drummer of the special *kugbɔkithɔ* music for their weeding company—a great honour he was at first diffident in accepting. He was also one of the chief drummers at the important boys' initiation dances where his *ŋkali* drum was considered essential. As he summed up his experience in drumming 'it was the dead who told me to drum, and my heart.'

Karanke therefore was paid general respect for his artistic achievements. He was still regarded as a young man, so had as yet no weighty voice in the discussion of law cases and formal reconciliation of opponents. But he could already 'speak' to smooth out quarrels between the younger boys or clarify some point of dispute among his contemporaries. He himself described his early attempts to contribute to a formal discussion of a dispute before the chief—'my heart was afraid to speak, but I dared a little, for I knew a little how to speak.' In addition Karanke had the socially recognized power to 'speak' in the context of the important smith's rituals; he could, for example, invoke the dead owners of a 'swear' with the correct formulas and intonation, and, with appropriate phrase, gesture, and control, set it to pursue its victim.

Unlike Niaka and Karanke, Dauda Konteh came from a larger and more moneyed village, Kamabai, on the main road north. Now a man in his forties or early fifties he had spent some years in Freetown where he had had work connected with the army which involved a certain mastery of Krio and urban ways. It was while in this job, he said, that he suddenly became blind; and he has remained so ever since. He returned to his home village where his father held a respected position as one of the senior and influential elders and where there were many relations to help him. In spite of his blindness Dauda continued to work on the farm, help with house-building and even dye the native

[1] A *sansa*-type instrument with nine bars mounted on a metal box.

cloth red according to the traditional skill that not even all Limba men can master. He was continually busy and full of energy, and people regarded him almost with awe because of his determination and the way he had almost overcome what is generally, in Limba conditions, one of the most extreme of all afflictions.

Dauda was particularly fond of telling stories; indeed once he had begun it was hard for anyone else at all to get a tale in. He made much of the point that 'Kanu does not take two things'; meaning that though his eyesight had been taken he still had left his ability or intelligence (*funuŋ*), and in this way was able to 'think out the stories in his heart'. He used to tell his stories with peculiarly beautiful gestures and strikingly mobile face, and had up to a point developed an individual artistic style of his own. As described later[1] certain phrases and motifs occur and recur in most of his stories, whatever the plot or topics; he frequently added to the vividness of the narration by adding in an aside that he had been there at that point, standing silently by and observing with his own eyes—blind though his listeners knew them to be in actuality—the fantastic doings of animals or of Kanu. The main feature of his stories was his singing which he had developed to a special art, so much so that it usually dwarfed the actual narrative of the story, but was nevertheless immensely popular as the audience around him joined in repetition after repetition of the songs he was leading.

Details about the singing, speaking, and drumming of these three story-tellers may seem rather far from the main subject under discussion. But Limba story-telling involves the ability to speak skilfully and to lead people in song, and the qualities which make a good speaker, singer, drummer, and story-teller are often in practice united in one person. As mentioned already, the Limba themselves associate together spoken and sung art, and the latter in particular is closely related to the idea of drumming, and dancing; songs occur in the stories and people often tend to move a little in a rhythmic half-dancing manner as they sing. It is not then surprising that those skilled in one aspect of Limba artistic expression may also at times excel in another.

The description of these three individuals has also touched on certain ideas which are discussed more fully later in connexion with the genesis of Limba stories. The story-tellers are all *individuals*, individuals who perform on specific individual occasions. There is no joint common 'folk' authorship or set form of performance dictated by blind tradition. The stories are, naturally, composed and enacted within the limits of the social background of Limba life and literary conventions; but each individual performer has his own idiosyncrasies and unique fund of experience, interests, and skills.[2]

[1] See below, pp. 94–95.

[2] For further details on narrators see Appendix II.

4. STYLE AND TECHNIQUE IN STORY-TELLING

Since the style and delivery of each story form an important part of its impact, some account of this is called for here. Questions of style naturally lead to a consideration of the characteristics of the language and the conventional ways of heightening effects. Within these limits the individual story-teller can embroider, expand, dramatize, or exaggerate by the various means of language and technique at his disposal.

The vocabulary of the stories is much the same as that of ordinary speech used in day-to-day conversation, reporting of some special event, or the formal speaking at law cases or funerals. In this respect spoken narrative is in contrast to songs, both those interpolated into the stories, and, even more, most of those sung independently; these are often in obscure or unusual language. Sometimes only a few people know their real meaning; sometimes, so it seems, there is no clear meaning at all, the attraction being in the sound, rhythm, and dance rather than in the sense. In the stories however, no specialized technical or esoteric vocabulary is introduced (apart from songs within the narration).

Similarly the syntactical structure of the stories differs little from that of ordinary speech. The stories very frequently include direct representation of the greetings, remarks, and conversations of the characters portrayed, and this speech is exactly like that which can be heard at any hour in a Limba village as people go about their work or stop to greet or argue. As events are reported or discussed in real life, so they are too in the stories. The closing sentences in a story sometimes seem to be rather more complex and long-drawn-out; but this too resembles the similar diction used in generalizing funeral harangues or the comments made by moralizing elders in summing up law cases.

There are, therefore, no striking differences in the language of the stories from the vocabulary or structure of other forms of speaking. However, there are certain ways of heightening effect which are used by a good story-teller by playing on the potentialities of the language and sentence structure or by using various dramatic techniques.

Before discussing these various devices, it may be helpful to make a few points clear about the general structure of sentences in Limba.

The framework tends to be paratactical rather than compound: sentences follow on one after the other as parallel formulations complete in themselves rather than making up long periods of complex subordinate clauses. The sentences are therefore in a sense rather short, but they are also often spoken very fast, one straight on after the other, so that just how they should be separated up in a written form—whether, say, by a comma, semi-colon, or full stop—is not obvious; the whole idea of 'sentence' in Limba is only a relative one.

Parataxis, therefore, is a typical Limba feature, and most of the stories are made up of what could be regarded as short, apparently abrupt, sentences. However, these are bound together by various connecting devices. People often, for example, use words like *wuna*, that is why, therefore; *mɛna*, then; and so on; the interjection *awa*, well, is also found very useful to mark a new stage in story or argument. The connexion of a new sentence or move with what has gone before can also be made clear by short interjections such as *huna*, *wuna* (that is it, that is why) at the end of a piece of direct speech to show that it is now complete, or the common word *kumaŋ*, a term I have translated as 'behold', when a point as yet unknown to the agents in the story is being introduced or referred to. Sometimes an explicit connexion is made by taking up a phrase in the previous sentence and repeating it, in such examples as 'she went in. Going in, she said . . . .' (*wundɛ bii. Wundɛ mabii ma, wundɛ dome*). Another way of pointing the sentence structure is by the device sometimes called epanalepsis, taking up with a pronoun some noun that has been previously referred to; as, for example, 'that boy—no one must now see him' (*na hato wobɛna, na wumɔ wumɔ sa nda niŋ kutiɔkɔ*). Certain other particles such as *thɔŋ*, just, immediately, *nda*, already, or *nɛnɛ* to introduce a new point are also used to clarify or point the sense in Limba though they cannot usually be directly translated into English.

Another effectively used particle is *na* (and its negative *kute*) which stress the preceding word, thus making it possible to point the meaning of the sentence more simply and effectively than can be done in translation. In the story of the *Four wives*, for instance, when the hero is found dead because he had disobeyed the prohibition to see a stranger, the girl who was found the next morning with his dead body replies briefly to her questioners with the simple *mathimo na bilɛ bali*, literally 'love *na* owns thing'; in an English rendering the economy of the phrasing is lost and one has to choose between such unsatisfactory alternatives as 'it was love that caused it', 'the real reason was love' or just '*love*'.

The Limba also tend wherever possible to report direct speech, a very simple construction in their language. It is introduced by *na*, and this word is repeated before each clause, group of words, or even single emphatic word of the speech, so that the fact that the words are still part of the speech is never for a moment lost to the listeners; even where no verb of speech is explicitly included, there is no confusion. People are always reporting others' direct words or suppositions in everyday conversation and in story, and, as described later, particularly effective use of this construction can be made by story-tellers.

There are many contexts in Limba where the syntactic features mentioned above can be observed in use. In formal speeches, reporting of news, and the everyday interchange of information, Limba make use of the mainly paratactical form of sentence, interspersed with various connectives and the quotation of others' direct words. Parataxis, it is clear, need not imply a confused or unpolished diction, but can be pointed and embellished by the devices described above, among others.

These basic features of Limba are all to be observed in the stories, often used with vivid or intensified effect. When further special vehemence or emphasis is required there are other ways in which a skilful story-teller can add to this basic structure. These elaborations do of course occur in all kinds of speaking, but appear most strongly in the telling of stories.

Repetition is commonly employed. Often this serves to bring out some point in the story more dramatically. In *The story of two women*, for example, the exacting nature of the examination of the first woman is indicated by the questions being asked twice over in the same words, eliciting in each case the same reply. Repetition of a long phrase or sentence may bring out not only the dramatic importance of a certain episode or saying, but also suggest the length of time it continued, or the concentration of the actors.[1] Great excitement too can be directly expressed by the use of repetition as, for example, in the indignant and agitated refusal by the first wife in *Four wives* to allow another woman to join them, 'No, no, no, I won't agree' (*na hali hali hali, na yaŋ sa me*). Sometimes a phrase is repeated again and again at various key points in the story. In the two stories, for example, where Kanu is shown going round on earth looking for hospitality, his perseverance and weariness are hinted at through the continual repetition of exactly the same words after each episode—'he went on' (*ndɛ daŋande*).

In a much less elaborate way, and one which commonly occurs in every kind of speech, single words are themselves often reduplicated. Sometimes this is really a standardized form which can properly be written as one word, though it may be pronounced with special expression or effect by a skilful story-teller, for example *gbɔkɔgbɔkɔŋ*, rub in, *ŋkinikini(ŋ)*, pity. Certain superlatives are commonly expressed by repetition of a word separated by the particle *o*; this is sometimes stressed or prolonged for effect, specially in story-telling, thus giving yet more emphasis to the superlativeness already inherent in the phrase, as in *mbɛ o mbɛ*, everything, *kamɛ o kamɛ*, everywhere, and so on. In addition a repetition of a single word or root is also used by story-tellers to create certain effects. This sometimes gives a more extreme sense: thus *yete* means 'small', whereas *yete yete yete* means 'very very small indeed'; *wunde ke* means 'he went', *wunde ke ke ke ke ke ke ke* in *The story of the great witch* is a conscious exaggeration meaning that she persevered in

[1] For example Siema's repeated sentences when left alone on the bank in *The hunter and the three twins*.

going over a great distance for a long time without stopping even once; *piripiri* means 'all night', *piripiripiripiripiripiri* in the telling of a story conveys the idea that someone continued in his struggle for absolutely the whole length of the night without ceasing for an instant. This sort of exaggerated repetition is a favourite one among some story-tellers, and always creates an effect among those listening.

Besides repetition of words or phrases, constant use is also made of *parallel phrasing*. This also involves repetition of a sort, but with variation of certain key elements.

Sometimes this occurs in a very minor way. Thus two brothers, in *The white and black brothers* are simply presented in parallel phrasing as 'the one white, the one black' (*woi wo fufɛ, woi wo bɔlɔ*), and the names of three twins are given as 'one Luseni, one Koto, one Siema' (*woŋ Luseni, woŋ Kɔtɔ, woŋ Siema*). But even these minor examples can at times be used in a purposeful and expressive way to set the scene or produce an impression of the opposition or interdependence between the individuals thus introduced.

Lists of objects or events using this device of parallel phrasing are very popular. They are often recited with a conscious air of comprehensiveness or climax. This may be an enumeration of exciting events, as in *The man killed for a banana*, where the Limba is so much more terse and rhythmic than any possible English translation: 'he was seized, he was thrown down, he was killed, he was skinned' (*ndɛ boho, ndɛ toŋo, ndɛ koro, ndɛ seŋo*). The idea of the care and single-mindedness with which a difficult task was meticulously completed is indicated in the list of actions taken by one twin to revive his father in *The Hunter and three twins*, where he is depicted, in parallel phrasing, as dripping the medicine on all parts of his father's body in turn—on his ear, on his nose, on his eyes, on his brains, on his mouth, on the soles of his feet, on his arms. Long lists of people or objects are also appreciated. These too manifest a type of parallel phrasing, and are delivered *as* lists, with an intentional stress on any parallelisms of rhythm, tone, or meaning. In *Kanu and palm wine*, for example, the various tapping instruments brought by Kanu are carefully enumerated. In *The stomach is chief of the body* the various parts of the body in the story are listed at both the beginning and the end. In *A story of witches*, the climax is, as often, introduced after a list of parallel phrases: the boy concealed in the cotton tree has his attention called to those dancing round him in witchcraft, with 'You see your mother? you see your father? you see your brother? you see all your relatives?—to kill you!' (*yiŋ kute nanda na? yiŋ kute fanda na? yiŋ kute wɛnda na? yiŋ kute bia nda hooma?—na ba kɔra yina*).

In a more extended sense parallel phrasing is also used as part of the wider structure of a story, and the same patterns of phrases or sentences may recur over and over in the various episodes of the story.[1] This structural device of placing successive episodes side by side, as it were, each showing development in one aspect only while the rest remains unchanged, is very different in scale from the more limited application of this feature. But, from another point of view, it is analogous both to the common use of parallel phrasing in the more restricted sense and to the paratactical structure of Limba in general. Each episode is related as a unit, and this full repetition of nearly similar events is one among the several means by which a skilful story-teller effectively heightens the tension and climax in his narration.

A certain amount of *imitation* or *mimicry* is also used to make the narration more vivid. This may involve direct imitation of what is understood to be the sound of animals speaking. The words of an insect were pronounced by the narrator in a kind of buzzing voice to represent its sound, and the monster's sniffing of a human in *Sira and the monster* was depicted as *inf inf*, then the breathy snuffing iteration of *furu yumba furu yumba* ('a human's smell, a human's smell'). The sound of dogs is imitated in various ways: *krrr krrr* for their growls, *wo wo wo* for their barking. Representations of the sound of birds' voices or flight also sometimes occur, as with the vulture in *Two friends*, which was made to speak in a kind of high monotone.

Mimicry is also employed in the sense of imitative gesture or expression. The Limba use this in many contexts, and hunters particularly often imitate the stance and walk of the animals they are describing as they tell tall hunting tales to entranced audiences. This kind of mimicry is readily imported into story. The shy nervous peeping out of the antelope was simulated; so too was the staggering walk of the spider as he was dragged along by the ropes that bound him to his bowl of rice, or the variety of ways in which different animals are depicted as eating. Imitations of human protagonists are also common. Sara's action, for example, in *Kanu and palm wine* was portrayed by the narrator's mimicking the way Sara tapped sharply on Kanu's knee to wake him up; and in *Four Wives* the teller vividly depicted how the father and mother of the dead boy went up eagerly to the fire to save him, but each time were driven back against their will by the fierce heat of the flames. Characterization is also often conveyed by facial expression or gesture, as, to quote only one of many examples, with the obstinate and rather sulky daughter in *The story of a millionaire*.

Certain conventional gestures are also often used. The Limba have several very stylized gestures, but these are commonly made to convey information *without* words and do not occur particularly often in the stories. A few such gestures do, however, occur in story-telling, for example the representation of eating by making as if to take a ball of

[1] See the following section on style and form.

rice in one's right hand; the click and downward sweep of a hand to indicate anger or beating; putting a hand to one's mouth to express extreme astonishment; pointing by pushing out the lips and moving the head; or pushing the elbows slightly out from the body to suggest chiefly dignity and pride. Other less formalized gestures used by story-tellers include pointing to the sky to show the angle of the sun (hence the time) at a certain point in the action; indicating the height of a child or of the rice by holding the hand a certain distance from the ground; or illustrating the size of a knife by measuring off its distance on the arm from the finger tips.

Besides mimicry, a story-teller often uses a form of *onomatopœia* to embellish his narration. This in part overlaps with the imitations mentioned earlier. In addition there are certain words which to the Limba always represent some particular sound. These include such obvious examples as *biŋkaŋ* and *gbaŋ*, resonant representations of the sound of a shot; *prrr* the whirr of a bird's feathers in flight; and *gbiŋ gbiŋ gbiŋ gbiŋ*, the loud beat of a chief's drum calling the people. Sometimes the words which to a Limba self-evidently express some sound are to us strange and unsuggestive; thus *digbi digbi digbi digbi* is said to be the noise, rather like a great wind, made by the spirit Kumba in passing, and *dɔiŋ dɔiŋ dɔiŋ dɔiŋ* is the sound made by a rat as it runs. Sometimes the expressive auditory words are used with a verb of the same root, thus apparently making the basic action more vivid or more amusing. A donkey is said to shake itself (*yikinɔkɔ*) as *yiki yiki*, a spider crunches (*gbɛgbila*) a bone *gbɛgbɛlɛ gbɛgbɛlɛ*, a man knocks (*gbagbasi*) at a door with a *gba*. Perhaps related to this is the way in which some words are occasionally used which are thought in themselves to have some funny sound without necessarily being imitative of any particular sound, and such words are always likely to make an audience laugh—*kuyakayakaŋ*, a useless stupid man, *dɛmpɛŋthɛŋ*, a scrounger, or *yumumumu*, secretly and furtively.

In addition to these words, which convey acoustic effects, there are also in Limba apparently set phrases which seem to qualify a verb and, by their sound, are thought to represent certain actions. Sometimes the actual sound of the action is directly represented. Sometimes the phrases are used to suggest some related quality such as sharpness, suddenness, or completeness.

These phrases are introduced by *na* followed by the term representing the sound or quality. *Na tiriŋ* and *na tiraŋ*, for example, indicate the splashes made by two people as they dive successively into a pool; *na tiiŋ* is the quiet, intent, and prolonged way in which a leopard or lion is frequently made to regard its prey; *na raa* gives the long diminishing sound as a galloping horse or running bush cow covers the distance.

When a leopard scratches at the ground, the awesome effect of the scrapes is conveyed by *na ruki ruki ruki ruki*, while *na kɛlɛthɛ* represents the light way in which the spider soundlessly lays himself down. Similar phrases seem to suggest some impression of sound to a Limba listener, though to a foreigner they may appear to refer to some quality not normally associated with sound at all, and thus, for us, do not serve to make the description vivid in the same way. Thus *na kudu*, 'all night', in Limba suggests the whole long length of the night; *na fuu* or *na gbuu* are used to represent the slithering movement of a snake coming towards one, *na bɔdɛ* something stealthy and quiet, *na bis* the sudden and unexpected encounter of two people face to face. *Na gbɛti*, 'precisely', is always uttered with a sharpness that suggests to any listener the sudden sound of cutting something exactly, an abrupt refusal to include one single item more or less—thus, in Limba 'precisely' seems to be used as an auditory word. Phrases such as these are used both in everyday speech, and, to a much greater degree, in the stories, and are often used and pronounced with a vehemence or long-drawn-out exaggeration that brings a delighted response from the audience.

Tone (or pitch) is sometimes used in a special and exaggerated way for effect in the stories. This is normally thought very effective or amusing by the audience. An exaggeratedly high and prolonged tone is not infrequently used by a clever story-teller to represent some absolute extreme. Thus, whereas *wuyete* means 'a little', *wuyeéete* is used to mean 'very, very little indeed', and, as well, serves to make the audience laugh or react. *Bemandi* means 'many' people, *bemadándi* means 'very, very many'; in, for example, the story of *Two friends*, the teller uses this method to hint at the vast number of suitors who were, one after the other, and with no exceptions, and over many years, killed by the powerful spirit: all this is conveyed merely by the high, long tone in the clause 'many people were killed there' (*bia bemaáandi bindɛ koro nde kɛndɛ*). This, then, is another example of the way in which any *written* version misses the impressive yet economical flavour of the original narration.

The superlative force of a high long tone can be applied to other words besides such adjectives of quantity. One common term, for example, is *haŋ*, which means 'for a long time' or 'over a long distance'. In the stories this is frequently heightened and prolonged to give the idea of a great length of time or distance. 'He went *hadaŋ*' means that he travelled for a long long time, he went a long long way. *Gbɛŋ*, 'the whole day' is often similarly treated: *gbɛ́ɛŋ* stresses the great length of the whole day, dawn until dusk. Special violence is also often comically given in story through the pitch or length of such common exclamations as *ee* or *ha*, a vehemence impossible to convey in a written translation.

Such differences in tone and the use of mimicry or onomatopœia are all means by which a story-teller in various degrees produces variety and colour. Other ways of producing effect through *variety* are also evident in the use of unexpected interpolations or exaggerations as well as in variations of tempo or volume.

A sentence beginning with *kumaŋ*, 'behold', is often used to momentarily interrupt the consistent flow of the narrative with an aside; it introduces some fact as yet unknown to the characters in the story and thus produces a reaction from the audience. Unexpected exaggerations about events or objects in the stories are also appreciated—for example the references to 'a thousand boxes', the 'hundred thousand people' killed by a witch, the vast number of gold ornaments, or even, in one story, to 'one million of money' and a 'millionaire'. 'England' sometimes seems to be in the same category, representing some exaggeratedly far-away land suitable for a fantastic story.

Variety is also produced by exaggeration or alteration in the tempo or rhythm. The way in which changes of speed may be used for emphasis has already been mentioned in the sense of prolonging or pausing over certain words such as *haŋ*, 'for long'. In a more elaborate way speed seems to be used to suggest excitement, as when the succession of dramatic events which befell a trouble-maker was narrated with great speed—'he was seized, he was knocked down, he had his throat cut' (*bayaŋfa boho, wundɛ lɔpitando, wundɛ fayo, The boy that talked with animals*). The lengthy exchange of greetings between characters in a story is often run through very quickly, as, for example, in Dauda Konteh's narration of *Daba the snuff-taker*. At other times, a sentence is pronounced slowly and lingeringly to give better expression to its meaning, as in phrases like 'he wept' (*wundɛ bereŋ*), or the slow pathetic tones in which Sara complains that however often he goes to try to find Kanu asleep, he has never yet succeeded. The sad opening of Sangbang's story about the toad bringing death was spoken very slowly and sorrowfully—'the toad, ah, the toad did not love us'. An abrupt stop in mid-sentence is also sometimes used as a most effective means of violently stressing the following word and riveting the audience's attention on it, as, for instance, with 'they—*ran* away' (*bindɛ—thare*), or 'he—*dashed* him down' (*ndɛ—lɔpitande niŋ*), where the violent emphasis gives the implication that he both hit him very hard and caused him sharp sudden pain. This emphasis is conveyed both by the stress on the verb itself, but even more by the abrupt pause before it, sometimes followed by a clap to give yet more emphasis.

Changes between loud and soft are also used for effect in both public speaking and story-telling. A few sentences may be practically shouted, with great vehemence, then the voice suddenly dropped to little more than a whisper. Timidity, for example, may be expressed by suddenly introducing a very quiet tone, as when the narrator describes how the wife went and peeped in at her dead husband (*The man killed for a banana*), or when the boy Bayo nervously replied almost inaudibly to the monster's challenge to disclose himself.

The atmosphere of a situation is also often vividly suggested by alterations in the speed or tone. This can best be illustrated in some detail from part of one story, told by Karanke Dema. At one point in *The story of Deremu*[1] he gave a clear picture of the hero standing alone on the far bank of a wide river, with all his followers now on the other side, as he waited isolated and in suspense for the fateful moment. The slow, quiet way in which this picture was drawn, as if with breath suspended, then suddenly gave way to the loud, rapid, violent narration of the struggle between hero and spirit when all was blood and turmoil and Deremu had to draw knife after knife before at last conquering. Then the story returned again to the slow prolonged hushed suspense felt by those waiting on the bank, how they began to weep hopelessly—then their sudden breathless realization that Deremu was safe; the tense quietness of the description is violently broken by the loud and vigorous representation of their noisy relief as 'they began to dance with joy now'. A similar contrast in speed and tone of narration was made as Karanke went on to describe the sad anxiety of the mother as she waited at home, replaced first by her quick excitement and obstreperous happiness when she heard that her son was safe and was coming home, and then by the rejoicing and dancing by all the villagers and the followers of Deremu. The vigour of this dance and the excited description of the mother's ecstatic joy are then momentarily interrupted by the story-teller's sad, reflective interpolation about what is then seen to underlie the noisy rejoicing, 'behold she is to die. She the mother was very glad. Behold she is dying. . . .'

The use of *direct speech* introduced by *na* has already been mentioned. This is especially popular in the stories and is a means by which the action can be advanced and presented through a quick exchange of greetings or questions. The voice, character, and bearing of the protagonists can be dramatically represented, and effective use made of the common exclamations of surprise, shock, or admiration—*ha*, *e*, *ε*, *iyo*, *ye*—which are often delivered with great vehemence and effect. Through the simple device of merely prefacing the remarks by *na*, the action can be portrayed as a kind of drama rather than a mere straightforward description. Thus, for example, a character's feelings at some point in the story are very seldom conveyed by any direct statement about his inner experience,[2] but rather by some exclamation put into his mouth. To express surprise, the story-teller does not say 'he felt puzzled, confused', etc., but merely the direct and aghast exclamation *ee!* Similarly the

[1] See Part II, pp. 113 f.

[2] Exceptions are references to the heart (*huthukuma*) and to fear (*palɔ*).

pleasure of meeting after long separation is shown not by any description of feelings but by the direct exchange of greetings, such as 'Father', 'Oh', 'Greetings', 'Yes', in *The hunter and the three twins*, where the narrator can convey by his delivery all the drama and excitement that are missing in the written version. The thrill of surprise and joy felt by the girl who had refused all other suitors when at last she saw her ideal husband shining in the distance is not expressed through any account of her emotions, but by the uncontrolled excitement of the actual words she is portrayed as uttering, ecstatically calling her mother: 'Mother mother mother mother mother! The man I was talking about, the one I was talking about, he has come, it is he who will marry me; I said before that the one to marry me must have no blemish; now he has come, *he* is the one I want, he has come' (*na ya na ya na ya na ya na ya, na wundɛ yaŋ dɔŋ, wundɛ yaŋ dɔŋ, na wundɛ tɛŋ, na ndɛ na ma dɛŋ; yaŋ tepe nde ba dɔma na wo na ma dɛŋ na wo ka iŋ hubima; na na wundɛ tɛŋ, na wundɛ na thimo yaŋ, na wundɛ tɛŋ, Sira and the monster*). Sometimes, as for example in *Sara miser and Sara scrounger*, *The finch's loan* or *Ninkinanka*, much of the story is presented through the conversation of the chief characters, so that their aims or successes or disappointments are dramatized through the content and tone of what they themselves say rather than described from the outside by the narrator.

As already mentioned, *songs* are commonly introduced into many, though not all, stories, to be taken up and repeated by the listeners. Sometimes the songs take up the major part of the story; more often songs occur only at certain points in the narration. The exact meaning of the words often seems obscure even to the singers themselves and sometimes to be without any clear sense at all. This tends to be a characteristic of songs of all kinds. They often open with, or include, more or less meaningless sounds such as *o ye o*, *ya wo ya*, *woya*, *iyo*, *awaio*, etc., often sung in rhythmic chorus by the audience, spectators or dancers. Even where the words do have a meaning, this may be expressed in difficult or obscure language. However, where they occur in stories, even where the precise meaning of the words is difficult, the general purport of the song is usually clear. In *The story of an orphan*, for instance, the boy sings to his dead mother; the point of his song is clearly to bring her out from her grave to help him, and he sings and sings the song as she rises gradually from her grave in answer. In *A story of witches*, the witches are depicted as replying with the chorus *yɔ yɔ yɔ*, which is then taken up by the audience, while the narrator, representing the woman Mamakoto, sings 'in the nook, in the nook' (*ka ŋkumba ka ŋkumba*) as she tells the truth to the boy hiding in the cotton tree watching the witches dancing and singing. In other stories, for example *Sara and the guinea fowl* or *Kanu scatters his children*, the words of the song are somewhat more intelligible, and have an explicit connexion with the action at that point; each of the parallel episodes is marked by a parallel stanza. As remarked before, a story-teller's skill in singing is an essential part of his art and one which is highly appreciated by his audience who both listen and take part in the music, sometimes dancing or half-dancing as they sing.

Sometimes quotations from characters in the story are intoned or repeated in such a way that they seem almost a type of song. The sentence, for instance, semi-chanted by the mother to soothe her fatherless child 'hush child hush, your father was killed for a spinach leaf' (*kɔntɔkɔ oo kɔntɔkɔ, fanda nde koro ba ŋkereŋkereŋ*) calls to mind the songs commonly used by Limba mothers to amuse or lull their children. In the story of *Sira and the monster* both Sara's call to his dogs and their reply as they come bounding to his rescue are half-sung, and repeated several times by teller and listeners. These too, then, have the effect of decorating the narrative and enhancing its effect.

From this, as from other elements in the style and technique of delivery, it is clear how impossible it is to convey in a written version the vivid and varied representation of scene or atmosphere which can be evoked by the spoken narration and enactment, particularly where the story-teller is skilled in this art. This illustrates once again the point that any bare synopsis of plot or any written translation, whether literal or paraphrased, can never catch the flavour of the actual occasion when the story was performed with and to a group, nor fully represent what, for a Limba, is assumed to play such a large part—the actual dramatic process of story-telling.[1]

5. STYLE AND FORM

The question of form or structure in Limba stories cannot be wholly divorced either from the nature of style and presentation just discussed, or from the account, given earlier, of topics and treatment in the stories. However, a more direct discussion of some of these points here may help to illuminate certain aspects of form in Limba oral literature.

The openings and conclusions of most stories are marked by certain formulas or stock phrases. Occasionally these are not used, but in most cases the story is presented as a unit with clear beginning and end marked by these conventional phrases.

The openings vary to some extent. Generally these do not in practice include the teller's name or village. The most common occasions of story-telling are to friends and contemporaries, and the Limba, unlike some peoples, do not seem to have well-known story-tellers who would

[1] In the notes to the stories in Part II I have added a few remarks on the delivery; these are examples only as similar comments could have been made on every narration.

tour the country and thus wish to include their names for identification or prestige.[1]

Very often there is no formal title,[2] and the teller either plunges directly into a sentence about one of the characters, or opens formally with the announcement that he is going to tell a story: 'a story' (*mbɔrɔ*), or 'a story for you' (*mbɔrɔ bena*). Sometimes there is a kind of title, though this in practice can be closely bound up with the following sentence which begins the narrative proper. Thus, for example, a story may open: 'Kanu and we in the old days, we Limba had then no food' (*Kanu iŋ miŋ nde miŋ do Yumbɛŋ miŋ ka nde iŋ muthɔŋ*); 'a story of hunger—the spider and his wife and all his family . . .' (*mbɔrɔ ki ta kɔnthɔ, wosi iŋ yɛrɛmɛ nama niŋ kɔhɛ nama foma*); 'a monkey and a chameleon, they went travelling' (*bakɔ iŋ yɔŋkɔ binde kai huthahine*). Such quasi-titles are usually a reference to the two or three main characters of a story, most commonly in this case animals.

Very often the story opens directly with a sentence about one of the characters, usually the hero. He may be specified only by some general description such as 'a man', 'a hunter', 'a woman', without any more exact name. Thus typical introductions to a story are 'someone was once born' (*wa na kio nde*), 'a chief once had a child' (*gbako nde kiɛ nde hato*), 'a hunter once came out' (*badonso na huŋɛ nde*), or 'a man once came out in the world' (*wa na huŋɛ nde kahai*). Sometimes this general introduction of a character is followed by the proper name, as in 'someone once bore a child. That child was called Deremu' (*ndɛ na kiɛ nde hati. Hato wobɛna ndɛ na dɔma Deremu*), or 'twins were born; one was Koto, the eldest; one was Yemi; one was Luseni' (*bathemɛŋ bina kio nde; woŋ Kɔtɔ, wothanthɛ woŋ; woŋ Yemi; woŋ Luseni*). Occasionally the name of a character is not introduced until later in the story, in parenthesis, but here either the name or the particular character is not usually of great importance.

In these introductory formulations, the verb *huŋɛ* (or *fuŋɛ*) 'he came out' is very commonly used. This, in various forms, is a frequent term in Limba. In practice it can also be translated as 'was alive' 'lived', 'existed in the world'. It also has the implication of being 'in view' or 'in the light', as distinct from those who are dead or unknown. Various modifications of the same root (e.g. the causative forms *fuŋuŋ*, *fuŋutu*, 'bring out', 'make to come out') occur in many contexts, notably of the way in which Kanu is said to have given or created certain objects and customs for the Limba—'he caused rice to come out for them', 'he brought out chiefship', or 'he made the Limba people to come out'.

[1] The relative frequency of names in the texts I have recorded is not typical but arose from the field situation where people wanted to explain their correct names to me, and this habit then persisted, specially when I was recording on tape.

[2] Titles for the stories in Part II are my own.

Similarly Kanu 'brought a man out into the light', or 'a man came out into the world here', that is, was born, lived, became known, was active, perhaps became famous for some skill like hunting. It is in this sense, apparently, that a character in a story is introduced as 'coming out'.

The word that I have usually translated as 'once' in these introductions is the Limba *nde*. *Nde* is commonly used with a verb to specify that an event took place in the distant or fairly distant past. In the stories it sometimes occurs just once in the first sentence to place the whole tale firmly in the past where the events of stories belong, and the subsequent narrative then often runs on without further specification of time. However at the outset of a story *nde* seems almost obligatory and occurs in every kind of opening formula—'an elephant once called together the animals' (*kampa na thuŋkunande nde mamɛŋ be*), 'there once lived a man called Sara' (*wɔ na dɔŋɔi nde ko dɔma Sara*), or 'once we were together with Kanu above, we were all together here below' (*miŋ do nde iŋ Kanu wo kabegede, miŋ do kathabanthe hooma kapothi*).

The closing phrases of a story tend to be in some ways more formalized than the opening. In this stories resemble speeches where the speaker also ends by complimenting his listeners and stating that his words are finished—'that is it, it is finished' (*huna hoho, lɔŋtha*). Often a very brief phrase concludes the story. 'The story is finished' (*mbɔrɔ ki pati*), 'it is ended' (*kiŋ pati; wuŋ pati*), 'that is it, it is ended' (*huna, wuŋ thaŋki*), or, most commonly, *lɔŋtha(ŋ)*, a very formal term which also appears in religious contexts, and which I have translated throughout as 'it is finished'.

Sometimes a more elaborate sentence is used, referring either to the audience in general, to certain people by name, or to the generalized 'you' used for pointing a moral or generalization.[1] Frequently the narrator says something to the effect that since he had heard the story, he wanted to tell it to the present company—'as I heard it, I had to tell it to you. It is finished.' The listeners too are sometimes thanked for hearing the teller with patience, or giving him support in their 'replying' by song or word. 'Since I heard that story, I told it. Kapoingpoingbang [the friend who had 'replied' to him], you patiently heard me. Saraio [the narrator's brother] who is sitting there, by your grace too I told the story. I told it to Yenkeni. It is ended for me, it is finished (*mɛnɛ yaŋ yue nde mbɔrɔ kibɛna, Kapoiŋpoiŋbaŋ e ma thuŋka yuya, na awa, thɔkɔ ba ka Saraio wo dɔŋɔi woŋ, mbɔrɔ kibɛna a tepe ki Yeŋkeni na. Bɛnɛ huŋ thaŋkɛ ma, lɔŋtha*).

In these standardized ways the story is verbally brought to an explicit ending and the speaking of the narrator formally concluded.

The kinds of *situations* with which stories end have already been

[1] This also occurs in the common phrase 'you see now' (*ba nda kuta*, etc.) used at the beginning as well as, more frequently, the end of stories

discussed.[1] These include such situations as returning home, winning a wife or chiefship, eating or being left hungry, announcing, thanking or giving blessing, and outdoing another in cunning or revenge. These are often accompanied (or replaced) by a moral, a generalizing comment, an ascription of origin or a dilemma. All these are assumed to be natural ways for a story to end, and the action is thus brought to a pleasing and final conclusion.

Apart from these ways of marking the unity of a story at beginning or end by verbally standardized phrases or conventional situations, stories also often exhibit an inner structure. At times, it will be clear from the earlier discussion,[2] the actual topic of the story provides its framework. Thus in the stories about Kanu's teaching the Limba how to cultivate rice (*Kanu gave food to the Limba*; *The dog and the rice*) the operations of the rice-farming year provide a clear structure for the action of the story, each new episode opening with a reference to the next phase of the year. Similarly in stories about a 'company' of deceit and revenge the story often begins with an episode about the ill deed performed by one of two travelling companions or acquaintances resulting in the distress of the other; this is answered by another, similar episode in which the second pays back the first in much the same coin; and the story is then closed by some moral or comment about the dangers of trying to hurt a companion (for example *The monkey and the catfish*; *The monkey and the chameleon*). In other stories the action falls within the framework of a series of cunning acts performed one after another as in, for example, *Sara and the greedy chief* or *The spider and the leopard.* Or each of several characters will in turn do 'his part', then retire to make way for the next; this is especially marked in stories about the various co-operative actions performed in turn by each of three twins (as, for example, in *Three twins woo one girl*; *Three twins and an elephant*), but it occurs also with animal characters in *The girl taken by Kanu.* Rather similar series of actions in stories are also described in the framework of a character's successive efforts to win, or to cheat, a wife, trying to get the better of someone in regard to food, travelling round from one place to another, or the successive efforts made by the competitors in a tale such as *Contest in strength.*

Sometimes, then, a series of successive and comparable actions, the framework within which the narration is presented, is imposed by the standardized topic of the story itself; form and content are here necessarily and closely intertwined. However, even in cases where the theme of the story as a whole does not necessarily give rise to this clear framework, presentation in the form of a series of parallel episodes is still very marked. These may be on varying scales. The wider framework I have mentioned already is itself a series of parallel actions. So are the smaller-

[1] Above, chapter 3. [2] Chapter 3.

scale repetitions by which, for example, the hero calls his dogs several times over (*Sira and the monster*) or the episode within *The story of Kubasi* in which first the mother and then the father go to throw themselves into the fire and fail, finally to be followed by a similar but successful attempt by the girl. In a general way, each story, whatever its main topic, tends to move through a series of parallel actions which provide the main structure of the story. This is a typical feature of Limba stories at every level.

This characteristic form in Limba stories has to some extent been made clear in the translations in Part II by my use of paragraphs which clarify the underlying structure in a way not, of course, directly dictated by the teller in his oral narration; this paragraphing in a sense replaces a more lengthy commentary on the structure of the stories. However, there are also various characteristic ways in which new parallel episodes are introduced or linked which it may be worth noting here.

The most clearly marked structural points in the stories are those indicated by the introduction of songs. In *Sara and the guinea fowl*, for example, each of the series of parallel episodes in which Sara progressively cuts up, prepares, and eats the guinea fowl, is marked by basically the same song by the bird, with the chorus taken up by the group of listeners; when that is finished, the next move in the story is then presented. Similarly in *Kanu scatters his children on earth*, Kanu sings a song to accompany his action as he takes each of the peoples on earth to hurl them in turn to their present dwellings. In a lesser way a half-chanted phrase can recur as part of a minor series of parallel actions within a complex story, as with the phrases interchanged between Sira and the bumps as she gradually realizes her husband's true nature in *Sira and the monster*.

There are also standard verbal ways in which a new move is introduced. This is often a reference to time. The stories abound in phrases like 'the sun rose' (*kaŋ wo puthɔi*), 'in the morning' (*saŋkala ba*), 'the night passed' (*wuŋ furu*), or 'after some time' (*wuŋ nambe*), and often the several episodes in a single story are each introduced by an identical phrase throughout. Often these introductory phrases are to do with travel or movement—'he went on' (*ndɛ daŋande*), 'he went' (*wundɛ kai*), 'he got up' (*wundɛ ŋale*), 'he began to go' (*wundɛ thunuŋ ba saa*)—or serve to bring in a new character in the form, for example, of 'the bush cow came . . . the leopard came . . . the chimpanzee came . . .', etc., the element of a series of successive actions of characters being brought out both by the similar phrasing and, sometimes, by adding 'also' (*hɛlɛŋ*) to the later moves. In a corresponding way the ends of episodes are often marked by someone's going away, returning, eating, going hungry, being formally thanked, or by some other phrase that keeps recurring throughout a given story. In all these detailed ways, then, the basic form of the story is made clear as it moves in the main through a series of parallel episodes.

Within this very common basic framework there is great opportunity for the narrator to expand or compress. Stories can be longer or shorter according to the number and nature of such parallel moves introduced by the teller. One person, for example, may be content to say merely 'every animal came' without any further detail, another may recount what happened to two or three animals in turn, another still may bring in as many as six or seven. In, for example, *The spider and the bearded cave* the story could have been told by introducing just one or two animals to be killed by the spider before the final episode of the antelope's triumph, or it could have gone through ten or twelve—yet the basic structure would have remained the same.

Besides the possibilities of expansion or otherwise, the basic form can be made more or less complex, and be more or less embroidered by the narrator. Apart from the questions of style, mimicry, etc., that have already been mentioned, there is what might be called a common fund of standard events, turns, or runs which occur in many stories, not so much as part of the basic plot or form as a potential elaboration of it. These include such common episodes as, for example, the trapping of an enemy up a tree by persuading him to go further and further to pick some leaf or fruit so that he is finally stuck at the very top; the series of increasing demands for payment by a group of musicians, proceeding through the list, also common in other contexts, of a hen, rice, a goat, an ox, and a wife (or occasionally something even more), the articles increasing in value as the story proceeds; a girl running away from a man who may marry her if he can catch her; a travelling Fula tricked by the hero into being thrown into the river in his place; someone dying, then being revived by leaf-medicine (*mafɔi*); a character who helps some animal or spirit and then hides, too fearful to discover himself. Sometimes the standardized elaborations are on a much smaller scale: the blood on the floor after someone has been killed, or the flies buzzing over it; the surprise when someone is apparently sleeping too long in the morning; someone sharpening a sword, the stock way of indicating a dangerous situation to come; a character's being marooned in the cane-grass, a place of barrenness or despair; or the interchange of words and greetings. All these, and many other short events or turns, occur and recur in different contexts in many of the stories, elaborating or embroidering the basic structure of the tale.

There are, then, various senses in which Limba stories have a clearly distinguishable form imposed by the action and the plot itself, by a succession of parallel episodes, or by certain stock openings or conclusions. These can be embellished or made more complex in various ways —by the choice of character and content, by the style of delivery, by expanding or contracting the course of the narrative, or, finally, by introducing one or several of the stock turns which, in various degrees, can be built into the basic outline of the story. The basic form may be similar in many stories or performances, yet the treatment and content may be very different.

In this discussion of the structure and potentialities of Limba tales, I have been forced to write as if there were in some way *the* basic form or structure of any given tale which, once laid down and learnt, could then be improved or expanded. This of course would be to give a false impression. There is no *one* form of any Limba story that could be called the fixed or 'correct' one, and even if some tend to recur more often than others in roughly the same form, yet even there each performance is in a sense a unique composition by the narrator. There is a common fund of plots, stock openings and conclusions, actions, and characters, but, as will appear more fully in the next chapter, the exact nature of the story itself in each case depends on the individual occasion and individual narrator. Similarly, I have perhaps written as if there were a fixed structure which must be imposed strictly on every Limba tale, and from which there is no escape for the narrator. But, with Limba stories, the use of parallel episodes, stock openings and endings, etc., is not obligatory; there are no fixed rules but rather tendencies in story-telling which allow a great deal of flexibility. A Limba who has grown up hearing many stories will, when he tells stories himself, tend to use these conventions. But there are no rigid and absolute laws or formulas. This indeed will be immediately obvious to anyone who considers the complexities yet similarities of the many stories given in Part II.

5

THE GENESIS OF LIMBA STORIES

LIMBA stories, then, must be seen from two points of view—literary composition and performance before an audience. We cannot separate these two elements in practice, as we can in written literature: the Limba work of art is the story actually presented on a particular occasion by an individual narrator. There remains therefore the question of how far there can be individual variation, innovation, or creation within the traditional framework of these two facets of story-telling; a discussion of this problem recalls many of the points raised earlier.

The whole question of the genesis of such stories has, in a sense, been confused by much of the writing that has touched on the subject. Assumptions about 'folk' or 'common' authorship tend to obscure the part of the *individual* narrator in non-literate societies and concentrate on what is—or is thought to be—common to all the tales in question. Furthermore the concept of 'oral tradition' is sometimes interpreted so as necessarily to imply fixed traditional forms handed on word-perfectly from generation to generation with little or no possibility of individual variation; but although this may be so with *some* types of oral tradition, it is not a necessary property of all oral literature; it is certainly not the case with Limba stories. Similarly too easy ascription of crude psychological or sociological explanations for the content of oral literature means that questions about the scope of variation tend to be neglected for what seems fixed or traditional. The analysis of texts in written versions only has further contributed to this neglect. Even the investigation of the origins of particular stories, plots, or motifs can be misleading owing to the apparent assumption of a fixed prototype or model of the 'correct' or 'original version', as if items of oral literature could be isolated and traced back in the way that is feasible in the case of a manuscript tradition in written literature.

The discussion of the importance of style and delivery as an essential part of Limba stories should make it clear that such approaches ignore certain aspects of the stories that are of real significance when they are treated as living art and not just an abstract frozen 'text'. Even apart from questions of the techniques of delivery, it will be clear from any study of the stories included in Part II that there is no exact verbal correspondence even between different versions of what could be called 'the same' story—even when, indeed, they are delivered by the same narrator. The idea of word-perfect verbal identity does not, in fact, seem to be a Limba concept at all.

When I refer to the 'genesis' of Limba stories, I am not intending to treat general questions about the ultimate origin of their content. It is quite clear that many of the plots or episodes I recorded among the Limba also occur in various forms in many other parts of West Africa and further afield.[1] But how, where, or why they first came to the Limba is not a question I intend to raise. All I am concerned with is to distinguish something of the way in which, given the present way of life, current interests, and literary conventions of the Limba, stories are in this context produced, changed, and engendered, the contribution made by individual narrators within the traditional limits, and the way in which the Limba themselves view this process.

I. INDIVIDUAL AUTHORSHIP AND TRADITION

The area within which individual creation is possible is clearly twofold, covering both style of delivery and content. Though it is impossible strictly to separate these two, it is clear that as far as the oral *performance* of a story goes each occasion is, almost by definition, a unique artistic creation in that the narrator himself enacts the tale, depicts the action with more, or less, characterization, mimicry, exaggeration, and effect through the use of tones, length, speed, singing, or onomatopœia in order to make his narrative vivid, attractive, and amusing to his audience. The means at his disposal for producing these effects have already been discussed; they are traditional ones, laid down by convention and the potentialities of the language. But the use a particular narrator makes of them on any given occasion is an individual one, and may even vary from narration to narration. The dramatizing part taken by the teller as well as the answering participation by the audience are essential elements in the narration.

A more complex but related aspect is the content; in this I also include questions of plot, theme, treatment, and the general framework in which these are expressed. As already pointed out there are certain literary conventions about the kinds of topic that tend to occur in stories—those about, for example, wooing a wife, cunning, a 'company' of revenge, and so on—certain conclusions that are generally found pleasing, various stock characters, and a general type of framework within which these tend to be presented. This, then, is the background, the fund of common literary materials. The story-teller can choose one stock character rather than another, or introduce one with an otherwise unknown

[1] For example the plot of *Three twins woo one girl* and the popular episode about a man's being tricked into letting himself be thrown into a river will be well known to those familiar with the *Arabian Nights* and *Grimm's Tales* respectively.

name; he can include many or few episodes; he can embellish the basic structure with songs, with special details that attract him, or with some episode that another teller might have avoided; he can choose to bring out one or another aspect of the narrative as a whole by his free choice of the kind of conclusion, whether a moral, an explanation, a comment, or a question, and by the exact forms in which he decides to express these. As will be clear from the texts I give, certain plots seem to recur in a rather more consistent form (as far as content is concerned) than do others. But in all of them, and perhaps particularly in the longer stories about people, the material has a large degree of fluidity, and the story is not a fixed product which should be described as 'The Limba Folk-tale', but the individual creation of a particular narrator on a particular occasion.

The way in which the material, treatment, and delivery may vary can best be illustrated by discussing some individuals, stories, and occasions in a little more detail. These three aspects will be treated in turn.

After one records several stories by one individual, their own idiosyncrasies of style, interest, and emphasis begin to become apparent. The elder Bubu Dema, for example, always tended to tell stories in which the generalizing or meditative element was paramount, being sometimes as long as the narration of the plot itself. He used to stress in particular an image of Kanu that was a compound of fatherliness, understanding, and resignation, and was always pointing out, in general conversation as well as in many of his stories, that without Kanu a man can do nothing, without Kanu you cannot predict how things will turn out. His habit as an elder of speaking quietly and persuasively between people to reconcile them came out too in the stories as he ended up time after time with an emphasis on some moral or generalization illustrated by the events of the story. By contrast, Fanka Konteh, a younger man who had had more contact with urban ways but had no particular position of authority in his village and little interest in moralizing, laid more stress on the actual course of events in the plot; he enjoyed portraying exaggerated surprise, amusing episodes, mimicry of animals, the dramatic representation of eating, hunger, or beating, yet on the whole his tone throughout was rather quiet, consonant with his own personality. Suriba Konteh (or Nevertire) differed yet again. When *he* exaggerated the superlative force of some word or phrase (in particular his favourite '*everything*'—*mbɛ ooó mbɛ*) this was done with immense force and effect; his narrations were the extreme of vivid and vigorous dramatization, full of vehement surprise, clever characterization, and, at the end, passionate and committed generalization or moralizing. Dauda Konteh was more interested in the artistry of the delivery and, above all, the songs than in the plot or its details, and many of his stories consist mainly of singing. He had built up a peculiarly individual style of his own—greatly developed even in the couple of years between my two visits—with typical phrases and motifs; these included frequent references to his blindness (a point greatly appreciated by his friends listening to him), to the way in which he himself was an eye-witness to the events he described, and to the period when these events took place, when 'the earth had not yet begun'. Niaka and Karanke Dema have also been mentioned earlier. Both tended to prefer longer stories and used the possibilities of expansion and embroidery, often combined with a certain amount of singing or chanting. Niaka particularly enjoyed repetition, whether of episodes, sentences or single words, as in his story of the 'great, great witch', and made much use of his favourite phrase 'it is good' whenever, as often, he hesitated for the next word or sequence. Karanke, on the other hand, was rather more fluent; his stories tend not so much to conclude with a long elucidatory comment tacked on to the end, as to contain the comment within the framework and emphasis of the story itself, giving an impression, perhaps, of a more integrated unity than in the case of some other tellers.

Much more could be said about individual characteristics; people varied, for example, in fluency, some hesitating for words and having to fill in with some stop-gap such as 'well' (*awa*), or 'someone', 'something' (*wanini*), or being inconsistent in detail; others tended to stress particular aspects or topics which appealed to them individually—the element of paradox or reversal in a situation, for example, the amusement connected with hunger and food, the didactic element, or the imitation of the animals portrayed; and so on. To assume, then, that the performance and composition of Limba stories could be treated as something so fixed and traditional that they are not significantly affected by the personality or originality of individuals would be to misunderstand the whole nature of their oral literature.

It would have been possible to have included many different 'versions', each in a sense unique, of what could be regarded as the 'same' Limba story as far as the basic plot was concerned; this is clearly a matter of degree with many stories exhibiting similarities more or less marked in plot, motif or form. The best commentary on the degrees of variation and similarity is the texts themselves. However, a brief discussion of two stories in which the plot *was* very similar may help to illustrate how far, even in this case, variations of details and emphasis occurred between different narrations.

The man killed for a spinach leaf and *The man killed for a banana* are clearly, in one sense, merely detailed variants of one basic plot, and include many resemblances. They were told by two story-tellers (Karanke Dema and Dauda Konteh) from adjacent chiefdoms and in rather different dialects (Yaka and Biriwa). In the first version the girl consults only her mother about her plan to avenge her father; in the second she goes to the finch for advice through divination. In one her various suitors are called by the names of actual chiefs in real chiefdoms, in the other not. In the Banana version, she first prays to Kanu to forgive her before killing her new husband, and after his death there follows the episode about the children peeping into the hut and treading on the blood, then the discovery by his senior wife, and the girl's ruse to trick one of the chief's followers who was pursuing her by her pretended advice about the best way to kill her. In the Spinach version, there is no mention of any prayer or of the children; instead, in a vivid piece of description, the chief's cousin is made to find him lying dead with the flies buzzing around him; when the chief's eldest son gallops after the girl, she beguiles him by her beauty into giving up his plan of revenge in order to marry her. Even the concluding remarks are different. In one, the story is used to give a justifying explanation for the fact that the women now have their own special women chiefs—a custom introduced into the Biriwa chiefdom to which the teller belonged about two years before: 'If you should hear now that a woman has been made chief, well, that was through the girl, it was she began it.' In the other version, the conclusion is not to do with the girl herself at all, but consists of advice to a chief not to take violent action against someone who has committed only a trifling offence: 'Even if you are a chief, don't kill him for that.' Thus, quite apart from the differences in the style of delivery and the inclusion in Karanke's narration of many small subtle touches, there was also considerable divergence in the detailed course of the action.

Another similar example is of the three versions of the brief story about how death first came to mankind through the toad (*The toad did not love us*, *The toad and death*, and *The toad and the snake*). In the first version, the whole story was told with great sadness and with few of the usual effects of vivid dramatization or mimicry. Sangbang's interest seemed to be mainly fixed on the present tragic situation in which people so continually die, and the paradoxical reversal by which 'the one who loved us then, well, when we meet him now, we kill him. We do not kill the toad. Well, Kanu looks at us for that.' In Fanka's version, on the other hand, the main emphasis was on the actual action of the story, the interchange of words between the characters, the way in which the toad put the medicine on his head, jumped, and spilt it. The interest seemed to be concentrated much more on the animals concerned than in the previous story, and less stress was laid on Kanu's intentions and the sad result of death for human beings. Karanke's narration, *The toad and the snake*, differed yet again. The plot was somewhat more elaborate as an additional point about the snake was introduced; Kanu had intended that the snakes as well as humans should not die, and the snakes in fact succeeded in obtaining their portion of this 'medicine'; that is why snakes do not die but when they become old merely change their skin for a new one. This version also, unlike the others, included a reference to the common point in Limba stories about the unfortunate results of disobedience, in this case the toad's. Thus, in spite of the plots of the three stories being so close—and this is a plot that seemed to be among the better known ones—the tone and emphasis of the three narrations were noticeably different when told by these three individuals.

Many other instances could be given of the way in which the same plot continually appears in different guises, with varying concluding comments or different emphases, determined by the personality and interest of the individual narrator. These variations can also sometimes be traced to the particular circumstances of the occasion or audience. At times a whole story may seem to be partly just an excuse to bring in some special moral appropriate to the occasion or on which the teller wishes to expatiate, so that the plot may then be kept to the minimum; or, alternatively, the speaker may wish to amuse or shock his audience and may, perhaps especially if young, lay great emphasis on some one funny episode without much thought for any moral or generalization. Some apparently ridiculous conclusion may be drawn from a story just to provoke laughter in some particular group of listeners. Thus, to give an example, one version of the common plot about a chief's killing his own son after a forbidden knock at his door[1] was told with riotous success to the group of which I was one, because instead of resting content with some expected moral or generalization at the end, that it is wrong, say, to be too hasty, the story-teller made everyone laugh by adding with great rapidity and mock seriousness 'and that is how the man got much money from a dead body, and that is how the Europeans got their money'. Sometimes the actions or disposition of a particular person in the audience are obliquely referred to or a recent event in everyone's minds is used to give extra point to the plot or to the enactment of the story; one example of this was *The dog and the tortoise* whose race recalled the recently fought local election for chiefship. This illustrates how a particular form may arise from a direct desire to exploit a special occasion or to amuse or tease a particular group of listeners. Such elaborations are admired as a manifestation of the teller's ability and would not be thought of as involving any 'incorrect' rendering of some original tale.

Quite apart from any direct reference to the audience, the occasion also gives rise to variation in the sense that the telling of even the 'same' story by the same narrator tends to vary from narration to narration. Though certain individual tricks of style and motif certainly recur as well as the general framework, one cannot expect exact verbal identity.

[1] See *A clever husband* for another version of this theme.

People occasionally related a story for me twice over, the second narration being immediately after the first, and even in such circumstances the second narration differed from the first, often being less full. Even the general presentation and detailed ordering can vary to some extent as I discovered when, for example, I recorded a second version of Karanke telling *The man killed for a spinach leaf* about two years after the first. There is no careful verbal reproduction—even of one's own art.

Each story, then, is expressed in the actual *narration* which to the Limba is so important, and thus has its genesis in a particular situation —the audience is such, the teller is such, and the occasion is such—so that one could say that each telling of a story, each rearrangement or embellishing of the traditional themes, is itself the creation of a new story.

2. 'NEW' LIMBA STORIES

This aspect is even more evident in the stories which have a modern setting or refer to the more recent innovations. It would be quite wrong to wish to exclude these from a collection of Limba stories as if they could be regarded as in some sense 'foreign' or 'unLimba'. They are, after all, what Limba stories have presumably always been—expressions of conventional themes and styles using details which are of current interest to teller and listener. In, for example, the story of *The dog and the wheel*, the whole flavour is most certainly Limba even though the plot is concerned with the invention and behaviour of lorries. As in many stories, it begins with Kanu and the varied qualities of certain animals, then goes on to account for certain attributes of man, or of white man, with an amusing interpolation, to make the audience laugh, about his propensity to go bald on the top of his head. In the story already mentioned, *The dog and the tortoise*, the traditional theme of a race was used to refer to a contemporary incident, and for this reason was received with extra interest by the audience. *The story of a millionaire* is another example of what might seem in certain respects a 'new' story but is yet neither unLimba nor untypical. Certainly many of the things referred to in the story, like diamond, bank, cheque, or millionaire, are ones which arise out of certain recent circumstances and were not, in fact, directly familiar to the bulk of the audience (though with the contemporary interest in the diamond-digging in the south many people have heard of such things). In addition to these references to the modern means of wealth, the story is set in England. This is mainly because England is a good far-away land in which to set a fantasy, and it was also perhaps in reference or response to my presence. But in spite of these elements, the basic conventions of setting out the story, with its parallel episodes, vivid dramatization of the dialogue and its exaggerated replies, and the amused and delighted reactions of the listeners, are all characteristically Limba. So too is the theme which it contains, of the obstinacy of 'our young girls now', a common complaint among older Limba people, represented in the story by the chief's daughter's far-fetched demand for six diamond combs before she would be married to her husband. In spite of certain elements in the content this is clearly very much a Limba story and must be classed as such.

The way stories arise and are put into a Limba framework may also occasionally be observed in the treatment of biblical and other foreign stories which they may hear. Schoolboys returning home for a short visit, for example, may tell their friends some of the Christian stories in Limba and these may or may not be taken up and remembered; in the remote village in which I stayed, for example, the young son of a sub-chief had told his friends the biblical creation story, which they recognized when I mentioned it later. Several of the other stories included here have plots which in some ways directly recall certain biblical themes (e.g. *The white and black brothers* and *The jealous mothers*), and may well have arisen from similar contacts, though there is no means of ascertaining the date or details of this. In any case the way in which these are treated in a Limba context is all the more interesting if these stories were in fact originally prompted by Christian teaching. In the first story, for instance, it is typical of Limba story-telling that stress should be laid on the very common moral that *yaŋfa* (talking behind someone's back) may have far-reaching results, in this case affecting the whole destiny of white and of black men. In the second, there is the characteristic reference to quarrels which are likely to arise between co-wives over their *children*, and the direct reporting in a Limba manner of the spirited argument between the two mothers in the presence of Kanu in his role as Limba arbitrating chief.

As an example of the way in which a 'foreign' story can become a really 'Limba' one I have included among the stories in Part II Karanke's narration of 'Adam and Eve'. During my first visit I had once told him this story in a short and straightforward version. Over two years later he volunteered to tell it to me, as a story which he had in the meantime told several times to a group of Limba; when asked where he had heard it, he said, he had replied that it was from me, but had told it in his own way, and according to the conventional Limba forms. In many ways it had become a typical Limba story, both in the obvious sense of the techniques of style and delivery and the verbal formulas at beginning and end, and also in certain of the motifs he employed—a wife betraying her husband to her lover (the serpent) so that, rather as in *Kanu and chiefship*, the husband did not get the benefit of Kanu's intended help; humans going to Kanu to complain of hunger and ask for food; someone hiding, too frightened at first to come out; and the conclusion with an attribution of origin, alluding, as so often in the stories which state an origin, to the present hard condition of the Limba: 'And that is why we Limba have hard work—it began from the snake, and from Adam and Eve.'

Sometimes a deliberately Christian reference is used to create the desired effects of vividness or amusement in what may be, in other ways, a traditionally Limba situation. In one version of *Kanu and palm wine*, for instance, the teller described Sara's final success in finding Kanu with the vivid little picture of how he came on Kanu asleep, his eyes shut, sitting with the big Bible open on his lap. On another occasion I witnessed, a pastor preaching in the Limba Church in Freetown gave a dramatic rendering of the story of Elizabeth and Zacharias to a spell-bound congregation who were reacting with interest and interpolations in a way not untypical of Limba audiences in a situation of story-telling. He first read the passage from Luke in both English and in Limba, then told the story in his own words; he was speaking in English accompanied by a simultaneous sentence-by-sentence translation into Limba by an interpreter who imitated his gestures, tone, and expressions. He recounted how there was once a poor man who had no child, alas, his wife still had no child (a standard tragic situation in Limba story and experience), how the wife prayed and prayed to God (Kanu) to give her a child; when her husband went to the temple to see if it was his turn to sacrifice 'the lots all lay down flat' (a common term in Limba divination of the thrown halves of kola nuts), but because he doubted this answer he had received through divination, when he came out he was dumb. The people then all began to talk about him, saying he must be a bad man: 'he has no children', 'now he is dumb', 'surely he is bad'. But in the end his wife got a child; so did Mary too because she trusted in God. Therefore, he concluded, one ought to be kind to others and (again a typical Limba moral) not speak bad about them behind their backs. The whole occasion of this sermon strongly recalled that of any other Limba story-telling: the pastor used many gestures, shouting excitedly, then dropping his voice to be very low, quiet, and moving; and the whole was portrayed with great effectiveness, stressing the drama of the narrative rather than moralizing, and the listeners were clearly intent on the story.

Unfamiliar plots from any sources may be taken up and repeated or changed by one of the hearers. The story of *Kanu and palm wine*, for instance, was immediately retold with great vigour by an old man who had just heard it for the first time from a fellow Limba. Limba travellers who have come back from work or school in Freetown, the diamond area, or even further afield retell and exploit in a Limba idiom stories they have heard while away. Such new stories are often found particularly attractive by listeners; they are not to be regarded as 'unLimba' once they have been told by a story-teller in the characteristic Limba manner and according to Limba literary conventions.

In practice then one could say that from the point of view of content, as well as style, a story may have its own genesis in the occasion on which it is told, as well as in the participation of audience, actual performance, and the manner in which the story-teller improvises, rearranges, or expands the traditional themes. Any one Limba story is not immutably fixed, and the repertoire is continually growing and changing as new plots, episodes, situations, or jokes are bound into the traditional material and form.

3. THE GENESIS OF STORIES—THE LIMBA VIEW

The contribution made by individual story-teller and occasion is quite clearly recognized by the Limba. As already pointed out they stress the artistry of a particular individual performance rather than any verbal 'correctness' of rendering, and they more often praise a narrator for the verve or drama of his delivery than for the content of the plot itself or his clear memory of it. They speak of the way that children grow up hearing stories; some, they say, are not even capable of reproducing a plot with consistency or organizing the material sensibly. But even those who can manage that aspect—and up to a point most can—may still not be able to 'speak' the story satisfactorily so that the audience can hear clearly and with pleasure.

Good story-tellers hear stories, and also think them out again themselves (*simɔkɔ*) before they speak to an audience. A thoughtful narrator may himself stress his own contribution by remarking that he has been 'thinking out' a story for several days, perhaps while working or chasing birds in the fields, before he attempts to tell it in the evening. Or he may say that while he heard the story in the first place from 'the old people', he had himself 'added a little' (*ndinti, thi wuyete*), or told it from his own 'heart and intelligence' (*huthukuma iŋ funuŋ*). Very occasionally an experienced story-teller will even, on some occasions, claim that he himself was responsible for some story as a whole, that he had thought it out in his own 'heart'.

Nevertheless the Limba are at the same time clear that the basis of the stories is a traditional one. If a Limba is asked about the origin of any particular story the most common reply is always 'I heard it from the old people.' In this phrase the old people may be either those elders now living who tell the stories to their children or, more often, the dead, 'those who lived in the old days'. It is the dead who, in the last analysis, are responsible for the existence of stories: they handed them down through their descendants until finally they reached the present generation; that is how an individual now may be able to hear and retell a story, and why one of the most common formulas for ending is 'since I heard it, I had to tell you that story'. It would not be said of a Limba narrator that he had 'made' (*leheni*) a story in the sense that, say, a smith makes or mends a tool. A story-teller either 'speaks' (*gboŋkoli*) or 'brings out' (*fuŋuŋ*) a story. He 'carries it forward' (*kati ka kɔtɔkɔi*) so that others may hear it. The story is a *mbɔrɔ*, an 'old thing', and he speaks it 'by grace of the old people'.

The Limba therefore recognize what we, in referring to the genesis of their stories, might call their dual nature: that there is continual re-creation or improvisation and yet that this takes place within the framework of traditional style and theme. For at the same time as being strongly aware of the significance of individual performance and artistry in the current performance of any story, the Limba quite definitely make the claim that their stories are *old*, and form a part of their traditional heritage, a heritage which they explicitly assert is an ancient one, sanctioned by the dead. This conjunction between the exhibition of what may be new and personal in the practice of story-telling with what may in fact be old and traditional and is always claimed to be so, is expressed by the Limba attribution of the stories on the one hand to the old people from whom they were first heard, on the other to the individual performer and composer who speaks them and thinks them out. In the Limba phrase, the story-teller is 'taught by the dead and his own heart'.

4. GENERAL CONCLUSION

These chapters form only the introduction to the literature that follows, and the stories included here are only a small sample of the innumerable Limba tales that, within the context of the traditional settings, are all the time being told, performed, and enacted, using experience both new and old to entertain or enlighten the group of listeners. To regard the present texts as in any sense definitive or comprehensive, merely because they happen to have been recorded in writing over a few months in 1961 and 1963, would be to miss the fluidity and life of the actual practice of Limba literature as it now exists.

Regarded as literature, and not merely as some kind of cause or result of social structure, the Limba stories can be seen to have their own literary conventions about the kinds of characters, topics, form, and conclusions that are acceptable. In their concept of *mbɔrɔ*, a term with a wide range of applications which all more or less connect with its central meaning, there seems to be suggested a view of literature that is not unfamiliar to us—as a reflective comment on human life and action in terms in some way removed from reality. Limba literature, being oral, is also dramatically presented by the narrator in the very act of his simultaneous composition and performance. Hence the importance of style and technique of delivery and of the part taken by the audience.

It is within the context of the social and physical background and of these literary and dramatic conventions that the individual story-teller composes and performs with the help of those who hear and 'reply' to him. The stress is on the importance of the traditional and age-old nature of the stories; but it is by using these aspects that each narrator produces on each occasion his new and individual creation. In the towns and villages and farms of northern Sierra Leone the Limba meet together in their groups to pursue the joint and pleasing activity of story-telling, and possess a conventional medium through which, in the traditional manner, individuals formulate and mediate their experience in the form of literature.

PART II

THE STORIES

INTRODUCTORY NOTE

1. METHOD OF RECORDING

THE stories given here were recorded in three ways: on tape, in dictation, or, in a very few cases, written by my assistant Suri Kamara. In each case the story was originally told in Limba and later translated by me.

About one-third of the stories were recorded on tape. This was the most satisfactory method in capturing the atmosphere and encouraging a full narration. But it presented great difficulties in transcription; narrators tended to speak very fast at times, or to move, or move away from, the microphone while speaking, and thus were not always very audible on the tape. The differences in dialect also increased the problem as the Limba I was able to train to help in transcribing did not always speak the same dialect as that of the recording.

Many of the texts (just under two-thirds) were therefore taken down directly by myself. This was often done in the evening in the presence of several people all of whom were also listening and reacting to the stories. Though not altogether satisfactory this did up to a point reproduce the story-telling situation as I soon acquired the habit of taking down the story very rapidly. However, it has doubtless led to the omission of possible expansions, imitations, and singing. My habit was normally to take the texts down rapidly at night, then write an English translation the next day, inquiring about the parts I could not readily understand and normally checking through the text itself again with my assistant.

Only a few stories are included that were written for me by Suri Kamara from dictation. I found this a less helpful means of recording as I had no opportunity to see the story itself enacted by the narrator.

2. TRANSLATION AND PRESENTATION

I have tried to make the translations relatively literal so as to preserve something of the flavour of the original, while at the same time not rendering them unintelligible to an English reader. Limba sentences, and their sub-divisions, are sometimes delivered in a somewhat abrupt way with the phrases following on one at a time, as it were, rather than built into a long sustained unit; this has been partially indicated in the punctuation, for example by rather more frequent commas than might seem suitable in an English sentence. I have adopted certain conventions throughout, such as always rendering *kumaŋ* as 'behold', but otherwise have not been entirely consistent. Ejaculations such as the Limba *e*, *he he*, *ha*, *ye*, etc., have sometimes been left in their original form, sometimes replaced by English exclamations. Where the actual Limba terms have been used, usually those representing some sound, these are given in phonetic spelling[1] and italicized. Names of people and places have been given in their English spellings. Phrases where I am particularly doubtful of the translation are omitted (marked by dots) or, more frequently, enclosed or followed by question marks.

The titles and paragraphs are my own. Interpolations by listeners and the many repetitions of the songs have not generally been included in the text given here but are sometimes noted in the commentary. Otherwise, apart from the occasional phrase that was inaudible or unintelligible (in these cases I have marked the omission) and the compression of certain of the long preambles sometimes introduced before the beginning of a story in compliment to myself, the stories are given just as they were recorded; I have not in any case tried to paraphrase or 'improve' them.[2]

A few texts with word-for-word literal translations are included in Appendix I and may be of interest to some readers.[3] In both these texts and the Limba terms that appear in the translations the orthography is based on that used by Professor Berry in his articles on Limba.[4] In general the vowels have the so-called continental values, the consonants the English. In addition *ɔ* and *ɛ* represent the open *o* and *e* respectively; *gb* is a labio-velar plosive (normally voiced, occasionally, in some dialects unvoiced); *ŋ* is the velar nasal; and *th* a voiceless interdental plosive distinct from the palatalized *t*.

In all I recorded a little under two hundred stories and heard many more. In making the selection for the present volume I have tried to include stories which were both popular with a Limba audience and would read well in an English version. However, not all those included are necessarily to be thought of as the best or definitive examples of Limba literature; in a volume of this sort stories by the ordinary as well as by the specially gifted narrators are of interest. Indeed it is perhaps in these that some of the more typical characteristics of Limba stories and story-telling come out particularly clearly; and they too are representative of Limba literature as it is practised and living at present.

The stories are presented in three main sections, followed by a brief

[1] The orthography is discussed below.

[2] The only story of which I have not got an exact Limba text is that of *The dog and the rice*, on which see note *ad loc.*

[3] The complete Limba texts of all but the sixteen stories collected on my second visit are to be found in my Oxford D.Phil. thesis *The Limba of Sierra Leone with special reference to their folktales or 'oral literature'*, 1963. It is hoped to publish these and other texts elsewhere at a later stage.

[4] *Sierra Leone Studies*, 11 (1958) and 13 (1960).

section on shorter forms. Within each group I have placed together a few obviously similar versions of the 'same' plot which it may be of interest to compare. I have also grouped together the stories about very much the same characters or subjects, for example those about hunters, orphans, twins, or the spider. This arrangement, however, is merely for convenience and there is no special merit in the order I have chosen.

LIST OF STORIES

1 · STORIES ABOUT PEOPLE

The story of Deremu

KARANKE DEMA. *Dictated* 29.10.61

Deremu is attacked, through a spirit, by his own mother—a situation of tragedy, for a mother is usually the one person a man expects to be able to trust fully. Deremu protects himself, conquers the spirit, but kills his mother; then he gives her a magnificent funeral. It was told as a sad story. The moral is stated—you should not plot against someone behind his back, especially a mother against her child.

A WOMAN once bore a child. That child was called Deremu. When she had reared him and he was grown, his father put him in the men's society. Deremu came out.[1] He went down to Freetown.[2] She the mother was left behind. She was dyeing clothes indigo.

The dry season came. The cane grass was burnt. The indigo came out in new leaves. The woman went out, going to look for indigo. She went. She searched, but she could not find any. There in the middle of the cane grass,[3] the water was mostly dried up; for the sun was very hot. Thirst distressed her, the woman. She came to a big stream bed. But there was no water there. She sat down—*wɔ hɔŋ!*[4] Then she said, 'Ah me! how I have suffered today since I came into this cane grass to search for indigo. I have not found any. Thirst is distressing me. I have searched long for water, I have not found any. Alas, Kanu, if only, here where I am, here where I am sitting, if only water was to come forth here.'

Then the spirit of the place came out. He said, 'If water comes out, will you pay me?' The mother said, 'What will I pay you?' The spirit said, 'A man.'[5] The woman said, 'I—after the long time I have spent searching round for water, if I find water now, *whatever* you say I am willing to give you.' Then the spirit said, 'A man.' She said, 'I accept.' Thirst was distressing the mother. She accepted there. When she had accepted, the spirit said, 'Go to one side here.' The woman got up from

[1] From the bush, after initiation.

[2] Many young men go off to Freetown, often before marriage, hoping to accumulate money for bridewealth.

[3] Cane grass (probably *chasmopodium caudatum*), frequently associated in stories with barrenness, harshness, drought.

[4] Noise of sitting, flopping down tiredly.

[5] On a spirit's help and payment see p. 22.

where she was sitting, and sat there. He went. He sat on one side. Water came out, brought out by the spirit—much water. The spirit said, 'Mother, here is the water. But I will not let you drink it, unless you pay me what I asked.' Then the woman said, 'I bore a child; his name is Deremu. But he went to Freetown. When he returns—take him! I give him to you. For you helped me with the water. I would have died, but you helped me.' The spirit said, 'I accept. All right.' The woman drank the water, she bathed. She went away.

And for that the spirit sang to tell his children:

'Deremu *yo*; Deremu *be ye*, Deremu *yo*, Deremu is mine. If there is a Susu there, Deremu is mine; if there is a Koranko there, Deremu is mine; if there is a Mandingo there, Deremu is mine; Deremu, Deremu is mine. *Ye!*' The spirit stayed there. All the time the spirit was singing this song.

Now Deremu was in Freetown. He thought about going up [to his home]. For where he was now in Freetown, he had become well off in the work he did there. He was a diver, working underneath the water. He had been made a chief there. He had now many followers, wives and all, musicians and all.

He said, 'I want to go up to my country; to see my mother.'[1] But he went first to a diviner to ask, 'Will I go up in peace? I want you to look about that for me.' The diviner looked. He said, 'Ha! if you are intending to go up, harden yourself. Your mother is keeping war for you,[2] at the river, in the middle, in a deep place. If you think of going, go to a blacksmith, for him to make you many knives. Take them to a leather worker and have them sewn [into sheaths] for you, and fasten them to a big gown, and let this be the gown next your body. One knife take to a moriman, so it may be worked on, for it is to be your life. That is what you will do.' He said, 'All right.' He went to the blacksmith. He went and told him, the blacksmith. He made the knives. One of them was a small one, he gave it to him. He took them to the leather worker. The leather worker sewed them. He fastened them in his gown. He took the one to a moriman. The moriman went and wrote much on it, so that it would help him to kill the spirit who lay in wait for him. He wrote on it, with *manasi* water.[3] He gave it to Deremu. Deremu fastened it on to a big gown. When he had put the gown on, with a hat and all on his head, and the knives all over it, he thought about coming up.

They began to come; they, musicians and all, wives and all, young men and all, they came. For he was a chief. He was riding on a horse.

[1] A common reason given for a visit home.

[2] Lit. 'you are having war kept for you by your mother'; the term is that for the usual gift of food in welcome.

[3] 'Medicine' made by a moriman (Muslim expert) writing words from the Koran on a piece of wood then washing them off into the water.

When they were about to set out, from where he was in Freetown, when he had thought about coming, he had sent a message to his mother here. 'I am coming this month.' The mother heard it. She was glad. But she had not acted well. For she had given him to a spirit. She was thinking to herself 'I have not done well.'

When they set out to come, they came to the river.[1] He knew, he Deremu, that it was at the river he had been told that war was being kept for him—that it is here. He stopped. He got down from his horse. He said to them, 'Go across.' They crossed by the bridge. He stood on the far side [from them]. He put on his gown, the one with the knives. He called out, he Deremu, 'You, you who stand on the other side, you whom I brought here; for me, it is here, that if I am to find life, it is through Kanu; if I don't find life, all right.' The horse was taken over. He stood on the far side. He said, 'When the bridge breaks under me and I am thrown in the water, if you see red blood, weep, my time is finished. If you see black blood, rejoice, I have not died.'

He started out. He reached the middle of the bridge. The bridge split in two. The spirit had broken it. Deremu fell into the water. The spirit seized him. They began to fight there. The spirit was struggling to kill him. He was struggling to kill the spirit. He drew one knife, and cut at the spirit. The knife broke. He drew another, he cut. It broke. He drew another, he cut. It broke. A hundred knives—they were not able to kill the spirit! The spirit meanwhile was struggling to kill him, Deremu. He drew another, the one he kept against his stomach, that the moriman had worked. He thrust it in here at his throat, he cut through the spirit's throat. He thrust it in here [back of neck], he cut it through. The spirit was unable to kill Deremu. Deremu won in killing the spirit.

Those who were standing here on the dry land—when Deremu fell into the water, their hearts were sick. They thought 'Deremu will die today.' They were weeping now. Behold Deremu had hardened himself. They saw the water now: it was black. They danced with joy now—Deremu had not died! They danced with joy now. Deremu lifted up the spirit, he pulled him out, dead. He brought him out on to the dry land. He split him open. He took out the heart, and the gall. He said, 'My mother bore me; she brought me up, but—that is what is meant by bearing a child—but you will not know what is in her heart. For my mother intended to kill me. But by Kanu's grace I did not die. But for her—where she wanted to send me, I will send her there.'

He bathed well. He put on his fine clothes. He took the gall and heart. He split open the heart, he put the gall in it. He closed it over. He gave it to his wife, 'Take this with you for me.' The wife took it. Deremu mounted his horse. They set out. The musicians played.

[1] On the delivery of this and the following episode see the description on p. 83.

When they came to the bush by the side of the village, he sent on his messenger. 'Tell my mother I have come. Deremu is here, to see you.' The messenger went, he went and told her. For he [Deremu] had sent a boy before[1] to announce that he was going. She—her heart was bad,[2] for she had given him to a spirit. But when she saw the messenger saying, 'Your son has come', she rejoiced, she danced now. She swept the whole village. She said, 'Well, let him enter.' The messenger came back and said this.

They began to enter the village. The musicians played. Deremu was riding on his horse. They entered the village. His mother rejoiced now. They were now all dancing around him. After a long time, he got down. He went into his lodging-place. There as they danced he gave his mother gifts. Behold, he was thinking about killing his mother; for his mother had intended to kill him; but he had hardened himself. When he got down, he brought out the heart, with the gall. He told his wife, 'Cook a little rice for me in a small pot. Boil the heart, prepare it. But don't eat it! Don't taste it!' The wife prepared the heart. She cooked a small bit of rice. She gave it to Deremu. Deremu took it; he called 'Mother, come here.' His mother came in. He said, 'Here is what I brought for you; for it is long since we parted. This is what I have brought you, for you to eat, it is good.' Behold she is to die. She the mother was glad. Behold, she is dying. For she would have killed Deremu. When she had taken it, she ate it. When she had finished eating it, they came out to dance outside. The musicians played. They danced beautifully. His mother was rejoicing now.

When she had danced a little only, she fell. When they went near to lift her up, she was dead. The musicians stopped playing. They all gathered at the place. Deremu got down from his horse. He said, 'Mother, you bore me; I did not act badly. You brought me up. But when I went down to Freetown, you heard that I had become well off. I was sending you everything. But you did not notice that, you were thinking about killing me. You gave me to a spirit. Behold, by Kanu's help, I am here. I too have got a child, but we will not know what is in his heart. Now the place you wanted to send me to, you have gone there first yourself.'

Then he got up. He said, 'Dig the grave.' It was dug. He took her, he put her in a chest, so that the earth would not touch her body.[3] He took gold and put it on her mouth. He took more gold, he put it in her left hand. He took more gold and put it on her right toe. He said goodbye. Saying goodbye to his mother: 'Mother, you will not say of me that I

[1] i.e. from Freetown.

[2] Guilty and anxious.

[3] Usually the dead are buried only in white cloth; to use a coffin, gold, and large quantities of shot indicate the magnificence of the funeral. To hold the 'wailing' after only a month is also exceptional.

did not think of you. If I had not hardened myself I would have died. But all right. I . . . (?) If you bear a child, you too become well off. But you did not think of that with me. But since you have died, I will bury you well.'

She was buried. He brought out gunpowder and gave it to the people—'Fire!' For seven days they fired that gunpowder. After one month had passed, he held a wailing for her.

So, if you bear a child, do not work against him,[1] for you do not know about him. If he is to become poor—you do not know. If he is to become well off—you do not know. If he becomes well off, it is you who owns it. But if you work against him, that is bad.

Now you have heard the story. I Karanke Dema, I wanted to tell it to you on this day, for you are setting out to go. It is finished.

Sira and the monster

KARANKE DEMA. *Recorded* 4.10.61

A long story with several themes that also occur elsewhere, for example the girl who insisted on finding her own husband (*The girl and the spirit*), the three dogs saving the hero's life (*The hunter with three dogs*), the pretended farewell while really calling for help (*The child and the hunter*), and the insistence on climbing higher and higher up a tree (*The man killed for a spinach leaf*, etc.). These are all bound together to make up the present integrated story, ending with a suitable general comment.

Thumpu, 'monster', was sometimes said to be a spirit, sometimes an animal. He comes into several other stories, for example *Bayo*, where he helps the boy.

The extreme personality of the girl in the story, whether in joy or sorrow, was conveyed by the mode of delivery as well as by her words and actions, and the whole narrative was made dramatic by the narrator's presentation and acting.

Karanke said that he had heard the story from the old people and had 'added a little' (*a thi wuyete*) himself. He had been thinking about it for several days in the farm before telling it.

I, KARANKE DEMA, I want to tell Yenkeni[2] a story. Well, cousin Konia, well, you will listen to me well, won't you? I am going to tell Yenkeni a story. If it pleases her—all right; if it doesn't please her—all right. But you will reply to me, won't you?[3] By grace of all who are sitting here.

[1] Lit. do not do *yaha* (*yaŋfa*), i.e. plot secretly against him.

[2] My Limba name.

[3] i.e. formally 'reply' (*me*) to his words. Konia did this, commenting, prompting, and reacting audibly throughout.

Someone once bore a girl. Her name was Sira. But that girl, she was amazing.[1] When she was in the belly still, her mother went to bathe. She said to her mother, 'Eh, mother'—that her mother was not to scrub her too much, 'Don't scrub me too much.' Her mother said, 'Eh! my child, will you at last come out? Child, are you my child?' 'I am your child; but there is one word I will tell you'—it was the child speaking —'when it happens that I come out in the world, I will not be wooed in marriage by anyone. I will choose for myself the one to marry me, someone with no blemish.'[2] She said that. Her mother remembered it.

She came and bore Sira, her first child.[3] That Sira—Kanu did not give her suffering. She grew up very quickly. She [the mother] bore a second child. His name was Sara. That Sara, he had no suffering.

Well, then people stood up, everyone got ready to woo Sira for himself. But when you go and announce your purpose, she says, 'I—the one who will marry me (for my mother is not concerned for my bridewealth)[4] —the one who will marry me is to have no blemish.' When she said that, everyone went away. Oh! they were not able to marry her.

The monster heard that. Then he was told about it. He said, 'I will marry her.' He was thinking about her. He came out. He began to come, to come for Sira, saying, 'I will marry her.' He borrowed a gown, that of the green *bahande*[5] snake, the small one. He put it on. He borrowed a gown from the cobra. He put it on. He borrowed the *baŋkiboro* snake's gown. He put it on. He borrowed the iguana's gown, he put it on. He borrowed the python's gown, he put it on. He borrowed the *waŋkana* snake's gown, he put it on. He borrowed the mamba's gown; that was the last one he borrowed. That is the one that shines beautifully.

When he had borrowed them, he began to go. When he appeared in the distance, she Sira was pounding rice. As soon as she saw him, she threw down the beater. She ran to her mother. 'Mother, mother, mother, mother, mother! The man I was talking about, the man I was talking about, he has come. It is he will marry me. For he has come. He has come. He is the one who will marry me. I said before that the one to marry me must have no blemish. He has come, he is the one I want. He has come.'

Her mother came outside. She looked at him. 'My child, you said

[1] *hugbanaŋ*—cunning, wily, far-fetched.

[2] A weal or bump on his body.

[3] Her *first* child; Karanke pronounced this quietly and tenderly to convey that the mother loved her very much indeed.

[4] i.e. her main concern is not the property for bridewealth but the qualification of being unblemished—not a usual situation.

[5] He borrows the skins of the various snakes to make himself look smooth and gleaming. The *bahande* is said to be a thin green harmless snake about two to three feet long; the *baŋkiboro* a 'beautiful' one living on the top of palm trees, spotted and very long; the *waŋkana* small and red.

before, "No other man will marry me." Now since he has come for you, since you have said "This is the one I want," I will not argue.'

The rice she [Sira] had been pounding, the *disi*[1] rice, she put it down there. She took the monster's bundle. She took him into a room. 'Well, here is where you can stay.' She took out the rice she had been pounding. She said, 'Mother.' 'Yes?' 'The *disi* rice is not what he should eat. Go and get some *mɛrikɛ* rice.' The mother got some *mɛrikɛ* rice, she came and gave it to her. She pounded it. She produced the hen she had had for long. She caught it there. 'The one who is there, whom I have come to want—he will eat it.' She caught it, she Sira. She killed. She killed it. She pounded[2] the rice. She cooked very well for him. She brought him in, into where he was to lodge.

Now he, the monster, he is *very, very* ugly. In the whole world, he is the ugliest thing, more than all other animals, more than all Limba people. The monster is the ugliest of all. We Limba, everyone among us —no one is near him, the monster is uglier than all, because his body is all over bumps.

She took him in—but that monster will never eat rice. When she took the rice in for him she said, 'Here is your food. All the people have been coming here for long. But I don't want them. You are the one I want. You have come today. You will marry me. Tomorrow I will be taken to you. But before you announce what you came for, if it was for that you came, before you say why you came, we will first make food for you.' She gave him the rice.[3] Now the monster will never eat rice. She took in water. She came out, she Sira. Then he stood up. He cut a piece from the rice,[4] he dug in the cooking place. He buried it there; for he does not eat rice. But he cut a piece from one side, so Sira would not know that he had not eaten. He covered it in the earth; so Sira would not know. He called her: 'Sira.' Sira came. 'Well, here is the food [that is left].' Sira came and said 'Oh! eat some more.' He said, 'No. I am satisfied.' Sira took the rice away with her. He announced why he had come: 'I came for you.' Then Sira said, 'I.' Sira said, 'I, now that you have come—my mother says, "I am not concerned about the bridewealth."[5] I too, I am not concerned about the bridewealth. But now—you and I. I will not be left behind.' Behold she did not know that he had a bad disease.

[1] The *disi* rice is regarded as ordinary, the 'American' (*mɛrikɛ*) as the most valuable, white and filling. The girl insists that her suitor must have the very best.

[2] *yoŋoni*—the word implies that she pounded it extra well.

[3] Giving him rice and water suggests her willingness to be his wife.

[4] The monster is not human and does not eat rice. He buries part of it to conceal this from Sira. Not eating the rice she gives him also implies that he has not really accepted her as his wife.

[5] Usually the formal announcement by a suitor would be followed by some discussion, implied at least, about the bridewealth. But in this case Sira quite unconventionally neglects all the usual arrangements.

When they began to go, he came to the mamba. The mamba said, 'Oh cousin, what a long time ago you came and borrowed my gown. It is my only gown. Oh, you caused me trouble. These three days the tiny flies have been eating me, the *bawɔnɔ* flies have been eating me, the mosquitoes have been eating me. Well, you won't take it with you when you go, oh! Take it off.' The monster took it off. Then said Sira, 'Oh!' The bumps spoke, 'What Sira, what Sira; what Sira, what Sira.'[1] Sira said, 'No, it is nothing. I have forgotten my head tie. That is what I thought of.' The bumps said, 'Yes Sira, yes Sira.'

They began to go. They met the python. He greeted him 'Greetings, cousin.' The python responded, 'Yes. Cousin, welcome.' 'Yes. Thank you, thank you, thank you, thank you.' 'You went and brought a wife. But you have given me trouble. The three nights you have gone and spent I stayed here, eaten by worthless creatures—the mosquitoes have been eating me, the gnats eating me, the flies eating me. The gown—you will not take it with you when you go, oh! Take it off.' He took it off.

Everywhere he had borrowed the gowns, they were taken away from him, all of them. When Sira was surprised, 'Oh!', the bumps spoke, 'What Sira, what Sira; what Sira, what Sira.' She said, 'No nothing. The bead loin cloth I wove yesterday, that's what I had forgotten. That was why I showed surprise.' The bumps answered 'Yes Sira, yes Sira.'

When they entered the house, they went and took her into the house, she was brought into a room. She was brought into another room, she went through. She was brought into another room, she went through. She was brought into another room, she went through. She was surprised 'Oh! oh!' The bumps asked 'What Sira, what Sira; what Sira, what Sira.' Then Sira said, 'No, nothing. I am only thinking about my lodging-place. That is why I showed my surprise "Oh! oh!"' The bumps said 'Yes Sira, yes Sira.'

When she was brought into that lodging, there was a mirror lying there. She could not go out anywhere; for wherever she goes, the monster will know. If she goes out to spit,[2] the monster will know. If she is told that he has gone to hunt in the far distance, if she even goes outside the house, he knows. She stayed there in that jail.

When two months had passed, then Sara said, 'E, mother.' 'Yes?' 'Sira, whom he came for in marriage, where she went to—it is long since I have seen her. My heart is not resting. I want to go to find her.

[1] The exchange between Sira and the bumps recurs several times in a kind of chant. The bumps (on the monster but apparently with a kind of life of their own) reply to her surprised exclamation as she sees that her husband's gleaming body is not as she had thought. In each case she then tries to cover up her remark.

[2] People often go outside to clear their throats and spit. This can also be used as a euphemism for urinate, as later in the story.

So I may see where she is staying.'[1] Then his mother said, 'All right. My child, what you have said, it pleases me.' Sara went out. He used to train dogs—three of them. One was Kondengmukure, one Sosongpeng, one Salialoho,[2] the three dogs. He trained them well.

When they began to go, they went in—he Sara. He arrived, in the afternoon. He came and gave a greeting. His sister replied where she had gone, the one called Sira.

If you were to see her now, the one called Sira—her body is not well. But there was no chance for her to return to her parents. She was thin and not right. For as soon as they reached there, when she came with her husband, the bumps were all over the house! Anyone who is married there is bound to get those bumps. When she reached there and was given the kola for marriage—two bumps. She slept there two nights—four bumps. Before her brother had found her—the one called Sara—she had six bumps on her body, she Sira.

Sara, when he came, he did not (?) recognize her at once (?). He asked, 'E, Sira, what is the matter with your body?' She said, 'Ah, ah, my father.' She fell at his feet, she wept, wept, wept. 'I have come within a rope. It would have been better for me not to have done it—saying I will not have a husband found for me, I will find one for myself. Well, I have got a husband. It is bringing me suffering. But brother, since you have come, sit in the courtyard; don't come inside. In here a human will not come. If a human comes here, he will kill him.'

Well, Sara sat in the yard. He had his dogs with him. The monster set out from over there. He had a dream[3] that Sara had come here. He stood up from where he was staying to hunt, he began to come. As he arrived at the bush near the town, he smelt the scent. He said, 'E? *Inf.*[4] A human's smell, a human's smell.' He reached the compound. He called, 'Sira. Sira.' Sira answered, 'Yes?' 'A human's smell!' He looked round, he saw Sara sitting there. He said, 'Sara.' He saw him sitting. He said, 'You. What have you come for?' As he asked it, the dogs began to growl. 'Krrr, krrr; krrr, krrr'—for they had heard the name Sara. For they are dogs trained thus. He [monster] moved back. He had been thinking that if he saw a human there he would kill him. But the dogs spoke, he was afraid. Then said Sira, 'I don't know him; since he came

[1] There is normally a close bond between brother and sister; they tend to visit and help each other even after her marriage.

[2] Dogs often have names, sometimes with special meanings. Here Salialoho means 'jumping well' and was uttered here and later with lingering affection by Karanke, implying how rightly fond Sara was of him. The recurrence of these unusual and attractive names seemed to be one of the effective points about the story for the audience.

[3] The power to see with 'eyes' in a supernatural way is fairly often expressed as seeing 'in a dream'.

[4] The sound of his snuffing, carried on into the next phrases.

here I have not learnt his name. I have not yet greeted him. He did not greet me. He sat there where he is sitting. I don't know his name.'

He asked 'What then you? Why have you come here?' Then Sara said, 'My name is called Sara.' 'What have you come for?' 'I have come to see my sister. The one you married is my sister, the one called Sira. She is my sister, that is why I have come to see her.' But he, he the monster, was thinking; his heart was delighted—to eat him. But no chance to eat him! The dogs were guarding Sara. When he made to come near, the dogs growled. He lodged him in a room. He, the monster, on one side, Sara on the other. He took him in there.

It was a time like now [late evening]. He was thinking about eating Sara as he came out from where he was lying. But the dogs were ordered by Sara. He set them at the door. The dogs themselves knew well too. When he opened the door, the monster, to come where Sara was lying, the dogs growled 'Krrr, krrr; krrr, krrr.' He went and knocked at the door. 'Hey, brother-in-law, brother-in-law, brother-in-law,' calling Sara. Sara answered. He seemed like one sleeping. Behold, he was not asleep. He answered 'Mmmm?' 'Ha! Those strangers[1] you brought with you, ha! those strangers, ha! I am beginning to be a little afraid of them. A man won't be able to go outside to spit.' Sara said, 'No. Only lie down again. If you don't knock into them, there where they are lying, they will make no trouble for a man.' He went out. He didn't pass water. He went in again. Behold, he was preparing to eat the man, Sara.

When he had gone and slept a little bit, he took a sword, he went out. As he went to a stone to sharpen it—as he pulled the knife once on the stone, *gbaka*, the dogs growled. What he was doing was pulling the sword back and forward, *gbaka gbaka*, to sharpen it, for him to go and find where Sara was lying; to go and cut him up. The dogs growled 'Krrr, krrr; krrr, krrr.' He said, 'E.' There where he was standing, he was afraid to go in. He did not dare to go inside. 'Cousin, cousin. Ha! the strangers you brought today, well? The strangers are cruel. I think they have not eaten today.' Sara said, 'No, that is not why. Only come inside, and lie down. If you don't knock into them, they will cause no one any trouble.' He went in.

The whole night, he spent all the night struggling to kill Sara; but he was unable to kill him. He thought, 'Since I am not able for him at night, tomorrow morning, I will be able for him.'

In the morning he said, 'Sara.' Sara answered 'Yes?' 'I have got a kola tree, it has many kolas, but I cannot pick them. Come, come out and help me to pick them.' Sara said 'All right.' 'But don't take the strangers you have with you today.' He Sara, when he first came, his

[1] It is clear from his tone that he is very afraid of the dogs, but he tries to conceal this by making a kind of half-joke about their being 'strangers'. Sara is not deceived but pretends to make a helpful reply.

sister Sira had told him everything, that 'He, he the monster, he will not see a human without eating him.' Then Sara said, 'All right.' When he was told this that morning by the monster, he said, 'Sira.' Sira answered, 'Yes?' 'Cook well for the dogs, and let them eat. Put in the palm-oil in plenty so they may be satisfied.' When Sara said they should go, what he [monster] had told him was not to take the dogs. He said, 'All right; I will tie them up.' He told Sira to tie them. Sira went and tied them with raffia leaves. He [Sara] was thinking to himself 'My life—it is the dogs are to save it.' He didn't refuse; he left them behind there.

When they went to pick the kola, they reached the place. The monster loaded his gun, to kill Sara. For a human may never come to his house. When they had reached there, he said, 'Here is the kola tree. You will climb it.' Sara said 'I?' 'Yes.' He was determined to kill Sara at once. For he had been unable to kill him by night. Sara climbed up. He came to a kola nut. 'Is it this one?' 'Not that one.' Sara went a bit higher. 'Here?' 'Not that one, climb further on.' Sara climbed right to the top. When he reached it, the monster said, 'Master,[1] there where you are high up there, your time is finished. At night, I tried to get you, but I was unable. But now your time is finished. I am going to shoot you.' Sara said, 'What, me?' 'Yes.' 'All right. No matter. But before killing me, wait, let me say goodbye to Kanu.' He was thinking about his dog's names. He shouted 'Kondengmukure, Kondengmukure; Kondengmukure, Kondengmukure; Sosongpeng; Salialoho.'[2] The dogs were: one, Kondengmukure; one, Sosongpeng; and one, Salialoho. 'Kondengmukure, Kondengmukure; Kondengmukure, Kondengmukure; Sosonpeng; Salialoho. I will say good-bye to Kanu six times before you shoot me.' The twice he called out, the dogs heard it over there. They broke all the fastenings. Kondengmukure was in front, for he was the oldest. He sang, 'You are called, you are called, jump—*sɔyɔŋ!* you are called, you are called, jump—*sɔyɔŋ!* you are called, you are called, jump—*sɔyɔŋ!*'[3] . . . When they reached there, as soon as they came and stopped, Sara shouted out and told them, 'What you find there is your food!' Before he had finished saying it, the dogs had fallen on the monster. They bit him open and tore out the flesh. They bit him open and tore out the flesh. They split him all up, they scattered all the bits.[4]

When they had finished destroying him, Sara arose where he was up above. He picked all the kolas. He came down. He found the monster lying there. 'Master, you wanted to finish my life. I am called Sara.

[1] This term is often used between opponents in the stories; cf. the various parts of the house threatening the witch in *The story of the great witch*.

[2] He calls the dogs in a kind of song.

[3] This was sung, Karanke singing the first two phrases, the chorus coming in with *sɔyɔŋ*, and the whole was repeated about eight times.

[4] This episode was recounted with great vigour and excitement which the audience found very effective.

Mine is not finished, yours is finished. The kola, I will take it away when I go.' He picked it. When he had picked it all, he wove a basket.[1] He tied it up for Kondengmukure, he put it on his head. He wove a basket—for Sosongpeng. He put it on his head. He wove a basket—for Salialoho. He put it on his head. He began to go.

He reached the village. 'Sira.' 'Yes?' 'My sister, now you understand that I am more than you. Well, let us go; I was able to free you. I was nearly killed for you. But it is all right. For you, I am the senior to you.[2] My sense is the senior's. I am called the man, and I have more sense than you. Let us go.' Sira, at what Sara spoke, there where Sira stood she trembled. She lay at his feet, she wept. 'My father,[3] I am less than you. You told me at the beginning, but I would not listen. Now I leave it all to you. You came and saved my life.'

They went. They went and told their mother. 'Mother.' 'Yes?' 'Here is Sira.' The bumps on Sira, the bumps were six. But he was able to go and take Sira from where she was, with the monster. His mother said, 'E, my child. Thank you, thank you, thank you. At first when you spoke about it, I did not at once allow you. But now, you were able to free your sister. I am thanking you for that.'[4]

Now for Sira, before she could find a husband, it was Sara that had to say, 'Here is the man you will marry.' Kanu Masala saw this. That is what he told us in farewell, we Limba. Even if it is only a small boy, and you are the first born, you the woman, if he says to you, 'Here is where you will be married', you the woman—agree to what he says. Even if you are known to be the older, you the woman, you will not be able to stay in marriage by your own power. You will not be able to save your life. Stand behind what the boy says. He is able to speak for you. Since Kanu told us that, all of us Limba, now we follow that. The boy says, 'I am able to speak for you, to say where you will be in marriage. Even if you are older than me—here is where you will be in marriage.' She will agree.

Yenkeni, since you have come to be taught Limba, and say that whoever knows a story should tell Yenkeni the story, I am telling it, I Karanke, I heard it from the old people. Konia, you consented to listen to me, I talked and you answered me well. By grace of all who are sitting here, well, that story is finished, it is ended by your grace.

[1] To put the kolas into and get the dogs to carry. In real life dogs are never used as beasts of burden.

[2] In years he is younger but by intelligence senior.

[3] She calls him this in entreaty and humility.

[4] Thanking is one of the suitable conclusions to a story.

The girl and the spirit

BANKOLO MANSARAY. *Dictated* 11.11.61

A similar plot to that of *Sira and the monster*, but with a rather different ending; there is no explicit moral, but a typical Limba conclusion of a return home, coupled with a (somewhat half-hearted) attribution of origin, that of gold. The plot is a common one, and I heard still other stories based on it though there is not room to include further examples here. In one version the girl's obstinacy in marrying a spirit 'with a body like a white stone [diamond]' results in the deaths of her parents, swallowed by the spirit.

In this version the girl is saved by her small brother who had 'clear' eyes and so was able to perceive the spirit Tintilongo's acts. Typically exaggerated numbers are used to describe the bridewealth and the size and food of the hen left to guard the girl. In his delivery the teller used a particularly large number of onomatopœic words and phrases in the form of, for example, *na berede*, plainly; *na frrr*, the sound of gold being thrown through the air. He also used a number of unusual words taken directly from English—those, for example, for 'rent', 'watchman', and 'salt water'.

A STORY. A girl was once born. She would not listen to what her father said. She would not listen to what her mother said.

She grew big. She became full grown—with full breasts, *yɔkɔrɔkɔrɔ!* One chief got up to marry her. He went to her father. Two hundred pounds! 'I love your child.' 'I don't love you. Whoever marries me—he must have no weal.' The chief went away. Another chief heard that. He counted out forty pounds, he tied five horses, he tied a hundred cows, he took out five pounds for her mother's dress. The girl refused. Her mother said, 'Alas, Kanu.' Her father too said, 'Alas, Kanu.' 'Get out from there! The one who will marry me—he must have no weal.' Everyone in the country came—she refused.

A monster heard that—Tintilongo. He was—like from that forest there to Kabala.[1] The animal turned into a human being. He borrowed a fine shirt. He put it on. He borrowed fine trousers. He put them on. He borrowed a long gown as well. He put it on. He set out, coming for the girl.

When he had reached like to there, the girl saw him, plainly. 'Ah! Father, mother, the friend who is coming, he will marry me.' Her mother said, 'Oh! All right.' She went and caught a hen, she went and killed it. She cooked rice. She went and gave it to the man. The man did not eat rice—he was a spirit! E! He took a little bit. 'Since you love me so much, well, let us go.'

[1] About fifty miles.

She, the girl, she had a small brother, one so high.[1] The child said, 'I will follow you.' 'Ah! You will not follow me, you are dirty.' The child said, 'But I will follow you, whatever happens.' Behold he [Tintilongo] and the child saw each other—plainly. She said, 'All right.' They set out. They went for far. The child followed. She beat the child. But the child still followed.

Well, they came to one village. He went and took off one shirt. He gave it to the one he had borrowed it from. He went for far. He took off the trousers. He gave them to the one he had borrowed them from. They went off.

They went and rented a house. He went and left the girl there. He went off to the bush. He found a hen as big as the house! He went off to the bush. She cooked, she the wife, she put it on the child's head [to carry]. 'Well, take the rice to where my husband went to work.'[2] The child went. As he was standing here, he saw him [the spirit] red—bright red! He called. '?Numu (?) come here, here is your rice.' The spirit came. He took a little bit. 'Well, take it to your sister, it is you who matter.' The child sat down. All of it—he ate it. He went. 'Thank you,[3] thank you, the one who cooked. You are thanked oh! But tomorrow, we will go together to take the rice.' 'All right.'

All night. In the morning she cooked. 'Well, today we will go, so that I can go and see how much my husband has cleared.' When they went, as far away as here, he said, 'Look now at your husband, the one you love, he is that redness!' She looked. Ah! She fell down.

She urinated [from fear]. She hid. She was afraid. She said to her brother, 'Let us run off.' Then her brother said, 'Wait for me.' He took the rice, 'Come, let us eat, this is rice cooked for workers. We will be spending the whole day going, all all day.' 'I will not be able to eat it, I—what I saw, that is why!' The child sat down. He ate it—all of it.

They set out. They came to the village. Then he said to his sister, 'Wait for me.' He took out rice, a hundred full bags. He piled it up in a heap. He took out guinea corn, a hundred full bags. He piled it up in a heap. He took out millet, a hundred full bags. He piled it up in a heap. He went and found the spirit's hen; for the hen was the watchman. The hen came out to eat—*sɔkɔdɔ sɔkɔdɔŋ kɔlɔi hɔ hɔ hɔ*.[4] 'Well, let us go' —speaking to his sister. They went, taking fast steps—*ragba ragba ragba ragba rrrrrr*.[5] They went. The hen finished the rice. They went. The hen finished the hundred bags of guinea corn. They went. The hen finished the hundred bags of millet. They had now crossed the salt

[1] i.e. about four years old.

[2] She assumes her husband has gone to clear a farm, as a human (Limba) would do; instead he has gone off to the bush, the place of spirits.

[3] i.e. her husband has sent her thanks.

[4] The sound made by the hen's pecking as it ate.

[5] The sound made by their hurrying footsteps.

water for England. There it was near now, there the girl had been born. The girl undressed. 'Let me bathe, you go on to the house.'

The hen said '*Kokoroko.*' 'What? What?' 'Oh! That Sira—you will have to take another.'[1] Then he came out from there—*soo!*[2] He stood now, he saw Sira over there, on the other side now. Then he pulled out gold—*tiɔ!* He threw it—*frrrr*. It went and stuck on a lobster, fast, *tabi!* Well, that was gold.

The girl went off now. When she reached her father's feet, there she went and fell down. 'Give me in marriage. I agree completely. The friend I followed then—he was a spirit.'

Her mother—the man she saw with weals, the one she had said before, there she went and gave her. It is finished.

Two friends

FANKA KONTEH. *Dictated* 3.11.61

A story of the affection of two friends: one willing to suffer blindness (a relatively common affliction in Sierra Leone) for his friend, the other to sacrifice his first-born to restore his friend's sight. The story ends with an implied dilemma about which of them loved his friend more. The plot is a common one, and, in various versions, I heard many stories based on it. Friendship between men is important among the Limba, specially between those initiated at the same time; a man specially likes to have the support of a friend at the time he is wooing a wife.

The delivery of the story served to bring out the highlights—the atmosphere of quiet when all people slept and the man waited alone for the stealthy coming of the spirit, the exaggerated portrayal of great numbers and of the suddenness of the friend's restoration of sight, and the vivid imitation of the vulture's rather nasal way of speaking.

A GIRL was once born. Whenever any man went to woo her, Tintilongo[3] killed him. Many[4] people had been killed there. A man arose with his friend saying, 'Come with me; I am going to woo a woman, the one up country.' His friend said, 'All right.' He agreed to go with him.

They went on their journey. They spent the day travelling—all day.

[1] He tells the spirit that since his wife Sira has gone, he will have to find another wife.

[2] Coming very fast and directly.

[3] A powerful and well-known spirit (or animal), who also appears in *The girl and the spirit*.

[4] The great number of people killed is conveyed by the length and tone of the adjective as pronounced by Fanka.

They came to a big cotton tree.[1] There an elephant and a vulture always spent the night. There they went to spend the night, those who were going on their journey.

Then the vulture said, 'Greetings to you. If anyone is there who wants to sleep, when you go on your journey, when you come to a village tomorrow, you should have a sword made there. Well, that sword—when you go to that place where you are going to woo a wife, well there lie down on the veranda. The sword which you are holding, as soon as people are sleeping, come out with it stealthily, go round to the back to the cooking place, go and stand behind the door, you will see a thing that has come for your friend, where he is lying there with the woman. At that moment, just as he puts his neck over the door, strike him. When you have struck him, your eyes will be blind. All right.'

They went on. What the vulture had said came to happen. When they arrived, they were given a lodging-place. They explained why they had come. They [the parents] answered, 'Our daughter will not have bridewealth put for her; you are to go and sleep in the small hut, you and the woman. Well, that is the custom when a daughter of ours is wooed.'

When they went to spend the night, his friend spread his mat on the veranda. He saw the animal, Tintilongo, about to come. He killed him [Tintilongo]. When he had killed him, his eyes were blind.

In the morning, when he got up, he took them water to wash their faces. He went and woke them. They got up, both of them, the husband and the wife. That caused amazement. 'What! This man alone—he was not eaten by the animal because of the woman.' They took and gave the woman.

They were given the woman, they went and spent the day again travelling—all day. They went and spent the night again by the cotton tree in the wilderness. The vulture came. He perched up above on the cotton tree. The elephant came, he stood there. The three people were also there by the cotton tree.

The vulture said, 'Elephant, greetings.' The elephant replied, 'Yes.' He also greeted the three, 'You who come travelling, greetings to you.' They were afraid. The vulture said, 'If someone is there to sleep, well if his friend's eyes are blind—for the sake of his friend who went to woo a wife, and many people went there to woo the woman but they did not return, they were eaten by Tintilongo; but you who went for her, since no bad thing caught you, well, when the wife becomes pregnant and bears a child, take that child from its mother, call your friend, and go to where the roads meet. Take the child and kill it. When you smear the blood on his eyes, he will see. For it was for you that he went and became blind before.'

[1] Cotton trees are often associated with witches or magical happenings.

They went on. After long, the wife became pregnant. The wife gave birth. He took the young child from its mother, he carried it to the roads, with his friend whose eyes were blind. He went and killed the child. He took the blood, he smeared it on his friend. His friend saw, brightly, *wa ke!*

They greeted each other—*tipa!* clapping.[1] 'Ah! comrade, you love me!' His friend said, 'You loved me more. You were the first to suffer for me.' He said, 'No. The wife whom you have just married, when she bore a child, the first child of all—you took that child, you killed it truly, for me. You loved me most.'

The boy that talked with animals

BANKOLO MANSARAY. *Dictated* 5.11.61

A story that illustrates the common theme that someone who tries to make trouble for another behind his back (*yaŋfa*) in the end suffers himself. The neat way in which the boy turns the trouble-maker's ruse back on himself recalls that in *The goat, the leopard, and the lion.*

The succession of difficult tasks is rather similar to those in *The wooing of Sira* and *Koma tricks his brother-in-law*. Here they concern the cultivation of rice and the building of a house, both well known to the listeners as difficult and protracted pieces of work taking weeks or months to complete.

A MAN once left a child. He was a hunter. He said to his child, 'Here is the gun. But do not kill an animal that is behind you.'[2] The child said, 'All right.'

He died, the father. The child was left. He hoed a farm. The animals came out into the rice. The child took the gun to go and shoot the animals. The animals said, 'Sara, did your father not tell you not to kill an animal behind you?' 'He did say that. Well then, go away from my rice.' The animals went away.

There was a trouble-maker there. He went and told the chief. 'Sara's child is talking with the animals of the bush. His rice has not been eaten by the animals; but, chief, your rice is eaten by the animals. Say that he is to hoe a farm for you, in one day.' The child was fetched. The chief said, 'Tomorrow you will hoe a farm for me, in one day.' It was the

[1] The sound made by clapping their hands together as is often done in excitement, pleasure, or affection.

[2] I am not sure of the significance of this prohibition. It would be unusual for a man to have a gun and not be prepared to use it.

child who was told this, to hoe a farm, in one day. 'If you don't hoe it in one day, I will kill you.'

The child put his hands on his head.[1] The animals asked, 'Why are you crying?' 'The chief says that I am to hoe a farm for him in one day.' 'Friend, don't cry.' The colobus monkeys stood up. They cleared it all. The ants gathered the rubbish. The *dibi* birds[2] picked up the small sticks—all of them; by now the sun was coming out, so high.[3] The rice came up so high.[4] The sun came out. The rain came down. It was full of seeds. By the time the sun had reached so high, it was dry. By the time the sun had reached so high, it was dry. It was harvested. The birds thrashed it, rice as much as a house. He went for the trouble-maker. 'Come and look, here is the rice.'

The trouble-maker came and looked. He went to the chief. 'Ha! Chief. You have got rice now, this year there is none like it (?). Say that he is to build you a house in one day.' The child was fetched. 'I thank you, the one who hoed.' Then the chief said, 'But you are to build me a house, in one day.' 'All right.'

He said, 'Alas, Kanu! Alas, Kanu!' The ants asked, 'Why are you crying?' 'Because I am told to build a house in one day.' 'Don't cry.' The ants made the wall. The sun came so high [morning]. The woodpecker split the boards. The *thamgba* bird[5] went to Freetown for the roofing.[6] The woodpeckers came and put all the roofing up on the house, in one day. The *dibi* bird went to Freetown for gold, and smeared on all the gold, and fixed all the house, in one day. The child went for the trouble-maker. 'Here is the house.'

The trouble-maker went and told the chief. The chief came. The chief came with his wife, his favourite. Ah! They were amazed. A snake came out from there. It came and bit the favourite. The girl fell, she died.

The trouble-maker said, 'Let the child cure the favourite wife.' The child said, 'Father, I agree. I hoed a farm for you, in one day. I built a house for you, in one day. Now take hold of the trouble-maker, and cut his throat. It is with his blood I am to cure the girl, she will become well now.' The chief said, 'It is true.' The trouble-maker was taken, he was knocked down, his throat was cut. He went and touched the blood, he spread it on her. The girl stood up. She put her arm round the chief's neck.

You see now—the trouble-maker he was killed by his own trouble-making.

[1] In mourning.

[2] A small red bird.

[3] He points to the place in the sky—to indicate first morning (about an hour after sunrise), then midday, then afternoon.

[4] Showing a height of about 1½ feet.

[5] A small long-tailed bird.

[6] This is clearly a modern house built with 'pans' (corrugated iron) on the roof.

The man killed for a spinach leaf

KARANKE DEMA. *Recorded* –.10.61

The story of how a daughter revenged her father's murder. The plot is very similar to that of *The man killed for a banana* (for the resemblances and differences see the discussion on pp. 95–96), and other typical motifs also occur such as the episode about the tree and about someone apparently sleeping late in the morning.

The story was told by Karanke under the name of Yaling, and 'replied' to by his friend Niaka. People's actions were portrayed vividly, for example the way everyone was filled with excitement at the thought of marrying the girl or the gradual transformation of the chief's son from avenging anger to desire for the girl. The girl's character was conveyed with especial vividness by both mode of delivery and facial expression—her apparent innocence and quietness, concealing her real determination and cleverness.

I AM Yaling. I am going to tell Yenkeni a story. A story for you, Yenkeni.

A man once married a wife in a village. The chief there planted leaves for sauce—spinach. He said that no one was to pick that spinach. 'If you pick it, I will kill you.'

Well, the wet season fell. Now, the people were in the farm there,[1] the woman with her husband. [He said] 'I am going to go and beg for a spinach leaf.' When he came and begged for the spinach leaf, the chief said, 'That leaf, if you pick it, I will kill you. Of all those in the village, no one must pick it. It is the "sacrifice"[2] of the village.' The boy said, 'All right.'

Then what happened? When night came, the boy came from the farm. He came and picked the spinach, one bunch (?) of leaves. That one bunch he took away with him when he went. For if even one bunch of spinach leaves is picked you will eat it for two days while you are in your house. You shred it finely. That is what the boy came and picked—one bunch. He took it away.

When the chief heard this in the morning he looked. He could not see it [spinach]. He sent a servant for the boy. 'Go and ask there for the spinach for me—the spinach that he came and picked. If he was the one, let him confess. Let him confess.'

When the servant went, he went and asked him. The boy said, 'I went and begged yesterday, but he refused. So I went and stole it.'

[1] i.e., it is implied, they were poor.

[2] Trees are sometimes specially planted as a 'sacrifice' in the village. Here, however, it may be implied that the chief was trying to keep the produce for himself.

It would have been better for him not to have thought of it. For when the servant came and told the chief after he had left the farm, the chief set out from the village. He took his sword. He sat on his horse. He struck his horse *gbaŋ!* Then he began to go, galloping *raaa*, right to the farm. When he got there he asked. When he asked, he said, 'What about that man sitting there? I have come for you. You went today and picked the spinach. That is why I have come for you.'

When the man wanted to speak, he struck him.

Ah! when he had killed him, there was left his wife, a girl, who was pregnant. The young wife got up. She went far off. She said, 'I will not stay here, here where my husband was killed because of sauce. If I stay on here tomorrow, if I stay my child will be killed.' She went far away. She went and stayed there.

When she bore the child, she gave her child the name of Sira. That Sira—she began to bring her up. When the child began to cry then she began to pet her, 'Hush, oh, child, hush.[1] Your father was killed for a spinach leaf.' Always, always, always she told that to the child as she suckled her, till she could sit, till she could walk—always she would say that and the child would hear it. Till the child was weaned she told her that; when the child began to cry she said, 'Hush, oh, child, hush. Your father was killed for a spinach leaf.'

When the child grew and got sense, her breasts were filled—*berede!* everyone tried to woo her. She refused. When she was grown, she asked her mother. 'Mother, where did my father go?' Then her mother said, 'Your father was killed for a spinach leaf.' 'What was the name of that chief?' 'Ha! I cannot think of him again. For where I came from is far away, a long way to reach this place.' 'Well, show me the road to where you came from then.' It was the girl that asked. Her breasts were well filled oh! Her mother showed her.

Then she stood up. She put on beads, as far as her navel. She bought a hanging loin cloth, she put it on; she tied her head tie, and bound on a head band of beads, and hung beads on her neck, and covered [her wrists] with bracelets. She tied her clothes in a bundle. 'I must find the one who killed a man for a spinach leaf.'

When she set out, she began to go. She came to one village. All the people stood up, to look at such a lovely girl.[2] As she stood there they said, 'We will not ask yet (?) about her. She is a fine girl. When you see her, that woman is a perfect woman on earth, beyond all others.' They stood up for her.[3] They welcomed her. She came and entered the compound. She stood there. She was asked, 'Any trouble?' 'No, no trouble. I am travelling inquiring, seeking the chief who killed a man for spinach.

[1] The mother sings this refrain as a kind of lullaby to the child.

[2] The adjective is given the non-personal prefix here—*mulɔhɔi*.

[3] i.e. wanting to marry her.

When I hear of that man, he is the man who will marry me.'[1] Ha! all the people there, they wanted her in marriage. But they said, 'No, that chief is not here.'

She went on. She went for very far. She came to a village. They all welcomed her. She came and stood outside in the compound. They wanted to marry her there. Everyone was standing there, getting ready to put a first gift for her. When she was asked, 'Any trouble?' she answered, 'No, no trouble. I am here to make a free marriage with someone.' Ha! they all got ready. 'I love you.' 'I love you.' She answered. She had marriage gifts brought out for her. The kolas given for her came to one hundred. The money given for her came to £2. They were gifts for marriage.[2] They were first gifts of all. Everyone was bringing out gifts. Then she said, 'For me—all that you have given, I have looked at it all. But the one who is to marry me is the one who killed a man for spinach.' They said, 'Ah, but it is not here, he is not here.'

She went on. She passed through six villages. She asked for him. But he did not come out.

When she came to the village where the chief was—that chief was called Saio—she was welcomed well. She entered. She came right in. She came and stood outside the chief's house. At that moment, the chief's drum was beaten—*gbiŋ, gbiŋ, gbiŋ, gbiŋ, gbiŋ, gbiŋ, gbiŋ*. All the people gathered. The people came to look at her. If you saw that girl—there is no girl [like her] in the country. When she had had the gifts given to her—well, you know what power is like![3] they all thought that she had come to live with the chief, to stay in his house with peaceful heart. They brought out kola for her there, as the first gift. The kolas were two hundred. The money was up to £60—as a first gift! She took it. 'I have seen the money. It is much. It pleases me. But the one who is to marry me is only if I hear of the man who killed someone for a spinach leaf.'

Then Saio stood up from where he was sitting. His heart was eager to marry her. 'The woman I love has come, the woman I love has come. She, it is she who will look after me when I am old.'

He stood up. He came outside. 'Here I am!' He tapped himself. 'Here I am. I am the one who killed a man for a spinach leaf. My spinach here it was growing in my compound. That was what he came and cut. That is why I killed him. When he came and begged, I refused. 'My wife is hungry.' At night he went and picked it, one bunch, one bunch. That angered me, that is why I killed him. It was I, I Saio.'

The woman said, 'All right'—the girl called Sira—'all right, I have

[1] The girl is depicted as speaking rather slowly and solemnly as if making a public announcement.

[2] The list is given in an excited tone, emphasizing the great amounts that were being brought out for the girl.

[3] i.e. a chief has power and is more likely than others to get his own way.

found my mate. For he was the one I was seeking. It is you will marry me. I have come to the marriage.' Since the day she was born, she had had no husband. Then at that time she was angry.

Then the chief stood up. It was as you usually do—if a wife comes for you, a new wife, you take a hen to make sacrifice for her. It was a sheep[1] he went and bound, saying, 'Here is the sacrifice for her.' He gathered all his headmen and announced the news to them. The girl—the one called Sira—said 'It is good. I agree. I came for a marriage; now I have found the marriage. My mother gave birth to me there; they began to woo me there in marriage, they killed a cow for me. But I did not agree. I said I would wait till I heard of a man who killed someone for a spinach leaf. Now I have found the marriage. I am glad. With Saio here I will stay.' He was a great, great chief. Ha! He was called 'There is no earth.'[2] When he came to make the sacrifice, the sheep was killed. The girl was cooked for.

The time came. You know how it is with a new wife.[3] The chief said to the one who should sleep in his dwelling, 'You will not sleep here today. Go out today! Go out today! My new wife, Sira, will sleep here today.' She went in, at that time; they spread the bed for her. A new wife, sitting there in all her blackness[4]—well, that is what we call a fine thing! When they had spread the bed for her, he [the chief] stood up. All the keys—he gave them all to her.[5] Oh! the owner of the house, she is to get out! 'Now you are being left the house. You are the head wife. You will not have to do anything.' Everything, everything he could remember, he told her it all. All his powers of magic—he told her all. Sira said, 'All right.'

When they lay down to sleep, Sira thought, 'Behold, this man is the one who killed my father for a spinach leaf. That deed I will revenge.'

When they were going to lie down to sleep, they had not yet lain down, he said—for you know how it is with a new wife, how you talk to her; everything you are thinking in your heart you will say—he lifted the sword and he said, 'Here is the sword, the sword I killed the man with who stole the spinach. This is that sword.' Sira said, 'Yes, all right.' He leant the sword against the wall. He said, 'Do you see that horse outside there? It was on it I rode when I was going for him in the farm.' Sira said 'Oh.'[6]

When they had lain down to sleep, when the chief fell asleep, then

[1] i.e. something much more valuable than usual.

[2] His chiefdom was so big that there was no country outside it (?)

[3] The audience nodded and murmured in agreement.

[4] i.e. nakedness.

[5] He was making her his chief wife, in charge of the whole household, and tells the previous chief wife to go—a dramatically narrated episode.

[6] Sira is made throughout this episode to speak only in monosyllables, as if shy and obedient—the opposite of the truth.

she stood up. She took the sword—she Sira—she struck the chief with it 'for you killed my father for a spinach leaf'. She struck the chief at once.[1]

It was at night. Everyone was asleep. The servants that had been guarding him had been told by everyone, 'Don't stand here.' They said, 'No, all right.' 'Go to your houses today, a new wife has come to me today.'

When she had killed him there, she took the keys. She opened the lock on the door. She went out. Everything she had brought when she was coming she took with her—the gold she had been given, and the golden ear-rings. She did not leave it. She took [everything].

When she had gone off far away, in the night, going to return to her home where she had come from, then the light came.

When the light came they looked for their chief who always wakes early. The light became bright. The servants said, 'He will want to be going. Let us go and knock at the door. Oh! but a new wife came to him yesterday. You know what a new wife is like,[2] it is sweet. He wants to have much talk with her. It is a new marriage, is it not?' So they went away again.

They saw the sun rise higher. Now the sun was hot—very hot. Then the chief's cousin got up. 'Ha! let us look. I am going to look at where the chief is lying. Perhaps he is ill. One cannot be sure.'

What happened? They went and opened the door. All they heard was the buzzing—*gbuu*—of the flies. They looked—the chief was lying there. He had been struck. The wife had gone.

Then the cousin shouted, 'Hey! hey! hey! hey! something has happened. The wife that came yesterday to the chief, she came and killed him.'

The drum was beaten—*gbiŋ, gbiŋ, gbiŋ, gbiŋ, gbiŋ, gbiŋ, gbiŋ*. The people gathered. They came and looked—it is the chief lying there, their kind chief, the chief called Saio.

Sara, his son, he was sent off, 'Follow the woman.' He mounted the horse. *Gbaŋ*, he lashed the horse. It galloped—*raaa*. When he followed the girl, as the sun was coming to the mid point exactly, he came up to the girl—'Hey! you going there, you going there, don't move from where you are, it is you I am pursuing. Stand!' The sword had been given him. 'If you meet her, kill her to revenge what she has done to our father, our kind kind chief.'

What did the girl do? Before he could reach her, the girl took off all her clothes, she stood there. The man came up to her on his horse—

[1] This was related very quietly, conveying the atmosphere of night, sleep, and stealth.

[2] One of the audience interpolated in excitement and ironic sympathy 'Behold, the wife had run away!'

thadaŋ thadaŋ[1]—he turned his eyes, secretly looking.[2] Ha! the man got off his horse. His heart was pleased with the woman.

'You, you are the one I am pursuing. You killed my father. You killed our chief.' Then the girl said, 'Yes, it was me. I killed him. Is that why you have come?' 'Yes.' 'Is that why you have come?' 'Yes.' 'To kill me?' 'Yes.' 'But I will ask you a question. Which do you want—to kill me, or to marry me?' The boy—his heart went out to the marriage. The reason he had set out there was spoilt. He said, 'Ah, I want to marry you—even if it means I do not go back. If they want to, they can bury him without me. I am not returning—let us go, you and I, to your home. Even if they say that I have to go back with you, we will mount the horse together. I will go and say that you shall not be killed. But I will marry you!' The girl said, 'All right. That is good. I accept. But before you marry me, first pick me one leaf from there,[3] for I want to drink, I am thirsty.' The boy got down from his horse, he made the horse stand. He hung the whip there. He stuck the sword in the ground. 'Am I to climb now?' She said, 'Yes. But before climbing take off your gown, and pull your trousers off. Put them down with your cap and go and pick the leaf for me.'

The *kuwɔ* tree is very tall. It is tall like that *kusiridi* tree standing by the road. The boy began to climb, for his heart was now turned towards the woman as she stood there now in her blackness with her beads round her loins. That pleased him. He put his arms round the tree, he went up, he came to one leaf. 'Is this the one I am to pick?' 'No, not that one.' He climbed up, he came to another. 'Is this the one I am to pick?' 'No, it is not that one.' He climbed, he came to another one. 'Is this the one I am to pick?' 'No, not that one; the one on the very top.' The boy climbed up to the very top. Then she said 'Now you are right up there, now I am going, I who am called Sira.'

The girl mounted the horse. She took up the things he had taken off. She took the horse. She took the whip. She took the sword. She lashed the horse, *gbaŋ*, to go to her home. The girl went. She took the horse with her. As she set out from there, she was holding the sword, holding the whip, and the boy's things, that is what she hung over her shoulder.

She came in [to the village] with the horse. She stopped the horse. 'Mother.' 'Yes?' 'Here is the sword.' The blood was on the sword, the sword she had killed the chief with. 'Yes.' 'This is the sword, the one Saio killed my father with. I went and killed him. Here is the whip he was holding. His son Sara pursued me to kill me. But he was unable. Here are his things.'

Then her mother said, 'Oh my child, oh my child, I thank you. For

[1] The sound of the galloping.

[2] This point in the story caused great amusement.

[3] From the *kuwɔ* tree mentioned later (I am not sure what tree this is).

what you have done, since you have exacted revenge for what your father suffered, for the spinach leaf,—for that, wherever you stay, may Kanu give you a cool spirit.'[1]

Thus you see now, even if someone is called a chief, when people are told that something is forbidden and someone goes out who does not obey that word—even if you are a chief, don't kill him for that.

Since I heard that story, I told it. Kapoingpoingbang, you patiently heard me. Saraio, who is sitting there, by your grace too I told the story, I told it to Yenkeni. Since it has ended for me—it is finished.

The man killed for a banana

DAUDA KONTEH. *Dictated* 13.12.61

A very similar plot to that of *The man killed for a spinach leaf*, but with some differences in detail, tone, and conclusion (see Part I, pp. 95–96). The ending includes an explanation of the origin of 'women chiefs' (an institution introduced only a couple of years before to deal with disputes between women) and of the possibility of bearing 'a good child'; it has not a very clear connexion with the story; the second explanation is linked on by the not uncommon device of referring to those who 'tread in the footsteps' of some character in the story (cf., for example, *The story of two women*).

A STORY for you. A girl was once married. She became pregnant. She had a longing for a banana. Well. Her husband went to cut a banana for her. The chief had said that 'The one who cuts it down, I will kill you.'

When he had cut it, the chief came. He came and passed by, to look at the banana. He found it cut. He came. 'Who is it who has cut the banana?' The man said, 'It was I.' The chief got up, he called his servants. 'Seize him.' He was seized. He was thrown down. He was killed. He was skinned. His skin was hung up above the door.

The girl got up, she went off to her people. She came to give birth. When the child cried she said, 'Hush. Your father was killed for a banana.' This was what the child always heard. For long she was growing up, she was hearing what her mother said. She finished growing.

She said, 'Mother, I must return revenge for what was done then to my father for me. That is what I am coming to revenge.' When her breasts were full she said, 'Mother I will go today.' 'All right.' 'Let me go to the finch,[2] to have it divine for me.' The finch divined '*Se se*, put

[1] *thεbina lima*. The quiet conclusion with announcement, thanks, and blessing is a characteristic ending.

[2] The finch is often depicted as a diviner in stories. Here it might seem

good, put bad, shaking the stones I was left by my father.' He got up, he said, 'You are to go to a smith,[1] you are to have a knife made for you, a sharp one.' When he had made it, it cut the wind (?). When he had made it, it cut the sun (?). She was told to go to a moriman, to get a white cloth[2] and a basket for her to take with her. That basket—the loads that would fit into it were as much as one thousand boxes! She was told, 'All right, you can go today, on Friday.'

She set out, she set out on the journey.

She came like to Bumban.[3] Pompoli got out mats, fifty of them; he laid them down wherever the girl passed. The girl passed. 'I love you, to marry you.' The girl said, 'I also love you. But you have to tell me what you have done before now.' He said, 'I beat people. I do wicked things.' The girl said, 'Father; there is no chance. I will not live with you.'

She got up. She went to Binkolo, to Kose. Kose got up, 'I will marry you.' Kose said, 'I will give fifty cows, so that I may marry you.' She said, 'No. Unless you tell me what you have done before now.' Kose got up, 'I abuse people, I beat them, I tie them up.' The girl said 'No. I am going on.'

She went, like to Makeni, to the chief there. The chief rejoiced. 'I have got a wife.' The girl said, 'I am not concerned about bridewealth being put for me; you are only to tell me what you have done.' The chief got up. 'I, I beat my mother, I beat my father, I beat my brother and sister; that is what I have done.' 'No never. I am going on.'

She came and went like to Masongbong. She came to the chief there. The chief rejoiced. 'I have got a wife.' The woman said, 'Do not rejoice yet. I do not want bridewealth, I only want you to tell me what you have done before now.' He said, 'I once planted bananas, saying that no other person should cut them. As soon as I had gone off on a journey, a woman became pregnant and had a longing for banana. She said to her husband, "I long for a banana." Her husband got up, he went and cut it. The wife went and took it, she came and boiled it. She ate it. The chief[4] came. As he got down from the hammock he went to the bananas. "Who cut a banana?" The husband got up, "It was I." The chief beat his drum. They gathered, he told the hammock men "Seize him." He was seized. He was killed. His skin was hung up.'

The girl said, 'Aha! All right, you are the one I love. I will live with

unsuitable to introduce a bird as an actor into a story otherwise about human beings. This illustrates yet again the impossibility of a complete distinction between stories in terms of their characters.

[1] A smith or a Muslim are often asked in stories to aid the hero.

[2] Sacrificial white cloth used in many rituals.

[3] The names are of actual places in or near Limba country, and the chiefs are contemporary ones known to the listeners.

[4] A switch in the chief's speech from the first to the third person.

you.' A sheep was caught for her. It was killed, as sauce for the wife. She ate. Two nights passed. She had an ox killed for her, rejoicing for the wife.

When one night passed, she thought to kill the chief. When the night came, the people had all lain down. She came. Every possession of the chief she took and put in her basket. The loads were over two thousand. When she had finished packing, all the gold, all the magic of the chief, she put it in the basket. She got out the knife. She got out the white cloth. She said, 'Hear me Kanu, may you leave me free. It is the evil deed he did that I am coming now to revenge. For my father was killed for me. My mother was pregnant for me. It is that evil deed I am coming to revenge today, on the Friday.'

She pulled the chief towards her, quietly. She laid him on the ground by the bed. She took the knife, she killed the chief. She took the white cloth, she rubbed it in the blood. She took the white cloth and knife, she put them in the basket. She went out, at night. Well, there were roads joining there, twelve roads. She set out, on the left hand. She followed the road on the left. She went through about fifteen villages in the night.[1]

The sun rose. The children set out to greet their father.[2] The mothers said, 'Go back.' The children refused. 'We will go and greet father.' They found the door open. The oldest child went in. He went and trod, he looked—blood. He peeped in, he saw his father lying on the ground by the bed. He came outside, he cried. 'Mother, father is dead.' They seized and beat the child, 'Stop lying.' The child said, 'Look then at my foot. Is that not blood?' They looked. The oldest wife, the one who was in charge of the marriage, she got up, she went there, she went and peeped. She saw her husband lying on the ground by the bed. She wept, 'Alas! What is this? The father, here he is, lying dead.' The drum was sounded. All the people gathered.

Well, the chief had twelve horses. The men came and divided out the horses. Each one had a gun and a sword. They went on the roads to follow the girl past the fifteen villages. There she was found.

The boy was going to shoot the girl. The girl said, 'Don't shoot me.' The boy got down from his horse, he drew his sword to strike the girl. The girl said, 'Don't strike me. If you want to kill me, undress, take off your trousers, take off your shirt, take off your cap, and climb up for a leaf.' A *kuwɔnɔ* tree stood there, huge, tall. She said, 'Climb up', saying that the boy should go and pick the leaf up there right on the topmost twig. 'If you pick it, that is what can kill me.' When he had climbed up

[1] As often, distance is conveyed by enumerating the number of villages passed. (On this point see also J. Littlejohn, 'The Temne House', *Sierra Leone Studies*, 14, 1960.)

[2] Children normally go to greet their father in the morning.

to the top twig, she put on the shirt, she put on the cap, she took the gun and put it on her shoulder. She took the sword, she slung it over her shoulder. She took the bag, she tied it round her waist. She lifted up the basket, she put it on to the horse. She took it, she mounted the horse. She struck the horse. The horse ran past about ten villages. She shouted. She said 'Where you are perched up there on the top twig, you will never now eat rice again; the amount you ate yesterday—that is all there is for you.'[1] She mounted the horse again. She struck the horse. She was beginning to come near to her mother. She sang, 'My father was killed for a banana, at the first (?); my father was killed for a banana, at the first (?).'

She went and dismounted. She and her mother exchanged greetings. The drum was beaten. All the village gathered. She came to open her basket. All the village came out to see the boxes in the basket. When they were taken out one by one, it came to about two thousand boxes. She brought out the white cloth, she brought out the knife. 'Mother, by grace of the village I went and returned revenge, revenge for what was done to my father for me. So that you may believe—look at the blood; look at the knife.'

Well, if you see the chiefship going to the women, it was that girl who made it that chiefship came to the women. If you should hear now that a woman has been made chief, well, that was through the girl, it was she began it. She was beautiful. Her tracks where she trod, whoever passes [there], it is they who through (?) the girl bear a good child, those who tread in her tracks. It is finished.

The story of a hunter

BUREMA DEMA. *Recorded* 21.5.61

The story of a hunter who understood the speech of animals. He nearly died for the sake of his wife, but, it is implied, the wise words of his dog saved him. It includes the common motif of someone giving help and then being called out of his hiding-place to be thanked. The episode about cutting a deer for two pythons also comes into another story (not included here) but there the pythons in fact later tried to kill the man instead of helping him.

WELL, now—a hunter came out. He used to go hunting. Well, at that time he went out, he went to the wilderness. When he had gone and

[1] i.e. he will die, and so no longer eat rice.

climbed a tree,[1] well, two pythons came out there, they were hungry. They caught a deer. When they had caught this deer—but one of them got up, he swallowed the head end; the other got up, he swallowed the leg end. They met in the middle! Well, they were not going to have a chance to eat it! They parted.

When the hunter saw this, then he said, 'Wait. Let me go and part it for them.' He came down. He came and cut it in two. He pushed the two bits apart—one to one side, one to the other.

Well, when the pythons came from there again, one began at the head end, he swallowed it, the other began from the leg end, he swallowed it.

Well, then they said, 'E! Ha! The man who did this work for us, ha! he has done good work for us. He has done good work for us. Well, what we want is—if anyone is here nearby, let him come down so we can show him medicine. Well, whatever it is, you will not ever again be distressed.' Well the hunter was afraid to come down. 'Perhaps if I come down, well, they will come and swallow me.'[2] Well—but they begged him to come down if he was near there. From the place he was sitting, he stood up, he came down.

Well, when he had come down, they said, 'Was it you who did this work for us, so that we were no longer hungry?' 'Yes.' Then they said, 'Ah! We will show you medicine. We will put it on your ears; you will not again be distressed in your hunting.' Then he said, 'Well, all right. That is good.' They took and searched for the leaves [for medicine]. They put them in a funnel.[3] They dripped them in one ear, they dripped them in the other ear. 'Well, every animal that talks in the world you will understand.' They thanked him there many times. He said, 'I accept.'

Well, from that place where they were he started coming to the village —quickly, *buu!* He came on pigs in a swamp farm. Well, as soon as he came on the pigs, he shot at them. Then they said, 'E! what is that thunder that fell on us?[4] Well, what we will do—let us run to the pile of sticks to hide ourselves there.' He heard that, for he had had the funnel put to his ears. He heard it. He went there. He went first and waited there. As they were arriving there, he shot. They said, 'E! What work is this we see? Let us climb up and go behind the hill.' He heard that. He went up the hill, he went and sat there. As they were arriving there, he shot. 'Ah! This is our end!' They parted, they ran away—*wus!*[5]

[1] Hunters sometimes go up a tree to look round for game or to lie in wait over a track.

[2] Pythons are very much feared.

[3] A funnel-shaped tube made from a leaf is often used to pour in 'medicine'.

[4] The wild pigs that he found destroying someone's swamp farm are represented as speaking with a funny voice and words.

[5] *Wus*, i.e. shaking the leaves *wusu wusu wusu wusu*. The hunter, it is implied, has killed several of the pigs.

He now, he was tired. He went away. He came to the village. He came to announce his news to the chief.[1] Well, the chief let him have people. All the animals were skinned—completely.

Well, when they were in the village, he took the meat, he gave it to his wife. He said, 'Well, let us go to your parents.' When they went out now, they went to her parents. Well, they went and announced [it], they said, 'This is what we have brought you.'

Then the mother-in-law got up. She leant the ladder.[2] They were to take rice. As she was placing the ladder, behold she placed it on a small ant. The ant wept. 'Oh you! Oh you! This hag[3] has tramped on me. Look how she put the ladder on me.' The hunter laughed. For that was why he had had the funnel put on his ear, so that whatever animal talked, he could hear. He laughed. Oh! The mother-in-law climbed up, she took the rice. She said, 'No matter! I that you laughed at. No matter. I only know that you have peeped secretly at me.[4] That is what you laughed at.'

When she had come down with the rice, she also, the mother-in-law, she had only one eye. So, when she came down with the rice, she went and spread it out. As she spread out the rice, the hens came out there to eat the rice.[5] When the hens tried to come, she chased them. When the hens tried to come, she chased them. Then one hen said, 'Friends, let us not be troubled, let us go to the side of her blind eye, so that *it* may look at us!' Well the hunter heard that too. He laughed.

Oh! Then the mother-in-law said, 'Oh you! We have come to quarrel now, you and I. You laughed at me when I put up the ladder. You laughed at me when I spread out the rice and sat down to chase the hens. Now'—she took up the rice—'Now, you will not take the woman with you when you go—you will not ever take the woman unless you tell me why you laughed at me.' Then the hunter said, 'No matter. I will show you why I laughed. What you demanded I must show you. Well, before I show you, you must call your people.' The mother-in-law gathered her people. The hunter too gathered his people.

Well, the drum was beaten now—he was to show it. The hunter had rice cooked for him by his people 'For you to take to the place of the dead. If you show it [the secret] you will die. Well, here is the rice.'

[1] i.e. tell the chief formally that he had killed big game; as is normal, the chief then sent people to help him to skin, cut it up, and bring it to the village.

[2] A notched stick used to climb up to the platform under the roof where the rice is often stored. She is going to get rice to cook for her visitors.

[3] A very rude term indeed.

[4] i.e. when she was up the ladder. This would be thought bad with any woman, but especially so with a mother-in-law. She was depicted as exceedingly indignant.

[5] It is normal to spread the rice outside the door to dry, and then watch it to drive away the hens that come to eat it.

They killed a hen for him. Well, when he sat down to eat the rice, when he had eaten so much[1]—he had a dog there. He took a handful of rice—*gbi!* he put it down for his dog.

Well, there was another hunter there, he was a stranger. He too had a dog. When the hunter's dog began to eat, the hunter who was about to die, his companion's dog got up there and sprang, it went and bent its neck to eat the rice. Then the hunter's dog said, 'I beg you, don't trouble me; for my part, the life of my [master] is finished today. For he was told that he was not to reveal the words he heard to anyone. But he has been made to forget this (?), he has to reveal them. Well, now, if he reveals them, he will die. Well, it is for a wife he is being destroyed.'

The other hunter's dog said, 'Move aside, let me eat. What—are there no other wives in the world? are there no other wives? If it happens that he goes hunting and kills meat, will he not sell it and look for another wife? Will he die for this one wife?'

Well, now, since Yenkeni said she wanted to be shown stories, stories of the Yaka[2] people—that is it. It is finished.

The hunter with three dogs

SELI KONTEH. *Dictated* 28.11.61

A story of a man who married a spirit who wanted to destroy him. The situation is, in reverse, like that of *Sira and the monster*; the episode about the tree and the dogs is almost exactly the same. In this version the dogs take a central part—unlike the hunter they have names—and the concluding comment is about the value of dogs. As with many Limba stories the action ends with a return home and formal announcement to his parents of the protagonist's acts.

A STORY. There were once people. One came out as a hunter. He trained three dogs—one was Denifela, one Sangsangso, and one Tungkangbai.

He came and saw a beautiful girl. When he came and saw her, the hunter said, 'It is she—I must marry that girl.' Well, that girl was evil. Behold she was a spirit. She used to come; when she came and saw him, her heart rose for him at once.[3] When the boy, the hunter, saw her, he said, 'She is the one I am going to marry.' 'Well then, if you are going to marry me, you must see the place where I live.' The boy said, 'All right. I, I will arrange to marry you.' He fixed a time for the marriage.

[1] A very little, as demonstrated by the narrator.

[2] The branch of the Limba living in and near Kakarima.

[3] i.e., I think, to eat him.

'But I want first to see the place where you live. But if I am going to see it, I want to gather the property for the bridewealth before I see it.' He gathered all the bridewealth. He was looking at her now. He was looking as well at it, the bridewealth, he and his people. From that they knew that he loved the girl.

He got up. He took his gun. 'Let us go today. Let me go and see where you live.' They went for long. They went and came to a cave in the middle of a rock. She the girl, she started, she turned into a breeze. The boy stood outside. The girl entered. She went and opened one door. She went further, she went and opened another door. She went further, she went and opened another door. She went further, she opened another door. Six doors to the house before you come into the house!

Well, she came out then, coming to see the boy. He was standing there. When she had come out, she turned into a human being again. But the hunter, he did not know at all (?) what it was (?).

Well. She got up, she came to the hunter. The hunter took his dogs, the three, Denifela, Sangsangso, and Tungkangbai. She said, 'Let me leave them behind.' Well! He said, 'I will not leave them. For I am a hunter. Wherever I go, well, I will not go if the dogs are not there.'[1] She said, 'For me, in my house—ha! dogs cannot go there.' She said, 'Well, all right then.'

When the dogs were taken to the door, she opened the first one. They went in. It shut behind them, *gbambuŋ*. They opened another. It shut behind them, *gbambuŋ*. They opened another one. It shut behind them, *gbambuŋ*. They opened another. It shut behind them, *gbambuŋ*. They opened the last one to go into the house now, the house belonging to the girl.

When they reached there, they went and found differences there from here. They went and found a different air there. For they had gone and found a new world. When they went and sat down, everywhere there was cold on their bodies. The boy who loved the girl, he stood, he was worrying in his heart. She said, 'Since you love me, well, this is my home here. The food that you gave me there, I do not usually eat that kind of food.[2] For I am not accustomed to that. But since you say that you will marry me, well I, I have come to show my country and my home, since you love me.'

The hunter sat down there now. She went and got him food, the kind they usually ate there. He looked. He did not like it. For he had not ever eaten it before. But what he had done when he was taken there, what he did—he took the food he usually took for hunting. He fastened it on to the biggest dog, Denifela.

Then the girl said that he should go with her to pick her kolas. Ah!

[1] A hunter is normally followed everywhere by his dog(s).

[2] She is not human and does not eat human food.

she said that he was not to bring his dogs, that she would tie them up. When she had tied them, they would go to pick the kolas. She stood up, she tied them. She said that he was not to take his gun. When they had gone for long, about one mile, they came to the kola tree. She said, 'Climb up.' Oh! He said, 'What! how should I go up?' 'If you don't go up—well, here where we have come, you are to abide by my words. You saw all the doors which you kept going through? Well, only I can open them for you. It is what you have come to for love, that is it! Well, here, here where we have come, it is truly my kola. If I send you for them, well, you will have to do it. If you do not do it, well, the marriage will not last. Well, that is all I have to say to you. Well, you will not know where to go.'

Ha! The boy stood there thinking. He said, 'Ah! It was love that put me here. If it had not been for that, I would not have come here.' He climbed up. As he was about to pick one kola, she said, 'Go on up for that other one, the one up above.' As he was about to pick it she said, 'Leave that one; pick the one up above.' The boy—that hurt him. He said, 'Oh! What are you doing to me today? Ah! Ah! that hurts me. But there is no alternative.' She said, 'The top one, that is the one you are to pick.'

She looked at him now. 'Ha! Well, your time is finished. Say goodbye to Kanu. If you stand there and see someone beautiful, you insist on marrying her. Well, it is a spirit you have married. For I, I am a spirit. When you saw me before, saw me clearly, well I had turned into a woman. Well, I was a spirit all the time. There where you are perched up above, say goodbye to Kanu.' Then he said, 'What! Is it today? I am to say goodbye to Kanu—for what?' 'Your life is finished. Have you ever before come to all this country?' 'No.' 'Well, you have come to a new country. Have you ever seen doors like these ones?' 'No.' 'Well, it is the end now. You will never again see a beautiful girl ever. Why I told you to say goodbye to Kanu—you are to die now. I am killing you.' 'Well, all right then. I will say goodbye to Kanu.'

You see now, what he meant by his Kanu—where they had gone, his dog had carried his food, the one called Denifela, it was he whom he called in saying goodbye. He called 'Denifela Denifela Denifela Denifela Denifela Denifela Denifela Denifela Denifela Denifela.' He began again. He called.

The dogs heard where they were standing. They were tied with wire, chains. They broke them. They stood again, listening on the path of the calling. They heard the calling 'Denifela Denifela Denifela Denifela Denifela Denifela Denifela Denifela Denifela Denifela.' They began to run. She said 'Twice. The third time I will kill you.' He called once. The second time the dogs heard. The third time they were almost there. They found the girl. The man perched up above, as soon as he saw the dogs coming, he said, 'The thing you find below, deal with it.' They found the girl standing there, still speaking. The dogs went and fell on her. They bit her in pieces. They chewed her all up. They scattered her all.

He came down. For she was finished, she the spirit. The dogs had killed her. The hunter was saved.

When he was saved, and he came down, he came, he came now to the house. All the gold he found there, he took. Everything in the house, he took. It became his own house now. For him to be shown the doors, how they opened—he knew it now. He tied up all the things, he put them on the dogs—a load for Sangsangso, a load for Tungkangbai, a load for Denifela.

They came. When they arrived there, they came to the door. They opened it. It shut behind them, *gbambuŋ*. He opened another door. The dogs went through. It shut behind them, *gbambuŋ*. He went and opened another door. The dogs went through with the things. It shut behind them, *gbambuŋ*. He went and opened another door. The dogs went through with the loads. He left it. It shut behind them, *gbambuŋ*. He went now and opened the last one. They all went through. He left it. It shut behind them, *gbambuŋ*.

They came and found their world now. When they came to his people, he came and told them what had happened. 'Love would have killed me. Behold, that girl was a spirit. If I had not taken the dogs, I would not be here. Well, all the things I found there, the things the dogs have brought, they are her things.' He opened them all. He showed them to his people. 'But for her—the dogs killed her.'

If you now ever see a man training a dog—a dog helps you, he saves a man. In the evening, if you sleep and he is at the door, if a thief goes there, he barks; if a witch goes there, he barks. That is why we like a dog. That is it. It is finished.

The hunter and the forbidden forest

DAUDA KONTEH. *Recorded* 20.1.64

A story told with some of Dauda's characteristic motifs. As often, he begins by calling people's attention, stating his name and alluding to the wisdom found in stories. Then he sets the story in a period when 'the earth had not yet begun', a period only he can understand. During the action of the story he adds to its vividness at certain important points by speaking of how he stood to one side and himself observed what was happening.

It is the normal custom for a hunter new to a district to come first to the chief; certain areas are closed to hunting or even to entry. A 'forbidden' forest of a rather different kind also occurs in one of Dauda's other stories.

Probably no one present had ever actually seen a lion though the term is a relatively common one.

The story ends with a reference to a common sentiment in Limba: that you should take advice you are given or it may be worse for you.

ATTENTION, may you hear me this evening, me Dauda the son of Fane Konteh of Kamabai. I have come this twilight to come and bring Yenkeni Konteh a small story. Attention.

The earth had not begun. If I told you where the earth began and where it ended, you would not believe it—only I alone and my heart, I understand it. Well, you, if you are wise, may you listen. My father is here, you hear? my mother is here, you hear? my brother is here—may you listen. Why? So you may carry it forward.[1] May you hear the story of Dauda the son of Fane Konteh of Kamabai, he owns the story. Well, may you listen.

The story for you. Ha! the earth had not begun. The old people had a forbidden forest. Then a hunter came out, a famous famous famous one. The hunter came to the chief—attention—one like the one here. 'Chief.' 'Yes?' 'I have come to hunt in your country.' '*Ala!* I have heard [what you say]—but the forest is here and a stranger may not go there to hunt; a hunter may not go there.' 'Why?' 'It is forbidden.' 'Ah! chief, I am going.' 'E! Don't go!' 'I am going.' 'Ah! Don't go!' 'I am going.' The chief said 'All right. It is not my trouble. I will be silent.' The chief went inside, he went and lay down.

When the man got up, he went and took his gun, he went to the forest. Well, there was a lion there, we call it a 'lion', a lion—a dangerous animal in the cane grass, he is the chief of all the animals, he is called a lion. He had children.

Well, the man dressed himself up to go out with his gun. He set out. A bird said to him, 'You going there, where are you going?' He stopped. He took down his gun. 'You going there, where are you going?' He took his gun to shoot the bird. The bird said, 'If you spare me Kanu will spare you.' 'What is that truly, bird?' He got up to go further on. The bird said, 'You going there, where are you going?' He stopped, to shoot the bird. The bird said, 'If you spare me Kanu will spare you.' 'E! You! What are these parables in the middle of the bush?' Now I, Dauda, was to one side, I was silent, completely, *thekimu!* and was listening.

When he got up he went further on. Just as he met the lion's cub and the lion appeared in the distance and he came to shoot—the lion

[1] i.e. pass on its wisdom to someone else.

came and caught him. Then the bird said, 'You, lie there where you are.' He knew that death was coming close. He did not refuse what the bird said. He fell. The lion came and scratched at him to kill him. Then he [the bird] said, 'You who are lying there, if you have a sharp *kamaro* knife there'—(you know a knife? we call the European knives by one word, *kamaro*). 'Yes.' 'Act quietly.' Now the animal had come to catch him, to kill him. 'All right, when the animal scratches oh, take your hand and scratch him.' He did not refuse. When he was scratched, he took his hands, he began to scratch the animal. For long he scratched him, for long he scratched him, the animal lay down on one side. It pleased him very much, to be scratched. Now I, I stood to one side there and watched, I did not speak so I would not be caught. When he [the lion] had lain down and he was being scratched, the bird said, 'You, open your knife.' He opened it. 'Stroke the animal's neck, and scratch it.' He began to stroke it, he scratched it. When he scratched it, this pleased the animal very much. 'Now look for where the neck and the head are joined and strike there.' He looked, he looked, he looked. He saw where the head and the neck were joined. He knew that there, there, the animal could be killed. He [the bird] said, 'All right. Put out all your strength and draw the knife and strike him.' He took it, he began with all his power. He came and caught him—*bakaaa!* he killed him. 'Have you cut his throat?' 'Yes.' 'What of what I told you—that if you spared me Kanu would spare you?'

If you hear—that is why we children do not escape from troubles; when someone[1] says 'Stop that', [and you reply] 'I will not stop' and go on with it—you will see the result of that going on. What is the reason for refusal?

Since Yenkeni came this evening and said that Dauda Konteh was to tell her a story this evening in the twilight and dusk, I have come to sit on the chief's chair and lean back this evening. Since it has come to [the time for] me to finish this evening, that is it, it is finished.

The story of Kubasi

YAYA DEMA. *Recorded* –.5.61

A story about how a man, Kubasi, was helped by three women in turn; by their help he survived various hazards and in the end won chiefship. The story ends with a dilemma about whose child should succeed him, but this dilemma does not seem of great importance to the rest of the story.

[1] Lit. one of yours—i.e. a friend or relation, most often a father.

The early part of the story is rather confusing. It seems as if 'Hugboka' is really Kubasi (the boy). Apparently what happens is that the two children are not to be seen; the father thinks this means that it is Hukongko, the girl, who will die; in fact it is Kubasi—but this part is not clear to me. The general plot (very similar to that of *Four wives*) may well have been familiar to the listeners and they did not seem to be puzzled by the narration.

THE story. A chief once came out in the world. He had wives, many of them. He said that he had not got a child. For the child—of the two wives he loved, one wife went to a moriman. She called the moriman. He came, the moriman. He said to her, 'Yes.' He agreed. He said, 'If you have children, wherever you give birth, whatever name is easy, give them that name.' Well, she stayed in marriage with her husband; there was one other child born in the family: the name of one was Hugboka [or Kubasi]; of the other Hukongko.

When they were born, that is the name she gave them. Well, the moriman had also said when someone gives birth, no one is to see them [the children]. If they see them and the time has not yet come for them to be seen, they are likely to die.

Well, he was there. He said that he was going to make a sacrifice, with a white cloth. For the white cloth he called Kubasi—'Kubasi.' 'Yes?' 'I want you to go for me and buy me the white cloth.'

Kubasi went. As he went, he went and saw Hukongko. They did not know that ha! they were of one father. For whoever is born does not know of his companion's birth. Well, they went and met together there. Kubasi said, 'Ha! I love you.' Hukongko said, 'I am not to be seen. I am not to be seen by anyone.' 'Well, we have come and met together here. I too, I am not to be seen by anyone. Well, I have been sent by my father, to go and buy white cloth. It is for the white cloth that I went.'

When he returned, he came and told his father of it. His father said, 'It is all right.' As they stayed there, two nights passed. On the third, Kubasi went out, he died. When he had died, the chief did not rest. His heart did not rest. He called the moriman. 'Ha! the despair you have made for me! When I got those children, you did not say that that boy, Kubasi, would go out. He has died. I do not know what I am to do, for I have no child. The child you were thinking of, she is still in my compound. But he [Kubasi] has gone out, he has died. Ha! That, that breaks a man's heart!'

The moriman said, 'All right. Well, tell people to cut long sticks. When they have cut long sticks they are to get petrol—one drum—and come and put it down, and come and set it on fire.' He sat down. He made *manasi* water. He put it in a big tin. 'Well, set fire to the sticks.' They set fire to the sticks.

When they had set fire to the sticks, he said, 'Well, of you two people [father and mother], well, let one of you go out now, and go into the fire.' The moriman took his book. He put it down near the fire. 'When someone goes into the fire, Kubasi will raise his head again.' He spoke. The mother came out. She fixed her dress, she trembled at going into the fire. She could not. She fixed her dress.[1] She said that his father should go. He went. His father took off his trousers; he took off his robe, all of it; his cap—he put it on one side. He trembled at going into the fire. He could not. Then Hukongko said, 'I—so sweet is love, right from here as far as the place of death. Kubasi, I love you here right to the place of death. Well, Kanu has come today to take you. The moriman came and said that if someone goes into the fire, you will raise your head again. So that time has come now. I love you beginning from the world here as far as the place of death. So let us go together, I and you.' As she fixed her dress she went into the fire.

No person could know what happened to the fire. He raised his head again. Ah! Kubasi spoke! 'It is good. I will not stay here. My father did not love me. He worked for me indeed, but he did not love me. I am going. Let me go and search for where chiefship begins and where chiefship ends.'

He went. He met Bongaio [another woman]. Bongaio was carrying food. Her people were clearing a grass farm. For this clearing, she had her brother, her younger brother, he was helping (?). She came and met them. She said, 'Ha! I, I love you. May you take me with you where you are going.' He said, 'No. I am starting out to where I will get chiefship, to where chiefship begins and chiefship ends. I am not seeking a wife. It is the chiefship I want.' Then Hukongko said, 'No. I, I want not to have to travel alone. Travelling with one person is not good. So for that, let her go.'[2] 'Well, it is for you [to say]. Let us go.'

As they went, they went and came to water, much water, a river. No one can cross it unless someone is left behind there. They went and came to the water. Then Bongaio said, 'I love you, Kubasi.' They went and came to the water. She took her brother, her younger brother, to throw him in the water. They threw him into the water. As they threw him into the water, the water divided in the middle, right across. It was a river—a big river, what is called a river. They crossed.

He went and came to the place where the chiefship begins. He went and found a sword there. The sword was standing where the chiefship is sought. But the chief there had been there for long. He had

[1] The hesitation of the father and mother is brought out by the reduplicated forms of the verbs used here—*kɛmɛkɛmɛŋ* (fix or tie one's skirt), *yɛkiyɛkinɔkɔ* (tremble), *karakaraŋ* (take off trousers).

[2] Hukongko, the first wife, is eager to have others to help her; this is a common attitude among senior wives.

taken and killed many people there. For if you arrive there, he gives you the sword to point it somewhere. If you don't see the chiefship, ha! you are killed. The chief, he remains there.

Then Kubasi arrived. He wanted the chiefship. He slept the night. On the second day, he was told 'Well, seek the chiefship.' Where he went, there he found the *basaraka* girl,[1] the *basaraka* of the chief who owned the village there. Whatever they perform in the village, that girl is called. She is the *basaraka*. She went and said 'Kubasi, I love you. I love you today, I love you tomorrow, right from here as far as the place of death.' Kubasi said, 'Yes. But I have not come to seek a wife. I have come to seek chiefship.' Ha! Hukongko said, 'Kubasi, ha! don't refuse her, saying you don't love her. You love her. Living with one person is not good. Living with many people—that is good. . . .'[2] Kubasi said, 'Yes. Hukongko, if you agree—'. 'I agree, by grace of Bongaio.' Bongaio said 'I agree.'

They said, 'Since you have said that tomorrow you are seeking the chiefship, if you do not find it, you will be killed.'

In the morning, the chief beat the drum. They were called. He came and sat down. They filled the whole compound, they came and sat, very many of them. They were coming to try to seek the chiefship. The chief there, the old one, the one who had spent long killing people there, he said 'If he is not strong in seeking the chiefship—we will kill you.'

He [Kubasi] pointed to one side. What had helped there was that the *basaraka* had come to love him. The *basaraka* had said, 'Wherever tomorrow you see me shake out the broom, well there is the chiefship. There is the chiefship.' Kubasi had said, 'Yes.' He had remembered carefully: when the sun rose, the *basaraka* would go out to go and sweep; she would go to sweep, and go and point the broom to the chiefship.

The sun rose. There Kubasi went and pointed the sword. As he pointed the sword, ah! they lifted their hands up. 'He [the old chief] has finished among the people—he has spent long putting an end to people's lives.' Then, at last, they caught hold of him. They tied him, tightly, *dɛŋ!* They went and tied him to the cow-post where he had often tied his companions. There they tied him.

They said Kubasi was to be taken behind the house. When he was taken right behind the house, he was taken and bathed. Big gowns were now taken, the old chief's things, they put them on him. As soon as they had put them on him, they heard it being said that they would kill the old chief there now. Kubasi said, 'No! Do not kill him now. Wait. Wait for me to come. When I come, well, I know what plan I will tell him. For he is accustomed to kill people. But I will not kill him. If someone

[1] The *basaraka* helps the chief with certain rituals and is expected to be specially loyal to him; thus her love for Kubasi here is all the more striking.

[2] There follow a few words I cannot make out on the tape.

is accustomed to doing bad to people, if you say you will return the bad, you are acting the same. Don't do that.' He took him, he said, 'It is good that he should go and stay in the farm. But I will not kill him.' He took him. He took him to the farm, right to the farm. There he now stayed.

Kubasi came now, and took those three wives for long. Hukongko bore a child, a boy. Bongaio bore a child, a boy. The *basaraka* that he found in the village with the chief there, she bore a boy.

Kubasi went out, he died. When Kubasi died, those three all rose to claim the chiefship. Bongaio—Bongaio's child said he owned the chiefship. The *basaraka's* child said, 'I own the chiefship.' Hukongko's child sat there. He said, 'Well, is it false? is it not false? All of you, you speak truly, but if my mother had not gone into the fire for our father, he would not have reached here. We would not have been born. If you say that you own the chiefship—that is false. I own the chiefship.'

They sat down then there to decide that case.

Well, of those three people, of those three people, I want to ask you, who owns the chiefship? Who owns the chiefship of those three? Well, since Yenkeni said that I am to tell her this story, I am asking her that question.[1]

Four wives

FANKA KONTEH. *Dictated* 8.11.61

A very similar story to that of *Kubasi*; each concerns the way in which the hero is saved by the love of various women and wins the chiefship, ending with the same dilemma about whose child should succeed him. There are also various differences; the lack of proper names in this story, the different number of women concerned (in *Kubasi* the same woman, Bongaio, both gave the hero rice and helped him to cross the river), the absence here of the *basaraka* in favour of the chief's daughter, and, finally, the fact that in this story, in contrast to that of *Kubasi*, it is the wives, not the man, who are unwilling to add another woman to their number.

A CHIEF married a wife. He loved the wife. But they had no child. He called a moriman. 'Moriman! I love my wife, but we have no child. That is it. You are to help me, so that we may have a child, I and my wife.' The moriman said. 'Well, all right.' The moriman went into his room. He sat there for long, about a month. He came out. He said, 'You will get a child, you with your wife. But that child, no one is to see him, except you, and your wife, and the one who cooks for him—three people only.'

The wife became pregnant. She gave birth. The child was brought

[1] Most people agreed that Hukongko's child owned the chiefship as Kubasi would not have survived at all if it had not been for her.

into a house, up above, in an attic. There the child remained for long, he grew. For long he was there. The child learned to walk on his own. He was there in the house, high up. He came to be a young man, he grew up tall. When it came, at that time, he stood up above on the house, looking at the people below. For long he used to look at the people.

One day a girl came out in the village. She stood there. The boy came out above. He stood looking. They let their eyes meet, she and the boy. They saw each other. The boy had been told that he should not be seen by any other person. They came and saw each other, he and the girl. The girl said, 'I must go and see for myself where that boy lives.' She went and searched for a ladder, she tied it—a long one. She went and leant it against the house.

The evening came. The girl went and climbed up. She entered. She found the boy there. The boy said, 'E! What have you come here for?' 'I love you. Since I saw you yesterday, my heart has not stood still. That is why I have come, I love you.' The boy said, 'But I should not be seen by any other person.' They lay down.

When the sun was about to rise, the boy died. She the girl she did not run away when the boy died. In the morning the woman who cooked for him brought water for the boy to go and wash. She found the girl sitting there. The child, the boy, he was dead! She went and called the chief and his mother. 'Come here! come here! I have seen something amazing. The boy has died. But I also found a woman there, sitting there.' The chief went with the mother. He went and saw the boy who had died, and the girl sitting there. He said, 'E! Have you killed the boy, our son?' 'Yes. It was love that caused it.' 'Well, all right.'

They called the moriman. 'Ha! the child you struggled for us to get, that child has died.' The moriman said, 'Well, all right. Let me have men now to go and cut wood and bring it to the village.' The men went to cut wood. They brought it to the village. They came and put it down. The moriman said, 'Have you here a can of kerosene?' 'Yes.' 'Well, fetch it.' It was fetched. He came and put kerosene on all the wood. He struck fire and put it on the wood. The fire caught.

'Aha. Chief, do you love your son?' 'Yes.' 'Well then, go into the fire.' The chief went up, but the fire was hot.[1] He went back. He went again. 'Ah ah, the fire is hot indeed.' He went and sat down. He wept. He said, 'Ah! chief. You do not love your son.'

He called his mother. 'Do you love your son?' 'Yes.' 'Well, go into the fire, so that you may be burnt with your son.' His mother went up too—it was hot. She went back. She came near again. The fire was hot indeed. She said, 'All right. I will not be burnt too. I will leave it as it is.' 'Well, all right.'

[1] The narrator mimed very vividly the way in which the heat of the fire drove back the two parents against their will.

The girl was called, the one who went and found the boy and caused him to die. 'Girl, do you love the man?' 'Yes.' 'Well then, go into the fire, so you may both be burnt.' The girl leaped into the fire. They were both burnt, the two of them.

The fire died down. The moriman took the ashes. He entered his room. He was there for one month. He made a woman and a man, complete. He brought them out as Limba people. He said, 'Aha, chief. The work you called me for, I have finished it. Here is the man, and the woman.' The chief said, 'Thank you, thank you, thank you.' He paid the moriman. The moriman went off. The boy came out with his wife. He said, 'Father, I will not live here. I will go up country, far away.' 'All right, my son, all right. Go, with your wife.'

They went off travelling. They spent the day travelling—the whole day. The man—hunger seized him. He was not able to travel. He was weak all over. There was a woman who had ordered out men, to have a swamp cleared for her. The men went to clear the swamp. The girl stood, she cooked rice with meat—much of it. She put the rice on her head. She set out, taking it to her workers. They came and met with the man, the two of them, he and his wife. 'E! this man is fine, isn't he! I will follow him in marriage.' The other girl said, 'No! No! No! I won't allow it.' 'E! If you agree for me to follow him in marriage, I will take this rice and give it, and he can eat it—the rice for my workers. I am not giving the rice to them.' The other girl said, 'All right.' She gave the rice. They sat down, they ate. 'All right. Let us go.'

They set out to go. They went and met a woman at the water, a mother of a young child, washing. She said, 'E! that man is fine! I will follow him in marriage.' The [other] girl said, 'I will not allow it. No! No! No! I took my rice, the rice for my workers, I gave it to the man, he ate the rice, my workers were left like that, I did not give them the rice. Now you come to say just like that you love the man. I won't allow it.' The girl said, 'If you allow me to follow him, and for him to marry me—you see this water here, this big river? Here are many crocodiles. No one can cross here without giving a person and throwing him in the water, so that the crocodiles may take him to eat. All right. If you are going to cross over quickly in the boat, well the crocodiles will not catch you, I will take my child and throw him to the crocodiles. Well, let us cross.' Then the other said, 'All right. Throw in your child.' The mother took and threw her child into the water. They got into the boat quickly, they crossed quickly. The crocodiles did not catch them. They started going.

Well, in the village to which they went, the chief there was by now old. But a stranger could not enter there unless he could show where the chief's afterbirth was [buried].[1] When they reached the village, the

[1] It is common for the afterbirth to be buried with a kola or other fruit; the tree that grows on the spot belongs to the child.

chief's daughter, his first-born, she said, 'E! ha! I love the man who is come to our village. I will go there to marry him.' Then said the other 'No! No! I won't agree. I took my child whom I bore, I threw him to the crocodiles in the river, we got into the boat, we found a chance to cross. Now we have reached here, this village here, you come to say you are coming to our husband to marry him. I won't allow it.' The chief's daughter said, 'Oh? If you allow me to come in marriage to your husband, I will show you the secret of the village. So that your husband may not be killed. Whenever a stranger comes here, to this village here, he has to show where the afterbirth of this chief is buried. Well, if you agree for me to come to your husband in marriage, I will show him tomorrow.' 'All right.' 'Tomorrow morning when he gets up in the morning and he stands on the veranda, and he stands and looks, and I will be sweeping the compound—where I beat out the broom, that is the place. I will do that as much as six times, let him look there.'

Well, when he was asked by the old people of the village, 'Stranger, well, a stranger cannot come to the village here unless he can show where the afterbirth of the chief is buried. If you do not know the place, we will kill you'—the man said, 'Oh, well, all right. Everything there is, is as Kanu wills.' He went and showed the place 'Is it not here?' 'It is there.'

The old chief of the village died. The stranger who had shown where his afterbirth was, when the chief died, he was taken as chief. He remained for long in this chiefship, he bore children by all of his wives. He lived long.

The chief came out then, he died. His wives were left with the children, those whom the chief had borne.[1] Then they got up. The one who had gone into the fire with the man said, 'My child owns the inheritance.' Then another said, 'It is not your child who owns the inheritance; my child owns the inheritance—because I took my rice, for the workers I had called and had cooked for them. I gave that to the man, for he could not go because of the hunger that oppressed him. My rice saved him. I left my workers.' Another said, 'No. That is not so. My child, I took him, I threw him to the crocodiles in the big river. We got a chance to cross in the boat. If I had not done that, we would not ever have crossed the river. The crocodiles would have eaten you.' Then said another, 'E! What about me? I came and showed my father's afterbirth, so that the stranger would not be killed. He saw where the afterbirth was buried. My father died. Now, since you come and say it is your child who owns the inheritance—it is my child who owns the inheritance.'

Well, of all these women, the wives, whose is the one child who owns the inheritance?

[1] *Kiɛ*-bear, beget. The same Limba term is used for both men and woman.

The forbidden forest

DAUDA KONTEH. *Dictated* 28.11.61

A story of how a girl's breaking of the rule of the forest stopped her from either eating or going to her lover until she had returned to it again. The theme of a failure to destroy something, even by employing the most extreme means, recurs in several stories. One of the points of the story seems to be a kind of parody of the normal situation of love.

A STORY. A girl came out on the earth. She went escorted [to her husband]. There was a forbidden forest. No one was to go there to the bush there.[1] If you go in there, what you leave there will turn into a human, following you, singing, 'Hamusa, *nɛŋgbɛ*, *nɛŋgbɛ*, *nɛŋgbɛ*. I am pursuing you, don't leave me behind. If you leave me, I will pursue you.'

When she arrived there, she took it,[2] she got water, she rubbed it in the water. She set out to go. It turned [into a human] it followed her. 'Hamusa, *nɛŋgbɛ*, *nɛŋgbɛ*, *nɛŋgbɛ*. I am pursuing you. . . .'

When she arrived, she found fire. She took it, she put it in the fire. It burnt. She took the ashes, she took them to the water, she rubbed them into the water, the water took them off. It began to follow her again. 'Hamusa, *nɛŋgbɛ*, *nɛŋgbɛ*, *nɛŋgbɛ*, I am following, don't leave me behind.'

She came and arrived to her lover. She took it, she held it, she wrapped it up in leaves. She tied it up. When she was given food, she was beginning to eat, the bundle got up saying, 'We will both eat'; the form (?) came out saying, 'We will both eat the rice that was cooked for you by the man.' She seized the form, she tied it. It brought her shame. She was not able to eat. Her lover asked, 'Why are you not eating?' 'My head is sore.' She said goodbye. 'I will go back home.' 'Oh! stay the night!' 'No chance.' 'I beg you.' 'No chance. My head is sore.'[3]

She set out to go. 'Well, goodbye to you.' The girl had set out,[4] going to be escorted. The girl was beginning to talk with her lover, and the form said, 'Don't leave me behind in your talking that you are talking.' The form got up to embrace the girl, 'You are not the only one that came here yesterday. It was two of us! Both of us are to embrace the girl.'

They [the girl and the form] began to go back. She came to the forest. where she had defecated the day before. The form was left behind there.

[1] Euphemism for defecate.

[2] i.e. her excrement which follows her and which she tries continually to get rid of.

[3] Euphemism for menstruate; she is using this as an excuse to go.

[4] This paragraph is a recapitulation of what had happened thus far.

'Well, all right, you and I have parted. Let me be left in my own place.'

The man came now. The form was left there now. It did not follow any longer.

Since I have finished it, well, it is finished, I have ended.

The story of the great witch

NIAKA DEMA. *Recorded* 6.10.61

The story of a witch who tried to prevent her daughter marrying, first by pursuing the couple, then by turning herself into a young girl who comes to marry and then attempts to kill her daughter's husband. The witch is treated as something not quite human, and at one point is called a 'spirit'.

Karanke, one of the listeners, 'replied' to the story throughout by grunting at intervals, prompting the teller, or asking questions to elucidate or emphasize certain points; he also thanked Niaka when he ended the story.

Niaka makes great use of the phrase I have translated as 'It is good'; sometimes this fits well into the context, at other times it seems just to be used to gain time for thought. There are a number of obscurities, often due to the ambiguity of the Limba word for he/she, and because of the same word being used to describe the witch's daughter and herself in the form of a young girl (I have differentiated these in translation). A few sentences which were, to me, very obscure have been omitted; this has been indicated by dots.

I HAVE come to talk with you. Well, Maheni, by your grace. Karanke, by your grace. Well, Yenkeni came here, coming to hear stories.[1]

Well, a witch once came out on the earth. She was called Kologbang-tang,[2] the greatest of all the witches. Well, she finished [killed] all the people. What did she do? She went and built herself a house, she alone, a farm-hut. When she had built her house, the farm-hut, she alone—well, her daughter, she was called Yonkomaring. Her daughter—the witch's. Now the old woman had been using magic for long, she had now killed many people, ha! over three hundred now. When she had now killed a hundred thousand people, well, she said, 'It is good, now, for no one to come to my hut here.' Then the girl said, 'It is good, mother—ha! I am a young girl now; I want now to find my husband,

[1] At this point Karanke asked if he should 'reply' (*me*); he was told he should to which he answered 'I accept', and 'replied' throughout the story. (On 'replying' see pp. 67–68.)

[2] The word, I was told, means a 'great witch', but it seems to be used here (the only context in which I met it) as a proper name.

the man who will love me and I will love him. But for me to come and live here by myself—ha! that does not please me.' Then she [mother] said 'I will not allow it. I, I will not see a human come here.' Whenever she saw the tracks of a human, she shot.[1] Whenever she saw the tracks of a human, she shot—the great, great witch, the old, old woman. Then the old woman said 'Well, now, rather than have you get a husband, I will kill you first!' Then the girl said 'It is good—well, if you are going to kill me, all right.'

Now she [the girl] went and met with a man—his name was Momodi. 'Well, it is good, Momodi, for you to come to me.' The man came there in a free marriage.[2] When he came, she said, 'Well, come and stay here with me.' He came, he came in a free marriage to her, 'so that you may know the witchcrafts of my mother'. Well, he came. What did the girl do? She said, 'It is good, I am coming to you in a free marriage.' The boy came to her home, to her witchcrafts. In witchcraft, there they [mother and daughter] were now quarrelling.

The girl said, 'It is good that my mother should not see you. Well, let me put you in a cigarette cup.'[3] She put him in a cigarette cup. Well, they said, 'It is good.' They cooked millet. When the millet was cooked, she said, 'But my mother is cruel.' 'It is all right.' Well, when they had cooked the millet, she took pepper as she stirred. Where she stirred, there was the pepper—taking some to give the boy a handful. When she had taken a great handful of food, she dipped into where they were stirring. Her mother asked her, 'What are you doing there?' 'Nothing. I am squeezing the pepper.' Behold, she was taking some, behold she was giving it to her lover! Well, the boy was filled, completely.

[The girl said] 'It is good—I want to go with you. I want to go with you now. It is good—well, my mother is cruel, she has many, many, many, many, many magics, she has many, many, many, many, many magics. It is good, that when the night comes, I will tell you the time.[4] When I tell you the time, when the time comes, then it is good.' Now the girl too—when a witch brings up a child, then the child is complete too [in witchcraft], twice or three times [over]! She said to him, 'It is good, I will give you what will save you.' She said, 'I will watch the time.'...[5]

[1] Witches are sometimes said to kill their victims by shooting them with a magic 'witch gun'.

[2] i.e. without payment of bridewealth.

[3] Cigarette cups (tins for fifty cigarettes) are very much in demand as containers. The girl's magical powers are demonstrated by her ability to conceal Momodi from her mother in this small tin.

[4] i.e. the best time to go, when her mother would be asleep.

[5] Then follows a short episode which I cannot fully understand and have omitted, about raffia which the mother had apparently travelled to a great distance to fetch.

She gave him ashes, she gave him a rope, she gave him mist—to her lover. 'Well, it is good, well, when my time comes—'

They slept for long, for long they slept. When they had slept for very long, she put down the raffia ribs—'No, the time has not come yet.' They slept for long, they slept. 'How is it?' 'No, the time has not come yet.' . . . When the time had now come, 'It is good—well, let us go, you are to take me to marry you freely.'

They set out to go. They went. The woman [witch] now—she was still asleep. She had travelled far, as far as from here to Freetown, as far as from here right to where the country ends. She had been travelling all the time—*thɛ thɛ thɛ thɛ thɛ thɛ thɛ thɛ thɛ thɛ.*[1] It had been far—for eating food. Where she had lain down, she had travelled far, she had not been thinking about where she lived here.

They set out to go. When they had gone about thirty miles, her mother began to wake a little little bit—*sɛŋku sɛŋku.* They took—for someone brought up by Kologbangtang has great power—she left the mist, she put it down.

Then the woman, Kologbangtang, got up. 'It is good.' She woke up there. 'E, my child, my child has gone'—it was the mother-in-law speaking—'My child has gone.' She rushed in. She could not see her. Well, she set out to go. Now she had a knife, bigger than a cutlass. She went. She went, went, went, went, went, went, went, went, went, went, for far! As she went, she came to the mist. 'E! the mist—do not think that I will be unable. I am called Kologbangtang, the great one among the witches, I am called Kologbangtang, the great one among the witches. I will not fail. I have magic in everything.' Well, she went, she came to the mist. For about two months she went through it, and passed it. She went, went, went, went. She called 'You that are going—' She went. She had gone now about from here to Freetown, she said, 'Hey, you that are going there in front, ha!'

They put down the rope. That rope—she went for the whole day, she spent the day cutting through it. When she had cut through it, she saw them. 'It is good—hey, you that are going there, don't forget, I am coming. For you came and took away my child, and carried her off when you went.' What did she come to? Stones. Those stones—she had there the knife to cut the stones with. She took it. She cut a path through the stones, she went through them. 'You that are going, it is good, do not forget, I am coming. The man who came and took away my child, believe me, it will not be friendship between you and me.' She went, went, went, went, went, went, went, went. They came to the ashes. Well, they came now to the ashes. They went, they came now to where the man lived. 'Well, here is my place.' They lived there.

When they went in there, when they had gone in, she said, 'Well,

[1] Her quick footsteps.

it is good—I, I have come to you in a free marriage, to Momodi.' Well, Momodi said, 'It is good. That is true. For I brought you here now when I came. For me, that is good. For I took you away from Kologbangtang, the great, great witch. But come here to me.' They came and lived there.

When one night had passed the woman [witch] got up. She went out now. She dressed herself, dressed, dressed, dressed, dressed. She went out now—you would think it was a young girl that had just come out. It was the mother, Kologbangtang. Her mother, Kologbangtang, the great, great witch. She turned into a young girl. Her breasts—they became like a girl's just about to be given [in marriage].[1]

When she reached there, she said, 'I too, I have come in a free marriage to Momodi here. Here to Momodi, here I have come in a free marriage.' Before she had come, she had seen her daughter there, the daughter she had been bringing up, the one she had long been bringing up; for she had been seized and carried off to a free marriage. Well, when she [witch] had arrived, the stranger was welcomed, she was welcomed, she was welcomed![2] Then the girl [the daughter] said, 'That is my mother oh! That is my mother oh! Watch her!' She knew that she was her mother. She had now transformed herself, turned herself into a woman. The daughter now knew her, for they had known each other, for a long time they had quarrelled, the girl and the mother. 'Ha! If you don't watch her, you, ha! you will suffer. There will be cruelty here today.' Then the man said 'It is good. It is all right. Well, it is good for you to spread a bed for her. All of you, you will know, I will tell you.'

She [witch] had a hen killed for her. That hen was brought for her as food. She went and dug in the fire-place where she was sitting in the room. She took the food, she buried it.[3] When she was burying it, she divided it; when she had divided off half, she buried that food. She said, 'It is good. Come for it.[4] I am filled.' Behold, she had buried it. For she did not eat people's food—only humans, that is what she ate, *rɛki!* That is what she ate, *rɛki!* Then the girl said, 'It is good—when people go to sleep, well, I want them to go and spread a bed for you (?) to one side in a room.' She [witch] said, 'No. I am going to sleep with my husband tonight.' As soon as she had arrived, as soon as she had

[1] This is a fairly stock description of the attraction of a young girl who has just come out from initiation. It contrasts with the withered breasts of the old witch in her proper form. (For another description of a young girl dressing with care to attract a husband she is planning to kill see *The man killed for a spinach leaf*.)

[2] As a new wife—not realizing that she was the witch.

[3] Concealing that she was not fully human. Cf. the spirit in *Sira and the monster*.

[4] i.e. for the food she had left, her hunger being, in theory, now satisfied.

arrived, before she had been told 'Here is your lodging' she had said, 'It is good for me first to sleep with my husband.' She had not had a sacrifice made for her, a hen had not been killed to welcome her,[1] she had said 'I want today to sleep with my husband.' Behold—she was wanting to kill the man, so that (?) she could go home with the girl.

Then the girl said [to Momodi] 'It is good—you know what you will do?' She was watching her now very, very carefully. 'When you lie down, do not refuse her. When you lie down in the clay bed there, you are to call blessings on the rafters saying, "Well, I am lying down by your grace; hut-supports, I am lying down by your grace; thatch, I am lying down by your grace; eaves, I am lying down by your grace; rope, I am lying down by your grace."' He said 'All right.' He guarded against her completely, he the man.

When it came to the first hours of the night, the woman got up very carefully, *yumumumu*,[2] to fall on the man in the night. Then the hut-supports said, 'Ha! Master. If we fall on you, you will not go home safely.' 'All right.' She lay down there. She slept, slept, slept, slept, slept. She got up again, carefully, *yumumumu*. 'Ha!'—the rafters got up, 'Master, if you do anything, if we fall on you here, we here on you, that will not be good, you will not go away.' She lay down. She slept. They slept, slept, slept, slept. She arose again quietly, carefully, *yumumumu*, to fall on the man. Then the thatch said, 'Ha! Master. You here today, the same as the rafters said, we here know how to fight you a very, very good way.' She lay down. She slept, for long she slept. Ha! they went on sleeping for long. She got up again quietly, carefully, *yumumumu*. The ropes said, 'Ha! I too, master, I own this house. It was I who let them build it all here. If we fall on you here, we and the rafters, we will both fall on you, for I am wrapped round them.' 'All right, for me, I will lie down.'

The sun rose now. Then she said, 'Ha! I spent the whole night, all night, in trouble, I spent the whole night in trouble. What is good—ha! I, I want to go. I want to go.' She had not been able to kill the man, Momodi. 'It is good—I want to go.' Now the girl, she knew. She [witch] said, she said to her husband 'Escort me'[3]—as far as from here to the place where the goats are beyond the village—'Escort me to there.' Behold she was thinking of killing him there. They went for far. The woman said, 'It is good that when you reach that big tree, you should stop there.' When they had gone for long, they came there to a ripe *here*-fruit. 'It is good for you to climb for it for me, Momodi, please. Please climb for the *here*-fruit for me, I am hungry.' Momodi said, 'You

[1] i.e. none of the usual preliminary formalities of marriage had been performed.

[2] With great stealth and care.

[3] Go with her a little way in honour—a request that should not be refused.

spent the night full fed.' 'I did not eat. I—it was trouble that I found here today. But it is all right. I am going. Well, when two months have passed, I am coming back. Please climb up for the *here*-fruit for me.' When Momodi climbed up for the fruit, he climbed, climbed, climbed, climbed, climbed. 'It is this one I am to pick?' 'No. Up at the top, that is the one you are to pick. That is where you are to go, to the top.' 'All right.' When Momodi had climbed up far, what did the woman say? She cut it all away underneath. Behold she was a great, great spirit. When she had cut it underneath, all the forest became red, *wɔki*. 'Ha! Master, there where you are standing, ha! you are finished. You are finished. You today, your life is finished. Ha! I spent the night troubling for you. I spent the day troubling for you. Ha! I was not able for you. But now, I have been able for you.'

Behold, the girl—for she knew her mother, for she had brought her up—then the girl who was left behind, she took her head-tie. She [witch] was cutting it [the tree] all, all round. The forest was now all red. Then the man said, 'E Kanu! Today I will die.' Then the girl took her head-tie quickly, she threw it to him. When she had thrown it to him, the head-tie went and brought the man down from there. The man came and sat down quietly here with the girl. Then the woman said, 'Ha! I brought up this girl for very, very long. So I have now become!'[1] Ha! She went off now, crying. She had been unable to kill Momodi. The girl had saved Momodi.

Well, when he came, the girl said, 'Were you able?' 'Ah! by your help. I, I was not able—but by your help oh!' So, they came and lived there....[2]

Well, since I came and was told that story, and Yenkeni came to learn stories, that is it, it is finished, by grace of Karanke, by grace of Maheni.

A story of witches

FODE KAMARA. *Recorded* 6.12.61

A story about how witches joined together to kill the child of one of their number and how he escaped through the help of the woman Mamakoto. The narrator commented on the story that 'usually a mother, if she bears a child, would never, never kill it. But a witch—you see a witch has no sense and would kill her own child.' In the story all the family have gathered together to kill the child—the ones, who, above all, should be his protectors; in the end he is saved by someone who is not a relation at all.

[1] i.e. she is now childless and helpless.

[2] Then follows a short and obscure sentence about spirits.

A similar story where the point is partly made by the reversal of the usual behaviour of a mother is *The story of Deremu* where a mother also tries to kill her son. In each of these stories the mother is herself killed as a result.

I was told another story (not included here) based on very much the same plot, though with differences in detail: much stress was laid on the fact that the boy was her only child; he was hidden in a pile of thatch rather than a tree and his fear as he sat there listening to the witches and wondering whether he would be discovered was vividly depicted; he and the girl had lived together for some time; the song of the witches was different; and the story was concluded by a long episode about how the boy ran off with the girl who saved him and escaped.

The present narrator had been employed as a cook for many years; hence the precise times mentioned in the story.

THERE was a woman, and she bore a child, one only, a boy. But she was a witch. Well, the father of the child was also a witch. The mother's brother was a witch. The one who bore the mother's brother was a witch. Well, they formed a company,[1] one for eating each other's children in witchcraft.

He set off, her child, and he ran away to a far country, right away. Well the mother, she stayed behind. But she did not cease from her company with these witches, those who stayed behind. What they did was the eating of each other's children. When they killed one child of one of them, they killed also that of their companion. Even if it was as many as forty that they all came to, each of them had to give a child for that company. You cannot eat your companion's child and not have your own eaten. Well, she was always going to eat her friends' children, all the time.

Well, it came to her [turn]. They asked her, 'What about your child? so that we can eat him; for you have long been eating ours.' She said, 'My child is not here now. When he comes back, we will kill him all right. By then he will be very big and fat. Well, we will eat him, and he will all be sweet.'

Well, the child arose, he came and arrived. Well, they said, 'Ah! Good! the child has come. Let us now reap the benefit of our company. For you have long been making us eat [our children]. Your son has come today. Well, let us fix a time for us to kill him.' Well, they went to the secret bush, they went and sat for the discussion. They fixed the time when they would come and eat. 'Well, but let us dance today.'

Well, they began the dancing. But Mamakoto[2] alone, she did not want the boy to be killed. In the afternoon, she came, she knocked on the

[1] A 'company' (*kunɛ*) is frequently said to be formed by witches; each in turn gives one of his own children to be eaten by all.

[2] *Mamakoto* is probably the name of one of the witches, though the word seems sometimes to be used with an article as if a general not a proper noun. If so I think it must mean woman or girl (Wara Wara Bafodea dialect).

door. The boy said, 'Who is it?' 'I.' 'What is your name?' 'Oh! open to me.'[1] The boy got up, he opened the door. Well, Mamakoto went in. As she went in, he said, 'Oh, mother![2] what is it?' 'Boy, I want to take tobacco.'[3] The boy said, 'Oh, mother, I have no tobacco here, for I do not take snuff. But wait for me. Let me go and buy.' He went to buy tobacco, he brought it and gave her. He got up, he took out money, two shillings; he added it as well on top of the tobacco, saying, 'When this is finished, buy more.' He got out one head-tie, he gave it her as a present. Mamakoto said, 'Oh my child, I thank you. Ha! I will tell you something; but you are not to tell anyone.' The boy said, 'No, I will not tell it.' 'Well, in the evening I will come and take you to a place. But when I hide you, don't you laugh! don't be afraid.'

When the boy had come and sat down in a nook,[4] the witches all gathered together, they held their discussion. They said, 'What we will do—well, half-way between eight and nine, well, let us kill the child. At nine o'clock let us bring him, at half past to eat him.' Well, Mamakoto got up, she said, 'Here, wait here. I rejoice much, ha! for killing the boy. Well, I am about to sing a song, one which I like, to rejoice for the eating of the child.' Behold, Mamakoto was making a chance to save the child, so that they would not kill him. That was why she came and hid him, so that he would hear his father and his mother and all his people arranging to kill him. Well, so that he would also see all these people who were trying to kill him. But the witches—they did not know that Mamakoto was saving the child so that he would not be killed. The witches thought that Mamakoto was rejoicing for the killing of the child. Behold, her idea was really to save the child! That was why she gave the song, the song of the nook. She told them to answer in chorus '*iyɔ yɔ yɔ*'. She sang 'In the nook, in the nook.' Well, the witches answered the chorus for her *yɔ yɔ yɔ*. Well, the boy was in the nook, she was telling him, 'You see your mother? you see your father? you see your brother? you see all your people?—for killing you.'

Well, they danced for a long time. The witches were pleased with the song, they danced to the song, the song that Mamakoto was singing. They did not know that Mamakoto was saving the boy. The boy now was seeing, he was hearing, ha!

They said, 'Let us go first to our houses, let us go and rest a little; then let us come to kill him then.' They thought that the boy was lying down in the house. Behold, there he was, sitting to one side of them! But they did not know. Well, as they were going to go and seek him in

[1] She is impatient at the way he is keeping her out with his questions when she has come so urgently.

[2] A term of respect.

[3] Women often take snuff.

[4] The boy is hidden in one of the great nooks so often to be seen in the huge trunks of cotton trees.

the house, the boy escaped. Well, they said to the mother of the boy, 'What about your son?' His mother said, 'I don't know.' The witches said, 'Don't say that now, we won't accept that. We were rejoicing over killing the boy, and you hid the boy again. Ha! You have long been killing ours. When *your* child comes, you deceive us. We rejoiced over the child, you hid him. We won't accept this from you. We will have to kill you.' There was no escape. They killed her.

Two co-wives

KOLOI DEMA. *Dictated to Suri Kamara*, –.9.61

A story illustrating the moral that co-wives should not quarrel. The quarrel begun in the story by the elder wife ends in the death of her own child—a motif that recurs in *Jealous mothers*.

SARA wooed wives. When they had been wooed, they went and lived together. They were quarrelling. The younger one stood up, she went to the water, to wash out the calabashes. But the water was much. She lost her co-wife's calabash.[1] She went to her co-wife, she went and told her, 'I have lost the calabash.' Her co-wife said she was to return the calabash. Then she said, 'Ah! I have come into trouble.' Then her co-wife said, 'You are to return the calabash.' She went to her parents. Her parents went and found many calabashes. She [co-wife] was shown them. 'Come and see which one you want.' The co-wife said that she did not want any of them, only her own. The girl said (?), 'Let me go, so that it may not be bad behind me' (?). She, the girl, went to the bank of the stream. The girl went into the edge of the water, she sat at the edge, she wept for long. She began to go, she was singing a song '*Bilɔ bilɔ nàɛ, ko riŋ ko rena ye woi ko riŋ ko kabayerena ko riŋ ko*'.[2] She came to many calabashes. There was a woman there underneath the water who held every calabash that was carried away by the water, keeping them. When the girl came to her, she said, 'All right, come and look at the calabashes and take whatever calabash you see.' The girl took the calabash. She brought the calabash to her co-wife. She said, 'Here is your calabash.'

Now the girl had beads that she was stringing. Her co-wife's child came and took one bead, he swallowed it. The girl said that they were to return the bead that had been swallowed. Her co-wife offered many

[1] A calabash could easily be washed away in the wet season when the rivers and streams are flooded.

[2] A song with no apparent meaning to the words.

beads—no! only her own! They begged her. Only her own! They had to go and open up (?) the child, going to kill the child, and take out the bead to give to the girl. The girl said 'It is finished.'[1]

Thus a co-wife should not do bad to a co-wife. It is finished.

The woman with four lovers

NABENI DEMA. *Dictated* 28.10.61

A story that ends with a dilemma asking which of the people who had all acted in an improbable or amazing way was the most remarkable. The woman not only had four lovers at once, cooked for all four at the same time, and went directly from one to another, but she was able to cook different foods together in the same pot yet serve them separately—something known to be impossible. The men, apparently, are to be thought remarkable because they accepted a situation with so many known rivals; at the end of the story, one produces a pipe which takes them across the river by its smoke. The general verdict after the narration was that they were all equally amazing, and the telling generally caused much amusement.

The emphasis on the woman's cooking for her lovers and on the formal verbal interchanges between them are characteristically Limba. The woman gives the rice—unquestionably for a Limba the best food—to the man she loves the most. The woman and the men are depicted as behaving in the typical way for Limba lovers—she cooks for the men, they bring her wine, gifts, and pleasing words.

YOU see now—a girl was bound in love with four men. They got up to come and sleep. She stood up, she put on meat.[2] She stood up, she put on leaves. She stood up, she put on beans. She stood up, she put on ochra. The time came close for her to cook. She mixed them all up in cooking. The maize and the rice and the guinea corn and the millet—she cooked them together.

She stood up to help it out. She helped out the cooked rice, what had been cooked together! When she had helped it out, the scrapings of the rice, they came out, from a shilling pot![3] She stood up, she helped out the maize; in one pot, there it had all been cooked! When she had

[1] i.e. the case (or quarrel) is formally ended.

[2] She cooks first the meat, beans, etc., for the sauce, then later begins to cook the four basic foods, maize, guinea corn, millet, and rice.

[3] This is intentionally ridiculous as a cooking-pot big enough for all this food would cost several pounds. On the special significance of the 'scrapings' see p. 9.

helped it out, she took, she scraped out the scrapings. She took, she helped out the guinea corn, she scraped out the scrapings. She took, she helped out the millet. She took out the scrapings.

The lovers came. She took the millet, she brought it to one. 'Here is what I have kept for you today.' She was thanked. She came and took the guinea corn. She brought it to another. 'Here is what I have kept for you today.' She was thanked. She took the maize. She brought it to another. 'Here is what I have kept for you today.' She was thanked. She said, 'I will first rest a bit now'—for she knew that she would bring food for the one she loved very much. Then she said, 'I will rest.' When she had rested, she took the rice, she brought it. 'Here is what I have kept for you today.' 'Thank you.'

The men—they had brought wine. The one who had had millet cooked for him, he came first. 'You,[1] by your grace, I have come here to sleep today. That is the word.' They passed the word between them,[2] saying, 'That pleases us.' They took, they drank it. The one who had had guinea corn cooked for him came. 'You, by your grace, I have come here to sleep today. That is why I have come.' They passed the word between them, saying that that pleased them. They drank. The one who had had maize cooked for him took wine. 'You, by your grace, I have come here to sleep today. That is the word.' They said, 'That pleases us.' They passed the word between them. They drank the wine. The one who had had rice cooked for him, because he knew that he was the most favoured in the love, he took wine and added a dress to it as well; for they loved each other. He came. 'You, by your grace, I have come here to sleep today. That is it. Here is a dress. Here is wine.' They passed the word between them, saying, 'We accept.' They drank.

The woman got up, she went to the one she had cooked the millet for. She went and spent time there, for long. She got up from there, she went to the one she had cooked the guinea corn for. She went and spent time there, for long. She got up. She went to the one she had cooked the maize for. She went and spent time there. She got up. She came and sat down a little first. For she knew that she would go to the one she loved. After some time, she went. She went and slept there.

The sun rose. Each one of them, he set out to go. Each one of them, he went and left her something. They began to go. They came to a river, a big river. 'How will we cross here?' The smoker, he smoked. The smoke which came out, by it they crossed the river. They went.

Now, of them and the girl, who is the greater?

[1] He calls her by name.

[2] In an exchange of formal phrases of announcement, thanks, and acceptance.

The boy who got a wife from a bird

GBELU WUTIA. *Dictated* 2.10.61

A far-fetched story of how a child won a wife, the most valuable of all possessions, from a small bird (normally merely a child's plaything). The idea of killing one half and leaving one half that recurs throughout the story is intentionally comic. The story moves through a series of parallel episodes, the boy gaining more and more valuable things as he proceeds. It concludes with the typical Limba ending of being given a wife and returning home to report on his actions.

The story was told by Gbelu, prompted by the younger Kumaru Dema. They said they had heard the story from the old men who told it in their compound.

A STORY for you. A woman once gave birth to a child. After she bore him, she went to gather cane grass. She came on a bird there. She caught the bird, catching it for the child. When she had caught it, she met the child. She gave it to the child. When she had given it to him, the child said 'Mother, I will get a wife from this bird.'

He set out to travel. He met a blacksmith. His name was Sara. The child said, 'What! You are looking after those things,[1] but will you not make a sacrifice?' He said that he should kill the bird one half and leave one half. Well, he killed the bird—the whole of it! The child said, 'Oh! the bird that was caught for me by my mother when she was gathering cane grass!' He said, 'It will have to be a knife.' [He was given the knife.]

Well, he came on people who were cutting raffia ribs,[2] splitting them with their teeth. He gave them the knife. 'Split one half, leave one half.' Well, they split them, they broke the knife on them. Well, then he said, 'Oh! the knife, the knife that was made for me by Sara the smith; Sara the smith who ate my bird; the bird that was caught for me by my mother when she was gathering cane grass! It will have to be the raffia ribs.' He was given the raffia ribs.

He came on people who were weaving baskets—weaving from cane grass! He said, 'Split the raffia ribs one half, and leave me the other half.' Well, they split one half—they finished the whole lot! 'The raffia ribs that I was given by the people cutting raffia! It will have to be a basket.' They gave him the basket.

[1] i.e. the secret implements in the smith's hut which need a special ceremony performed over them about once a year by killing a bird, normally a hen.

[2] The ribs from raffia leaves are split lengthwise into four or six pieces to make the long curved framework for big baskets. Cane grass, mentioned in the next episode, is not suitable for this, being too brittle.

Well, he came on people who were carrying home the rice.[1] He said, 'Take the basket and carry home half, leave me half.' They carried it all home! They were told, 'The basket I was given by those weaving baskets! It will have to be rice.' He was given the rice.

He came on people who were making a sacrifice.[2] He said, 'Take the rice. Sacrifice with half.' They took it all! They sacrificed it all! He said, 'Oh! The rice I was given by those carrying rice! It will have to be a hen.' One of them caught a hen, he gave it to him.

He came on people who were mourning, mourning with a small *kuyele* bird.[3] He said, 'Take the hen. Make a sacrifice with one half.' They killed it—all of it! He said, 'Oh! The hen that was caught for me by those sacrificing! It will have to be a goat.' They caught the goat. He went off.

He came on people who were mourning. They were mourning for a chief, with a small hen, a very little one. He said, 'Kill the goat one half.' They killed it—all of it! He said, 'Oh! the goat that was caught for me by the mourners! It will have to be an ox.' They caught the ox.

He came on more people who were mourning, mourning a great chief with a goat. He said, 'Kill the ox, one half.' They killed it—*all* of it! He said, 'Oh! See, it was the ox I was given by the mourners! It will have to be a wife.' He was given the wife.

He came and said, 'Mother. I found that the bird came to be a wife. That is the announcement I have for you.'

Since you said you wanted a story, that is it; it is finished.

The wooing of Sira

KARANKE DEMA. *Recorded* 27.9.61

A story about the difficulties encountered in winning a wife. The formal discussions between the suitor and the parents are typically Limba, with interchanges of, for example, 'I accept', 'announce', 'passing the word' which are all essential parts of the formal negotiations with parents-in-law. It is also characteristic for a young man to have to work for his wife's parents. In the story the tasks he is set are apparently impossible

[1] i.e. carrying the main bulk of the rice harvest to the village—a large task, involving many journeys. Rice is usually stored in the large baskets already mentioned.

[2] Rice is sometimes used for 'sacrifices' (*saraka*).

[3] In mourning ceremonies a large sacrifice should be made, preferably of at least a goat, or, for an important chief, many cattle. A *kuyele* is a small wild bird, unsuitable even for a minor sacrifice.

ones. But the hero succeeds and says that henceforth everyone will have to work for their parents-in-law just as he did.

In the middle of the story there is a digression from the main narrative when the narrator apparently turns aside to refer to an episode he had not inserted earlier. Apparently the chief went to a diviner before leaving home and was told what to expect; we gather that on the journey he met and fed some ants with the millet he was carrying and thus earned the help they gave him later. The narrative thus seems rather confusing to one who is not acquainted with this or a similar plot.

The themes of wooing a wife and of being set difficult tasks to finish in a set time recur in several stories.

I NOW, I am going to tell a small story, for Yenkeni to hear.

A chief once came out. He came and lived. A girl was born. Her name was Sira. She was the only one from her mother's womb. She was beautiful. Her mother said, 'This girl, no one will marry her, at the time now when she is small, no one will woo her, not until her breasts are full. When she is full grown, someone will be found to marry her at that time.' Her father said, 'It is all right.'

They lived. They brought up the girl. She became big. She came to be full grown. She [mother] had a swamp farm, a big one. She said, she, the mother, she with her husband 'I, I—even when it is said that someone will marry our daughter, of whatever I say, "That is what you will do", that is what he will do. If he is able to do it, all right, he will be able to marry my child.'

Then a chief came out. 'All right. I will go for the girl, the one called Sira. I will marry her.' At that time, he began to come, he brought sugar cane, it filled a bag completely—*diŋ!* He put it there. He started coming. He was bringing millet, very much millet. He began coming. What happened? He began coming.

He came. He came to a swamp. He found cane rats there. They were sitting sadly.[1] He raised them up. 'Any trouble?'[2] 'I have just come here. I have come to woo the woman who is called Sira. But the ones who own her they say that we will not be able to marry her.' He asked them [rats]. 'E! Why are you sitting here?' Then they said, 'Ah! Our father![3] We have stayed here long in suffering. Look now at us. Here where we are staying, there is no grass here, there is nothing for us to eat.' 'Is that what makes you unhappy?' He took out the sugar cane. 'Here is your food.' The cane rats clutched it to them. They ate it. They called

[1] Sitting in the stock posture of despair or unhappiness: with arms crossed, or head or chin in hand.

[2] The cane rats greet him in the usual phrase.

[3] 'Our father'—used in address to express entreaty, sadness, or respect. The rats' despair was mimed with great vividness by the narrator, as was the way in which they clutched the great armful of sugar cane they were given.

blessings on him, 'Through Kanu, the thing you are going for, may you not fail in it.'

He passed on. He began to go. He arrived. When he had entered, what did they come and do, those who owned the child? He came and sat when he had come and entered. He brought cattle. He brought sheep. He brought goats, and a hen, and a bag of salt, and a pan of oil. He came and was asked, 'Any trouble?' He was told, 'No, no trouble.' 'I—why I have come, it is a woman I love—Sira.' Then her mother asked. 'Will you be able?' 'E! I will try.' 'Will you be able?' 'E! I will try.' 'If you will be able, you will go and clear a swamp. When you have spent the night, when the night is passed, tomorrow morning, I will show you the work. But before the night has passed, I will give you work to do in the night.'

Now he, when he was thinking of coming . . . he had gone to a diviner, to ask him to divine. 'The thing, will I do it? I want you to go and discover how it will go.' [The diviner said] 'The woman—the man who will marry her—if you want the woman, that night you will be given millet, two great baskets full, and it will be scattered all through the village; when it is scattered, through the night, until the sun rises, you are to finish picking it up. When you have finished picking it up, you will marry the woman.'

He now had heard this before. What did he do? When he arrived in the village, wherever the ants stayed, he gathered them all together, saying that they were (?) his people and were (?) taking him on his journey. He came and said, 'Wherever you go, tell your companion, whoever you meet, that they are to help me, so that I may not find shame.'

When he came in, he went and was asked [his purpose]. He announced his purpose. 'Why I have come—it is for Sira. I want to marry her.' Then her mother said, 'I—Sira is here. She is the only child of my womb. But if you want to marry her, whatever I say, that is what you must do.' She said 'I—my part, I the woman, I have a swamp farm; I have no one to clear it for me. The rice is not much. If you are able to clear it in one day, you will marry Sira.' The chief said, 'I accept.' When she [formally] passed the word to her husband, then her husband said, 'For me—so it is.[1] Sira is my daughter. I said that the girl will not be married when she is small. Now at this time whoever wishes to marry her—a "sacrifice" came out in this village: to scatter millet, two large baskets full; if you pick it up in one night, all night, and you finish picking it up, you will marry Sira.' The chief said, 'All right. I accept.' Then they said 'All right. For us, we accept.'

When they were there—you see, the chief, he had come with one follower. That was the one he had brought when he came. He had no

[1] He agrees with what has been said by the mother.

one [else]. They—when the time came near, the sun set. He went. He said, 'I, the thing I came for, Sira, I came and heard all, all that I have to do—I have come [to do it] now. I want you to go and show me the farm. When I have been shown it, and looked at it, I will come back to the village. If I will be able tomorrow, no one will know [yet]; if I will be unable, all right, I will go home.'

He went. He went and was shown the farm. That farm, that is what is called a big thing! It began as from here right to Kamasapi, one farm, right to Fadugu, one farm, right to Kafoko,[1] one farm. Flat bush only. 'If you only clear it in one day, you will marry Sira.'

In the evening he went and was shown the farm. Then he got up, when they were about to return, and said, 'It is all right. I am going in to bathe here.' He went in there to look at the farm. When he looked at the farm, there he met a cane rat. He greeted him. Then the cane rat said, 'Well, the place where you went, well, was it all right?' Then he said, 'So it is. E! It is not yet right. They came and put me to difficult work. Ha! ha!'[2] Where he was standing saying, 'Let me cut a small place, here I will come and begin tomorrow', that was where the cane rat found him. He asked him. He said, 'The work I came for yesterday —here is the farm I have to clear. This is what I have been set to clear.' Then the cane rat said, 'E! Give me the knife. Go and bathe. What you did for us then—we had not eaten anything, you came and saved us. We would have died. We will thank you for that. Let us come for the work that you were set, work which we know.[3] You will not be troubled for that. You, go to bathe, and go to the village. It is all right. When the sun rises, we will meet. And when you meet us tomorrow, from that you will know that you did a good thing on the earth.'

He gave him the knife there. As he turned his back, the cane rat went round the country, to all the cane rats. He spoke. They came. All night . . . before the sun rose, even before it reached the first light of sun, the farm was finished. They went off back into the bush.

Now the chief, he came back to the village. When he entered in the evening again, he was told about the millet. 'Here is the millet.' He was told 'To scatter it in the village—will you be able?' The chief said, 'Well, all right. If I am unable, I will cease.' The millet began to be scattered, all of it. When it had been scattered, the sun set. The moon shone. He came and bent, the chief, to pick up the millet. So he picked it up. He began to speak to himself, 'Alas, I, the old man[4] the work I have come

[1] Villages between three and seven miles from Kakarima where the story was being told.

[2] Expression of sad resignation—a kind of sigh.

[3] The cane rats' power to cut through vegetation is only too well known to the Limba; they are among the main destroyers of rice crops.

[4] He is weak and sorry for himself.

and set for myself today! Where will I be able to see the millet in this darkness, all that has been scattered in the village? I came, and I will not be able to marry Sira. For me, if I spend the night here, if I am unable to finish it, well, all right. But I will try for Sira.'

The ants heard that. They came. One came and said, 'E! chief, why have you come bending down here?' When Sara said, 'Ah! my father, that is how it is. Where I passed you yesterday, I have come today to what I told you. That is what I have been troubled by tonight. The millet has been scattered all through the village, I am to pick it all up. If I finish picking it up and it fills the two baskets, I will be able to marry Sira. But if I am unable, I will not be able to marry her.' Then the ants said, 'So it is. Thank you. E! chief, when you went and acted to us before—we had not eaten anything, you went and did good to us. A full bag of millet, we ate that. We finished it. For the two baskets, will we be unable for that? It is all right. If you are unable for that, go for the baskets and come and put them down.' The chief went for the baskets, he came and put them down. 'All right. Go in and sleep.' The chief went in.

All night, all all all all all night, as it reached midnight exactly, it had hardly passed midnight, they finished picking up the millet. They filled up the baskets—full.

What happened? In the morning, the light came. He called them. He said to his follower, he the chief—he took out a token gift—'Here is a token gift. In the evening here I said that I wanted to marry Sira. But for all that I was told to do, before I will announce my purpose, before I will announce my purpose, let them go to look at the work. Here now is money, one pound. If I was able, all right. If I was not able—let them come and look.'

When the chief [of the village][1] went and had that message brought in to him, he came. He said, 'Good. I, for my part, that pleases me. The amount of millet you have picked up for me, now, unless I am unable for the future (?), there is no quarrel with me now. For my part, I accept now. For the task in the village, the sacrifice is finished.' Then he passed the word to his wife who had borne Sira. Then the woman said, 'That is it now. For your part, it is finished. But I have not yet seen the work for me. If it is all right, or if it is not all right, I do not know yet. But let me go there and look, so that I may know what word to speak.' The chief was told her words. He said, 'So it is. All right then.' They began to go [to the farm]. Before they had arrived it was finished. The amount they had said, it was completely cleared.

Then he took out more money, one pound. 'But I love Sira, I want to marry her.' Her mother was [formally] told of that gift. Then she said, 'For my part here, your work is finished. I have seen that you have

[1] The girl's father.

brought great possessions. But I do not want that. But, for the amount of work you came and did, your task is finished.'

Then Sira was told. She was given to him. Then he said, 'Yes, I came and tried hard for this. I, I am a chief. All night, I spent the night bending down to pick up millet. I spent the night clearing a farm, I was able to marry Sira. Did I not marry her? It was not bridewealth I set for her. What I have done, that is what you are to do for your mother-in-law and your father-in-law.'

When he was given Sira, he took her. He went and married her.

Since I heard that story, Yenkeni, since you came to say—whoever thought of a good story of his, all right. That is it. It is finished.

Wooing Sira

DAUDA KONTEH. *Recorded* 17.1.64

Another story about the tasks demanded by parents-in-law before a wife is given. This story contrasts vividly with the much longer and more sustained narrative by Karanke. In the present version the plot seems of little importance and a great proportion of the actual narration was taken up with introduction, conclusion, and singing. The song, a rhythmic and melodic series of words without any clear meaning, was sung attractively by Dauda and echoed over and over by the audience. Though at first Dauda had some difficulty in calling people's attention to his story, by the end all were intent and joining enthusiastically in the singing.

AHA, attention—attention. You see, among us humans if you want to beg wisdom from someone, listen to him. Why? To carry [the wisdom] forward. If your friend talks, remember it in your thoughts and your wisdom. You see—you take it to your friend. Well, since Yenkeni Konteh came, coming to say that I should bring her a story, well, attention, may you listen oh!

Aha. Well, a human once came out on the earth here, Sira. Sira. 'Whoever marries her must reap my millet in one day and pick the locust beans in one day.' The locust tree stretched like from here right to beyond England. Its branches were like from here right to beyond France. The millet—if you measured (?) it, it was about from here to where the sky ends and where the sky begins—the millet.

Then he was told 'All right. All right. Well now—if you want to marry Sira at all, well now!'

He bent down [to work], singing, '*Fiki fiki fiki, o dɛŋgbɛluma dɛŋgbɛluma, thɛmɛsi thɛmɛsi, dɛŋgbɛluma, dɛŋgbɛluma.*'

Then her mother said 'Ah! Thank you. I have found the man who will marry my daughter. Why? Because he was able to pick the locust beans in one day, and to reap the millet in one day; my heart is content for him to marry my daughter. Yes, Well now.' (Now I, Dauda Konteh, I stood behind there, where they were speaking. I stood behind there, I Dauda. Then I listened.) 'Well now.'

He began [again] '*Fiki fiki fiki, e dɛŋgbɛluma dɛŋgbɛluma, thɛmɛsi thɛmɛsi, dɛŋgbɛluma dɛŋgbɛluma.*'

Since I heard that [story]—The girl was given to him, since he had picked the locust beans and reaped the millet in one day. Then he was told, 'Since you have done that, you will get Sira.' Sira—when Sara[1] had finished reaping, she was taken, he was given Sira.

Since I heard that [story] and Yenkeni Konteh came and said 'Let Dauda bring me a small story'—well that small story has come today, this evening. I Dauda—since it is ended by me, that is it, it is finished.

The woman who wanted to be greeted

SANGBANG YELEME. *Recorded* 27.9.61

Another tale about the difficulty of winning a wife from her parents, specially her mother. The mother insists that she be greeted all day, and only the monitor lizard can succeed in this, and so is given the girl. The importance of greeting is brought out very clearly—even, says the mother-in-law, if her son-in-law is too poor to bring her the due presents, she will at least be sure of receiving honour from his greetings. The necessity of greeting a mother-in-law is one of the requirements of Limba marriage.

YOU who are sitting here, I am Sangbang, I have a story. At Kakarima, that is where I am, the son of Sabena and of Tene Benkutu. My mother—Tene is my mother. Sabena, he is my father. I am going to tell a story—you that are sitting here. My father-in-law[2] Bandi—a story. (All right)[3] Ningte—a story. Saiong—a story. The man Korombo—a story. Maheni—a story. Semanka—a story. Mboliking[4] Nabinde—a story. Neni—a story. Koloi—a story. Nabeni—a story for you all.

A child was once born. When she was born, everyone came.[5] She was a fine girl. She became full grown—full. She was light skinned.[6] They

[1] The man's name is introduced here for the first time. The general plot is so well known that there is no confusion.

[2] Or brother-in-law.

[3] Interpolated by the listeners.

[4] A funny name of special friendship for Nabinde.

[5] To woo her.

[6] Lit. red.

told her she was to be married. Her mother said that she was not one to be married. 'What? What reason is there for her not to be married?' 'The man who will marry her—the one you will meet tomorrow with a heavy mouth,[1] who does not greet me all the time, I will not agree to that. Before she will be married, if he gives bridewealth or (?) if he does not give bridewealth (?), I must first hear how (?) he acts.'

The *kolokolo* bird came. He failed. The rice bird came. He failed. The bush cow came. He failed. The bush buck came. He failed. The porcupine came. He failed. Ha, every animal came, and failed. The goats joined together. They failed. Every animal—the monkeys in the bush, they failed to marry her, to find a chance to marry the girl. They failed in that.

Then the mother said, 'Huh! You came in vain. The one for me to pick out tomorrow saying, "This is the one will marry my daughter"—you were not able for my demand.[2] No, you will not marry her.' 'E! Even when we have gathered together? Try us now.'

She said, 'What I say is that it is the one who spends the day greeting me; when he reaches the side of the bush, for a whole day he is to spend the time greeting me, all day. Because I do not want bridewealth if I spend all day being greeted. You meet some sons-in-law, when you approach them, they will not greet you. For that tomorrow I will give judgement. For a son-in-law who does not greet you, how will he give you something?[3] For me now, I must have someone who can greet me all the time.'

Every animal came. They failed. The monitor lizard came. 'For me, for me, I love you.[4] I love the woman.' Her name was called Sira. Her name was Sira. He, the lizard, he came. [They greeted] 'Yes.' 'Yes. I have come, to spend the day greeting by the side of the bush'—he the lizard—'The time we are to meet, on Sunday when we are to meet, that is when we will meet. Just when the sun has reached the middle here,[5] we will meet. Then you will hear.' (The way I sing,[6] you are to reply to me. That is the word for you, Maheni, whatever way I sing, so you reply, so you reply.)

He came to the edge of the bush. He stood. The mother-in-law did not know it.[7] But she heard the day that was said. Then she came, she stood by the edge of the bush. He sang,[8] '*Eye*, mother-in-law, greetings.'

[1] i.e. slow in speaking and greeting.

[2] sc. to greet her all the time.

[3] i.e. if he does not even greet her, how can he be expected to give her gifts?

[4] 'You' plural. As often, the suitor is professing his respect for the whole family not just for the girl herself.

[5] The speaker points to the place in the sky to indicate the time.

[6] The teller asks his friend to be sure to 'reply' to the song he is going to begin.

[7] i.e. if he would be capable of the task.

[8] The phrases were sung in turn by the narrator and the chorus of listeners, repeated eight or ten times in all.

'*Eye*, lizard, welcome.' '*Eye*, mother-in-law, greetings.' '*Eye*, lizard, welcome.' '*Eye*, mother-in-law, greetings.' '*Eye*, lizard, welcome.' '*Eye*, mother-in-law, greetings.' '*Eye*, lizard, welcome.' 'For the whole day the *kuwolo* tree—no one passed.'[1] '*Eye*, lizard, welcome.' '*E*, mother-in-law, greetings. . . .'

So he did there for long—*wrrr!* He did that for the whole day, until the sun went.

When the sun was set, he came. He said, 'Yes, I have come for the wife.' Then she said, 'I—what you have done for me, I know now that he will not fail. For he spent the whole day greeting me, all all day, all night, you went and greeted me. You did not fail in the task. If I meet you tomorrow, even if you have nothing, you will be able to greet me. For you came and spent the day greeting me . . . since the morning (?), and when the sun set, darkness came, you were there greeting me. I know that tomorrow he will not fail me. If you are not able to get anything, but if you greet me all the time, if a son-in-law greets you, he is good. Since you did that, I thank you. I—' she called the girl, 'Sira!' 'Yes?' 'Do you see him, did this man not come for you?' 'Yes.' 'When you go, if he sends you for anything, perhaps he says "Go there for me" perhaps "Wash for me"—whatever he says, . . .[2] if it is one of his people, do that. So that they may make the marriage, so that they may not be judged tomorrow in the council.[3] This is what I respect—that he did not fail in what I told him.'[4]

That is it—since Yenkeni said she wanted to hear a story, and I spoke it, so I had to tell it. That is it. It is finished.

Marriage and a bush cow's milk

FANKA KONTEH. *Recorded* 6.1.64

This story had recently been told by the new chief, Alimami Seku II, just after a wife had been brought to him; the purpose was, I was told, to warn wives how to be obedient to their husbands. The story particularly pleased those who heard it, and I heard it repeated several times, in various versions, over the next few weeks. In the present version there was little stress on the moral of the story, as the actual narrative was of more interest to this particular narrator.

[1] Part of the song—it seems to have no real sense here.

[2] I have omitted a few words I could not catch.

[3] The usual way of referring to the new official Chiefdom Court.

[4] i.e. it was his *greeting* that impressed her enough for her to give him Sira as wife.

A CHIEF once married a wife. The wife—she changed so that she would not listen to the chief's words. It was the chief that had married the wife. The wife would not listen to the chief's words. The chief said, 'I will turn my back on her for she will not obey me in anything, she will not obey me when I tell her to do something. Well, I will turn from her.'

For long—much time passed. Well, she no longer saw his heart (?) loving her. Well, she saw that now. She went to a moriman. 'Moriman.' 'Yes?' 'Ha! I—the chief married me long ago, but he does not love me now. He does not include me in anything now—only those who came last, after me, to live with him, he includes them! That is the reason, I ask you to write *manasi* for me, I beg you, so that the chief may love me again.' Then the moriman said, 'I am to write *manasi* for you, am I?' 'Yes.' 'All right. You are to look for the milk of a bush cow.'[1] 'What! the dangerous bush cows? I will not be able to get their milk!' 'If you can get it, you, you will speak lovingly with the chief again.'

She went, trying to go to find the milk of a bush cow. She followed them for seven days. On the eighth she was able to get the milk of a bush cow. She struggled for long, stroking the bush cow. The bush cow lay down. It slept. She went on stroking the bush cow's calf, she went on stroking the calf, she milked the milk little by little by little by little. After a long time she filled her gourd. Just as the gourd was filled, the bush cow got up, running *diki diki*. She too, she got up. The bush cow ran off.

She went back to the village. She came to the moriman. 'Moriman.' 'Yes?' 'I got the milk of a bush cow, that is it.' The moriman said, 'Oh? You got the milk?' 'Yes.' 'All right. That is good. Well, put it down. Well, go. I will write the *manasi*. But, well now, as you acted to get the milk of a bush cow, thus you must go and always act to the chief. Thus you must act, you must go again to struggle.'

When she arrived, she went into the chief's room. She went and found him. She went and found the chief's clothes, his dirty ones—his gowns and all, she took them. She went and washed them quietly. She came and spread them out [to dry]. She finished, they were dry. She came and ironed them. She went and put them back. In the morning she got up, she heated water for the chief.[2] She went and told him. The chief came and bathed. She swept—she did everything for the chief. During a long time, whenever the chief called her for something, even if he then did not say a word to her she did not complain, she went. The chief said, 'All right. Come.' For a long time, he acted like that. She struggled for the chief, she returned to being obedient.

[1] When people go to a moriman (Muslim expert) or a diviner to ask for a charm they are commonly told to come back with some necessary ingredient. Here the wife is asked for the near-impossible milk of the fearsome bush cow.

[2] Only very honoured people have water heated for them to bathe. Ironing clothes is also something rather special.

Well, after long, the chief's heart came and turned to her. Whatever the chief did now, he called her. She saw that 'Yes!', the chief's heart had turned to her.

She went to the moriman. 'Moriman' 'Yes?' 'Ha! The chief—his heart has turned to me oh!' 'It has?' 'Yes.' 'Well, all right. That is good. Even if you had not had *manasi* written, it would not have mattered since you acted as you always do [now]—that is good.' She went.

'Even if you had not had *manasi* written', the moriman said, 'well, since you struggled to get the milk of a bush cow, if you act now to your husband as you acted then, you will win his heart. But if whenever he tells you anything, you refuse, you will not win his heart. But since your heart has returned to please him, the chief too is pleased with you.'

You see—the chief came to take her again; as he had treated her first in his chiefship, so he treated her again. As the senior wife she went first again among the people. That is it, I Fanka.

Sara and the greedy chief

KELFA KONTEH. *Dictated* 2.1.61

Stories about trickery and success are always enjoyed. The narrator of this one was particularly applauded because of the vividness of his many onomatopœic words and phrases and his exaggerated representation of the anger and surprise of the cheated chief.

SARA and the chief who wanted everything. One day a chief lived in his country. He had very many children. The oldest son, he was called Sara. This Sara was known for his cunning.[1]

One day this chief came out, he died. His property was divided among his children. Sara said that he did not want anything, only a cow. Sara was given the cow. The children who were left were given the possessions that were left.

It happened then that all the chiefs in the country, they came to the mourning for Sara's father. When they were sitting there, one chief saw —the cow that they had given Sara, it was excreting gold! It went *puri puri puri puri!*[2] The chief asked who was the owner of that cow. It was said that it was Sara. He sent for Sara to be fetched. Sara came. The chief asked him if he owned the cow. Sara said 'Yes.' The chief said, 'I will give you my possessions, and divide my country in half and give it to you.' Sara agreed. The chief took away the cow. When the cow

[1] *hugbanaŋ*—trickery, cunning, rascality, wickedness.

[2] The sound and flash made by the gold as it fell.

excreted—it was cow dung! The chief said, 'Hey! hey! Sara has tricked me! The cow does not excrete gold!'

This angered him. He said, 'I will go to kill Sara.' He got ready his warriors. As soon as Sara saw them, he thought—*tɛ!*—a plan. He filled a bladder with blood. He hung it on his mother, on her neck. When the warriors and the chief came Sara said, 'Wait a little now.' He called his mother. He killed her—*fa ka ha!* the bladder was burst! The blood came out splashing—*pɔrɔbɔsi!*[1] from her neck. The people said, 'Hey! hey! He has killed his mother!' Sara said, 'Wait for me a little. I will waken her.' He dipped a broom in water. He hit her with it—*pɛŋ!* His mother woke—quite, quite well.[2] The chief said, 'I will not kill you now. If you show me the medicine to kill someone and cure him, I will give you many possessions and give you many horses.' Sara agreed. He gave him the broom and taught him—all nonsense! The chief gave him those things. He went.

When he [chief] went, he met his mother. He killed her. He killed his father. He killed the sub-chiefs in his country. He was left now with only a few people. When he said that he would waken them, when he hit them with the broom—the flies went *oooo!*[3] He said, 'Hey! hey! Sara has deceived me. Now I will go and kill him.'

When he went, he found Sara. He tied him tightly—*thebiŋ thebiŋ*—he put him in a basket. He carried him on his head.

When they had gone a little way, the chief said that he was going to the bush. Sara was put down near the road. It was not long, a Fula[4] came. He said, 'Sara, what is this that you are bound for today?' Sara said, 'Alas! I am to be taken up to the chiefship. But I refused, that is why they bound me, taking me up to be chief by force.' The Fula said, 'Well, bind me. You take the things—the head-dress, shoes, Fula gown, and the staff.'[5] The Fula was bound, tightly—*thebiŋ!* Sara took these things. He went off.

When the chief came now with his followers, they took up the Fula. The Fula began to talk, '*e fɔthɔ yai e dorotho fɔthɔ yai. . . .*'[6] The chief

[1] The splash of the blood.

[2] *Keŋkeŋreŋtheŋ*—intentionally exaggerated and funny word to express her complete recovery, and the others' surprise.

[3] A common way to describe death in the stories—the flies buzzing over the dead body.

[4] The Fulas commonly travel through Limba country with their herds of cattle and wearing their own form of clothing. They are often represented as a kind of travelling gipsies in the stories.

[5] All marks of chiefship. The giving of a special head-dress (*nɛmu*) is in some chiefdoms, specially those in the west which are more influenced by Islam, a necessary part of the investiture of a chief. A long gown, shoes, and a staff are also thought typical possessions of a chief.

[6] An imitation of the sound of Fula. I could not catch all the sounds, but they

said, 'Not even if you speak Fula today—today we kill you!' The Fula was put into the pool—*pɔkɔɔŋ!*

Not long after Sara came to the chief. He said, 'E! chief! The place where you threw me—it is a good place. My father is there, my mother is there, behold my brother is there. See these possessions—everyone there has these in peace and happiness.' The chief said, 'Bind me. Let us go to where Sara has come from.' The chief was bound. He was put into the pool—*pɔkɔɔŋ!* His followers said, 'We will go where our father went.' They all went. They threw themselves into the pool.

Sara said, 'All the ones who hated me, they have all died. Bring me the drum.[1] Beat it.' They beat it—*gbiŋ gbiŋ!* Sara was raised to become chief.

Koma tricks his brother-in-law, Sara

KARANKE DEMA. *Dictated* 15.10.61

A story of cunning with some points of resemblance to *Sara and the greedy chief*. The tasks set a suitor occur in many other stories; here they consist of familiar operations but ones known to take a long time. The story ends with Koma winning the chiefship, and an explicit moral.

SARA once wooed a wife, Sira. Sira had a younger brother, his name was Koma.

Sara wooed her for long, till she was full grown. He said she should be given to him. When the time was fixed, and it came near, then Koma said, 'We will go where you are going, to the marriage. But before we go, Sara is to find a [cotton] seed, and plant it, and let it grow and get big and bear and laugh[2] and be teased and wound and carded and spun and laid out and woven and sewn; and that cloth is what you will wear when you go.' He was meaning Sira. When he said that, Sara said, 'All right.' He worked at that. Kanu helped him. The cloth was brought.

Then Koma spoke again. 'I have got the cloth. But for Sira to go, Sara is to take millet and go and hoe it so it may grow big and get seeds and be dry and be cut and thrashed and heated and pounded and cooked; that is what Sira will eat when she goes to marry you.' Sara said, 'All right.' He did it. When Sara came he said, 'I, I want my wife.'

Then Koma said again, 'If you love your wife, go and get *sasi*,[3] go and

are in any case meant to be unintelligible. They also amusingly suggested to the audience the clipped speech of the Fulas.

[1] The chief's drum, sign of authority.

[2] The seeds split open.

[3] A kind of plum.

plant it, let it grow and become big and bear; when it is ripe, that is what Sira will eat as she goes to marry you.' Sara said, 'All right.' He went and looked for it. He brought it. When Sira had eaten it, she was taken to the marriage.

Then Sara said, 'This child [Koma] has been acting proudly to me. I will go and throw him in the river.' He took a mat, he tied him in it, he carried it on his head. He went and put it down at the side of the water, at a big pool. As he returned to his house, there Koma was lying on the bank of the river. A Kebu Fula man stood up and said, 'Who is over there?' (?) When he came close, he found Koma lying there. He asked, 'You, why did you lie down here?' Then Koma said, 'I am going to be made chief. If you want to, all right, I will let *you* go and be made chief.' The Kebu put down the sticks[1] he was holding. 'Well, unloose me.' He was unloosed. 'Lie down here.' He lay down there. Koma tied him. He took the sticks, he went off to Freetown.

When Sara came, he came and took the bundle. He thought it was Koma. He threw it into the river. He went home.

Koma—where he went to, he became well off. When he came [back], he went to his sister, to Sira. He came in and entered the house. He was asked, 'What is your name?' He said, 'I am Amadu.' If you were to see him now—he is dressed beautifully.

After two nights had passed, Sara set off to go to the river, to go and pound rice-flour as an offering to Koma.[2] For he thought, 'it was Koma that I threw into the river then'. It was not Koma! When he had set out to offer the rice-flour, he Sara, he crouched down[3] there. They went and fetched Koma—but they did not know it was Koma. When Sara crouched down he began, '*Ka harika wo lɔŋthaŋ*; you Koma. . . .' Then Koma spoke from where he was crouching, saying, 'You, Sara.'[4] Then Sara said, 'Oh? stranger, what is it?' Then he said, 'No, nothing.' He began again to make the offering '*Ka harika wo lɔŋthaŋ*, you Koma. . . .' Then he said from where he was crouching, 'You Sara.' Sara said 'What! Stranger, why have you got up?' Then Koma got up from where he was crouching. He said, 'Sara. Here I am. You thought you had killed me. But I went and got chiefship. Here now I am.'

Sara said, 'I will go too to find chiefship.' Behold Koma had not been thrown into the river! Sara said, 'Let them tie me.' He was tied. He was thrown into the water. He died.

After a few nights had passed, the month came to an end. The chief came and heard about it. 'I too will go and have my chiefship increased.'

[1] The sticks sold for cleaning teeth—valuable merchandise.

[2] As one of the dead.

[3] As is usual for praying.

[4] The amusing point of the episode is the way in which the man being prayed to as if dead was actually present and answered the prayer.

Koma said, 'All right.' When he had been bound, he was thrown in. He died. Four nights passed. The sub-chief stood up. 'I will go where the chief went, to follow where the chief went.' He was tied, he was thrown into the river. Behold, Koma was working to have the chiefdom left to him. When they had finished doing all that, Koma was left with all the wives, he was left with the village.

So if you hear of a child in a village, don't molest him; for long ago Koma got the chiefship by his cleverness. Since I heard that story, Yenkeni, I had to tell it to you.

The jealous husband and the chief's son

BANKOLO MANSARAY. *Dictated* 13.11.61

The story of a clever man who turns to account his wife's infidelity (expressed, as often, in terms of food), revenges himself on her lover and, as well as going free himself, tricks others into becoming his workers to protect themselves, as they think, from the vengeance of the chief; finally the chief himself is the one held responsible for his son's death.

The plot is a common one and I heard several stories based on it; the details and emphasis varied in each version; in one, for example, the stress throughout was on the tragedy of the chief's wife—she had borne a child after many years of waiting, then comes his death, and the tale closes with her weeping over the boy. The tone is very different from the version given here where attention is concentrated on the clever and amusing tricks of the husband. Another version is also contained in the following tale, *A clever husband.*

A STORY. A man once married a wife. She made love with the chief's son. Now he [husband] was a hunter. Whenever he killed, the meat, the good food—she would cook rice and put the meat there. She took it off to the chief's son. As for the husband, it was the bones she gave him in the evening. *Always* she did this.

One day now he went and killed a crocodile. He came and skinned it. He took out the gall. He went and opened the box.[1] He found the rice for the chief's son. He put in the gall—all of it.

The boy came. She took out the rice. She gave it to the boy. The boy ate. The boy died. The wife cried, 'Oh! I have killed the chief's son. The rice he ate, rice of mine, that was what killed him.' She went and cried to her husband. Her husband said, 'Go for your father. Go for

[1] Women often have their own private boxes. She hides the rice for her lover in her box.

your mother. Go for your brothers, all of them. Let them come and live with me, let them stay to clear the farm.' The girl went for them all. They came and lived there.

He put the corpse on his back. He went out to go, at night. He saw people who were getting honey, there, far off.[1] 'E, greetings to you! Give me some honey.' They replied, 'Die there where you are standing before I will give you honey!' He dropped the corpse there. He climbed up a tree. They came there with fire, those who were getting honey. 'Oh! It was the chief's son that we told today to die! We are in trouble. We will soon all be killed, all of us.'

Now that chief had made a law; if you go and knock at his house—*gbɔ gbɔ*—he will shoot you.

When the hunter heard that from up above, he came down. 'Greetings to you.' 'Yes, greetings. Ah! we have come into trouble. Behold, it was the chief's son that was greeting us. We said "Die!" And he died!' Then the man said—the hunter— 'If I save you, you are to give me your people, your brothers, for them to clear a farm for me.' It was the one who had married the girl oh! They went for their people—one hundred. 'Well, here they are.' 'All right. Ha! It is the house that is on top of the hill, go there for me now and stay there, and go and wait for me.' They went.

He put the corpse on his back again. He went. He reached the chief's hut. He knocked on the door. He took and stood to one side. He put down the corpse at the door. There was a little hole—so big—in the door. He knocked again. The chief took his single barrel,[2] his gun—*kaaaɔɔɔɔ*, he shot it!

He [hunter] went off to his own house. He went and found two hundred people there. And now, if he says they have to clear the farm all day, and if the one who was getting honey wants to refuse, he says, 'I saved you from slavery.' If his wife now wants to refuse to work, he says, 'I saved you from slavery.' They have no choice—but to work and finish it all.

A clever husband

SURI DEMA. *Recorded* 4.2.64

Another version of the same basic plot. Although the framework is the same and the episode about the honey and the chief's door almost identical, there are several differences; the earlier episodes differ considerably; in

[1] The great distance indicated by a raised tone.
[2] The English term is used.

this version the man is represented as farming with his wife rather than hunting and the way in which he kills his wife's lover is different; there is also the additional episode about the fish trap, and the paradoxical touch at the end about how it was the murderer himself who was sent for to act as the mourner for the one he had killed.

A STORY for you. Well, you see—a man once got up, saying, 'I will work.' The woman [his wife] said, 'All right.' They began to do the work. They cleared, they set it on fire—the farm did not burn. The man said 'It is good—to go out into the cane grass.'[1] Well, the woman said, 'No. Let us not go into the cane grass, let us try a little bit here.' Behold the woman had a lover. 'Well, it is good—you, you will reburn the sticks in the day time; I, I will reburn them at night.'

Now behold, the woman and her lover, they had come and loved each other. Then the man [husband] went and spent the whole day till sunset; he left. The woman came. When she had come, well, her lover came to reburn. While he was reburning she brought him food; he ate. Always now, when the man, the husband came, in the morning, he was delighted. 'E! my wife is able to reburn! She is better than I am.' Behold it was a lie! It was her lover who came to reburn at night.

Well, the husband sat like that, thinking, *sooŋ!* 'Yes, tomorrow, tomorrow, because of what is puzzling me, I will go to the finch, I will go and have it divined for me.'

'Finch oh! I have come to have divination made.' '*Se se seŋ.*'[2] He [the finch] looked at what he divined with. 'The good, the bad—which do you want?' He said, 'The good.' 'The good?' 'Yes.' 'You know the good one—(?). When she has gone to reburn at night, go out in the evening at dusk, well, go and cut a forked stick.'

The man went out. He went out to reburn with his wife. Well, the man who had married the woman, he cut a forked stick. When he found the lover reburning, he took the stick, he pushed him into the fire, he shoved him into the burning sticks.

While that happened, the girl was spending long making the food. She did not know that her lover had been thrown into the fire. When he had been thrown into the fire, she was cooking the rice. She brought it. When she came and looked now—no one there. She came and looked now—no one there. Now she saw the man lying in the fire. Now she cried out there, she cried, 'Hey! hey! see him. I have come into trouble, I have come into trouble. Hey! hey! Sara the son of the chief, his own son, it is he I have come and burnt here. E Kanu! I have come into trouble.'

The man came out, her husband. He asked, 'What is it?' '*Ala!* my

[1] Farms made in the grassy areas burn more readily.

[2] The finch's answer as he divines.

father, I was sleeping among the crops (?), I was afraid to tell you, I have had a lover for long, it was he who always came here to reburn at night. After he had reburned at night, when you came in the morning you thought it was I who had reburned. Behold it was my lover; but here he is (?), he was burnt in the fire.' Then the man said, 'Was that why you were crying? Is that what you are crying about?' 'Yes.' 'Stop crying now.' She stopped crying.

Well, some boys had laid down fish traps. [They had said] 'Whoever approaches them let him be bitten by the *baŋkiboro*[1] snake and let him die.' The man said, 'All right.' He went and put the man there, the dead man, near the trap. He took him, he went and put him down at the trap, he went and put him there. When he had put the dead man down there, he pulled at the trap. He put him down there. When the boy arrived he saw the man lying there. He cried out there 'Hey! hey! Our father, hey! hey! our father[2] has come into trouble. For he came to where I had made a trap; in the fish trap I put down I said that whoever came and looked at it was to be bitten by a *baŋkiboro* snake. It is the chief's son who has suffered it. He has died, utterly.'

'What? Well—' The man had come out. 'What is it? What is it?' '*Ala!* He came to where I had made a trap here, [I said] that whoever came to the trap, an animal was to bite him.' 'Well, if I save you, will you agree?' 'Yes.'

He took the [dead] man, he put him on his head, he carried him. He went for far. Well, he came, he came to people gathering honey. That honey—he shouted out there, 'You, greetings. Greetings.' 'Yes. Who is it?' 'Me. E! please, give me some honey. I have a longing for honey. Please, give me some.' Then they said, 'Ha! if it is for the honey, the good honey—die there, oh, die, if it is for the honey!' He lifted off the dead man; he lifted off the dead man; he went, he hid on one side. When he had hidden on one side, they came back from gathering honey. 'E! Hey! hey! Hey! hey! Our father has come into disaster. Hey! hey! our father has come into disaster. Sara the son of the chief, behold, he begged us for honey today, he came out here, he died! E! our father has come into disaster. What will he do then?'

Then the man came out. 'What is it?' 'My father, he has brought us into disaster. He shouted out here, "Give me honey." What we said was, "Die there, oh, die!" Here he is lying here now, he is dead.' 'What?' 'Yes.' 'If I save you, will you agree?' 'We will agree.' 'Well, but you must stop crying.' They stopped crying.

The man got up now, the one who had killed the man. He put him on his back. He took the dead man, right off, far away to the chief here.

[1] They have laid a curse, or 'swear', on the trap so that if anyone interferes with it he will be bitten by a snake and die.

[2] The chief, their 'father', has lost his son.

So—now the chief's door was not to be knocked on. He had said that whoever knocked on the door, well, he would shoot him. Well, at that time, whoever came to knock on the chief's door at night he would shoot. Then he [the husband] said, 'All right. This chief will stop doing that.' He took the dead man. He came. He found the door shut. He took the dead man. He put him down, propped up against the chief's door. Well, he stuck him like this to one side of the door. He held the dead man's arm. Well, the man who had died—he made him knock, *kɔŋ kɔŋ kɔŋ kɔŋ kɔŋ, kɔŋ kɔŋ kɔŋ kɔŋ kɔŋ*.[1] The chief did not stop to ask about it oh! He took his gun with cartridges, he fired—*boo!* he shot the boy. When he had shot, behold, before the bullet reached him, he let him go; the boy fell—*piri!* He opened the door.

Behold the mother now who had borne the child who had died cried out 'E! This has come to trouble, this has come to trouble. [It is] because the chief would not have his door opened, because the chief would not have his door opened at night. If you are known to own the country—if you had been gentle about it oh, if you had been gentle about it oh, you would not have killed your child.'

There she mourned for long. Well, the one who had found the boy, the man, he came back. He came and asked, 'What is it?' '*Ala!* My child has died here.' 'Oh?'[2]

The man who had put him into the fire was the one fetched to mourn for him, to mourn him! When he came, he came and mourned him. The ones he had saved—they gave him presents, goats, cattle, giving him presents.

Well, since I have come this evening saying I would bring Yenkeni a story, but only a short one, well, since I have told it, that is it; it is finished, I have told it. The story is ended.

A cruel chief

BOKARI SAIO. *Dictated* 20.10.61

The story of a chief who, because he refuses to take advice and acts with extreme harshness, loses his chiefdom to the boy Kukune. The impossible tasks he sets his wife—to plait hair on a shaved head or grow and prepare rice in a single day—are surpassed by the tasks set in return by the child Kukune—to carve a comb from solid iron or make nails bear fruit.

[1] The standard sound to represent a knock.

[2] He is depicted as pretending to be innocent and surprised.

A CHIEF once came out who was very harsh. He said that where he wooed a wife, she was not to have love made to her by any man. If anyone made love to her, he would kill her [? him]. The father-in-law heard that, and her mother.

Their daughter was Sirande. She came and had a lover. When they looked at the girl, they saw she was pregnant. Then her father said, 'E! You have brought us into trouble. The chief will not see his wife made love to.' Then her father said, 'Her mother—well, you are to take your daughter to her marriage.' Then her mother wept much. She said, 'All right, it is fair. For I bore the girl. Since the girl has come and put her hand on us,[1] as for me, however, it turns out, I will go.'

When she set out with her child, as they came halfway on the road, her belly began to hurt the girl. Her mother said, 'E Kanu! We have run into trouble on the road. The girl has borne a child!' When she had borne the child on the road, then the child sneezed, *thisio kukunɛ!* Then he said, 'Mother, all right; leave me in the yams' hole.' 'All right.' 'Take my mother to the marriage.'

As they went on, escorting themselves,[2] they came to a very big river. He, the child that had been born, behold he had gone first in front, he passed his mother, he went to the river. He said—his mother wept again; when they came near to the big, big river, then the child said *thisio kukunɛ!* All the river dried up—completely. His mother went across. When the child went off, he went and sat close to the chief's court, behind.

Then the chief sent his wives. 'Go for water, then come and cook with your companion.'[3] They took the things. When they went to the water, they found it dried up. They returned. 'The water is dried up!' The chief said, 'E! It is because you are at peace, that is why you do not want to see someone else.'[4] Then he took his whip, he chased after them.

He sent his messengers. 'Go for water.' When they went too, 'There is no water oh!' The chief said 'What! No water?'

The senior wife stood up. 'Because you [other wives] are full fed, that is the reason! That is why it is! Get out from here!' Then the chief said, 'Ah! The senior wife—go for the water.' The senior wife went too. She came too. 'There is no water there.' Then the chief said, 'It is because I am training[5] you, that is why!'

He, the chief, took his horse. He went to the water. The finch came

[1] i.e. brought us into trouble.

[2] They have to 'escort themselves'; usually a new wife has relations to 'escort' her to the marriage.

[3] To cook the food of welcome for the new wife and her mother.

[4] He suspects his wives of not wanting a new co-wife in the house.

[5] An abusive word, normally used of training and caring for an animal.

too. The water was dried up. He said, 'E Kanu! What made this big big river to dry up?' Then the finch came out there. 'Chief, it is because you are harsh. Send someone now to the back of your house. Whatever you find at the back of your house, bring it and lead it here.'

When they found the child, he was led outside here. When he was brought, then the finch said, 'Make a sacrifice for him, the one standing there.' He went in. He took out a gown, he took out trousers. Water was fetched, the child came and was bathed. When he had been bathed, the child said '*Thisio kukunɛ!* Well, go for water.' Before they had reached there, the water filled up there. There was no longer a place for someone to cross. Then the chief said, 'E Kanu! Thank you. Go to cook food for my mother-in-law.'

When they had finished cooking for them, when they had eaten, she went to announce their purpose[1] to the chief. 'But the girl has brought us shame. That is it. Father, here is the woman.' At the first light, the mother ran away.

Then the chief said, 'You, you have been brought as my wife, you will not spend the day here. You are to go to the farm.' He went on in front. Kukune followed behind. When he reached the farm, the chief took her child. He shaved his head. 'Go to Sirande. She is to plait your hair!'

When the child arrived there was no hair on his head. He said, 'Sirande, you are greeted by our father. He says you are to plait my hair.' Sirande wept. Kukune stood up there. There he spoke *thisio kukunɛ!* He took out there a piece of iron. 'Take this to the chief. This is it—the hair would have been plaited today, but there is no comb. That is the reason—the chief is to cut a comb[2] and come, so that the child can come and be plaited.'

When the chief came out for sacrifices, he came to split the iron for the comb. Every knife he cut it with—it broke! Then the chief said, 'All right.'

He took a little rice in the morning. 'Take it to Sirande. She is to go and hoe today and it is to become dry and she is to harvest it and thrash it and dry it as cleaned rice, and bring it here to the village in the evening. Say that he is putting rice-flour for his people.'[3]

Then Kukune came again. *Thisio kukunɛ!* He took out nails from his pocket. 'Take them to the chief. He is to go and plant them in the sacrifices. When it grows and it spreads and it bears fruit, he is to pick it and take it to the water; when he has put it in the water, he is to bring a gourd. There Sirande will put the rice-flour.'

When he had spent the day turning over the nails, they had not

[1] i.e. to announce formally that the girl has been brought as his wife.

[2] Native combs are usually made of wood, not iron.

[3] In sacrifice to his ancestors.

grown! He said, 'E Kanu! All right. Who is the one who owns this way of acting?' 'It is Kukune.'

Then he called out [the men of] a village to bring thatch to his village. He went for very many hunters. When he had lined up the hunters, there was a hunter who was a warrior, a great, great warrior. They went and tied the thatch, they put the hunter inside in the thatch. 'This is why, this is the word—let no one take this bundle! It is Kukune that is to come and take this one.' When Kukune came he [Kukune] said, 'No one will carry a load and not know what is inside.' He had a very long iron, he stuck it into the thatch. The hunter died inside. He carried the thatch. The chief cast his eyes there. That was blood there in the thatch! Then the chief asked again, he the chief, 'Why is blood dripping from the thatch?' Then Kukune said, 'I thought that people were bringing thatch today.'

He the chief stood up. He said to his messengers, 'Tie Kukune.' They tied him, tightly—*deŋ!* Then he said, 'Take him to the water.' When they came and started, he said, 'There is a deer[1] lying over there.' They cut off its head. They went to cut up the animal. Then the chief's son came. He was having instruments[2] played for him. Then he asked, 'Why are you lying here?' Then he asked the chief's son, 'Where have you come from?' 'I have come from Faransi.[3] I have gained power.' Then Kukune said, 'Huh! I will get that power.' He said, 'I am being carried where our father got chiefship.' Then the chief's son said, 'Untie him. Will a small one get power, and I the older one be left behind? Well, tie me now, me the older one.' He untied Kukune. The chief's son was tied tightly—*deŋ!* When they came from there with the meat, they put it down. They lifted the chief's son, they went and put him in the water. They carried back the meat for themselves.

When they saw Kukune riding up high on a horse, when he was in the distance by the side of the village, the chief said, 'Ah! Alas! It is he whom I see? I am unable for the chiefship. Tie me up!' The chief was taken. He was tied. The chief was carried to the water. When he was carried to the water, he was thrown into the water, with his son. They were lost there, disappeared—*yeŋ!* Kukune, he was left with the chiefdom.

Well, that is it. If you see a chief who will not be told 'Cease',[4] see, that is what made him unable for the chiefdom. He would not be told to cease about his wife. If you see something now in the country and are

[1] A deer would have much meat, worth stopping for.

[2] 'Balanjis' (a form of xylophone), associated with Koranko and Mandingo chiefs, not, usually, Limba ones.

[3] i.e. 'France' = Guinea, a place specially associated with chiefship and power.

[4] The chief had been given advice—something as valuable as good medicine—to cease from his anger and cruelty to his wife but he had refused it.

told to cease, he has given you medicine. For he was unable for power, for he did not agree to be made to cease. They were lost, he and his son, all of them.

Parents are closest

BUBU DEMA. *Dictated* 22.10.61

Parents always support you even if you do not help them as you ought, whereas others, even those in your debt, turn against you when difficulty comes. Some say that kinship does not matter, but as shown in this tale it was only the parents that came to their son's help.

Not closely similar in plot to any of the other tales, though a few of the motifs are familiar, e.g. the search for someone wise, the travelling round, and the comparison of people and places in the story to real ones known to the teller and listeners.

Some of the characterization came across effectively—specially that of the kindly father and the greedy and selfish people who were only interested in their own share of the meat.

A STORY for you. Someone once bore a child. When he had borne the child, he [child] came out as a hunter. He refused to kill now for his father. He got up, he went, like to Kawoya.[1] There he killed animals. There he killed. He killed there for long. He got up from there, he went to Kamamu. He went there and hunted for long. His father now was like at Kakarima here with the mother. He got up like from Kamamu, he went across to Yalunka country, killing animals! For long—ten years. He got up, he came to Kabala, killing bush cows, killing deer. He did not come visiting here to his father here. He was just travelling round! He was long there, Kabala—two years; killing animals! When he had done that for the two years, he was killing for people. His mother did not know about it.[2] When he got up from there too, he came to Konkoba. For long he killed there too, at Konkoba. Now his mother, who bore him, like at Kakarima here, well she was hearing that he was just killing! He spent again over two years.

Well, where he was there behind them, he said, 'It is hard, it is easy—but let me go back to where I came from, to my parents.'

[1] Kawoya (Bafodea), Kamamu (a Fula town), Yalunka (country of Yalunka people), Kabala, Konkoba: all places between ten and fifty miles from Kakarima, the village of the story-teller.

[2] A hunter should give away some of the meat he kills, particularly to his parents; he should also keep them informed of his actions and not go around in secret 'behind them'.

He came to Kasafroko.[1] He killed a bush cow there. They ate. He killed a deer. They ate. He killed a wild pig. Ha! for killing animals, you will not be able to count how many he killed! Well, what came now to happen? When he had shot the bush cow, then he got up at the edge of the village there at Kasafroko. When he entered the village with his hunter's dance,[2] it pleased them. They went and cut up the animal. They did not say that it was a bad thing. It pleased them, ha! very much. When the sun rose, he killed another deer. They ate.

When one day had passed and one night, then he got up again, he was going to shoot a bush cow. As he reached there, at Kasafroko, at the edge of the village, he shouted, 'I have come into trouble. I have brought someone into trouble. I have killed someone.'[3] He gave his name. At that those who had always been eating his meat said, 'Go and look for your own people. One will not be able to help that case—for you went and killed a man.' He said, 'It is all right.'

Then he got up, he came here to Kakarima. His father now, he resembled Sabena[4] here. When he went to the chief saying, 'I have come into trouble. I have brought someone into trouble', he said 'What?' 'I have shot someone.' The chief said, 'What! Go to your father. For you to have property—a man will not bypass the parents.' He said, 'It is all right.'

He came here to Kanda here. He came and wept much. 'I have come into trouble.' Kanda said, 'What?' 'I have killed a man.' 'You have killed a man? Ha! We want to save you;' he said, 'It is all right. Go to your father.'

When he got up from there too, he came here to Magba here. He came here too and wept much, and wept. Magba said, 'What is it?' 'I have brought someone into trouble.' 'Hey! hey! child! Even if a man has got a token gift [to open the negotiations]—your father is here.'

When he got up again, he came here to Bubu here. He came again and wept much. I said, 'What?' 'I have brought someone into trouble.' 'Quite dead?' 'Yes.' 'I am not able for that case. Your father is here. We own you, all of us, but you have a father.'

Then he got up, he set out. He went and wept much to his father, to Sabena. He was asked, 'What?' 'I have brought someone into trouble.' 'What? Where did you bring someone into trouble?' 'At Kasafroko. I got up from here, I went to Kamamu. I got up from Kamamu I went to Kawoya, killing animals! When I got up from there, I went to Kabala. I went there again killing for long, for long. For two months I was there.

[1] A small village a couple of miles from Kakarima.

[2] *Madonsia*—performed only when big game is killed; killing a bush cow is considered a specially fine feat.

[3] Hunting accidents are not infrequent.

[4] Sabena, Kanda, Magba, Bubu (the teller): all leading elders in Kakarima.

I will not be able to count how many animals I killed. When I came again to Konkoba—the bush cows, I will not be able to count them. Well, then I left Konkoba, coming to Kasafroko. When I came and entered there, I killed a bush cow. I killed a wild pig. They ate them then. I killed a deer. They ate. I killed a bush cow. They ate. I killed another deer. They ate. You know what a great hunter is like, don't you? You will not count in the small animals. When I had killed another bush cow again, they came and cut it up. They ate. When several nights had passed, several nights passed again, I killed a bush cow again. Then I wept much at the edge of the village. "I have brought someone into trouble." Then they said, they, the people of Kasafroko, "Even if you are able for the case, go and look for your father."'

Well, when he had finished telling[1] it all to his father, his father said, 'What! You are always going round the country and always killing; they did not refuse you [then]. I accept. I am the one who bore you.'

He took a gift of salt. Then he went to the chief. 'My child has come into trouble. He has shot someone.' The chief said, 'All right.' Then they raised the shout. 'He has come into trouble, he has come into trouble.'

Well, then he called his father. 'Father, I am testing the people—[testing] who is a wise man, who is not afraid of difficulty, who loves his child. I did not kill for you ever, in the whole country I was killing animals. But I was not refused because of that when it came to be said, "I have brought someone into trouble." Well, it is the people I am looking at, [to see] who is a wise man. For I did not kill a person, father, it was a bush cow I killed. When I brought the weeping "I have brought someone into trouble", well, when they refused me, the breast is not a light thing.[2] The people who were always eating my meat, when I came and told them a lie, that "I have brought someone into trouble", everyone said "Go to your father." Today did you not come and admit [for me]? If you say that parenthood does not matter—everyone refused me, though I was doing hunting work. Today, father, since you said just now "Let me go and admit" for the one I killed—it was a bush cow I killed.'

They raised a shout—for that pleased them again. 'Meat! A bush cow is killed oh!' But when they had heard that he had come into trouble by killing a man—only the father came and admitted. When they raised the shout now, they were rejoicing when they heard 'bush cow'. But in difficulty—only the parent admitted. No one agreed to it, only saying, 'Go to your father. We will not be able for the disaster—only the parent'—everyone who was told, except the parent. When the meat was

[1] The long description is typical of the way a son should report all his doings in detail to his parents.

[2] i.e. your parents will always support you and answer for you.

divided up . . . all those he was killing for, they were afraid. But his mother, when he came here 'no anger' (?).

So you see,[1] even in Limba custom, if someone does not eat with you, do not say that your relation does not matter. When the difficult time comes, your relation will say 'I own him.' Fortune is not like the time of difficulty. Since I heard that saying that for the breast, the one who bore you, that your father does not matter, your mother does not matter, . . . the one that says that your child does not matter. We the parents, even if someone eats something behind us, do not say that your child is no matter. You see, he accepted, for he bore him, everyone [else] refused. That is it.

The story of an orphan

KABI KANU. *Dictated* 10.2.61

The story of an orphan who was treated badly by his mother's co-wives after her death. The same theme comes in other stories and the figure of the friendless orphan is a stock one.

I AM Kabi Kanu. I have come to speak, here, at Kamabai. I have come to speak about a child that was left by its mother.

When he was left, the one who was bringing them up, the one who was bringing them up when his mother came and died, the one bringing him up said, 'Well, I am the one who is bringing you up. But as it is you have no mother. You know how I am treating you. All right.' His mother's co-wives began to speak; as they put their rice on to cook, they put in too much pepper for him.[2] Then the child said, 'Oh! If that is what it is, let it stop. If that is what it is, let it stop—putting pepper in the food you have cooked.' Then the child stood, the single child, for long. The one bringing him up,[3] him the single child, she brought him up, she gave him good food.

One day he got up, he said, 'All right. I have sense.' Therefore he

[1] This and following sentences are not quite clear. I have omitted a few words that are completely obscure to me.

[2] A young child is not able to eat as much pepper as adults. Not only do his stepmothers give him this unsuitable food but they throw it down for him roughly—*tɔŋie*, a word normally used of scattering food on the ground for hens.

[3] The one who is officially bringing the child up outside his own household looks after him well, in contrast to the co-wives there who *should* have treated him with the same care as his own mother.

went to have water looked for him, he went to the finch. 'Finch. I was left alone by my mother. Divine for me. When they cook they put in pepper. They will not give me much. I get only one handful. That is why I say "Finch, put good, put bad, but I have been left by my mother."' The finch said, 'You know what you will do—go and sit down at the grave.'

He went and sat at the grave, he began to cry pitifully. The finch said, 'You will see your mother coming out.' Then he stood up.

He went and sang, '*Ya yo de, thuŋ yɛyɛ thuŋ, iye Nayo,* you left me long ago. *Iye Nayo, thuŋ iye kulukutɛ keyo.*'[1] He saw her head, just a little. He rejoiced, he rejoiced, he rejoiced.

He sang again, '*Ya yo de, thuŋ yɛyɛ thuŋ, ya yo de,* you left me long ago. *Iye Nayo,* I have brought you something.' He watched until she came out, he saw her chest.

He got up, he sang again, '*Ya yo de, thuŋ yɛyɛ thuŋ, ya yo de thuŋ yɛyɛ thuŋ, iye Nayo,* you left me long ago. *Iye Nayo,* I have brought you something.' He watched, she came out completely.

He went and washed her. His mother said, 'Well, it was not death that I died. I was only watching to see how my co-wives treated you. But now I know it all. Well now, as it is you will not come to me, but go and wash.' He went and washed his mother. He rubbed her with oil. He sewed clothes for her. He did everything for her, he bought everything that his mother wanted. He took her to the house. She said, 'Well, don't yet take me out to the people. Don't tell them. Go and leave me first in the yard where they clean the rice, go and put me down there.' He went and hid her there 'so that I may see how you are treated'.

Then the co-wives stood up again. 'Since you have come again, you with your lack of upbringing, since you have come again—well, all right; what we will do to you—today we will not give you food. It is pepper we will throw down for you.'

When the evening cooled, they pounded the pepper, they gave it to the child. The child looked secretly at his mother in the yard. 'Do you see how I am treated? Do you see how I am treated?' His mother said, 'Don't eat it. Don't eat it.' Then he said, 'Here is the food you said you would give me—you put pepper. All that, let it stop.' Then his mother said he was to put it down for himself. When he put it down there, the mother came out. She came, 'Greetings to you. Behold! this is the way you are treating my child. You see, that is how death is. Let everyone believe in Kanu. If you see a child who is left an orphan, if you know how to treat him, he will not forget you. If you treat him badly in everything, tomorrow when he grows, tomorrow you start looking at him and saying, "Oh, we brought you up, we brought you up"—is that good?'

[1] The boy is calling his mother, and the stages by which she gradually appears from the grave are marked by stanzas of the song.

They started answering her, 'Oh.' 'No, no. I did not say you were to answer me.'

So that is what I have to say this evening when I came to speak, I Kabi Kanu.

The orphan child

KARANKE DEMA. *Dictated* 26.10.61

The story of a man who, although he was only an orphan, attained chiefship and riches through the help of a bird. But he lost all by failing to keep to the one condition imposed on him. The moral is drawn in conclusion that you should observe a prohibition laid on you by one who has helped you.

THE orphan child, he came out on earth. Just when he had been born, he had not yet been weaned, his mother died, his father died. He had been given the name of Sara. But when his mother died and his father, he was called Orphan Child. For he had no mother, he had no father.

When he was brought up, and he grew, he began to travel round in the cane grass. He came to an ant-heap. Animals were coming out from underneath there. He said, 'E, I have found an ant-heap where I will come tomorrow and set a trap.' He went back. He went and stripped out palm leaf fibre.[1] He twisted it, he tied it.

When the sun rose, he went. He went and set many traps. He went back. He came and spent the night.

In the morning he went to look. When he was still coming, he saw a white guinea fowl.[2] It had not died. He said, 'E! I have killed a guinea fowl!' Then the guinea fowl said, 'Loose me. Do not kill me.' He loosed it.

Then the guinea fowl said, 'Take me when you go.' He began to go with the guinea fowl. They came to a great rock where a high cotton tree stood. Then the guinea fowl said, 'Put me down.' He put it down. 'Climb up the cotton tree.' He climbed—up![3] 'Here?' 'No. Not there. Climb.' He climbed. 'Here?' 'No. Climb to the top.' Orphan Child climbed to where the cotton tree ended. It [guinea fowl] said, 'Let go.' Orphan Child was a little afraid, because of the rock below. It said, 'Just let go.' Orphan Child let go.

[1] The fibre is stripped out and rolled on the thigh to make a strong rope which can be used for snares.

[2] *Kusasikilɔ*—probably a kind of francolin. It appears fairly often in the stories, and is a popular food when it can be caught.

[3] The emphatic high tones of *duŋkɔ*, climb, indicate the height of the tree that he had to go up.

When he began to fall, just as he reached half way, he stood—lightly *yɛhɛdɛ!* on the earth. As he was saying 'E!',[1] he saw houses. As he was saying again 'E!', he saw people—thirty women. 'We have come to live freely with you here.' As he was saying, 'E!', ten men came, young men, 'We have come to stay with you.' As he stood there a little again, he saw fowls. As he stood there a little again, he saw goats. Every possession of humans came—pots, wooden bowls, chests, gourds, pans, spoons, they all came. Cattle, all. Orphan Child got chiefship.

The guinea fowl told him now, 'Since this has happened, you see, that small house you see there, locked, without a door—don't open that! If you open it, what you find, do not say that it was me.'[2] He said, 'Yes.'

When he had come to get the chiefship, many villages, countless wives, countless men, countless fowls, countless goats, countless cattle, sheep, all, he got them. He lived there in his chiefship with that honour (?).

When he lived there for long, everyone who came to him, he treated him well.[3] That helped all the country.

Then musicians[4] said, 'We will go and contest with him, for we hear that he is not poor.' When they went, they entered the village of Orphan Child. They went and beat their balanjis and their sticks, all. They praised and glorified Orphan Child. Orphan Child got up. He took a fowl, he measured out rice into a pan—quite full, *berede!*—and oil. 'Here, this is your gift.' They thanked him much. 'We accept.' They praised and praised. They called blessings on him. Then they said 'Orphan Child, do what your father did not do.'[5] Orphan Child got up again. He bound a goat, he put rice into a huge basket. 'Here is your gift.' They thanked him much. They praised that again. 'Orphan Child, do what your father did not do.' Orphan Child got up again. He went and bound a sheep. 'Here is your food.' They thanked him much. They called many blessings on him. 'Orphan Child, do what your father did not do.' Orphan Child got up. He bound a cow, and rice, four huge baskets. 'Here is your gift.' They thanked him much. They played. They called many blessings on him. They said again, 'Orphan Child, now, do what your father did not do.' Orphan Child got up. He gave them a wife. 'Here is your wife, who will cook for you.' They

[1] Involuntary exclamation of surprise.

[2] i.e. my fault.

[3] i.e. he gives many generous presents to them as befits a chief.

[4] Musicians coming to praise a chief and asking for great gifts in reply are rather more typical of the neighbouring Koranko and Mandingo than of the Limba. The musicians are depicted as 'contesting' with the chief to see if they can demand more than he can give. The stock list of increasingly valuable gifts is given: hen, rice, goat, sheep, cow, wife.

[5] They suggest he should emulate and surpass 'his father' (i.e. the last chief) in generosity.

thanked him much. They rejoiced. They said again, 'Orphan Child, do what your father did not do.' Orphan Child now, he forgot that 'the small house—I was told that I was not to open it'. He thought, 'I suppose there are possessions there more than what I have given to the musicians. Perhaps if I bring out the possessions from there, perhaps that will please them.' He got up, he Orphan Child, he went to the small house. He went and opened it.

As he opened it, there came there *gbiŋ gbaŋ!* Cane grass only now! He no longer saw a house, no longer saw a person, he was left, he alone again.

He began to come to his people. He came. He was asked 'E! Orphan Child, where were you?' Then he said, 'Ha! ha! my people. I was all the time walking through the cane grass.' He stayed there.

After a long time, he thought again, 'Let me go where I went before, to the ant heap.' He went there. He had palm fibre again. When he had put it down, he came home. He came and spent the night.

In the morning again he started to go to look at the fibre. When he was still coming again, he saw the guinea fowl, the white one. Then he said, speaking to the guinea fowl, 'Will I do as before?' Then the guinea fowl said, 'All right.' He took it. He came to the rock. He said, 'Will I do as before?' The guinea fowl said, 'All right.' He put it down. He said, 'Will I do as before?' The guinea fowl said, 'All right.' He climbed up above. He said, 'Will I do as before?' The guinea fowl said, 'All right.' He let go—*gbaŋ!* on to the rock! He died, he Orphan Child. Then he said, 'Oh! I, alas!'[1] there where he lay.

The guinea fowl got up. It looked for leaves. It went and squeezed them, it sprinkled him. He woke. Then he said, he Orphan Child, 'E! guinea fowl! You deceived me today.' Then the guinea fowl said, 'Was it I who ordered you today? When I told you at the beginning, what did you find?' Then Orphan Child said, 'I found good [fortune].' 'Well, what caused you to meet me again?' Then he said, 'Ah! my father, what you told me then, I failed. I opened the small house. Then I saw it all cane grass. I no longer saw a person. I no longer saw a cow. I no longer saw a sheep. I no longer saw a goat. I no longer saw a fowl.' Then the guinea fowl said, 'Well, you will no longer involve me in your foolishness! You see, I am going now.' The guinea fowl flew off.

He went again to make a trap for the guinea fowl. It would not come. He was always travelling around, he Orphan Child.

You see now, if someone helps you with something, and he says 'Do not do that'—that is a forbidden thing, you are not to do it. You see now, the reason that Orphan Child was not long in the chiefship, it was the musicians who came and contested with him.

Since I heard that story, that is it.

[1] Lit. 'E! me!', an exclamation of despair and, at the same time, of a sort of detached self-pity.

The orphan and the goats

NIAKA DEMA. *Dictated* 26.8.61

The story of a cunning boy who won goats from some Fulas by his clever riddles or parables (*thabɔrɔ*), then reversed the trick by which his mother's relations, to whom he had given the goats for keeping, tried to cheat him out of his due property. He triumphs in the end, is cured of his lameness, comes home with many goats, and is found a wife by his parents.

Basically the same plot was used in another story I heard (not included here), where several other 'parables' were brought in—the boy said his father had gone to 'meet together with the hills' (or high places), which meant that he had gone to mediate between the chiefs; his mother had gone to meet 'Satan', meaning that she had cooked rice for her lover and thus, if she met her husband, would be in trouble; and a pot had been 'made a widow'—i.e. it was dry and empty of water; this version ended with the boy's recovery of his property, cattle.

A CHILD once came out, an orphan. But he was lame. He lived as from here to the road there, coming from Ferengkai.[1] There he lived.

When Fulas came, bringing goats, they met him. 'E, friend, greetings.' 'Yes, greetings to you.' 'Well, where did your people go today?' Now he[2] had gone to make a bridge across a river. His mother had just finished her pregnancy and given birth. So when he came and was asked, 'Where did your father go today?', he said, 'He went to join together the earth.' They said 'Yes.' When they asked again about his mother, 'Where did your mother go today?', he said, 'She went today to bring together the earth and the sky.' When they had asked the boy, they said, 'E! What are these parables[3] that you showed us! Ha! Since we came out on earth, we have not yet heard these parables.' Then he said, 'It is good. I—for me to bring out my heart[4] for you first you must take one goat, a male, and take again a female.' He tied it. 'But you are to show us the parables you told us. That is what we want.' 'All right. You see—my father, whom you asked about today, he went to bind a bridge. For with a big river, when you come to it and there is no bridge there, will you cross there?' 'No.' 'That is why he went today to join the earth. And for what you asked me today saying, "Where did your

[1] About three miles away. Comparing the distances to ones known to the listeners, and setting the action, as it were, in the context of familiar places, is a common device in Limba story-telling.

[2] His father. The boy is called an 'orphan' at the outset—perhaps in this context it merely means 'poor' and 'helpless', i.e. the result rather than the condition of being an orphan.

[3] Or 'riddles' or 'stories' (*thabɔrɔ*).

[4] i.e. explain the parables.

mother go today?"—her belly pained her today, for childbirth. Thus both the sky and the earth. The parable I brought you today, that is it.' The Fulas said, 'It is true.' If you see a child, up or down, the child owned that speech. 'The two goats, I will take them to my people', to where his mother came from.

He took the goats. He went, he the lame child. He was not able to walk. He came in. 'E!' His people were surprised. 'Ha! You—ha! the cunning of yours that you have begun, it is not good.' Then he said, 'Only leave me alone.'

When the goats began to bear, as far as from here right to Kabala, if a goat gave birth now, he knew it here. He twisted a noose.[1] He put it down. When it became pregnant again, he knew here. When the goat gave birth like at Kabala, he knew here. He twisted a noose. He hung it up above. When the goats reached ten, he said 'Father. Carry me[2] now to my people, to the place where I am a cousin.'[3] He gave their names. His father put him on his head. He went. When they had just reached the bush by the side of the village, he was put down. He crawled now, he now entered the village. He brought four kola nuts, he said, 'I have come for the goats which I brought for you then.' The man said, where he had taken the goats to them, 'Ha! They are only males that the goat bears, these two. In these four years the he-goat has borne these.'[4] Then he said, 'Good. For me—it is all right. I will go. Father, tie the three male goats.'

When he went, he came to a river. He said, 'E! Father, I have trodden on a fish'—where he was carried on his father's head! Then his father said, 'How do you know that—to tread on a fish?' Then the boy said, 'You know, when I brought the goats here first, I was lame. Put me down now.'[5]

He took again now, he brought his cunning. He returned to where they had set out from. As he came in the distance from the bush by the village, he shouted. He cried. He came and was asked, 'E! Ha! It is hard! What is it?' 'My father's belly is hurting him—for childbirth'—because they had lied to the boy saying that the goat standing there, the male one, that that was the one that had given birth to young! When he came now saying, 'My father's belly is hurting'—'Why?'—'For childbirth', they said 'E! We have seen a parable, a male to give birth! Ha! It is hard!' Then the boy said, 'Cease now. Well, you told me that the goat I had brought, the female goat, that she had died. That this

[1] i.e. he makes a rope for each goat he owns.

[2] Because he could not walk.

[3] i.e. to his mother's relations.

[4] They try to deceive the boy by saying that only the he-goat has borne young—two—so that he only owns these two and their parent, instead of the ten really due to him.

[5] How he was cured of his lameness is not clear.

one, the male, had borne these ones. It is good—if a male does not ever give birth—to give me my goats. For a male does not give birth. I want my goats.' They took the ten goats, they tied them, they gave them to the boy.

He, the boy, brought them here to his father at the river where he had left him. When he came in the distance there with the goats, they now wept [with joy]. He the father, he began to go to welcome him. As he was coming to his father here, there were ten goats now! When he reached [his father] he announced[1] about the goats to him. 'Here is the journey I have been working at for them: at the time when you went to make the bridge, at that time Fulas came here, they came and asked me. "He has gone to fasten the earth." They asked again about my mother. Now my mother's pregnancy was completed. That is why I said, "She has gone to join the earth and the sky." I told them that parable. That is why I said to them, "Tie goats for me." They tied the goats. I took them now, those goats, I took them to my mother's people. Since those goats have become big now, let me announce about them to you. For a child, if you bear him, [even] if he is lame, and has no sense, watch him; if you say he has sense, he will help you. That is it. Here are the goats.'

The wife [his mother] was told about it. 'It is good that we, what we will do—the boy has told us a cause of complaint, ha! it is bad—he has not got a wife. It is good for us to woo a wife for him.' One goat was taken out, a female. It was given to her people. 'Here is this. I want my son to marry. At the time he went for the goats, then he was able to walk. He no longer stayed lame.' The boy—where the mothers[2] were asked they said, 'We agree. For he has bridewealth. For he also walks himself now.' The wife was given.

Well, now, since you said that someone was to give a story, well that is it, it is ended.

Three men, a boy, and a cow

FANKA KONTEH. *Dictated* 25.11.61

Like many of the stories which follow, this is an intentionally far-fetched tale. It concerns three men's greed for meat (a rare food in large quantities) which was so intense that they were prepared to travel many miles to avoid even a fly being there to share the meat when they killed their cow. They also tried to chase away their small brother when he followed

[1] He tells his parents formally what he has been doing, as is customary for a son.

[2] The girl's mother and her father's other wives.

them. But he in the end saved them by tricking the mysterious heads that had come to claim the meat; thus through the young boy's cleverness the older brothers were able to eat their meat after all.

The theme of great greed for meat is a popular one in Limba stories, and always a cause of particular amusement. Various of the episodes, such as travelling far to avoid the flies, also occur in other stories.

THREE men, they bound a cow. 'This cow, we will not kill it where there is a fly, but where there is no fly.' They tied up locust beans[1] in a bundle. They tied a rope to the cow. They began to go.

They went for far. They undid the locust beans. A fly flew around. They said, 'Let us go.' They went again for far. They undid the locust beans again. Their brother was there too, a small boy. He was following them. They said, 'If you come here, we will beat you!' The boy did not come near to them, but he was still following them. They went for far, they undid the locust beans again. The fly flew around. 'Let us go!' The boy was still following them—they said to him, they the elder ones, 'If you come here, we will beat you.' The boy did not come near them. They went for far. They came to a great forest. They undid the locust beans. The fly did not fly out round them. 'Let us kill the cow here, there is no fly here.'

They killed the cow. The boy came. He climbed up a tree, high up. They skinned and cut up the cow. As they cut off the first leg, and put it down, a head came out there from the hollow in the tree, 'I own the leg.' They cut off another leg, and put it down. Another head came out. 'I own the leg.' They cut off another leg, they put it down. Another head came out again, 'I own the leg.' They cut off another one. Another head came out, 'I own the leg.' It came to four. They cut off the head, they put it down. Another head came out, 'I own the head.' They cut the neck, they put it down. Another head came out, 'I own the neck.' They cut the chest, they put it down. Another head came out, 'I own the chest of the cow.' They cut the middle, they put it down. Another head came out, 'I own the middle.' They took the lower back, they put it down. Another head came out, 'I own the lower back.'

They sat there. The heads[2] took the meat now to take it away! The boy shouted, 'Elder brother oh! A woman has borne a child in the village, but the child that was born has no head. So seize one head now to take it to the village for the child that has been born without a head.' The heads heard. They left the meat. They ran off. Those who had killed the cow had a chance to eat the meat. The boy had made them able to eat the meat.

[1] The seeds of *parkia biglobosa*, which are eaten both raw and cooked. They are said to attract flies.

[2] No further explanation was given of these heads; the personal pronoun (*bindɛ*) was used to refer to them.

Sara miser and Sara scrounger

FANKA KONTEH. *Dictated* 29.11.61

Another tale about greed and, in this case, avarice. A miserly man is commonly blamed if he does not share his food with others who are present nor call them to eat with him. Correspondingly it is shameful to scrounge for food by always turning up just when food is ready, or by hanging round pointedly when people are eating. The story is thought funny both because of the greed with which the two Sara's behave (always an amusing topic), and also because of the almost inconceivable lengths to which each is prepared to go for the sake of the rice—pretending to die, and continuing to beg even after a friend's death.

SARA miser and Sara scrounger. Sara miser hoed a farm. After long the rice was ripe. At the time when Sara miser said he would harvest and eat, Sara scrounger went to greet Sara miser.[1] He found the wives of Sara miser harvesting. He sat down. They finished harvesting, they came and thrashed. Sara scrounger was there.[2] They dried the rice. Sara scrounger was there. They pounded it. Sara scrounger was there. They finished pounding. 'Wife, go and ask if Sara scrounger is sitting there.' 'Yes.' 'He is not going to eat this rice.' They put the pot on the fire. They went and asked, 'Is Sara scrounger there?' 'Yes.' 'He is not going to eat this rice today.' They cooked. The wife went and asked—'Ha! Sara scrounger is still there.'

Sara miser became ill. His illness did not last long. He died. His wife wept and wept. She called Sara scrounger. 'Sara scrounger, ha! Sara miser has died, oh! That is it. Let us go to the village, to go and tell the people that Sara miser has died in the farm.' Then said Sara scrounger, 'No. I want to be left with the corpse. A man should be left with the corpse. Send a child to call all the people in the village.' They let one child go, the child of Sara miser. 'Go to the village, and go and tell the people in the village—Sara miser, he has died in the farm oh!' The child went to the village. He went and said, 'Sara miser has died in the farm oh!' The people of the village set out, to come for Sara miser, to go and bury him in the village.

The wife of Sara miser saw the people coming, coming for Sara. She went to the corpse, she went and said, 'The people have arrived, coming for you. That is it. Have you truly died for the sake of the rice?' 'Well, if Sara scrounger is there, I will just die oh!' The people [came and] took Sara miser.

[1] Arriving carefully in time for food.

[2] Waiting for the rice to be ready.

Sara scrounger was told. 'Well, go on in front.' 'No, I will be left behind to make arrangements about the rice, for it to be taken to the village.' They took up the body. They put it on their heads. Sara scrounger followed behind with the rice.

They arrived at the village. They said, 'Well, let us go and dig the grave.' The wife went to the corpse. She went and said, 'The grave is just going to be dug, for you to go and be buried.' Then said Sara miser, 'Is Sara scrounger there?' 'Yes.' 'Well then, tell them to go and dig the grave.' The wife said 'What, is it because of the rice? Is it truly for that that you died?' 'Yes. If Sara scrounger is there, I am dead.'

They finished digging the grave. They came. 'We have finished digging the grave. Well, let us go and bury him.' The wife went again to ask the corpse 'They are starting out to go and bury you.' 'Is Sara scrounger there?' 'Yes.' 'Well, let them go and bury me.' Then the wife said, 'What? Is it for the sake of the rice?' 'Yes. Sara scrounger is not going to eat it.'

They came and took him, they carried him to the grave. As they put him inside the grave, then he said, 'Don't cover in the earth. Sara scrounger, oh you! you really beg from your friend! Well, let us go and eat the rice.' Sara scrounger said, 'All right. Let us go.'

They went and sat down, they ate.

Then Sara miser said, 'Oh you! you really beg from your friend! I died for the sake of the rice; you still said that even though I died, you could truly go on begging from me. Ha! you are a scrounger!' Then said Sara scrounger, 'Ha! You are truly a miser. Dying for rice! You are a miser. You are more of a scrounger than I.'

Daba the snuff-taker

DAUDA KONTEH. *Recorded* 19.1.64

One of Dauda Konteh's stories told with his typical style and characteristic introduction and conclusion. The story has little plot and the main attraction was his singing of the rhythmic song, taken up and repeated many times by his audience. One of the points of the story was its amusing exaggerations; many Limba take snuff but it is portrayed in an extreme and ludicrous light through the events of the story here. As often in Limba stories the scene is made more vivid and amusing by referring to the names of actual chiefs and places.

I AM Dauda the son of Fane Konteh of Kamabai. Hey! attention you. Let everyone come and listen. If you want to find wisdom—where your friend speaks, that is where you find wisdom. If you are very wise you will understand. I am Dauda, the son of Fane Konteh of Kamabai. I have come. Well, a story for you oh! Listen, won't you?

A human once came out on earth. Ha! The earth had not yet begun. If I told you where the earth began and where the earth ended, you would not be able to understand it, only I alone and my thoughts and my understanding—where the earth began and where it ended. A human once came out on earth. He was called Daba. Daba. Daba. He was a great great great taker of snuff, a great eater of snuff on the earth here.

When this Daba was brought out on the earth, he got up. He went out to go like to Binkolo. He said 'Ha! my brother whom I like—he must give me snuff, twelve housefuls of it!' He was brought out—'I am not speaking yet.'[1] He got up [and sang] 'Daba yo, Daba yo, Daba yo, in taking snuff, Daba yo, *marɔɔ*.[2] . . . Ugh—get out of the way here. Ha! The chief—he is not generous. See, what I want is—I want someone to pound me twelve great housefuls of snuff.'

He went away from there. He went like to Makeni. Well, the chief there, the one they call Bai Kobolo, he pounded Daba fourteen great housefuls. Daba got up, he came. One nostril sniffed it all up! 'E, chief, greetings.' 'Yes.' 'Have you not got anything for me?'[3] 'I have something for you. Look at that snuff—that is it.' 'You, you are not generous at all! I have often heard your name, but I have not found [reason for] belief in it. Why? Because where you are yourself, that is where you find out the truth.' He sniffed it with one nostril. Then he sang 'Daba yo, Daba yo, Daba yo, in taking snuff, Daba yo, *marɔɔ*. . . . E! get out of the way here. You are not generous. For me—I will stay in Makeni.'

In Makeni [he went to] the one called the chief of Makeni, like to Bai Sebora—'Give me something.' Bai Sebora had made him fourteen great housefuls for one sniff! When he came and arrived there, he said 'Bai Sebora, greetings.' 'Yes. Greetings oh.' 'Any trouble?' 'No, no trouble.' 'Have you got anything for me?' 'Yes, I have something for you.' 'What is it?' 'Snuff, for taking.' He got up, 'Show me it.' He was shown it, great housefuls. He got up. He came and sniffed—one nostril did not get any! Then he sang, 'Daba yo, Daba yo, Daba yo, in taking snuff, Daba yo, *marɔɔ*. . . . E! Stop! Ah, you! You are not generous.'

Then the chief of Port Loko got up. 'You, you are not generous, get

[1] He is not making any pronouncement of thanks, etc., until he has seen how much he is to get altogether.

[2] *Marɔɔ* signifies the sound that is made as his nostril sniffs up the snuff; it is still part of the song. After these words have been repeated several times by Dauda and the listeners, Dauda breaks in on the song in a louder voice with Daba's complaint about how little he had been given.

[3] This phrase—as with the other greetings in the story—is a common one by a visitor; here it implies great ingratitude after the large gift he had already been given.

out of the way there.' Then he got up, he pounded one bunch, about the thickness of my arm, mine, Dauda Konteh's of Kamabai, so much. 'E!' Then he came. 'Chief.' 'Yes?' 'I have come. Have you got anything for me?' 'Yes, I have something for you.' 'What?' 'A little bit of snuff,' 'E! This pounded snuff, is this it? Ha! Chief, you have no shame. I have often heard your name, but you, you have no shame here.' 'Well, all right, take it.' He came to take it to sniff. Now I, Dauda Konteh, the son of Fane of Kamabai, I stood behind and heard him, I did not speak a word. As I heard him, he came to sniff it. Then he sang, 'Daba yo, Daba yo, Daba yo, in taking snuff, Daba yo, *marɔɔ*. . . .'[1] *Gbudu!*—he fell. He died straight off Yenkeni!

I Dauda, if I am telling a lie, when I die let me not see those who carry me to the grave; but if I am not, if I speak the truth—those who carry me to the grave, who carry me to the grave, may I see them clearly, those who carry me to the grave. You hear—since you came and said to me this evening that I should tell you a story, since it is ended by me to you, Yenkeni Konteh, this evening, by me, Dauda Konteh of Kamabai, it is finished, that is it.

The story of a millionaire

SURIBA NEVERTIRE KONTEH. *Recorded* 21.2.61

A story set in the far away land of England, complete with the characteristics often attributed to Europeans—a 'millionaire', a thousand pounds, a 'king', diamonds, bank, cheque, and car. Many of these items would be known by repute among those who had travelled to, or heard of, the diamond boom of the mid 1950s when some individuals became suddenly rich through finding one stone. On the whole few Limba made money in this way as the diamond mines were outside their country and they took relatively little interest. However, many people who later travelled through or settled in the north had experience of the possibilities of sudden wealth.

In spite of the intentionally foreign setting, the framework of the story is set in the usual series of parallel episodes, the style and characterization are typically Limba, and the situation of a daughter being difficult about marriage or a man wishing to find 'honour' were familiar topics.

The story ends with an oblique comment on the situation in the Biriwa ruling house in which succession to chiefship alternates between two branches, comparing this to the apparently more economical system Suriba had heard of among the Europeans where the monarchy is in

[1] By now the song is very faint, almost impossible to hear, representing Daba's weakness.

one house. (He himself had contested a previous election in Biriwa and was said to have lost a lot of money by it.) The origin suggested for the European custom ('from his child then') is scarcely intended to be very serious.

I SURIBA Nevertire of Bumban, I am going to tell you a story—that if you see someone well off, he began as someone not well off.

Well, a poor man came out in England. He had nothing at all. But he was a fisherman. Well, his people had nothing. He lived there. He went to fish. He went there and caught two fishes. These two fishes, they had the stones called 'diamond'—twelve stones in the stomachs of the fishes. They had swallowed them. When he cut up the fish, he saw those stones. Well, those stones, he took them, he tied them in a cloth. He kept them.

Well, later, well the king's daughter was full grown. He wanted to give his daughter to her husband. Well, his daughter said, 'I will not go to the marriage unless you have made for me combs of diamond, six of them.' Well, the king had not got those combs. He sat and he thought. He called the whole country. 'Who will find diamond for me, for me to make combs to give to my daughter?' Well, this pauper, this poor man —for his people had nothing—he was called. He said, 'I have got something. I think it is what is called diamond.' He took the stones, he showed the king, two of them. The king was pleased. He took them, he said, 'Oh, what will I give you?' 'Well, I, I have nothing at all; I only have these stones; but I will sell them.' 'What do you want?' 'Look at me. I have nothing. I have no shirt. I have no money. I have no house.[1] I would like to see myself become well off.' He was given £600 for one stone. 'I refuse.' He was given £1,000. He took it. 'But now I have got this money, what will I do with it? Am I (?) to put it in my pocket when I travel? I have no house.' The king gave him a house, where he could stay. He gave him a car. On that day those who had laughed at him before were now pleased about this. He was loved by people. He began to see people coming to greet him.[2]

The stone was taken. It was taken to a goldsmith. It was worked. But it was not enough for a comb. The daughter said, 'I refuse, father, unless I get six combs.'[3] Well, the king said, 'I beg you, if you have one, sell me it.' He went again and brought out two. It came to the buying again! 'Ha! you will have to give me half of the whole bank.' 'Well, rather than that my child should be ashamed.' He gave him one bank. He gave him a cheque. All this money—'You own it now.' He stayed there. Well, that pleased him.

[1] He gives the list of his poverty in a pathetic sing-song voice.

[2] A mark of honour and position.

[3] The daughter is portrayed throughout as speaking in a plaintive yet completely obstinate tone.

What they did now—they went and made three combs. There remained three. The daughter said, 'Ha! father, I will not go to be married except for six combs. There remain three.' He was called again. 'Come here. I beg you, help me so that my child may agree to be married.[1] Go and give me what remains.' He went again and brought out three, two. There remained one. When he came, he was told. The king said 'What do you want?' He took banks, three of them and sold them to him! He gave him everything in the world, so that he could see his daughter go and marry.

They went and were worked. Two combs came from it. There remained one. Ah! He was called again. 'I beg you, help me so that my daughter may go to be married.' When he came he said, 'Oh, let me tell you—do you know what I want now? That we should divide the country, you and I. Even though I do not become a chief, let me become a leader in property, so everyone will give me honour. You love your daughter, may you also love me so that I may remain with honour. For at the beginning that I began, I had nothing. I had nothing at all. People used to laugh at me at that time. Today Kanu has given me one half. Now I wish that you and I—when your name is called, mine is also called.' 'Is that what you want?' 'Yes.' 'Well, we now, you and I, let us share the property in half. Well you—as your power is, so is mine. But you are not a chief.' 'What will you leave me for the help I have helped you?' 'I have told you, I will give you a name, you will be called Millionaire. The money in your hands will not come to an end. Everyone who wants anything will have to go and borrow from you.' He took the stone that remained, he gave him it. It went and was worked. The combs came to six.

Well, the woman was taken, she was given. As she was about to go to the marriage, then her father said, 'Ha! The money I have put down for you, it is much. I have divided my chiefdom with him, for your sake. It is good for us not to be changing the chiefship. If you bear a child, when you die, your child becomes chief. For the property is great, what we lost it for, for this chiefship, it was for your sake.'

If you see now, if you see that it is like this—the Europeans do not change round the chiefship.[2] It was the loss [suffered] from his child then, his first child, so as to give her to her husband—that is why they will not change round the chiefship. When one dies, the wife becomes chief. When the wife becomes chief, [then] when she bears a child, that child becomes chief.

Since I heard that, I Nevertire, Suriba Nevertire, I have told you that story, that is it, it is finished.

[1] The king is sounding very pathetic and helpless so as to persuade the diamond owner to help him.

[2] i.e. alternate succession to chiefship between different ruling lines.

The Story of Bayo

KARANKE DEMA. *Dictated* 15.10.61

A story which explains how it is that animals fear humans. It has some similarity to *Contest in strength* in which a human also triumphs through his power to kill. The episode about the monster resembles that in *The goat and the leopard.*

YENKENI, a story for you. A leopard, a lion, and a human child. His name was Bayo. He said, 'Let us form a company.'[1] In that company they said, 'We will not eat rice, only meat, raw meat.'[2]

When they had formed the company, they went to the leopard's farm. He now, he the leopard, used to catch animals. When he was told, 'Tomorrow we will hoe', he went in the night to catch animals. When he caught them, he brought them to the clearing by the farm. He came and put them down. When he had caught six animals, he went and lay down.

In the morning they came to the farm. They hoed for long. They finished. He got up, he the leopard, to bring their food. He brought out all the animals to the farm. 'Here is your food.' Now the child, the one called Bayo, he would not eat raw meat, for he was a human. When they ate—the leopard and the chimpanzee—the child took his share with him when he went.

When the sun rose, they were to hoe for the chimpanzee. That night the chimpanzee—for he has great strength—he met an animal. He took hold of it. He wrestled with it, he killed it. He brought it to the clearing. He came and put it down. He caught six animals. He went and lay down.

In the morning, they went to the farm. They went and hoed. They finished. He brought out the animals. 'Here is your food.' They ate. The child, however, the human, he took it with him when he went. They said, 'The day after tomorrow we are to hoe for you. For our food we will not eat rice, only meat, raw meat.' The leopard said, 'Now that we are forming a company, any place where we do not eat meat at the farm we hoe for—if we catch you, we will eat you.'

The child, he considered, he thought 'Alas for me! I am not a hunter, where will I get meat?' But he said 'All right.'

[1] A farming company in which the members go from farm to farm where they are fed in return for their work. In this story 'company' also has the sense of emulation and hostility.

[2] Rice is the natural food for humans, but the animals insist on meat, eaten raw.

When the sun rose, he went off to the bush. Whenever he came on animals, they ran away. Whenever he came on animals, they ran away. He went for far, he came to a small hut, belonging to a monster.[1] Now this monster was a hunter, a great hunter. His things were not to be touched by rain—his magic stones.[2] He had spread them in the sun and gone off to hunt, far away. When the child came and saw them, he sat down to rest a little. After a long time, the rain came. He got up, he took the things—the magic stones—he took them inside. The rain came down.

As the rain was abating, the monster ran, he wept, he thought, 'I have come to disaster today, for the things which I forgot have been wet. My life is finished today.' For if his things were wet, he was to die. He went and looked at the place where he had spread them. He did not see them. He said 'Ah Kanu! Who lifted up my things for me?' But the child was afraid, thinking 'Perhaps he will eat me.' He [the monster] asked. But the child was afraid to say, 'It was me.' The monster said, 'But if the one who lifted them up for me will only admit it, I will not hurt him. For he has saved my life today.'

The child came out. 'Me'—he admitted very quietly.[3] Then the monster said, 'Come out only; don't be afraid to come out.' The child came out. He said, 'Thank you, thank you, thank you. Today you have saved my life.' He asked him, 'Where are you going today?' Then the child said, 'I am going round today. I joined in a company with animals who are catchers; they said, "We will not eat rice, only raw meat." But I, I cannot catch animals. I have spent the day going round. As soon as I come on them the animals run away. That is why I have spent the whole day going round. I am unable.'

Then the monster said, 'Ah child, take heart. You saved me today. My life would have ended today but for your help. Now I will save you.' He gave the child a bag. He said, 'Now this—this is what you will carry with you. As soon as you come on them, drive them towards the farm. When they have reached the clearing there, you are to say "*Yɔri* to you oh!", they will all die. That is it.'

The child took it. He started to go. He came on a family of bush cows. He drove them along. They came to the clearing. He said '*Yɔri* to you oh!' They all died. He set out again. He came on a family of bush buck. He drove them along. They came to the clearing. He said "*Yɔri* to you oh!' They died. He went. He came on a family of pigs. He drove them to the clearing. As they stopped there, he said '*Yɔri* to you oh!' They died. Six families—when he had driven them, they all died. He went and lay down.

[1] *thumpu*—sometimes said to be a spirit, sometimes an animal.

[2] Hunters are often said to have magic stones (*sokoro*).

[3] Bayo here is made by the narrator to reply so nervously and quietly that he could scarcely be heard. He is depicted throughout as rather shy and quiet.

In the morning, they began to come to the farm. They went and stood there. The leopard began to sing. As he was singing, he was now swallowing his saliva for the child, wanting to eat him. Behold the child had been able to get the meat! He began to sing, he the leopard. 'I will not eat cooked meat—only raw meat.'

For a long time they hoed there, they finished. Now they stood there. They looked at the child. 'Well, show us our food.' The child said, 'Oh'— he seemed to be thinking. Then the leopard said, 'You, be quick. If you are not quick, we will eat you.' The child said, 'Come here.' He pointed to the family of bush cows. 'Come here too.' He pointed to the family of antelopes. He turned away. 'Come here too.' They went. He pointed to the family of pigs. Every animal he had caught—he showed them all. They *ate.*[1] They could not finish.

Then the leopard said, 'Oh, child, how did you get all these animals?' They wanted to ask the child to show them. The child refused. The child said, 'Kanu helped me.'[2] Then the leopard said, 'Let us show each other our magic.' The child said, 'I have no magic. I will just watch you.' The child stood to one side.

The leopard got up. He held out his tail—*pohoro* his hair stood up! He leapt on to a tree, to the top—frightening the child. But the child said nothing. He sat down again. The chimpanzee got up. He gripped the tree, he twisted it, he tied it in a knot. He sat down again. They said to the child, 'You? well now?' The child said, 'I dare not. I refuse.' They said, 'Try anyway.' The child said, 'All right. Stand over there.' He took out the bag. He said—there where they were standing—'*Yɔri* to you.' They all died!

They were lying there now. Two hours passed—they were lying there, they were all dead.

The child did not rouse them at first. After a long time, the child took a bottle with a small brush in it. He dropped *mafɔi* medicine on to the brush. He beat it on the ground—thus—where the dead animal lay. It got up now, *diki diki* it ran! Running to the bush, now fearing the human. He went to the leopard. He went and beat like this—at once it got up, *kidi kidi* it ran! Running to the bush, fearing the human. When they had all run away they went and met together, those who had fled. Then the leopard said, 'We, we are now afraid of humans. They have more cunning than we.'

If you see now, that animals do not dare to face humans—that is where it began, by the help of the child Bayo who joined in that company.

[1] The great emphasis given to the word 'ate' was thought striking in itself.

[2] In other words, he is not going to tell them the answer.

Two twins

FANKA KONTEH. *Dictated* 10.11.61

This and the following stories are about twins who, whether two or three, are often represented as possessing special powers. In this story one twin enters another world and brings back a wife. The story ends with the (implied) dilemma of who should have the wife, and after the narration was concluded the answer was quickly given by one of those present —Yemi owns her.

The plot is very similar to another tale about two twins, *Koto and Yemi*; it differs however, in that there Kanu is introduced as one of the characters and the conclusion involves the statement of an origin. The visit to another world and the help given there by various animals is also a common motif.

MILLET was once hoed by the mother of twins. She told Koto to chase the birds from the millet. There Koto went to chase. There was a pool there, to one side of the millet. In that pool there were then many girls. There was no man there. When Koto was left, when he went to sling stones in the morning, a girl came out from the pool. She greeted him, 'Greetings Koto.' Koto answered. He said 'Where do you come from?' 'Not from anywhere.' 'Well, say good-bye to me with food, cook for me.' When the girl had dried the millet, she pounded it, she began to pick leaves for sauce. She boiled the sauce. She stood, she cooked the millet. She helped it out. They sat down. They ate. When they had finished eating, the girl struck him. She began to run. 'Well, Koto, catch me, so that you may marry me.' They ran against each other like that. She went and entered the pool. When Koto reached there, he came to the pool. He did not dare to enter it. He went back. He came home to the village.

When the sun rose again, he was left to chase [birds from the crop]. He had just slung a stone, when the girl came out from the pool. She greeted him, 'Greetings Koto.' 'Yes. Come and pound millet for me.' She stood, she dried the millet. She again, she pounded it, she picked leaves for sauce, she boiled them. She cooked the millet. She helped it out. They sat down. They ate. The girl got up again, she struck Koto and said, 'If you are only able to catch me, well, I am your wife.' She ran. She went and entered the pool. When Koto reached there, he went and looked at the pool, he did not dare to enter it. He went home to the village. He came and told Yemi, 'A girl is going to (?) drive me (?) away in the millet where I am chasing; when she has finished cooking for me, and we have eaten, she strikes me, saying "If you are only able to catch me, well, I am your wife." When we run, she reaches and enters the pool. I am not able to enter it.' Yemi said, 'All right. Tomorrow we will go early, so that I can go and see.'

They went early in the morning, Koto and Yemi. They went to chase. Yemi went and sat in the farm hut. Koto stood to sling. After a long time, the girl came out. 'Koto, greetings oh! I have come today again.' 'Well, the millet is much there, dry it for me and cook.' The girl stood. She dried it. She pounded it. She picked leaves for sauce. She boiled the sauce. She cooked the millet. She helped it out. They ate it—the three of them now. The girl got up. She struck Koto. 'If you are only able to catch me, I am your wife.' They ran against each other. When the girl reached there, she threw herself into the pool. Koto reached there, he did not dare. He went back. Yemi came and said, 'Yes. I have seen her. Well, tomorrow I will be early.' They went to the village, Koto and Yemi.

In the morning, Yemi was early. He brought millet with him. He arrived. He slung. The girl came out. She thought that it was Koto. 'Koto, greetings oh!' 'Yes.' 'Well, I have come today again.' 'Well, the millet is much there. Dry it and pound it.' The girl stood. She dried the millet. She pounded it. She picked leaves for sauce, she boiled them. She took off the sauce. She cooked the millet. She helped it out. They ate. She got up, she the girl. She thought that it was Koto. Now Yemi, he was more clear-eyed[1] than Koto. She struck him. 'Well, if you are only able to catch me, well, I am your wife.' They ran. She arrived, she threw herself into the pool. Yemi reached there too. He threw himself into the pool.

He came and arrived at a village below in the pool. Yemi arrived there. They went and saw Yemi—a man! They were surprised. 'E! A man cannot come to our village here! What have you come for?' 'I am following a girl.' 'Do you know her?' 'Yes.'

He met a fly there. The fly said, 'Do you not know? Tomorrow the girl you are coming for here—if you do not know her tomorrow, you will be killed. But if you agree for me to eat and be filled, well, I will show you the woman tomorrow.' Yemi agreed, 'All right. Eat as much as you are able.' The fly fastened on him. It ate. It was filled. 'Well, tomorrow when the women are all lined up tomorrow, well, they are many, they are about two hundred, well, whichever one you see strike herself tomorrow, well, she is the one.' 'Thank you, thank you.'

He had rice cooked for him. It was brought. He sat down to eat—rice and meat. A dog came. 'If you give me the bone and I eat it, well, I will show you tomorrow the girl you have come for. If you do not know her, you will be killed. That is it'—the dog speaking. He gave him the meat; all the bones—he gave him. He ate. The dog said, 'Well,

[1] Able to see spirits etc.

tomorrow when the women are lined up, whichever one I jump up on, in the middle, well, she is the one.' Yemi said 'Thank you.'

He slept. In the morning, the girls were all early going to bathe. They came and stood. They rubbed oil all over them.[1] The girls—whichever one you looked at, they were all the same, their faces were the same. They were called. 'Girls, well, come and line up; so that Yemi may show the one he has followed here.' They were lined up. Yemi was called. 'Well, come and show the one you followed here.' Yemi stood. He began to walk along, going to look. Just as he reached there exactly—*yɔ!* —the fly bit the girl, the dog came too, he jumped up on the girl. Yemi came there to the girl. He said 'It is she.' 'Aha, yes.' The girl was told that it was her. 'Well, here is your wife. Take her.'

They went out. They came to the village here. Well, Koto came and said, 'I own the wife.' Yemi said, 'It is not you who own the wife. I own her. You—you did not dare to enter the pool. It was only I who went and entered. When I have brought the wife, you come and say that you own her—it is not you who own her. I own her.'

The hunter and the three twins

KARANKE DEMA. *Recorded* 30.6.61

A story of *hugbanaŋ*, cunning or amazingness, ending, as often in such stories, with a dilemma about which of the characters manifested most *hugbanaŋ*. This theme seems to be particularly common in tales of twins, usually three in number.

The actual episodes of the story are rather unusual. However, there are some similarities to those of other stories: the theme of a dead father whose children are brought up by a mother who reminds them of him so that when grown up they go on a journey for his sake, is reminiscent of the otherwise very different *The man killed for a spinach leaf*; the list of actions contributed in turn by the various characters also occurs in *Three twins woo one girl* and *The girl taken by Kanu*; the foods cooked together in one pot yet served separately also come into *The woman with four lovers*; and, finally, the framework of the story, a dilemma about *hugbanaŋ*, is relatively common.

The story was told by Karanke Dema, who preferred on this occasion to give himself the name of Yaling Koroma. (Koroma is merely another

[1] The mention of the girls' bathing, being anointed with oil, and lined up would, to any Limba, recall the situation of the final ceremony when the girls come out of seclusion, now initiated women and ready for marriage. The girls sit or stand in a row, their bodies glistening with oil, admired by the men there, and having speeches made over them by their fathers and future husbands.

form of his clan name, Dema; and people not infrequently decide to change their first names, specially if they go down country.)

I AM Yaling, Yaling Koroma. I am thinking of a story, one I have been hearing. . . . A story I have heard, that is why I thought of it. I want to tell Yenkeni it, today, this day.

A man once wooed a wife. He married her. Her husband's name was Koto.[1] He married the woman. The woman became pregnant. Now he was a hunter, the one who is called Koto. The woman became pregnant. He went to hunt in the middle of the water, by a big pool. He went and hung his hammock, hunting the hippopotamus. When he was hanging there, 'I am going there to hunt', he told his friend (?). 'We will finish his life. When he comes to shoot, there we will go and put him down.'[2] He did not know. He went and hung the hammock. When the time was near, when he had not yet shot the animal, the hammock broke when he was shot. The hammock broke. He fell into the water. Eh! the children now—the wife that he left behind, she had not yet borne him a child. He fell into the water, into the pool. If you go there you will not get out. He disappeared. The gun, he, the bag, all his things disappeared in the pool. They sank.

When it was like that, his wife that was left behind, her pregnancy came to end. She bore twins, Luseni, Koto, and Siema, three of them. She brought them up. Their father was not there. They came to be full grown. Then they said, 'Mother, what about our father?' Always when they were crying, saying 'Father father', the mother would say, 'E, my children, your father went to hunt without coming back, I have never seen him again.'[3]

When they had got sense[4] they asked, 'What about our father?' She said, 'Your father went to hunt, without coming back.' Then they said, 'We will go and look for our father.' They asked about the road. 'Show us the road that he followed.' Their mother showed that road.

Luseni, Koto, and Siema. Then Siema said to them, 'I, I will pick out the tracks of our father, the place he went then, I know those tracks. We will go to the place where his life[5] is.' They set out. He went in front. They went out for a long time. They arrived, they reached the pool. 'Here is the place where our father lost his life. Here is the tree he

[1] It seems that the father was also a twin and had the same name as one of his sons.

[2] This episode is obscure to me. Someone (the hippopotamus?) is planning the hunter's death as he hangs in his hammock waiting to shoot them. Therefore the hunter is shot (?), and his hammock breaks, and he is, as appears later, eaten by the hippopotamus and crocodiles in the pool.

[3] This sentence recalls the semi-lullaby chanted by the mother to her child in, for example, *The man killed for a spinach leaf*.

[4] i.e. were grown up.

[5] Lit. head (*huya*).

climbed. There he tied his hammock then. Here he found trouble. He fell into the water.'

Then Koto said, 'Siema, for what you have done for us, I thank you. We have reached here. I, I will go into the water, I will find where our father was lost, whether it was an animal that ate him, I will find out.' He said they were to take a mat.[1]

Then Luseni said, 'We will go in the water.' Siema said 'I found the way. When they go in the water, I will breathe for you.' He said, 'Yes, it is all right.' He took the mat. They went into the water.[2] Siema was up in the light. He started breathing, saying, 'I breathe for Koto, I am breathing for Luseni, I am breathing for myself. I breathe for Koto, I am breathing for Luseni, I am breathing for myself. I breathe for Koto, I am breathing for Luseni, I am breathing for myself.' That is what he did there.

Now Luseni, he entered the water, he went into the water, he with Siema['s help]. Koto went into the water, Luseni had a mat-bundle. Koto met a crocodile. He cut it open. He said, 'I am not looking for you, I am looking for my father.' Everything that he had eaten, it was brought out. He left him there. He met a hippopotamus. He cut open its stomach, saying, 'I am not looking for you, I am looking for my father.' Everything that he had eaten, it was brought out. Luseni put it in the mat bundle. Every animal in the water—he looked at them all. He took out the gun. He put it in the bundle. He came out. Everything that is [part] of a human being[3] was there—the head was there, the foot was there, the neck was there, the arm was there. He brought them all out. They put them in the bundle. He brought them out to a dry place. He came and breathed.[4]

Then Siema said, the one who was left outside who was breathing for them, 'Since you have brought out our father, we will not [yet] say that he is a person. But it is all right. You have come to me. I will join him together as a person.' He stood up. He joined him all together, he made him as a person, as a person is.

Then Luseni said, 'It is all right. You have joined him, you Siema. Now I, I will put breath in him, for him to breathe.' Well, he put in breath, Koto breathed, their father.[5]

Then Koto[6] said, 'They have joined him. He is breathing. I will find a funnel, with which I will drop medicine so that he may hear, open his eyes, stand up, talk, so that he may begin to go.' He took the funnel. He

[1] Mats are often used to wrap round things to make a bundle for carrying or storing.

[2] Apparently Koto goes right into the water, and Luseni is half-way in or by the side, holding the mat-bundle. Siema is out on the bank breathing for them.

[3] Lit. Limba.

[4] Or 'rested'.

[5] Their father (Koto) started to breathe again. That this is something wonderful to them is made clear by the tone of the teller.

[6] The son.

dropped the medicine on him. He dropped it on his ear. He dropped it on his nose. He dropped it on his eyes. He dropped it on his brains. He dropped it on his mouth. He dropped it on the sole of his foot. He dropped it on his arms.

Their father got up. They said 'Father.' 'Yes?' 'Greetings.' 'Yes.' 'When you went were we born?' 'No, I do not know you.' 'You bore us. We asked for our father. Our mother said, "Your father went to hunt then without coming back." We did not see him, that is what made us look for him. Here we are.' Their father thanked them.[1]

He left there. He started to come to the village. The gun was on their father's shoulder, the hammock and the bag (?). They entered their settlement.

When he was still far off, their mother came to meet them. She rejoiced, she rejoiced, she rejoiced, she rejoiced. She thanked them many times. 'Thank you my children, thank you my children, thank you my children, that pleases me.' Their father entered. They went and greeted each other. Then their mother said, 'It is all right, my children, this thing that you have done. I bore you. You have found your father. Well today, this day today, I will look for food for you to eat, all food for humans (?).' The children said, 'It is all right.' They stood [there].

Their mother stood up. She looked for rice, she looked for millet, she looked for maize, she looked for guinea corn, she dug yams, she dug small yams, she dug red bush yams, she dug other yams—all the food of humans, she found it. The pot—a little one, a sixpenny one,[2] it is like for one man's food, there she put all the things! She cooked them there. Each food had its scrapings—the rice with its scrapings, the millet with its scrapings, the maize with its scrapings, the guinea corn with its scrapings, the yams with their scrapings, the small yams with their scrapings, the red yams with their scrapings, and the other yams with their scrapings—she took them out. They ate them.

So Yenkeni, as you have come and I have heard this story, when you came and said you wanted to be taught Limba, I wanted to tell you it. Of these four people, their mother and the children, which was the most amazing? I want to ask you that. Since I heard that you asked me to talk, I Yaling of Kakarima, I have talked. I am asking you about those four people, I want to ask you. Since I have finished speaking, you have borne with me, no one has talked, you were silent; since I have finished talking, I have only to say thank you. You bore hearing me. Since I have finished speaking, I have finished the story. Yenkeni, I have to say to you, it is finished.

[1] The exchange of greetings, announcement ('here we are'), and thanks, are an important part of this episode.

[2] 'A sixpenny pot' is a joke. This would be infinitely too small to cook for a family in.

Three twins woo one girl

BANKOLO MANSARAY. *Dictated* 11.11.61

A dilemma story, the solution of which caused some argument, for each twin was seen to have been essential in preserving the girl.

The scene is partly set in England—a good far-away land for an intentionally fantastic story involving 'thousands' of pounds.

As often, the action takes place in a series of parallel events, each twin in turn taking part—leaving home, buying one article, helping to save the girl, and then claiming her love. The way in which at first they did not know of the others' love of the girl and then discovered at the moment of crisis is fitted into this parallel structure. Whatever the original source of the plot may have been, the tale as told here was a typically Limba one.

THREE twins were once born. They were full grown. There was a girl there in the village. Koto got up. He pledged[1] the girl to love. Yemi did not know. Yemi got up. He pledged the girl to love. Saiong got up. He pledged the girl to love. But none of them knew about each other.

Then Koto got up. 'Father, I am going to travel. But give me a thousand in money.' His father said, 'Yes.' He counted the money. He gave it. Koto went off. He went for long. He saw a glass. He asked, 'Old man, what is that hanging there? I want to buy it.' 'A thousand, that is the price I am selling it.' He counted out the money. He gave the old man the thousand. He took down the glass. He put it in his bag. He went off.

Yemi got up then. 'Father, I am going to travel. But I want you to give me one thousand.' His father counted the thousand in money. He gave him it. He set out to travel. He went for long. He came to a hut. He saw a tail[2] hanging up. 'Old man, greetings. Who owns the tail that is hanging up?' 'I do.' 'Oh, I want to buy it.' 'Well, there it is. A thousand in money.' He counted out the money. He gave it. The tail was cut down. He was given it. He went off.

Saiong got up there also. 'Father, I am going to travel. But I want you to give me one thousand in money.' His father said, 'All right.' He counted out the money, one thousand. He gave him it. Saiong went off. He went for long. He saw a skin hanging up. 'E, who owns the skin?' The old man said, 'I own it.' 'Will you not sell it?' 'I will sell it. But it is one thousand.' Saiong counted out the money, the thousand. He gave it to the old man. The old man cut down the skin. He gave it to Saiong. Saiong travelled on. He went off.

[1] A term used for giving a gift either to begin the official wooing for marriage or by a lover to a girl he loves. The girl's name is Kati.

[2] An animal's tail is frequently used in ritual and dancing.

They went for long—across the salt water, as far as London,[1] as far as Paris.[2] They went there. They began to come back, the three of them. They came to a road junction. Koto was coming from the road over there, he came like to here.[3] Yemi set out like from here, he came to the junction here. Saiong came like from that road here. They came and met each other all together, *gbegberise!*[4] 'E, Koto, greetings. What have you brought from your travelling?' 'A glass.'

At that time, behold the girl whom they all went to for love in secret (and none of them, the three of them, knew about each other)—behold, she died. It was in the far distance that the girl died, like from here as far as England.

Koto said, 'I got a glass on my travels.' Yemi said, 'Show me. Let me look.' He took it out. 'What is this for?' 'Oh, if you look here, you can see everything in our home.' Yemi put his eye to the glass. He looked at his own village. He saw the girl—she was dead. 'Oh oh! my love is dead.' 'Who?' 'Kati.' 'Oh,' said Koto, 'she is my love. What are we to do?' Then Yemi said, 'If we had something to take us there, if I could only reach there, she could be cured.'

[Saiong][5] said, 'Friend. Show me. Let me look through the glass.' He looked. 'Oh! It is my love. Come you two.' He opened out the skin. In one minute they had been brought to England! They found the dead body now lying near the grave ready to be put in. They arrived.

Yemi took out the tail. 'Don't bury her, don't bury.' He opened out the white cloth, all of it.[6] He covered the grave. He took out the tail. He struck the girl. The girl got up. She sat up.

Koto stood up there at once. 'E, she is my love. It was I who caused you to know that our love had died.' Yemi stood up there, 'E, she is my love. I raised her up.' Saiong stood up there. 'I brought you on the wind. I own her love.'

Of those three people—the glass, the skin, the tail— which is the one of those three who owns the love?

[1] People have sometimes heard of London as a far-off and mysterious place where strange things happen.

[2] Several Limba have themselves been, or know those who have been, to Guinea (previously French Guinea), often referred to as 'Paris'.

[3] The various directions are shown by gesture.

[4] i.e. at precisely the same place and time.

[5] The teller made a slip and said Yemi by mistake.

[6] The white cloth in which a corpse is wrapped for burial.

The oldest of three twins

KARANKE DEMA. *Dictated* 26.10.61

A story which illustrates how bad it is to abuse one who is older than yourself. Just before initiation in particular it is normal for the older boys, already initiated, to abuse the younger boys with words and blows, saying that they are impertinent to them ('abuse them'); it is required that the younger boys should not defend themselves against this—though in practice, specially in cases where they happen to be stronger than their tormentors, they do sometimes attempt to do so. This common situation would be at once recalled by the story when told in a Limba context.

The events of the story are intended to be fantastic, as so often with those in which twins figure—they cross a river by means of one of their legs, and Koto is miraculously able to appear in the hen cage though left marooned at the other side of the river.

THREE twins were once born. One—the eldest—was Koto; one Yemi; one Luseni.

When they grew up, the dry season came. The locust beans were ripe.[1] Now Koto was the senior. But he was not tall. He had not grown quickly. Yemi and Luseni had both grown quickly. They set out, they went to pick the locust beans, to pick them for the old woman, their mother. They set out. They went.[2] But there was a great river on the way. No bridge. When they had reached there, Yemi got up and said, 'I will take you across.' On the way they were going, there was a pool. Yemi put out his leg, and said, 'Go across.' They crossed. They crossed, all three of them. They went and picked the locust beans.

They started out to return. They came to the water. Then Luseni said, 'Yemi, we, let us not take Koto across. For he is always abusing us.' Then Yemi said, 'All right.' Now Koto was the oldest. When they abused him, Koto returned it; for he was the oldest. But he was not tall. They got up. They crossed. They left Koto there. As soon as they had crossed, then Koto said where he was standing on the far side, 'Luseni, when you reach our mother, tell her I forgot to free the hens.' They agreed, from the far side. They came. They left Koto there.

When they came in, they were welcomed by their mother. They put down the locust beans. Then their mother asked, 'What about Koto?' Then Luseni said, 'We left him there, on the far side of the water.' Then their mother said, 'What? What was the reason that you left him there?' Then Luseni said, 'He is always abusing us. That is why we did not

[1] The fruit of the locust tree (*parkia biglobosa*), eaten raw or cooked at certain times of the year,

[2] They went right off for far—this is shown by the high tone of *ke* (went).

bring him across.' Then their mother said, 'What! You did not do well. Because he abuses you, that offended you? But what if you abuse him, you the younger ones, because he is not tall? Yet he is the one that is the oldest.' Then Luseni said, 'Oh, mother! We nearly forgot what he told us, that he forgot to free the hens; that you are to free them.'

Their mother went out to free the hens from their cage.[1] She went and opened it—there she saw Koto, in the cage, the one for the hens, Koto who had been left on the far side of the water!

When he came out, then he said to Yemi, 'Yemi.' Yemi answered 'Yes?' 'You accepted today the deceit put to you by Luseni. But I have no case against Luseni. You are older than he is.[2] It is with you I am disagreeing. For I am older than you. For we were born on one day—I was born first, you were born, and Luseni was born, he was the last. He said a word to you: you agreed to it—but I did not think that you would do that to me. It is because I am not tall that you actually left me at the water, you did not bring me across. But I have shown you today that I am the senior.'

Then they were astonished at that. You see now, we Limba—the first born of your family, even if he is not tall, treat him well, for he is the senior. If he becomes—if he becomes well off, he will speak for you, saying, 'I am the older.' If you see now that we fear the oldest—that is from Luseni and Yemi. This—leaving their oldest brother at the water, saying 'We will not bring you across; you are always abusing us.' The younger boys abused the oldest: he returned the abuse, it turned into trouble for the younger ones.

Three twins and an elephant

KARANKE DEMA. *Dictated* 26.10.61

A story ending in a dilemma—which of three twins who all achieve impossible tasks was the greatest in 'cunning'? (I also heard a story with a similar plot told by one of the children from Karanke's village in which the plots of this and *The oldest of three twins* were run together to make one brief story ending with the boy's return home and no dilemma.)

[1] Hens are sometimes shut into a cage at night. These are much too small for a human to fit inside.

[2] He does not blame Luseni as he only did what his elder brother Yemi told him.

A STORY again.[1] Three twins again came out. One Koto, one Yemi, one Luseni. They were going to go to hunt, the three of them. They said, 'Let us go to hunt elephants.' They set out. Then Koto said, 'I, when we find the tracks, I will shoot.'[2] Then Yemi said, 'When you shoot there, and when it dies, and when we find it, I will cut it up, I alone.'[3] Then Luseni said, 'When you have cut it up, I will find something to carry it in.'[4]

They set out. They found the tracks of an elephant. Koto aimed. He shot. The bullet set out, it went, it came to the elephant. It entered there, the elephant died.

They set out, to follow where the bullet had gone and killed it. They went. For four days they went. They did not come to where the elephant was. On the fifth, they arrived. They came to the elephant. Then Yemi said, 'Yes, Koto, you have finished your part. My part, that is left now.' He took his nail, the first one [thumb]. He pulled it out, its full length. With that he cut up the elephant! When he had finished cutting it up, he piled it up. He said, 'I have finished my part.'

Then Luseni said, 'All right. Koto, thank you. Yemi, thank you. We did not bring each other into shame. Since we came out into the wilderness, if we had not killed—shame. Since you have come and done this, that pleases me.[5] My part is left now.' He got up, he Luseni, he pinched a small fly, he split it open. The empty skin, there he put in the whole elephant! It went in there.

When they brought it—of those three, Koto, Yemi, and Luseni, which one was the most in cunning? That is what I ask you, you Yenkeni.

Tungkangbei, Palongbei, and Yisinua

NIAKA DEMA. *Dictated* 20.10.61

As in other stories about these three twins, Tungkangbei brings the other two into trouble by his continual irresponsibility from which his brothers keep trying to dissuade him. Yet it is Tungkangbei who succeeds in winning chiefship and his brothers end up in his debt.The moral stated seems to be that you should obey the one who speaks and holds power.

[1] This story was told immediately after *The oldest of three twins*.

[2] i.e. aim and shoot when the animal itself was not visible, only the tracks.

[3] Skin and cut it up, a job which is usually reckoned to need a special expedition of many helpers sent out from the village.

[4] Carrying the meat home is also heavy work even for many men.

[5] The terminology used here is typical of formal thanking.

Stories about these three twins are popular and always cause great amusement. Part of the plot here occurs commonly. See also the following story.

KANU once bore children. They grew up, twins. One was Tungkangbei, one Palongbei, one Bantantiande [Yisinua].[1]

When they stood up, they began to travel round. They came to a chief. These men, all of them, they were well known. Everyone who saw one of them was afraid of the men. When they went to the chief, they went and found there beautiful girls, very, very, very beautiful. Tungkangbei, Palongbei, and Yisinua, they all found loves there. When they were cooked for, for each one they [the girls] brought a basin of rice to their room where they had lodged them. They ate the rice. When they had eaten the rice, they sat down. When sleeping came, they said, 'It is good that every woman that we have come and given a gift to, that we should have them to sleep here, to converse with.' They did not refuse. They went and lay there.

When it came to the middle of the night, Tungkangbei got up. 'It is good, Palongbei and Yisinua, that we should kill the girls.' That is what Tungkangbei said, 'Let us kill the girls.' Then Yisinua got up. 'E! You say—the ones who came and gave us the rice, those ones we are to kill? We will not do it.' When Palongbei heard that, Palongbei said, 'We were told that we were not to do anything bad.' Then Tungkangbei said, 'You! Father told us that we were not to refuse each other. That is what I tell you.' Tungkangbei said, 'Let us lie down.' As soon as they slept, he took a knife—they were now sleeping—he took the girls, he killed them.

When it was morning now at the first light of sun—there was a cotton tree there, like the tree growing here—that cotton tree, there was where the chief always washed[2] in the morning. The cotton tree was a hundred fathoms, very big. Early in the morning, they climbed up the cotton tree. They went and perched right up on the top twigs where the cotton tree ended.

When the light came now, they went. One woman got up. 'E, the young men and the girls, will they not wake?' When they opened the door, the blood was now on the floor. Then the girl put her hands up on her head,[3] she wept. 'The young men who lodged here, chief, they have come and killed our children, much mourning.' 'Oh, them!'—the chief wept. 'It is good for us to search where they went.'

The chief went and sat to wash. All his messengers now, they had

[1] Tungkangbei, 'Daring things', Palongbei, 'Fearing things', Bantantiande, 'Don't refuse' (throughout the rest of the story called Yisinua).

[2] Lit. rinsed his mouth, part of the normal morning washing.

[3] In mourning.

been sent all round on the roads, to find them, to come and kill them. Kanu now would have saved them. Tungkangbei got up; he said, 'It is good for us to urinate on the chief.' Then Palongbei said, 'E! You—here where we are sitting? So much now,[1] Yisinua.' Yisinua said, 'E! Tungkangbei, do not do that!' Palongbei had not yet finished saying this, when he undid the cord of his trousers, he pointed at the chief's head, he urinated on him! The chief saw now that it was the dry season, that rain was falling that dry season! He turned his eyes. He saw them. 'E! Here they are up above, the men.'

The chief was going to cut down the cotton tree. They came and stood, a hundred men, to cut down the cotton tree. Just as they had chopped one side, as they were coming to approach the tree to fell it, a lizard got up from there. 'E, they, children of my father, very, very fine children, they are going to die today.' He came and went right round it once. The cotton tree filled up there. It did not fall. They chopped again. The cotton tree would have fallen—the lizard came again, he went round again, the cotton tree filled up again.

Then Tungkangbei said, 'E! You. That man [lizard], let us strike him. He is bringing us suffering.' Then Palongbei said, 'E! You, cease! The one who has saved us, will you come and kill him? Don't do that! Ah! don't do that!' Yisinua said, 'You, cease! Thus we were told by our father, that destroying things is not good.' Yisinua had not yet finished speaking, he [Tungkangbei] struck the lizard. The lizard fell.

As the cotton tree was beginning to fall, there was an eagle there. When the cotton tree began to fall, then the eagle got up there—all three of them, the eagle caught hold of them. He embraced them with his wings. They went off, for far.

Tungkangbei said, 'E! men, have you found a good place to sit? I, here where I am sitting, there is a smell, its anus. I am going to prick it.' Then Palongbei said, 'E! You, you are a wicked man. Here where we are being flown, pricking the anus of our parents' man [the eagle]! Will we not fall?' Then Yisinua said, 'Hey! For that you are an accursed man!' Before they had finished that—he [Tungkangbei] had a nail, just as they reached to a rock, to the middle of it, he pricked the bird's anus. The bird let them go. They were crashed on to the rock. They lay there. They died.

When they had died, they spent there two days, they lay there, they were dead. Kanu now, he had sent a tortoise out; wherever it found someone dead, it went and sprinkled him with *mafɔi* medicine, he became well. When the tortoise found them, he said, 'E! The children—they are fine. Ha! It is a wonderful thing to me. I—it was for this I was sent by Kanu, wherever I find someone dead I am to sprinkle him with medicine.' He squeezed the medicine. He sprinkled Yisinua. He

[1] The formal phrase for 'passing the word' to Yisinua.

sprinkled Palongbei. Palongbei said, and he, Yisinua, 'Don't sprinkle the one lying there. If you sprinkle him, you will be his food today. It was he that caused us to be lying here. He has an obstinate heart.' 'E! what, the fine one here? I will sprinkle him with medicine.' He sprinkled him.

Tungkangbei got up. He sneezed, *thisio!* He said, 'I had a dream that I was just smashing a tortoise.' Palongbei said 'Well, friend![1] What I told you about has begun now!' He [Tungkangbei] seized the tortoise, he broke him on the rock. 'Men, hold the tortoise here for me, I am going for fire, so that I may eat him.' He would have died, but Kanu did not allow it—the healer, he was the one he was going to kill! He went off to fetch the fire.

Palongbei and Yisinua let the tortoise go, saying 'Run!' Behold the direction that Tungkangbei went in, that was where the tortoise went!

'Men, let go the one there now oh! I have caught another one here.' He went and smashed it. He ate it. 'Men, let us separate in this journey.' Tungkangbei went off to one side. Yisinua went up. Palongbei went down.

When Tungkangbei got up, he went to a great chiefship. The chief had a place where he bathed, a great pool. When Tungkangbei arrived there, he went and sat. The chief undressed. He went in to bathe. As soon as he had entered the water, Tungkangbei got up, he went and struck the chief in the water. He killed him there.

When he came out, he came and put on the chief's things himself. He put on his shoes, he began to come to the village here. He was welcomed. He came and sat on the chair. He was not known. They thought that the chief had gone and changed his skin, that he had come out as a young man.

He began to ask many questions. 'Since I went and changed my skin I do not know my cousins[2] now.' The cousins came out. 'E, father. Here we are.' 'Sit down. But I don't know how many wives I have.' The wives came out, they were lined up, more than fifty.[3] 'Sit down. But I don't know how many children I have.' The children all gathered. They came and lined up, more than sixty. 'Sit down. But I have forgotten now where my court is.' He was lifted up by the cousins, he was carried to his house. 'But I don't know now how many sub-chiefs I have.' The sub-chiefs came and gathered, more than thirty. They sat down. 'But

[1] 'Friend' or 'cousin' (*ka wo*), the usual term when the speaker wants to imply 'I told you so!'

[2] 'Cousins' (*sesaiŋ*), i.e. those in the relationship of classificatory mother's brother or cross-cousin. The members of all the non-ruling clans are sometimes collectively called *sesaiŋ*.

[3] All the numbers are exaggerated for effect.

I don't know now how many cattle I have, and goats.' They were loosed. He came and counted them, three hundred. 'Tie them up there.'

The chief had had cassava planted for him, it had grown very, very much. He went and was shown it.

Palongbei got up there, he was hungry, they were travelling around. He came to steal the cassava. He was caught. 'We are taking you to the chief.' Behold, that chief now—he was of one mother with him. When he came, 'Thief, sit on the chair.' He knew that it was his brother. When the sun rose, Yisinua came and was caught too at the cassava. He was caught there. [The chief said] 'Let no one come out!' They came and sat.

When they came and sat, conversing, Tungkangbei, he, when they came, he had gone and killed the chief. He was left with the chiefship there. He was left the [chiefly] staff now. He finished telling them all that. He took ten wives, he gave them to Palongbei. He took ten wives, he gave them to Yisinua. They sat down. 'See, men, who is the most of those born together, of us here, the twins? But I surpassed you. You would not have come to our home. But for me—I own this country now.' He took and said, 'For our father told us "Do not refuse each other"; but you were making me turn out useless; but by grace of the dead, I did not come out useless.' He took two villages, he gave them to Palongbei. 'Here are people to hoe for you.' He gave Yisinua three villages. 'Here are people to hoe for you.'

You see now, of [those born of] one mother, when one speaks or if one finds something, the one with strength—if he speaks, agree with him there. Perhaps the power that he has found, perhaps it will come over to you. That is why that is not allowed—if someone begins to find power, agree there. Perhaps if you bear a child there, perhaps that child will come out a chief, perhaps a great sub-chief.

Since I heard that, and you have come to be taught stories, that is it. It is ended.

The three rascal boys

KELFA KONTEH. *Dictated* 4.1.61

Another version of the same basic plot with several differences of detail, some additional episodes, and a different ending. The main point is the amusing narrative of the shocking episodes of Tungkangbali (the form of the name in the Biriwa dialect). The story was told with particular verve and drama, with great use of exaggeratedly high and lengthy tones and words used for their effective sounds. The title is that added by the English-speaking narrator.

THE story of three rascal boys. One day, three children were born. They had one father, but their mothers were different.

When they grew up, they said they would go to greet the chief. When they went, they were given a lodging. They were given food. The chief spoke well with them. When they had finished eating, Tungkangbali said that they should break the bowl. Palongbali and Wunekeria begged him, saying that they should not do that. But Tungkangbali said, 'Our father told us that we were not to refuse each other.' When they agreed to that, they broke the bowl, *wɛsa wɛsa!* Not long after, the girl who had cooked for them came for the things. When she saw that they had broken the bowl, that offended her. But they begged. They told lies, so they would be released. The chief released them. The chief told the girl to prepare food for them in a thick bowl so that they would not be able to break it. When they had eaten Tungkangbali said that they should break the bowl. The two boys who were afraid of trouble begged him not to do it. 'If we do that, the chief will kill us.' Tungkangbali said, 'What did our father say?' They broke the bowl. The chief—that offended him. He called his people for the boys to be killed.

When the boys were just about to be caught, they climbed up a cotton tree. The people began to cut down the tree. When they had been cutting it for long, the cotton tree was just about to fall, a lizard knocked on the tree, *gbɔ gbɔ!* The cotton tree became as it was before, completely! This happened up to three times. When it came to the fourth, Tungkangbali said, 'I will tell them what is preventing them, why they are not able to cut down the cotton tree.' His brothers said to him, 'If you do that we will fall with the cotton tree, and we will die.' Then he asked them, 'What did our father say?' They said, 'That we were not to refuse each other.' The lizard was killed.

The cotton tree began to fall. When it began to fall, a hawk saw them with pity. He said, 'Get up on to my back. Let me carry you to another chiefdom.' When they had gone for far, Tungkangbali said, 'The hawk's bottom—a smell is coming out.' He said they should prick it. His brother said to him, 'If we do that, we will be let go and fall to the ground.' Tungkangbali said, 'What did our father say?' They pricked the hawk's bottom. Just as they reached a flat rock the hawk felt the pain. He let them go—*gbaŋ!* They all fainted.

A tortoise came. When the tortoise came, he saw them with pity. He said, 'I will sprinkle them with *manasi* medicine so that they may be cured.' When the two who feared trouble were cured, they told the tortoise not to wake Tungkangbali. But the tortoise said, 'What! When I have wakened you, you do not want me to waken your companion?' Behold, a little of the medicine fell on him while they were arguing. Tungkangbali awoke. As he woke, he said, 'I see a tortoise.' His brothers begged him not to kill it. But he took no notice of them. He gave the tortoise to one brother to keep for him, so that he could go for fire to a farm hut. As he went, they let go the tortoise. He and the tortoise that had been let go met! He seized it. He said, 'Eat that tortoise there, I have got a tortoise here for myself now.'

Then they decided (?) to separate, for his brothers were so afraid of trouble. Tungkangbali went one way. His brothers went another way.

When he was going, he saw an adder. He killed this adder. He carried it on his head. When he had gone for far, he came to a smith. He said, 'Here is what I have brought you. I have come here to learn.'[1] That pleased the smith very much. He said to the other apprentices, 'You are not good. Look at this man here who has come just now, he has brought something with him when he comes.' Tungkangbali stayed there to blow the bellows. Behold, he was looking at the nails in the fire, seeing that they were red. Now the smith had a huge scrotum. Tungkangbali took a nail, he pierced the scrotum—*poo!* When he had pierced it, he ran away.

He began to be chased. When he was caught, he was beaten for long. He was sent with the children to chase the birds.[2] When they were there chasing, he pushed a child that was blowing the fire into the fire. The child was burnt completely—*mururu!* He ran away.

People began to look for him. Wherever Tungkangbali went, he called together all the young men and asked them which was the greatest rascal there. Some said, 'I defecate in the chief's court', or 'I abuse the chief.' But Tungkangbali asked if any had the daring to pierce a smith's scrotum! As he was making that boast, there he was caught. He was tied into a basket. He was put into a bag. When he was put down, they went to look for wood. Children came to look at him. He took out ground nuts, he threw them on the ground. When they were thrown, the children took them. He said, 'If you free me, I will give you very many ground nuts.' The children freed him. He tied up the children in the bag. When the people came back, they took up the bag. The children cried. But they took no notice of them. They threw the children into the fire. By that time, Tungkangbali had run away.

[1] i.e. he had come to be the smith's apprentice, normally an important and formal proceeding. A smith is expected to receive great honour from his apprentices, hence the specially shocking nature of Tungkangbali's attack on him.

[2] Chasing birds is the usual task to which enemies and children are said to be put.

Tungkangbei, Palongbei, and Yisahosaho

SURI DEMA. *Dictated* 10.10.61

Another story of the three twins, the third this time is called Yisahosaho, a nonsense name. The story is intended to be ludicrous and far-fetched, ending with the question as to which was the most amazing of all. It mainly seems to illustrate greed—first that of the three twins, who, in their excitement at the thought of the meat they were going to eat, all died as a result of their stupid absorption in the prospect of their meal; and, secondly, that of the mother who not only was able to eat a whole cow herself, but was unaware of the pains of childbirth, and of her child who, only a few days old, was able to finish off all the cow bones. The dilemma as usual gave rise to discussion, and was considered a 'hard' one, for both mother and child were amazing; several thought the child was more—'a small child, with no teeth, to eat bones!'

This plot is a very well-known one, so that it was understood at once, though rather sketchily told. I heard several versions of the last episode in particular (the pregnant woman and the bones), always ending with the dilemma.

A STORY. Three children got up. One was Tungkangbei, one Palongbei, one Yisahosaho. They came here to our chief here, to be given a cow, so that they would not kill someone. 'We are hungry—great meat eaters!' They were given a cow. They went—trembling with excitement! saying, '*I* will kill it.' Palongbei said, 'I will lie underneath.'[1] The cow was put on top. It was killed. He killed Palongbei with it! He lifted him up, he threw him to one side! He said, 'I am going for water'—trembling with excitement! When he went, he went and threw himself into the water! For those who were left behind—a deer got up from there. It came. It stepped on the meat. He[2] said, 'E! This person—he has taken the meat.' He followed it. He went and caught its foot. He sucked [the meat on] it! He was kicked. He died from the deer, it had kicked the human. Well, he died.

Well, the meat was left now. No one to eat it. A pregnant woman got up there, looking for yams. She came. She saw the smoke. She said, 'Greetings to you.' No one. She got up. She went and greeted. No one. She went, she found the meat. She ate it, all of it—the pregnant woman. She ate it, *all*! She bore her child. She did not know that she had borne a child! The bones, she put them in the basket. She took the child, she put it in the basket where she had put the bones. When she had put the child in, she put the child on her head, there among the bones in the basket.

[1] He wants to stay near the cow in his eagerness for the meat.

[2] The remaining twin.

Before they entered the village, the child—he was only little, he was just born—he took the bones, he ate the bones! They started to enter. She was welcomed. 'Greetings, digger of yams.' 'I did not find yams. I found meat. I ate it—a little only.[1] I put the bones in the basket. But wait, let me lower the basket now.' When she lowered it, the child had taken the bones, he had eaten them all!

But of the child, and the mother, which, Yenkeni, was the more? the one who ate the meat, the cow, or the one who ate the bones—which was more?

A dilemma about three smokers

FANKA KONTEH. *Dictated* 25.11.61

A well-known dilemma which I heard several times. It can give rise to fairly lengthy (but light-hearted) discussion.

THREE men. One had a pipe, but he had no tobacco. Another said, 'I have tobacco, but I have no match.' Another said, 'I have a match.' The one who owned the pipe said, 'Give here the tobacco.' The one who owned the tobacco gave it. The other said, 'I have a match.' He gave the match. He put the tobacco in the pipe. He lit it. They smoked, all of them, the three. They finished smoking. The one who owned the pipe took it, he knocked out the ashes from the pipe. A girl came out from there [the ashes], a beautiful girl. Of those three, which is the one who owns the girl?

[1] The whole cow!

2 · STORIES ABOUT KANU AND ORIGINS

Kanu and the python

DAUDA KONTEH. *Recorded* 20.1.64

A story which gives an explanation for why Kanu is now up above in the sky; in the old days he lived together with human beings and animals but because the animals refused to take his advice to stop their quarrelling he withdrew from them to where he now is.

On my previous visit two years earlier Dauda had also told me a version based on the same plot; this earlier narration, however, was much less full and did not contain the characteristic introduction or conclusion, nor any singing. I did not meet this or a similar plot elsewhere and other people did not seem to be familiar with it at all.

MAY you hear me, Dauda, this evening—Dauda the son of Fane Konteh of Kamabai, leaning on this chair oh! Well, may you listen to me. My father is from here; my brothers are from here; my mother is from here; well, my child is from here—may you listen to me. The reason is —to get wisdom in stories from your friend; if someone hears stories, if he is a very wise man he will remember them.[1] . . . Stand and listen. To let it enter your heart and to remember it—that is what is meant by a wise man.

Well, a story for you, oh! May you listen oh! Ha! The world had not yet begun! I am Dauda. Once we were together with Kanu above, we were all together here below; Kanu above and we were once together.

For you to see why Kanu fled from us—well, [because of] a python and a deer. The deer once set out. It went to travel among the bushes (?). Now a python was also curling along there, searching for something to eat. Well, it got up, searching for food for it to go and eat, it and the deer. It said, 'Deer.' 'Yes?' 'What have you come for?' 'Ah, I have come to look for something to eat.' 'Oh! What you have come for you will find yourself!'[2] 'E! Father. Don't do that!' 'I will do it.' It ran after the deer. The deer ran right off [to Kanu], singing 'Kanu yo, Kanu yo, Kanu yo, Kanu yo, Kanu yo, Kanu yo.'[3] Now I, Dauda, I too

[1] He adds a complicated sentence about a reference the chief had made recently about how he himself knew only the stories about the historical chiefs such as Suluku, and not the fictional (or 'lying') stories.

[2] i.e. the deer will be eaten itself.

[3] The words are half-sung and repeated at intervals throughout the story.

was standing there, I was peeping [at them], seeing where the world began and where it was going. Then Kanu said, 'Deer. Come and stand [here].' The deer stood. Ah! The python came. 'Python.' 'Yes?' 'What are you doing?' 'Father, this thing [deer] came and disturbed me. It was going to feed. I too was hungry, I too going to feed. When I said I was going to swallow it, it ran away. That is why we are quarrelling (?).' Kanu said, 'Ha! Python.' 'Yes?' 'You have started trouble. Cease.'[1] 'Oh! Father! No chance of that! I am not ceasing—I must swallow it.' 'Ha! Cease!' 'Ha! That? No, never!' Kanu said, 'Well—you have begun to lose me.' 'Father it must not get away.' The python seized it, it swallowed the deer. Now I was sitting there (?), leaning over and peeping!

When it set out now, it the python, it went to travel. Well, a swarm came out there, very, very, very many of them. They arose, those called ants. It came and disturbed the ants. The ants followed it. 'Python.' 'Yes?' 'You have disturbed me on my way. You—we must eat you all up.' 'E!' [The python] rushed out, running to Kanu. It set out, singing, 'Kanu yo, Kanu yo, Kanu yo, Kanu yo, Kanu yo, Kanu yo.' Kanu said, 'What is it? Stand.' It stood. 'E, well.' Kanu said 'Stand.' They stood. 'What is it?' 'Ah! It came and disturbed us—we must kill it, the python.' 'E! Ha! You have begun on an evil exchange[2]—to make me disappear.' 'Father.' 'Yes?' 'It is not an evil exchange.' 'All right.' They seized the python—*pɛ!* They ate it. Now I was there listening to them, I did not speak a word. . . .

When they set out after eating it, they left it, they set out, going to travel round. As they went into the bush a fire began there. The ants set out, running, chanting 'Kanu yo, Kanu yo, Kanu yo, Kanu yo, Kanu yo, Kanu yo.' 'Ha! What is it?' 'We went and disturbed the fire. The fire said it would lick us all up. Ha! That is why we have come.' Kanu said, 'E! What I was afraid of has happened. I Kanu, I have turned to being wept to.'[3] They said, 'No.' The fire seized them. The fire came up *dɛɛɛɛ*,[4] the fire licked up the ants.

The fire set out, going. The fire came out and met with the water, in the middle. Ah! It chanted, the fire, coming to Kanu—'Kanu yo, Kanu yo, Kanu yo, Kanu yo, Kanu yo, Kanu yo.' Kanu said, 'Stand, fire.' It stood. The water arrived there—*thɛŋbu thɛŋbu thɛŋbu thɛŋbu*. 'Water.' 'Yes?' 'Stand.' They stood. 'Ha! What is it?' 'The fire came and disturbed me. There is no other chance to end [the quarrel]—except to eat the fire.' Kanu said, 'Oh?' 'Yes.' The fire came and was pursued. The

[1] i.e. stop quarrelling—advice that should be taken.

[2] Lit. company (*kunɛ*).

[3] Kanu is 'wept to' in two senses: by the animals in the tale who rush weeping to Kanu to ask for help, and by human beings in the world now who cry 'Ah Kanu' when someone has died.

[4] The menacing sound of the fire coming; later the sound of the water is also imitated.

water came. 'You say you will make me disappear?' 'Yes.' The fire went there, *wuuuuu*. The fire was eaten up.

Kanu said now, 'Ha! Where I am staying, I see now—all right. For me, I am disappearing.' Kanu began, he went up above. He always turns his eyes on us. Why was it that Kanu fled from us to go up above and now sends us a way to weep? It was because of the obstinacy which the python began. From that it began that people were parted from Kanu, we who once lived together with Kanu Masala. No one then went anywhere, but lived together.

Since I have ended this evening, I Dauda Konteh, the son of Fane at Kamabai, that is it, Yenkeni Konteh. The story, this dusk evening, that is it. Since I have ended, it is finished, I Dauda Konteh.

True, true[1]—Yes—if I am telling lies, well, if I am telling lies, when I die, may I not find anyone to carry me to the grave; if I speak the truth may I see those who carry me to the grave—very clearly, I, Dauda Konteh. It is finished.

The toad did not love us

SANGBANG YELEME. *Dictated* 3.10.61

A story about the origin of death. The plot seems relatively common and I heard several other versions (see *The toad and the snake* and *The toad and death*). Sangbang's main emphasis in his narration was on the tragic aspect; the story was told with great sadness and quiet drama. The tragedy was both in the toad's hatred of mankind (thus resulting in our death) and also in the present paradoxical reversal by which men care for the one who hated them and kill the one who would have helped them.

Other stories which mention the origin of death, but in a completely different framework, are *The story of two women* and *Kanu scatters his children on earth.*

THE toad—ah, the toad did not love us. Kanu was squeezing out leaves for medicine. He squeezed the leaf-medicine. He wanted people not to see death. He said, 'But the medicine, who will carry it to the humans?'[2] The snake said, 'I will carry it.' Then the toad said, 'No. I will carry it for them. We are near to each other.' But he—ah!—he did not love us. He wanted to kill us all. He was told, 'Here is the medicine.' He put it on his head to carry it, he set out to go. When he jumped once—*tɔliŋ!*[3]—the medicine fell off, *bukute!*[4] He spilt it. Ah! It had been said

[1] Interpolated by one of the listeners; his point is taken up and elaborated by Dauda.

[2] Lit. Limba.

[3] The sound of the jump.

[4] The sound of the medicine spilling.

that if anyone carried this medicine, he was not to spill it. The snake who loved us, he did not allow him to bring it to us. The one who hated us, it was he who brought it. He went and upset it.

So, if you see us dying now, it is because of the toad. The white people and we the Limba, we would not have died but for the toad.

And now, this is how we and the toad are: where we build houses, he loves that place. That is why we drive him out. But the snake, who loved us in the beginning, he always pursues him, pursuing the toad. The toad runs to us. Well, the one who loved us then, well, when we meet him now, we kill him. We do not kill the toad. Well, Kanu looks at us for that.

Since you said you wanted to hear about it, that is how we are with the toad. That is it. It is finished.

The toad and the snake

KARANKE DEMA. *Dictated* 29.1.64

A slightly more elaborate version of the same plot as in *The toad did not love us* and *The toad and death*. Here an extra point is included about the snake—that when it is old it merely changes its skin and does not die unless it is killed by someone. This version also contains a rather more explicit reference than the others to the common Limba sentiment that disobedience to what one is told often leads to disaster.

WE Limba, we would not have been dying—for once Kanu loved us, he wanted us not to die, us and all the animals. He made *mafɔi* medicine—'I will give it to you.' He made it—two parts. For the Limba—one part. For the snakes—one part.

He said, 'Snake, you are to carry it to the Limba.' The snake said, 'Yes.' The toad got up—'*I* will carry it; for the way the snake goes is not good, going very quickly. He will soon spill it.' The snake said, 'I will not spill it. I will go quickly.' The toad would not allow it.

The snake took the one for them [snakes] saying he would take it. He carried it quickly, he did not spill it.

Now the toad—he took the one for the Limba, to carry it. Behold he was not able at all. He had just put it on his head, he jumped, when he jumped the second time he spilt the medicine.

He took the bowl.[1] He went back to Kanu and said, 'The medicine—it has spilt. Please look for more [medicine].' Then Kanu said, 'I will

[1] The now empty bowl which had contained the medicine.

not be able to get more now. I told you not to take it, you disobeyed, you went and just spilt it—I will not be able to get more now.' He did not give any more then, he Kanu, because of the disobedience of the toad.

You see now always—we Limba are always dying: it was the toad who caused that. He spilt the medicine for the Limba. But the snakes, those who did not spill it, they do not die except when someone kills them. But if you do not kill him, when he gets old he bathes in the medicine which they carried then, which they were given then by Kanu. Well, that is it.

The toad and death

FANKA KONTEH. *Dictated* 29.11.61

Another version of the same plot as in *The toad did not love us*, with a rather different conclusion, the paradoxical reversal not being included here.

KANU once said, 'If I make medicine for the Limba, who will take the medicine to the Limba?' The snake said, '*I* will take it.' The toad said, 'It is not the snake who should take it, I will take it.' The toad took the medicine, he put it on his head to carry it. He set out to come. When he had leapt once, and leapt again, he upset the medicine, he did not bring it to the Limba.

That is why the snake and the toad are enemies. Whenever the snake sees the toad, he catches him saying, 'It was you who did not agree to take the medicine.' Therefore the toad and snake are enemies. That is what caused the Limba to die. If the snake had brought the medicine, the Limba would not ever have been dying. But the toad did not agree. He upset the medicine on the road. That is why the snake and the toad are enemies.

Kanu gave food to the Limba

KARANKE DEMA. *Dictated* 15.10.61

A story about how the Limba were first shown how to prepare, cook, and cultivate their main food, rice. The whole story was told almost in the tone of a miracle, specially the part describing the people's despair as they farmed for the first time followed by the sun coming out to dry the forest and the rain coming at night. Karanke said the story was 'true' (*thia*); the old people told it to the children when they asked about how they knew about rice farming. He was told it a long time ago, but 'I am always thinking about it'. A somewhat similar story is included in C. F. Schlenker's *Collection of Temne Traditions*, 1861.

The descriptions of the various stages of cooking and, even more, of farming and the development of the rice would be particularly full of meaning to a Limba listener.

KANU and we in the old days: we Limba[1] had then no food. We just lived there. There was nothing. No water. No fire. The sun did not shine. The rain did not fall. The Limba stayed there, two of them; they stayed—ah! they thought about their hunger! But there was nothing. They sat drooping.

When Kanu saw that, he came down below. He asked, 'Why are you drooping here like this?' They said, 'Ah! our father,[2] we—you brought us out, but we are suffering. We have nothing to eat.' Then Kanu said, 'All right. I will help you for your food.' When he went back, he thought; he said 'I will give you something that will help you; but there will be a time when it will do bad, and you will not like it; but you will not be able to leave it behind anywhere, for it helps you.'[3]

After he had gone up above, he came down. He brought rice. He came and told them, 'Here is your food. Do you know how to work it?' They said, 'No; we don't know how.' He went and got a mortar and a pestle and a fanning basket. He put them all down. 'Well now, put it in the mortar. Pound it.' He [Limba][4] pounded, it broke up. 'Turn it out; fan it.' He fanned it. 'Put it in again.' He pounded, the chaff came off. 'Turn it out.' He turned it out. 'Fan it.' He fanned it. 'Put it in the mortar again.' He put it in. He pounded it. It was clean. He turned it out. He fanned.

He took—at that time there were no pots except clay pots—he took a clay pot. He looked for palm fibre—he Kanu. He went to a stone. He called them 'Look here.' He struck it with a knife. Fire came. It caught the palm tinder. He looked for wood, he put it on the fire. The fire blazed up well. He went to a big stone, he said, 'Kanu below,[5] I am begging

[1] Or 'humans'.

[2] 'Our father', a term used here, and in other stories, to indicate sadness or entreaty. It does not necessarily mean that they regard Kanu as their father.

[3] i.e. fire, which is both an essential tool in farming, and also destroys their houses etc. Matches are now common, but people still know how to make fire by striking a knife on a stone and catching the sparks on palm tinder, as described later in the story.

[4] The Limba personal pronoun does not differentiate between 'he' and 'she'. Normally it is a woman who beats and fans the rice, but this is not explicit from the language. The point here is that it is a *Limba*, not that it is a woman.

[5] 'Kanu below'—this phrase is seldom used, though it sometimes refers collectively to the dead, witches, and perhaps spirits.

you; let us help each other, so we may help the people; so they may not suffer. Send out something cool for them.' He dug in the ground. Water came out. It was very clear. He scooped it up. He went and put it in the clay pot. He made the fire. It lit. The pot boiled. He put in the rice, it boiled. It became dry. He helped it out. It cooled. He took it out, he Kanu. He ate. He swallowed. He said, 'All right, eat.'

When they ate, there where they ate, they sweated, their hunger vanished. Their bodies were all clear.[1] He asked, 'Well, was it good?' They said, 'Yes.' 'This is your food. The fire, it is your witness. The mortar, it is what comes first. The basket, it is your fanner. The pestle, it is your fighter. The water, it is your food. If you are lying ill, bathe, your body will be clear. If you are sweating, go and bathe, your body will be clear. But one thing I tell you—work.'[2]

He left them a little rice—so much[3]—in a pan. It is the rice called millet rice, because it comes quickly. 'Cut the forest. When you have cut it, I will help you so that it may become dry. When it is dry, put in fire. When it burns, go and sow, and hoe it. I will help you to let it grow up. When it grows up and is big, weed the grass. When it is in ear, drive away the animals. I will help you so that you will see the seeds become round. When it is dry, you will harvest it, and thrash it. It will be like this rice. It will be more than it. Well, that is *your* bank.[4] Every year, that is what you will do.' When he had said that to them, he went up above.

The time came near. They cut down the forest. They said, 'Ah, we! we have cut; but we will not be able to put in fire—it is soaked.' Kanu brought out the sun. It was hot. It shone for about a month. It became dry. They went and put fire. It burnt. They hoed. Then they said 'Ah, we! we have hoed; but it will not grow—there is only the sun shining.' Kanu said, 'All right. I will help you.' He brought out the rain. It came, at night. Before they had gone in the morning, it was soaked. They said 'Ah, Kanu; thank you.'

The rice—in six days it began to grow; in twelve days it had leaves. It grew big in two months. In the third it got seeds below. It was in ear. In one month it was dry. When it was dry and the sun was shining, the rice was opening up like this.[5] Kanu brought the rain. The rain went into the mouth of the rice. For ten days it drank all the water. In twenty days again it was dry. They went and cut it. They thrashed it. They dried it over the fire. They pounded it. They cooked it. As Kanu had

[1] Well and healthy.

[2] The Limba pride themselves on their capacity for hard work, and are also well known for this among other people in Sierra Leone, and by European employers.

[3] About one foot across.

[4] The English term is used.

[5] Opening its mouth—demonstrated by the teller.

shown them, so they all did. They ate. When they had finished harvesting, it was much now: more than what they had sowed. That pleased them. Therefore they said, 'Ah Kanu, thank you. We are saved by you since you helped us with the wisdom you showed us.[1] We, we are living here below now, we will not forget about you.'

If you hear that we work now, hoeing the rice—well, it began with those orphans who would have died from hunger.

Since I said that I would tell you a story of the wisdom Kanu showed us, that is it.

The dog and the rice

LAMINA MANSARAY. 10.7.61

I was not able to take this text down verbatim as the story was told to me in the course of a very hilly walk and I was thus only able to make brief notes. However, I have included it as this is a relatively common plot to which I heard references at other times too, though was never in a position to take down a complete version. Though I could not take down the story word for word, the sequences and framework here are certainly correct. The references are all to stages in the farming year.

KANU brought out the Limba people. He also looked for something for them to eat. In those days, the dog was able to talk. He was the messenger between men and Kanu. Rice was brought out. The people woke up and saw the rice. They took it. But they did not know then what to do with it. They asked. The dog spoke. He answered, 'I am able to discover. I will ask Kanu.'

So he went to Kanu and said, 'We have a thing here.' Kanu said, 'The thing you saw—you must take the seeds from it and clear a farm.' The dog said, 'All right. But where are we to get the implements to clear a farm?' Then Kanu took a round stone for them to blow on[2] and get iron in the smith's hut. So they got iron and implements to clear the farm.

They cleared the bush. When they had cleared it, they sent up the dog to ask, 'We have cleared the bush. What are we to do now?' Kanu said, 'Fire it.'

They fired it. It burnt. When it had burnt, they sent up the dog again. 'We have burnt the farm. What are we to do now?' Kanu said,

[1] Their present plenty is being implicitly contrasted to their hunger and lack at the start of the story.

[2] Smelting probably used to be done to some extent by the Limba, and certainly by the neighbouring Koranko.

'Scatter the seed and hoe the earth. And when you see the birds and the animals coming, take a stone and throw it.'

So they hoed the earth. The rice came out. It came out with weeds. The dog went and asked, 'We have hoed. What will we do now?' Kanu said, 'Go and pull up the weeds.'

They pulled up the weeds. When they had weeded, the rice came strongly and grew seeds.[1] When the seeds began to come, the dog said, 'The thing you have given us has borne children.' Kanu said, 'Now you must drive away the same animals as you did before.'

They chased the animals. Then Kanu sent seeds inside. Kanu said that the rain should come. When the rice had taken in all this water, it stayed there, it slept. But Kanu did not tell them that they must use it as food. It was still stiff and hard.

The dog went. He asked, 'What will we do now?' Kanu told the dog, 'Take it and cut it. Thrash it. Then beat it; dry it; pound it; put it in a pot over the fire. It will be cooked.' But he did not tell them yet to eat it.

They cooked it. They sent the dog again to ask. When the dog had gone, those behind did not wait for the dog. They took out the rice. It stood there for long—the dog had not come. They said, 'Let us eat. We have had much trouble for this rice.'

They took it and ate it. The dog came to say we were to eat the rice. But we had already eaten it! The dog went and looked into the pot. He saw only the flies going *weeee!* saying 'You got no food!' The dog backed away. 'E!' That is why the dog cannot speak. He says 'E!' He worked but he was not paid. He helped us. We know the dog helped us. That is why we give a dog a name.[2] The dog cannot speak but he can understand.

Thus Kanu brought us out, and thus he brought out food.

Kanu gives chiefship 1

KARANKE DEMA. *Recorded* 29.1.64

The story describes the origin of chiefship in a typically Limba way. The purpose of chiefship is implied to be to look after 'orphans' (those with no relations or guardians) and the sick. Sara is given the usual symbols of chiefship by Kanu, and, consistently with the normal Limba view about chiefship, it is the man, Sara, who deserves to be given authority, and not the woman, Sirande, who has failed in the duty of hospitality and courtesy to a stranger.

The plot is a relatively familiar one (cf. the following version also) and certain episodes within it also occur in other stories; for example that of

[1] Lit. became pregnant. [2] To honour him, unlike other animals.

Kanu going round to look for a wise man (*The stomach is chief of the body*) and of a wife betraying her husband (as in *Sara, the spirit, and the palm tree*, a story not included in the present collection).

This version was recorded on my second visit. Two years before Karanke had narrated the same story. The two versions were very similar in their general framework, but differed in details and stress. The previous version, for example, did not include the touch about Kanu recognizing Sara because he knew the gourd he brought with the palm wine, nor did it lay such stress on the way Kanu 'heard how the woman spoke . . . saw how Sara acted'; but on that occasion he laid more stress on the many different symbols of power which were given, one by one, to mark the chiefship and on the number of blows to be given—six for a man, three for a woman; the name of the wife was also different (Sira not Sirande). In the present version more is made of the moralizing conclusion which, on the first occasion, was stated much more briefly.

A STORY for you, you Yenkeni, I am going to tell you a story, one I have thought of, one I heard from the old people.

In the old days there was no chiefship. Everyone lived for himself. Then Kanu Masala stayed up above—thinking, *sooŋ!*[1] He thought, 'I will look for a wise man to whom I will go and give the chiefship. For I see how all the people live, I see this; they do not live in one word [in agreement]. I will search for a chief for me to take, a wise man.' When Kanu Masala set out from up above, what did he do? His whole body—a gown covered with sores, that is what he put on. If you saw him—he was like someone bad, all wrinkled. Behold it was Kanu Masala.

He came down. 'I am going to find a wise man for me to go and take [as chief].'

When he came down, he arrived. At the first place he came to, he gave a greeting. What did he find there? When he gave a greeting there the owner of the village, as soon as he saw him, said, 'Don't come in here, don't come in here you coming with sores, you coming with sores and scabs, don't come here oh!' He did not know that it was Kanu Masala. Kanu Masala said, 'All right.' He avoided [the village]. He went on.

When he had set out to go, he went for far; he came to another settlement. As soon as the woman [there] saw him she said, 'Do you see that man coming there with sores and scabs? Why has he set out here? Let us drive him away.' They drove him off from there with a stick. She did not know that it was Kanu Masala. Kanu Masala said, 'All right. I will search for a wise man.'

When he had gone on for far—passing five settlements, six, as many as ten settlements—he could not find a place where he was allowed to stay; from every place he came to he was driven out.

Then he came to one more now; he appeared in the distance. Now

[1] *Sooŋ* represents the quiet pondering and wondering to himself.

Sara owned the settlement there. As soon as he greeted him [Sara said] 'E! Welcome, welcome, welcome', welcoming the orphan who came with sores on him. Behold it was Kanu Masala; he did not know that it was Kanu, the one who owns us all.

When he had greeted him there, greeted him well, he said to his wife (she was called Sirande), 'Go for water for him to come and bathe.' Then Sirande said, 'Huh! Is it for the one sitting there with sores on him, for me to go and touch him? you say I am to go for water for him? I refuse.' Then Sara said, 'I will see now whether you refuse—if it is true that I have married you, you will go for me; if I have not married you you will not go for it.' She went for the water because of Sara's power, because of being married. Sara came and brought out soap, he bathed him completely.[1]

He caught a hen for him, saying that Sirande was to kill the hen for him. Then Sirande said, 'Huh! is it for the one who is sitting there all covered with sores, for me to kill him a hen? I refuse.' Sara said, 'No. You are to kill it. If I have married you, you will kill it; if it is not I who have married you—refuse!' She agreed to kill the hen, because of the power through the marriage, because of Sara's authority. Now Kanu Masala just sat there. He listened to how they talked together. When she had killed the hen, it was cooked well; Sara had told her, the wife; she cooked it well, the hen, and pounded[2] it well, through Sara's authority.

Sara went. He went and poured out wine. He brought it. He came and give him it, 'Here is your welcome-food.' He thanked him much. He did not know that it was Kanu. He drank two cups. 'Enough, I am full.' Sara drank what was left. As he was about to pour out what was left for his wife, what Kanu Masala had left when he drank, then she said 'Huh! is it what that man left that you are going to give me?' Sara said, 'All right.' Sara drank what was left. Kanu Masala was watching quietly, 'He is a wise man; he does not avoid an orphan.'

She cooked the rice. She went and took it in to [the room] where Sara slept. She spread out a mat for him. She put the rice down there. She drew water, she took it in. She called Kanu Masala—'Stranger come and eat. Here is your food.' Kanu went in. He went and took half. He was satisfied. He said, 'I am satisfied oh!' When he went out he called Sirande about what was left. 'Come and take what the stranger has left.' Sirande came and took it, she took it out. She came and put it before Sara. 'This, this that the man with sores has left—why do you give it to me? I will not eat it.' Sara said, 'All right.' Sara took the rice, he ate it. Kanu Masala just watched all that they did—Kanu Masala heard how the woman spoke; Kanu Masala saw how Sara acted.

[1] To bathe a guest, supply soap, and, as later, kill a hen for him is to show him especial honour.

[2] Meat is often pounded up and formed into balls for serving.

When they had finished eating completely then he spoke, he thanked them much. 'Thank you, thank you, thank you. I will not be able to give you blessing; it is only Kanu Masala alone that gives blessing.' Behold that was him! 'I thank you much for that.'

Then he said, 'When I set out to go I want you to escort[1] me.' Sara said, 'All right.' When he set out to go Sara began to escort him. Behold, Sara was going in front; his wife followed behind to watch and hear what they said. When they had come to a place after they had gone for far, he said, 'Sara.' 'Yes?' 'Well, on Wednesday let us meet. I want to meet you then, you and I. I travelled all round, I found you, you are a wise man. They did not know that I was Kanu Masala, that it was me. All these people will come and remain under you. On Wednesday, in the morning, have rice-flour pounded for you and a white kola and a white cloth and an egg,[2] and draw wine in the gourd you brought me and bring it with you; wherever you see a white cloth hanging up and a bell, that is where you are to wait for me, there we will meet, on the top of a high hill, like that hill there, a very, very high one, that is where we will meet.' Sara said, 'All right.'

Behold his wife heard that. She went out, secretly, and went and told her lover, saying that they, the wife and her lover, should come there. She did not want Sara to get the chiefship. She herself had heard the pleasing promise. She wanted to give her lover the promise she had heard, for him to become chief, to get chiefship over the whole country, and for all the people to stay in his authority. She went and told her lover, she went and recounted it all to him. Her lover said, 'All right.'

When the time came near, in the morning, she pounded the rice-flour, she Sirande, she finished preparing it all. She went and told her lover, 'Well, you, let us go first.' As soon as Sara had gone out to tap the wine, they set out, she and her lover. When they came, they found Kanu Masala there as they came. What did they find now? Chairs of gold; they found a staff of gold leaning [against a chair], and a chair, and a head-dress, and a gown and shoes, all the things of chiefship, and a scarf and all the things for a woman—her own chair for the wife and a dress ready-made, and a head-tie and all, a skirt and all, shoes and all—the things of chiefship, for her to be the senior wife now.

When they had come there they went and gave a greeting. Kanu replied. Then he said, he the man, the lover of Sirande, 'I have come because of what you said to me.' Behold it was not Sara! Kanu Masala thought it was Sara. He did not know it was not Sara for he saw the wife and he thought it was really them. Behold, it was a deceit. He stood there, he gave him the things of chiefship, he gave them all, completely.

[1] To 'escort' someone on his way is another mark of honour.

[2] All articles associated with ritual.

'When you go now, all the country will be under you, you are the chief.' When he had given him the chiefship there—the drum and all, xylophones and all, all the things of chiefship—he finished giving them to him. People were now following them in a throng.

Behold, Sara was coming now. While they were approaching from far, Sara went to draw the wine. He slung it over his shoulder. He brought all the things. When he was about to arrive there, as he appeared in the distance, behold Kanu was now setting out to go. He saw Kanu going. He greeted him—'Greetings you going, greetings.'[1] Kanu Masala stopped, he looked round. He replied 'Yes.' Sara said, 'E! I am coming quickly because of what you said to me.' Kanu came back. He came and greeted him. 'I have come, I Sara. Here is the wine I have brought with me for you.' Now Kanu Masala—he knew the gourd, the one in which wine had been poured out for him before by Sara. He recognized it. He saw the gourd. 'E! Is it you who have come?' 'Yes.' 'But your wife came and met me here, with a man like you. I thought it was you. I came and gave him the chiefship. Behold, you have come. I did not know. But it is all right.' Then Sara said, 'Well, that is why I have come; here is what I have brought for you.' Kanu Masala said, 'All right. Because of what he did, [what happened] between you, you and him, I will show you both, I will show you. Ha! I, I am not [any longer] deceived. They have worked in vain; that was how they went and got the chiefship.' Then Kanu said, 'All right.' When they had drunk the wine there, he and Sara, he gave him a whip. 'This is what you are to shoulder when you go. When you arrive there, as soon as you come to where they are, don't be afraid oh! Your wife—strike her first, *to!*[2] You will hear her cry out like a cat, she will turn into a cat. When you strike the other one sitting there, the man, you will hear him bark like a dog. Thus the chiefship will be left to you. I am called Kanu Masala. What I was doing yesterday was to look for a wise man. They did not know that I was Kanu Masala. Wherever I went, they drove me out. You alone did not avoid an orphan. You did not avoid a man with sores. You are now founding the whole country, and the chiefship, for ever. The whole country—you own it now.' Sara said, 'All right.'

He shouldered the whip. He began to go. When he appeared coming from there, then the wife got up, the one called Sirande. You see now, at the start of chiefship, all the people follow in a throng; the chief's drum was beaten; the xylophones were being beaten, up and down; the musicians were all playing.

The one who [really] owned the chiefship, Sara, appeared coming from there. Then Sirande got up and said, 'Oh no! Look over there at that fool coming there'—sucking her lips contemptuously at him,

[1] The distance Kanu has reached is indicated by the way the narrator made Sara call out loudly to him.

[2] The sound of the blow.

abusing him. Now Sara—he did not say anything about what he had been given when he went. When he arrived there, he came and raised the whip he had had on his shoulder, he beat and beat the wife—*to! to!* and heard her cry out *εεoo, εεoo*;[1] she turned into a cat. Sara said, 'Yes; all right.' He came near the man—*to! to! to!* He gave him six strokes; he heard the man bark like a dog now—*wo wo wo wo wo, wo wo wo wo wo.* He turned into a dog. Sara said, 'You were not able.'

All the things of chiefship—Sara was left them. He wooed a wife there; when he had got the chiefship there, he gave his wife the things for the senior wife. As for those who had tried to trick him for the sake of the chiefship—the woman turned into a cat (those are the cats that now wander around); the man turned into a dog.

If you hear now that a dog barks—he is barking now about the chiefship that he did not win. If you hear now what a cat says, *wεεŋ wεεŋ*—it was because she was removed from being senior wife. They thought they would bring Sara into misfortune. Behold, Sara got what he wanted, what Kanu gave him—the chiefship.

So now at this time, if you see that your wife is there and you have married her—do not reject a stranger; if you are known (?) and have something, take it and give it to the stranger. If you are said to be a [rich] man and you have won power, if you see an orphan—treat him well; if you see someone with sores—treat him well. But if you see me in power but not receiving an orphan—we Limba do not do that! We learnt that long ago from Sara and his wife. So now if you see that someone is considerate of an orphan, considerate of a man with sores—that is where he learnt that wisdom, from the old people, from Sara. Now chiefship is everywhere in the country, [chiefly] staffs are now plentiful in all the country. Sara was the first to get chiefship, because of his endurance, not avoiding an orphan, not avoiding a man with sores; when he sees a man with sores he loves him. Now when anyone gets power—do not avoid those that have something; but if you know about someone that he has nothing—show consideration for him! If you see that he has sores and you treat him well and if you have something and get it out and give it to him—Kanu notices it all. He owns us all. He sees how we all go around. You who do good—he sees you; you who do wrong—he sees you, right up till when the time comes near for you to die, and you meet him, him Kanu. At that time he will recount it all.

Since I heard that story, Yenkeni, I tell it this morning, I Karanke, Karanke Koroma,[2] of Kayaka, the son of Fane at Kakarima, Alimami Salifu's. Since I have finished the story this morning, telling you it, you Yenkeni, it is finished.

[1] A nasal sound representing the miaowing of a cat.

[2] Koroma is an alternative form of Dema.

Kanu gives chiefship 2

GBOSO DEMA. *Dictated* 21.10.61

A second version of the plot about Kanu giving chiefship; I have included it here for comparison. This one is much shorter. The conclusion is also different: here it is that the lovers now hate each other because of the woman's evil intentions in slighting her husband. The narrator's main interest was not, as in the previous version, in the nature and origin of chiefship, but in the amusing reversal by which the cat and dog, once lovers, now hate each other. He greatly enjoyed the paradoxical situation, commenting after he had ended the story that 'they once loved each other, behold, now they hate each other; when the cat sees the dog she spits at him'.

TWO people, they once lived together. When they were living together, that marriage was not pleasant. The woman did not love the man.

Kanu Masala got up. He had ulcers, all his body was thin. He came to the man living with his wife, the two of them. When the man had washed him all, Kanu Masala went. Behold, it was Kanu Masala. He said, 'For that, you, let me give you chiefship.' He said, 'Yes, it is all right.' 'The day after tomorrow, when the sun has just come up, you are to go to the top of the hill there, well, go and meet me.'

When the sun rose, at the time that he had been told to go to the hill to go and get chiefship—his wife told her lover, 'Go tomorrow morning to the hill. My husband has been told to go and get chiefship.'

Her lover went there in the morning. Kanu Masala said, 'Is it you who have come?' He said, 'Yes.' 'Well.' 'I have come for what you said.' Kanu Masala gave him the chiefship. Behold, it was not her husband.

The man who had been told to go to get chiefship, he heard the dancing now. When he came, he said, 'Kanu Masala, well, I have come now.' Kanu Masala said, 'What, was it not you today?' He said, 'No, it was not me. My wife caused me trouble. For her lover has gone and got the chiefship, she went to her lover.'

Kanu Masala said, 'All right.' He gave him a whip. He took out a kola as a token gift, he tied it up [in a bundle], he gave it to him. When he came to the village, he found people dancing. He said, 'E! They are the ones who are troubling me.' He took the whip. Where he was sitting in the hammock, he [husband] struck the chief. The chief leapt from there, he became a dog. He struck the wife. The wife became a cat. He said, 'See, Kanu Masala, I am the chief.'

You see now, the dog and the cat, they despise each other. But before they were people, lovers. But Kanu Masala parted them. One became a dog, the other became a cat. They were once people, lovers. But Kanu

Masala made them disagree—because she despised her husband very much, so that no one would ever do that, to despise her husband very much.

Kanu and palm wine

ABU KANU. *Recorded* 22.1.61

The story of how a Limba man first learnt how to tap palm wine, taught by Kanu in return for a debt he owed him.

The Limba are famous among all the peoples of Sierra Leone for their skill in palm wine tapping. In most parts of Limba country every young boy and man taps wine, climbing their trees in the early morning and the evening. The wine is used for many purposes, both greatly enjoyed for its own sake, and also as a gift that brings honour. The wine is drawn from the oil palm (*elaeis guineensis*), occasionally from one of the raffia palms. The men climb the palms with a climbing-strap to support them round their backs, pierce the trunk with two sharp chisel-like tools, insert a tube, and fasten on a gourd to catch the wine. Once the wine starts to flow it usually continues for two or three months.

Many Limba from the Safroko Limba chiefdom make a good living by travelling to the south and tapping and selling palm wine there; thus, like Sara in the story, they have 'become well off'.

I had the impression that the plot was unfamiliar to those who were told it at the same time as I, and one listener asked the teller where he had heard it. The episode of the palm tree resembles episodes in *The finch's loan*, and *The sun, the hawk, and the hen*, but a similar moral is not drawn here.

THE story. A man once lived called Sara. He had nothing. He begged Kanu, saying, 'Kanu lend me money, I am in poverty.' He went to the road junction. He found money there, 5*s*. He went to his house. He had just sat down, when Kanu came to him. He said, 'Sara, lend me the money that you saw a few minutes ago on the road.' Sara said, 'Oh! I had just come and sat down; I had begged money from you by your power!' Sara gave him the money. Kanu went off.

Much later, Sara got up and said, 'Let me go today and collect the money from Kanu.' He went. He greeted Kanu. He said, 'Papa.[1] I have come for the money.' Kanu said, 'The time you find me asleep, then ask me for the money; I will pay you.' Sara went off.

Much later, Sara went again. He went again to find him. Kanu was not asleep. Sara said, 'Oh, Kanu, you will never be asleep!' Kanu said, 'Go; when you find me asleep, ask about the money, I will pay you.' Sara went off.

Another day, when he was going along, a palm tree said, 'E! Sara.

[1] Common term of address to a father or chief.

You are always coming here. Why do you come?' Sara said, 'Kanu is to pay me, but he told me that when I find him asleep, I am to ask him about the money; but he does not sleep.' The palm tree said, 'Because you are untrustworthy—perhaps when I tell it to you, when you go to Kanu and, when Kanu asks you, you will say "the palm tree told me". At that time Kanu will soon be angry with me. But still I will help you. When you go to your house, go and sit down. In the evening when the sun is just setting, when you come to ask Kanu for your money, then at that time you will find Kanu asleep.'

Sara got up when it was evening. He went to Kanu. He found him asleep.[1] He tapped Kanu and said, 'Kanu, greetings.' Kanu woke. Kanu looked at Sara. Sara was afraid. He turned into anything you like.[2] Kanu looked again at him. He became again a human being. He Kanu asked Sara, 'Who told you about this time?' Sara said, 'The palm tree told me.' Kanu said, 'Well, let us go to the palm tree, so that I may pay you.'

They went to the palm tree. Kanu brought a gourd. He brought a chisel. He brought a spike. He brought a tube. He said, 'Sara, today I will pay you.' He climbed up above. He cleaned the palm tree. He finished completely. He stuck the tube into the palm tree. The wine passed into the tube. He took the gourd, he tied it to the palm tree. He came down below. Not long after, he sent Sara up. He said, 'Go and bring down the wine.' Sara went up. He came down with the palm wine. He put it on the ground. Kanu said, 'Pour it out, Sara, pour out the wine into a cup.' Sara poured it out. Kanu said, 'All right, drink it.' Sara drank it. Sara—the wine took hold of him. Kanu said, 'All right, that is your payment.' Sara came down with the gourd to the ground.

There Sara always does his work. He got clothes. He got much money. Always now he sold palm wine. Everyone saw that the wine was sweet. Sara became well off. All the Limba learnt this work of drawing wine. The other people do not know how [to do it]. Sara became well off. When Sara died, everyone saw how sweet it was.

The beginning of marriage

BIASI LOBA. *Dictated* 28.11.61

A story accounting for sex, marriage, and the present hard system (as it is considered at times) by which a man has to pay bridewealth, give gifts, and work to obtain his wife. The story was found very funny and light-heartedly indecent by the listeners.

[1] When the same narrator told the story on a different occasion he added the detail that Kanu had a Bible on his knee and was asleep over it.

[2] i.e. into some animal or other.

KANU brought out an old woman here on earth. This old woman, she went and wept before Kanu. 'Kanu, since you have brought me out, what is there for me to eat[1] here on the earth where you brought me out?' Kanu said, 'All right. I will give you merchandise[2] to sell. All right, go.'

Kanu went off and stood. He made two things. 'Woman', he said 'here is your merchandise.' The woman said, 'What? Well, how am I to sell that merchandise?' 'Well, hang one up here. The other—hang it up too, here. When people come they will buy.' Kanu went and stood again. He made a man. Here on earth there was then no man, not at all. He stood again. He made a girl also—a beautiful girl.

They set out to go. They came to the old woman who was selling merchandise. When the girl came—the first to arrive—she saw the merchandise hanging up. 'Oh? What is that?' The old woman said, 'Kanu brought me that merchandise. If you will buy it, all right.' 'But what if I buy it—where will I put it?' The old woman said, 'It's four pounds first!' The girl said, 'I agree.' She took out the four pounds, she gave it to the woman. 'Well then, take it.' 'But what if I take it—where will I fasten it on?' 'Well, fasten it on to some place.' She fastened it here [at breast];[3] it wouldn't stay. She fastened it here [waist]; it wouldn't stay. She took it and fastened it here [heart]; it wouldn't stay. She said, 'Mother, what am I to do?' She took it to another place. She fastened it here. Ah! It stuck on well—quite fast! You see, where she fastened it at the beginning—that is why a woman has breasts. When it had stuck here, she said, 'But mother—' 'Yes?' 'What if I decide for this? What will it do?' 'Go, go along the path; go and stand there.' The girl got up. She went on to the path.

When the man came, he saw something hanging up. 'Mother, whatever is that?' 'Kanu Masala brought it for me as merchandise.' 'I want to buy it. What if I do buy it? Where will I put it?' The old woman said, 'That is all right. I will show you where to put it. But it is four pounds.' The old woman took it down. She gave it him. 'Well now, where will I put it?' 'Fasten it on.' He fastened it on his chest; it wouldn't stay. He put it to his side. 'E! Mother—it is difficult.' 'Well, then, bring it here in front since it won't stick there.' He brought it to the front. It fastened—stuck fast, *gbɛpu!*[4] The three bits fastened together—*gbɛpu!* 'Since it has stuck, what am I to do?' 'Follow this path. When you meet a girl standing there, when you meet her, as soon as you see her standing there with her breasts all firm, *yakarakara*—then don't

[1] i.e. support myself with.

[2] *Markɛti* (from English 'market')—the word used of the gift often given by a husband to his wife for her to begin trading with.

[3] The teller demonstrates the first three places.

[4] This expresses the speed, fixity, and permanence of the fastening.

hesitate! When you see her, as soon as you reach her, then *wupu!* fall on her!'

The boy went and did that. Then the girl said, 'Hey! hey![1] See, I have bought good merchandise.' The man too said, 'Hey! hey! See, we bought good merchandise from the old woman.'

You see the man—the old woman's money, the four pounds, he refused to pay it to the old woman. The girl—*she* paid the four pounds to the old woman. The man, as soon as he went and knew it, then he had the knowledge. He took off the girl; they went. He did not pay the old woman.

The old woman said, 'Very well.' Because of that, that is why now we work for a wife. We, we were cursed by the old woman to whom Kanu gave the merchandise. The man refused to pay. Today we—if you want a wife, you have to give money. If you don't do that, you won't get one. That man used deceit on us. Now if you marry a wife, she just goes off! It was the curse that the old woman laid on us. She took the blessing and gave it to the girl. The money she gave then, she knows where she can get it. If you would like to marry you have to pay the bridewealth. Because of how marriage began, the bridewealth that he did not give the old woman, that is what we have to put for a wife, right up to this day.

The story of two women

SURI KAMARA. *Recorded* 9.12.61

A story which emphasizes the joys and sufferings of motherhood. The great value attached to children, and the sacrifices attributed to a mother for the sake of her children are typical; the point is dramatized in the repeated and emphatic questions which the old woman addresses to the would-be mothers. The two co-wives are contrasted in particular over their relative care of their clothes as compared to children.

The story also accounts, rather as an afterthought it appears, for barrenness among women, and the frequent deaths of their young children —both facts of much concern to the Limba.

I, SURI KAMARA, I am coming to tell Yenkeni a story of two women who wanted to have children. These two they came to be married to the same husband. They lived there in that marriage. They always asked everyone who came to the village where they were whether they knew a person who understood the medicine for having children. A man

[1] Expression of surprise and pleasure.

came from a journey. He came and told them, 'I met a woman, she is in one part of the village. That woman, Kanu came and gave her medicine for having children.' The two, each of them, their hearts came and rose up, to go to the woman so that the woman could help them to get the power to have children, so they could have children.

Then one of them came and stood up, the elder. She came to go. When she came to go, she came and found the village. The old woman who understood the medicine for having children was there. When she came and reached there, she told the old woman, 'Mother, well, here on the earth I was brought out by Kanu; but right up to this time today, nothing! I am unable to have a child. Well, I, I want to have children. That is why I am bringing you this gift, so that Kanu may grant me to have children, by grace of your power.'

Then the old woman said, 'Will you be able?' 'Yes.' 'Will you be able?' 'Yes.' 'Will you wash off its filth?' 'Yes.' 'Will you wash off its filth?' 'Yes.' 'Will you allow it to wet on you?' 'Yes.' 'Will you be able?' 'Yes.' 'Will you be able to be vomited on?' 'Yes.' 'Will you like the vomit?' 'Yes.' 'Well, sit down.' The woman sat down. She had food cooked for her. She finished eating. The night came.

Now the old woman—those who came to her to ask to have children, she had had a house built for her, and whoever came had to lie down in that house. In the centre of the house was an earth bed. There the person was to lie down.

When darkness came, then the old woman said to the girl who came to find children, 'Well, now, here you are to sleep. I will not be able to make you a fire.[1] You will sleep here alone. Whatever comes to you here, if you want to bear children—don't be afraid! Well, treat the thing well.' Then the girl said, 'All right, I agree.' She had a mat[2] spread for her on the bed, in the centre of the house. She lay down. The old woman locked the door. When they had slept for long in the first sleep, there the girl saw a great snake coming. The snake—it was huge; it crawled *fuuu!* She the girl, she stayed there. She welcomed the snake. The instant she took hold of the snake as if to put it on her knee, what did she see? A pillow. She took the pillow, and put it at her head. She kissed the pillow, kissed the pillow, kissed the pillow. When the time had gone on for long since she had lain down again, there rats came to her. The rats began to wet on her. She took her cloth,[3] her fine cloth, she opened it out, she covered herself with it so that the rats might wet the cloth.

[1] To be given no fire for heat or light at night is considered a real hardship, if sleeping alone in a house.

[2] One of the prized and decorated mats used for sleeping on.

[3] i.e. the cloth which women wrap round them as a skirt, their main garment. Sometimes a woman possesses only one and in any case the cloth worn for a visit would be a valued one.

When the morning came, the old woman went to open the door. The old woman asked her, 'When you spent the night here, what did you see?' 'Well, when darkness came in, what was the first thing to come to me?—a snake. That snake, it welcomed me and I put it on my knee. What did I see on my knee?—a pillow. Well even though it was a snake that came to me, it was with good intent; that is why I put it on my knee, a pillow. When I put it on my knee, when I saw that it was a pillow, that is why I put it at my head so you would know that I was thinking about the purpose I came to you. The rats too, when they began to wet on me—that is why I also opened out my cloth so that here where you spread for me, the mat would not be spoilt.'

Then the old woman said, 'All right. Well, wait. Now I am going into the bush, I will say good-bye to you.' The old woman went into the bush she went to pick the medicine for giving birth, all of it. She came back, she came and took it, she the old woman. She went alone into the house. She took a basket. In that basket, there she put a child, a girl, one with sores all over her body. She took medicine, with which the girl could cure the child she put in the basket. She put it inside. Then she picked up a little rice and a little of the medicine for having children, she gave it to her. 'Well, go. As you go, don't open the basket on the road. As soon as you reach the place, go to the waterside; don't send anyone else! You yourself are to go for the water. The rice—don't husk it. Come and put the cooking pot up on the fire. When you have finished cooking, when you are going to eat the cooked rice, then open the basket. The thing you see there, if it is something, you two, you and it, you are to eat the rice. If you see medicine there, it is that medicine you are to eat with the rice.'

The girl took the basket. She slung it over her shoulder. She went for far. She was not satisfied, for she thought 'Perhaps the basket will drop by mistake and be lost, and fall on the ground.' She took her cloth—which she no longer considered at all—she wrapped the basket in it.

As soon as she reached the place and went to the waterside, she took and put the cooking pot on the fire, she took the little bit of rice and put it in the pot. She cooked it well. She took the cooked rice, she helped it out. She took a pan and began to fan it so that the rice would cool. When the rice had finished cooling, then she sat, then she sat. She opened the basket. As she opened the basket, what did she see inside? A child, with sores, a girl child. She first took the rice, she pushed it to one side. She unloosed the child, she took the child, she put her on her knees. She first lifted up the child and kissed her, kissed her again, kissed her. She took the child, she took her cloth that she had bought with much money, she first spread it out for the child.[1] She left the child, she

[1] Sometimes old pieces of cloth or rag are used for laying a child on, but this girl uses a precious piece of material.

ran to the waterside. She came and put water on the fire for the child, she ran into the bush.[1] She went and picked her some [leaves for] medicine too for her sores. She came and took soap, she scrubbed the child. When she had finished scrubbing the child, she rubbed the medicine on the child. As she was rubbing her with it, then the child said, 'Mother. I, I am hungry now.' She put the child down, she took oil, she put it where the child was to eat. The child finished eating. She was satisfied. Once she scrubbed the child, the child was cured, the girl child.

That child—it did not take long, the woman conceived, a boy child. In two months she came and bore a child, a boy. It was a boy, a chief! The girl that she got when she was looking for medicine, she became the child's guardian.

Time passed, and the child grew. Then her companion got up, her co-wife. Then she asked her, 'Friend. Now we are co-wives, we two only that are married here. You, you went on a journey. When you went on the journey and came back, Kanu came and helped you. You came and bore a chief. I beg you now, don't think about our co-wifehood.[2] Show me now this path where you walked until Kanu gave you a child.' Then her companion sat down. She told her all, completely.

Well, she, the one who had borne no child, she was the one that was always the more loved; she was the one who always had clothes bought for her—the best ones, the ones of high price. She got up, she went and told her husband. The husband went and packed for her as the first had been packed for. She went. When she had gone, she came and found the old woman. When she found the old woman, the old woman asked her, 'Why have you come?' Then she said, 'Mother. I have come to find a way to bear children. I and my husband—we have travelled much, but we have not yet got children. That is why we are running here to you, for you to come and help us.'

Then the old woman said, 'Well I, I have heard. But I have something to ask you. Can you wash off the filth?' Then the girl said, 'What! Oh mother, it was not to wash off filth that I came. Look at my body. Does it look like filth? That remark, don't say that to me again!' Then she said, 'Well, I won't say that to you again. But what I have to ask you, I, I must ask you. Now, you, will you be able to wash off wet?' Then the girl said, 'Oh mother! I did not come here for a quarrel. Stop this! I did not come here to you for you to go and ask me to wash off wet. Look at my body, is that what my body is like? Is it to come and wash off wet?

[1] The girl's joy, speed, and energy in rushing round finding her child's necessities, pictures well the happiness and lightheartedness of many Limba mothers when they have a child of their own.

[2] i.e. even though co-wives are often hostile to each other, be willing to help me now.

Stop this, don't say that a second time!' Then the old woman said, 'Yes, but I have not yet finished asking you. What about you, will you agree to be vomited on? Will you wash off the vomit?' Then she said, 'Now, I will not answer you again. If this talk helps me, it is not proper. You are only talking at me. But these words you are saying to me, they are not entering my heart well. My heart is not cool. It is only because you are old—'[1] Then the old woman said, 'Well, all right, sit down now.' She was cooked for. She finished eating.

The darkness came in. Then the old woman poked her. 'Come.' It was to the bed where her companion spent the night, the one who came first. As they reached the place then she said, 'Well, I am giving you lodging in this house. When I give you lodging here, everything that comes to you here, embrace it with both hands, whatever thing you see here, since you are calling for children for yourself.' 'All right, I agree.' She lay down. When she had lain down, the old woman locked the door. Not long after, the snake came, the snake that had come before and found her co-wife there. It came again—*gbuuuu*. As it came, that instant it went right to her breast. She the girl, as soon as she saw the snake, threw the snake down. The snake went and fell. She took the spoon[2] that was leaning against the bed, she banged it on the snake's head. She struck it again. The snake died. The rats also began to come to wet on her. Then she stood on the middle of the bed, 'You, you, you, you! Your habits! Don't spoil my cloth.[3] It was bought for me for a high price by my husband. It was not to you I came. I came to the old woman for her to help me to bear children.'

The sun came to rise. As the old woman opened the door—*gburu*— she said 'Mother! Mother! So that is why you came and spread my bed here for me! The sufferings I have had this night—since I was borne by my parents, I had not ever seen such sufferings. But it is all right! But it is all right!'[4] Then the old woman said, 'Oh, friend, you have finished the night. Kanu said that nothing would hurt you. Now I am coming to say good-bye to you.'

Then the old woman went. The old woman did not show unfairness. What she had given her companion, that is what she gave her too. She went and picked medicine, she took a little bit of rice, she took a little medicine, took a basket, took a child and put them inside. But when she had put them inside, she showed her the rule. 'When you are going, if you open the basket on the road, what you see there—that will be your portion.'

[1] *sc.* that I put up with it.

[2] The large wooden spoon, sometimes up to two feet long, used for helping out rice.

[3] Her care of her cloth, both now and when she discovers the child, is contrasted to the other girl's.

[4] She speaks very sarcastically.

As soon as she went out, as soon as she had left the village, when she had been told good-bye—that instant she said, 'A person cannot be given something without looking to see what it is inside.' As soon as she opened it a little bit and peeped, she saw a shiny skin—shining. Behold, it was a snake! She tied and tied it in, she went. As soon as she reached there, she went and cooked rice. When she had finished arranging everything as she had been told by the old woman, as she was going to eat, she opened the basket. What did she see? A child with sores. Then she took the child, then she went for rags, the rags she wiped her feet on when she wanted to lie down! She went and took the rags, she rammed them into the child's mouth so that the child could not cry, so that the people would not know that the girl had brought a child with sores. She took her, she bound the rags on her, giving her pain all over on her sores. She put her back in the basket. She tied it all up, she went. She took the road back. As soon as she arrived, she did not even go right to the old woman's house, she dropped the basket. Then she said, 'I did not come to you to beg a child with sores.' She went back. As she went back, she died. No sign from her stomach even came to her first.[1]

That is why, since she died, the other women who live now in our country, whoever of them as they are walking round steps on the dust of the girl, the one who did not want children—that woman, right until she dies, Kanu will not give her any sign of bearing a child. From the snake that she killed—from that came death to the children. At the first, no child died; only the old people, they died.

Since I heard that story, and Yenkeni came saying she wanted to hear that story in Limba—that is the story. It is finished.

The stomach is chief of the body

NIAKA DEMA. *Dictated* 15.10.61

A story humorously explaining how it is that everything has to give way to the stomach. As in *Kanu gives chiefship* Kanu has to go round for some time before finding someone to give him hospitality. In the end he is depicted as calling each part of the body to him in a kindly and affectionate tone.

WINE-TAPPERS went out, they went and cleaned palm trees. They were the foot and hand and hips and neck and head and back and stomach. When they went, the wine came out for them; it agreed to

[1] i.e. there was no warning pain, she died instantly; or, perhaps, she never conceived a child.

flow. Now Kanu heard that they had a place where they were tapping palm wine. He said, 'I will go and ask for wine from the young men.'[1]

When Kanu came, he came to the foot. He said, 'Here is someone asking for wine.' The foot kicked out at him there—'I have no wine.' Kanu went on. He came to the hips. 'Hips, here is someone asking for wine.' The hips said, 'I have no wine.' Kanu went on. He came to the eyes. 'Eyes, here is someone asking for wine.' The eyes said, 'No wine.' Kanu went on. He came to the neck. 'Here is someone asking for wine.' It said 'No wine.' Kanu went on. He came to the back. 'Here is someone asking for wine.' The back said, 'No wine.' Kanu went on.

He came to the stomach. When he had come to the stomach (the stomach had been borne by a chief), the stomach welcomed Kanu. The stomach said, 'Here is somewhere for you to sit.' He brought down his wine, 'Here is your gift of welcome.' Kanu asked, 'How many people are there tapping wine?' The stomach enumerated them all. Kanu wrote it down. He drank the wine—he Kanu. He said, 'What you are to tell those tapping wine is that they should all meet on Thursday, in the clearing[2] where the stomach taps his wine. That is what you are to tell them. I will be coming, to come and choose one man as chief.' They accepted.

When Thursday arrived, Kanu came. He brought resin and the soft cotton from the palm tree. He brought ashes. When he had brought the ashes, he came and put everything in a pile. The people who had not given wine to the stranger that had come—they were now all bringing him wine, every one of them! They came and put it in a row in the stomach's clearing. They found Kanu there. He was sitting down. He had brought a gown of gold, and trousers of gold, a cap of gold. When they had come, they found there the one who had been asking for wine. He had not often gone there. Kanu said, 'Here is a good idea. I want to join you all together in one place. That is the idea I have come with.' This was told to them.[3] Everyone who had been tapping wine had the word passed to them. They said, 'We accept.' Kanu said, 'I want now to join you together in one place. That is the reason we have met here.' They answered, 'Whatever you say, we will agree to, because it was you who bore us.'[4]

He said, 'Hips, come here to where I am sitting.' The hips came near, and came and sat down. 'Leg, come and sit here.' The leg came. When it had come, he fastened it to the end of the hips. He rubbed the resin onto the end of the hips, the leg was stuck there. He said, 'Leg come,

[1] Young men are those who most frequently climb palms to tap wine, and they normally carry some of this back to the village to give the older men there.

[2] i.e. the place just below the tree where the young men like to gather to drink the wine.

[3] i.e. formally announced to them.

[4] Niaka tends to represent Kanu as a father rather more often than other story-tellers.

come and sit here.' He rubbed the resin again on the hips. 'Come.' He poured on the ashes. It hardened and stuck there. 'It is good; chest, come.' It came near. He stuck the resin. It was hard there. He took and said, 'Hands, come near.' The hands came near. He stuck the resin. He sprinkled the ashes. It was hard there. 'It is good—neck come here. I want you to come here.' He stuck the resin. He sprinkled the ashes. It was hard there. He took the head. 'I want you to come here.' He took the resin, he stuck it. He put the head on the top. He sprinkled the ashes. It was hard. You see the back—it is a man's covering. He took all the parts that he was fastening together, he sprinkled on ashes. He joined them there. It became hard.

'What is good is—here is your chief, the one sitting there.' 'Who is the chief?' 'The stomach. All of you are bad; you did not give me wine when I came before. But this man came and gave me wine. That is why I have come to give him the chiefship. The stomach outdid them. I am giving you the chiefship.' He took the stomach and turned it over on its front. He was the one with the resin; he sprinkled the ashes. The stomach was fastened now.

He asked them 'Who will sign[1] to obey your chief?' The foot said, 'Whatever you say.' Kanu said, 'Send out a cousin to sign.'[2] The foot said, 'Back, leg, hips, neck, eye, come here. I want to discuss something with you.' 'It is good.' They all sat down there, they began by quarrelling, they did not come near. Kanu said, 'I want those two, I want them to come; those four, the cousins. Ear, come, come here and speak for them.' He took the resin. He stuck it to the head. 'Ear, stay here, so that they may be heard. You are the small cousin. Eyes, come. I want you, because a chief will not live without a looker.' The eyes came. He took the glue, he stuck them both. The eyes hardened. He took the ashes, he sprinkled them.

'Now let me tell you all why I came. I came to look for a wise man. I found the stomach; he is the wisest. It is good for the eye to look for the chief. Wherever you say, "Foot that is where you will go"—you will go there. Neck—when the foot goes and then stops and stands and your hand takes something and puts it on the head—neck, then you are the carrier of the load for the chief. You are all the workers. Ear, if you hear that something is there, you will tell the heart, and the heart will tell the foot, "Well now, you go and find the thing." Head, you are the chief's cap. Chest, you are the chief's gown. Back, you are the chief's umbrella.' The back said, 'I accept.'

Whenever the stomach says—in the morning, or evening, or after-

[1] Probably a reference to the modern custom of signing under the supervision of a government official immediately after the election of a chief.

[2] The *sesa*, 'cousin', traditionally had special duties and responsibilities towards the chief.

noon—'I, I want to eat', then the foot stands up, and takes along with him the eyes, and the heart. When the heart says 'I will go there today', the foot will say 'All right.' It is the stomach that pushes them on saying 'I want the supply that Kanu told me of. I want you to feed me with food, so I may be filled.' So he is content now with the foot, and eye, and heart.

Thus I heard about the stomach and foot and ear and head and neck and arm. The chief of all is the stomach. That is it. Since I have ended—it is finished.

The story of palm wine

NIAKA DEMA. *Dictated* 24.10.61

This story was told in reply to my inquiry whether Niaka knew the story of *Kanu and palm wine*. Here the discovery of palm wine tapping is attributed to a spirit who is said to have shown the Limba the method for which they are now famous.

HUNGER once fell,[1] very, very great. A spirit went and cleared[2] a palm tree. The Limba did not know then that this thing was food. When he [a man] went to cut raffia ribs, he came on the palm tree. He climbed up. Hunger took hold of him now. He took the wine. He drank. He said 'E! This thing is sweet oh!'

Now the spirit had no family. When the sun rose again, he [man] came again, coming for the raffia ribs which he had cut the day before. He came again to get them. He went again to go and climb. Where he had climbed the day before, he climbed again. He was filled. He took the raffia ribs. He carried them on his head. He found strength again for carrying the raffia ribs, and for chasing the birds.

When the spirit saw that where he had cleared the palm tree, it was always being stolen, he got up now, he came and stayed underneath.

When the man was hungry again, he said, 'I, I am going again to where I was filled yesterday.' When he had gone and taken the climbing-strap and climbed a little, the spirit came out, for he was watching for the thief who had kept stealing there. When he found the man, he said, 'E! Behold, you have kept stealing here from my palm tree. I have caught

[1] i.e. in the wet season, when the rain falls, food is short, and the birds have to be chased from the farm.

[2] Clearing the undergrowth and trunk and making the first holes in the palm tree—the most difficult part; to climb the cleared tree later for wine is relatively simple.

you now today.' Then the man said, 'Oh, your things are sweet! When you drink your heart is good. Whatever you think, if you say it there is no shame.[1] I, I want you to show me how a palm tree is cleared and tapped.' Then the spirit said, 'I, ha! this work is painful. If you do not endure, ha! suffering! To come out in the rain—and if you don't cut a good creeper,[2] you will come drop off there, you will fall. But you will not die! But if you do not put on your hand,[3] you will die!' He said, 'I, I accept.' 'It is all right.' 'Well, it is good—I want to go and tap wine for myself, as you always tap it.'

He the spirit came. He climbed up. He the man came. 'I have come to beg wine from you, that you may fill me. We talked together today, I and you. Now I have come.' Then the man said, 'I want to climb.' The spirit said, 'E! Are you able to climb here?' Then the man spoke (his name was Sara). The spirit now had been left by his people. No mother. No father. No brother. No one at all with him. But Kanu had shown him this wisdom, to tap palm wine.[4] The man climbed up, 'You are to show me.' The man, he was (?) travelling about (?), he [too] was an orphan. No father. No mother. No brother. No half-brother. He was with the spirit now. The spirit had no one. He the man, Sara, he had no people. They were there now, those two people, they said 'Let us make a company,[5] so that we may not be talked about in the wet season.'

Then the spirit climbed, he [man] climbed. He went and drank. When the spirit tapped the wine, he [man] remembered. When he fastened in the tube, he remembered. When he had now finished learning from the spirit, there he was shown the medicine by the spirit. The spirit said, 'You are to pay me for my medicine—it has to be a child.' Then Sara said, 'E! don't do that! We two orphans together, let us not do that to each other.' Then the spirit spoke, he showed him the leaves, for him to go and clear the palm tree, so that it would agree [to give wine], so that everyone there now may drink the wine.

Then Sara went now and cleared a palm tree, one, two holes. But from those holes, it was like a drum for kerosene to be put, the gourd filled up there completely, it filled there. Every Limba now, there he will learn about drinking. The Limba would not have got palm wine, but the

[1] The man admits that the spirit has a right to say what he wishes since it is his tree.

[2] For the climbing-strap which supports him as he goes up the tree; a bad strap is often the cause of a fall.

[3] i.e. (?) use magic. It is occasionally said that people should have special medicine, or help from a spirit, to stop them from falling from a palm tree—a not infrequent occurrence. Later in the story the spirit shows the man the special *mafɔi* medicine for this, made from leaves.

[4] An orphan with no people to farm with is always regarded as typically helpless and hungry. Here the spirit has survived because he was able to get palm wine independently and so feed himself. The man, Sara, is also an orphan.

[5] To co-operate in work and food.

spirit showed Sara long ago how it is tapped. Semanka,[1] thus all now learnt from Sara about drinking palm wine.

Since you have heard—you asked today about Kanu and palm wine, I said 'No', that Kanu is not a tapper of palm wine, it was a spirit that began tapping. Sara went there and learnt. Sara got up, he taught all the country now.

Kanu scatters his children on earth

NIAKA DEMA. *Dictated* 29.10.61

A story about the origins of the various peoples on earth, and the clans of the Limba, concluding with an explanation of why people die one at a time and a generalization about the power of Kanu—only with his help can a man be successful.

Niaka commented that he had 'heard this story from the old people; for when as a child you go and greet them, they tell you a story and you will not forget it'.

KANU—long ago he bore many children, more than two hundred. They lived there. They could not endure [to live with] one another.

Then he said, 'Let us go down below.' To a small hill, there they went down. He said, 'I, I want to divide you out into the countries.' Now he bore the Limba, bore the Fula, bore the Europeans, bore the Gbandi, bore the Kebu, bore the Temne, bore the Indians.[2]

When they came to the hill, a man and a woman—he had glue there; when he took them, the man and the woman, he glued them together. He sang a song,[3] 'I fasten, yo! Yo Fula. I fasten.' He took, he hurled with his sling. They went and fell. They built a house. They went and made a village there.

He took these ones, the two, a man and a woman. 'I fasten, yo! Yo Temne! I fasten.' He put them in his sling. He hurled them. They went and fell. They built a village there.

He took again two, a man and a woman. 'I fasten, yo! Yo European!

[1] One of the listeners, specially fond of palm wine.

[2] These are mostly names of the various peoples in Sierra Leone near the Limba. The Kebu are the travelling Fula, Gbandi are the Loko. Europeans are called *Porotho*, a common term (in various forms) in Sierra Leone, probably originally from 'Portuguese'. The narrator had worked for a time in one of the Indian stores in Freetown.

[3] I am not sure of the translation of the song, which recurs throughout the story. It may not have any definite sense. The 'yo' is common in songs, often taken up by the chorus.

I fasten.' He put them in his sling. He hurled them. They went and fell. They built a village. They lived there.

He took again a man and a woman. 'I fasten, yo! Yo Indian! I fasten.' He put them in the sling. He hurled them. They went and fell. They built a village there.

He took again, two. 'I fasten, yo! Yo Kebu! I fasten.' He put them in the sling. He hurled them. They went and fell. They went and built a village. They lived there.

He took again a man and a woman. 'I fasten, yo! Yo Koranko! I fasten.' He took them, a man and a woman, he put them in the sling. He hurled them. They went and built a village.

He took again a man and a woman. 'I fasten, yo! Yo Loko! I fasten.' He put them in the sling, he placed them here. He hurled. They went and lived there.

He took again, the Limba, a man and a woman. For they were the ones he divided near here. He knew their clans. He took. 'I fasten, yo! Yo Dangkang! I fasten.' He hurled them to Kasasi. Those ones are the Dangkangs at Kasasi.[1]

He took these ones again, a man and a woman, 'I fasten, yo! Yo Ningka! I fasten.' He hurled. At Kasafroko, there are the Ningkas. They went and built a village there.

He took again these ones. 'I fasten, yo! Yo Yeleme! I fasten.' He hurled them, to Kawono. They went and built a house there.

He took again these ones, a man and a woman. 'I fasten, yo! Yo Konteh! I fasten.' He threw them to Tamiso. They went and lived there. They built a house.

He took again a man and a woman. 'I fasten, yo! Yo Warawara! I fasten.' He put them in the sling. He hurled. They went and built. They lived there, with Alimami Salifu at Kawoya.

He took these ones again, 'I fasten, yo! Yo Dema! I fasten.' He hurled. They built here, here where we are living, at Kakarima.

You see, we are all of one descent, Europeans, Temne, Loko, Indians, all, we are of one descent. Kanu owns our descent, all of us, from the power of Kanu. Kanu said, 'You whom I divided, when I come, I want to be paid. I, I take one.' You see, even with the Europeans, two people do not die, but one, one at a time. You see, here with the Limba, one dies in a day. Every person has his fixed time. Then he took, saying 'Monday, Tuesday, Wednesday, Thursday, Friday, Saturday, Sunday.' You see that people know how to reckon that—Kanu told it to them. 'Here are the days you will work.' Everyone remembers that.

[1] These and the following names are those of Limba clans and of the various nearby villages which they rule, including Bawoya (Bafodea) the capital of the large Wara Wara Bafodea chiefdom. The Warawaras are the name of a division of the Limba, not of a clan.

Since you have heard me come to tell you how the Limba and the Europeans and the Indians were made then, country by country—if someone says that it does not matter about Kanu,[1] that is not good. Kanu bore all people. If you hear about endeavours—if Kanu has not said, 'Here is what you will do', [even] if you take it with [all] your heart, it will not go forward. Even you, you Europeans, if Kanu has not said, 'Here is what you will do', you will not do it; if he has said, 'Here is what you will do', he will help you. If he has borne you as a fool,[2] you remain in that foolishness, you will always wander around. You will not become well off. That is it.

The white and black brothers

SURIBA (NEVERTIRE) KONTEH. *Recorded* 28.2.61

A story accounting for the differences yet resemblances between white and black men. They were full brothers but because of unfairness (*yaŋfa*) they received their present destinies. It is not quite clear in the story whether the father is the same as Kanu (*kia*, which I have translated as 'bore', can also mean 'put down') but it seems rather like it specially as he himself makes the book (cf. Kanu in *Koto and Yemi*).

The narrator told the story with great vigour and drama, and the audience were enthralled.

I AM Suriba Nevertire, of Bumban here. I am going to tell you a story about the Europeans and us, we the Limba. We are full brothers. A reason made us different, them to become white people, us to become black people.

Well, at that time, a man bore two children. Well, these two children, one had a white body, the other he bore with a black body. These people, Kanu made them, these two people he bore them in the light.[3] They lived there both of them in the world. They [the parents] had the two children. One was white, one black. But they were full brothers, one mother, one father.

But this child—his mother she loved the European, the white one. That pleased her. Now the black one—his father loved the black one.

Well, one day, he [father] said, 'Let us leave the earth', he and his wife. 'Let us see what the children will do in the light. But one day I

[1] i.e. that Kanu has no power.

[2] Foolish, useless, without money, wandering round with no permanent home to stay in.

[3] i.e. alive, on the earth.

will tell you, we will see what the children are doing in the light, if they are hearing what we told them.' That was their father.

He made a book. He wrote everything,[1] how to make a ship, aeroplane, money,[2] how to make everything. He wrote it in the book, to help the one he loved. He too, he took and made a hoe, he made a cutlass, he looked for millet, he made groundnuts, he made pepper, he made a garden, oranges, everything. He put them down, he gathered them into a pile. He took the hoe, he took the cutlass, he put them there.

If you see unfairness in bearing children, it is not today it begins. One man with two children—he likes to show unfairness to one.

At that time, well, the man said, 'We will hide now, I with you, to see what the children will do.'[3] Then the wife said, 'What will we leave for the children?' He said, 'No, I have got my plan.' He was the one who married the woman, he the man. Behold, he was wanting to act unfairly. He was going to take the book to give it to the black one, he the father. He wanted to give the book to the black one. The mother wanted to give it to the European, the white one, to give him the book. She said 'What will we do?' . . .[4] He said, 'We will bring what we are leaving for the children.'

Now their father could not see well. He could not see the children clearly. He said, 'Child, you, when you go to hunt, do not go very far.' He just turned round, he caught a sheep, he killed it. He [white one] came, he said, 'Father, I have brought meat. I went to hunt for it.' Well, that pleased his father. Because he could not see well, he thought he was lifting down the hoe to give the white one. Behold it was the book he took. 'Take the book for me.' The wife took the book. He said, 'Give it to the child, the one who brought the meat.' He was given it.[5] He was not afraid to peep at it. He started reading it. He started seeing the things, how to make an aeroplane, how to make everything, how to make a ship, he saw it in the book.

The black one came. He said, 'Father, greetings. What have you kept for me?[6] I have killed a bird. It is what I have brought.' He said, 'Ah, my child, you are left as a foolish man.[7] Well, take this hoe. Here is a basket, rice is in it. Millet is in it. Groundnuts are in it. Everything that

[1] Suriba exaggerates the length and high tone to almost ridiculous lengths to indicate that absolutely *everything* was there.

[2] All things for which the Europeans are specially famous among the Limba.

[3] This was spoken very quietly and surreptitiously, depicting the father's desire to conceal it from his children.

[4] A few words here and later are missing owing to a fault in the recording.

[5] It is not clear if it was the hoe or the child that the father mistook. In any case the book was given to the wrong son.

[6] A usual question asked by a friend or visitor, often only half-seriously.

[7] i.e. someone unable to become well off or gain honour. The word itself, *kuyakayakaŋ*, is thought a funny one.

you use when you go to work is there. But you are likely always to be left behind. He is more than you. Everything, if you want to get it, you have to ask your companion, the white one.'

You see us, the black people, we are left in suffering. The unfairness of our birth makes us remain in suffering. That is why they want to send us to learn the writing of the Europeans. But our mother did not agree, she did not love us. She loved the white people. She gave him the book. There they saw how to make everything in happiness [without suffering]. They were able to do that and to surpass us the black people. . . .

If you see the Europeans, everything they are doing, they have to put a black man there. He is a clerk; he sits in the store, he does everything. This is the way. Yesterday we were full brothers with them. We come from one descent, the same mother, the same father, but the unfairness of our birth, that is why we are different. We will not know what you know unless we learn from you. We are brothers of the same parents, that is why you learn from books, to teach us black people so that we may know. Why we are alike—we are full brothers.

I tell you the story, I Suriba Nevertire at Bumban here.

Koto and Yemi

BANKOLO MANSARAY. *Dictated* 13.11.61

Another story which comments on the respective natures and roles of white and black men. The white man has money and access to machines, and does not need or wish to work in the farm in the way characteristic of black men. At the end of the story the Creoles are also introduced; the Limba most frequently encounter them in the capacity of 'clerks'.

Koto and Yemi are stock names for twins, and are often characters in story. This tale resembles the plot (but not the conclusion) of *Two twins,* and also has something in common with *The girl taken by Kanu,* and *Kanu above and Kanu below.*

The beginning of the tale moves, as often, through the various phases of the farming year. The character of Yemi was portrayed vividly—first his off-hand refusal to help in the farm, and then his sudden interest, and even willingness to wake early in the morning, when he heard of the girl.

TWO children were once born. Koto said, 'I will hoe.' Yemi refused to work—he was having love affairs! As soon as he saw that anyone had a beautiful wife, he went and fell on her.

But Koto cut the grass on his farm. 'Yemi, come, let us go and burn it.' 'I am not going, I am having pleasure!' Koto burnt the farm.

The time for reburning came. 'Yemi, let us go and reburn.' Yemi said, 'I am having pleasure.' Koto reburnt.

The time to gather the sticks came. 'Yemi, let us go to gather the sticks.' 'Ugh! I am engaged with my love, I am staying here. Am I to leave this beautiful girl? I am not going there.' Koto gathered the sticks.

The time to collect the rubbish came. 'Yemi, let us go and collect it.' 'I am not going. I am having pleasure.' Koto collected the rubbish.

The time to rehoe came. 'Yemi, let us go and rehoe the grass; I have collected the rubbish.' 'I am not going there. Look at this—my hair style,[1] it is fine!' Koto rehoed the grass, all of it.

The time for chasing the birds from the new seed came round. 'I am not going there. What, am I to have my hair style soaked with rain? I am not going there.' Koto did all the chasing, completely.

The time of weeding came. 'Yemi, go and weed for me.' 'What, am I to go and dirty my hands with weeding? I won't do that.' Koto did all the weeding.

The time to cut the new shoots came. 'I beg you, Yemi, let us go and cut the new shoots.' 'But the moisture on my hands—as soon as you go *gbiŋ* to cut the shoots, the moisture falls on you. I would not do that.' Koto did the cutting.

The rice was in ear. 'Yemi, away to chase off the monkeys, the rice is in ear.' 'I am not going.'

The rice was all in ear. 'Yemi, go and chase the birds for me; there are many creatures there.' 'I can't go. For going early in the morning—before the sun has even risen, you have to go. I am not going there.'

The rice was all ripe. There was a great pool there. 'Yemi, the rice is ripe; come, let us go and see to it.' 'I am not going there.'

Now Koto had no wife. He went in the morning. As he took hold of the rice, and cut at it—*tau*[2]—a girl came out with full breasts, quite full, *yɛrɛ!* She came, she took a knife. But she did not speak. She cut all the rice. She thrashed it. She dried it. She pounded it. She cooked it. She boiled sauce. She helped out the cooked rice. She put it down for Koto. 'E, come, let us eat', said Koto. The girl did not accept. She did not speak. Koto said 'Come here.' She got up, she started to go away. Koto followed. She ran. She went and jumped into the pool. Koto returned. Koto came back again.

The whole night passed, *kudu*. When the sun rose again, Koto took a knife. As he went and cut again—*tau*—the girl came out again. She came and took the knife. She cut all the rice. She thrashed it. She dried it. She pounded it. She cooked it. She boiled sauce. She helped it out. She

[1] Limba men often spend time in cutting their hair or shaving parts of their heads with a razor.

[2] The sound of the first cut.

put it down. She began to go. They both began to run against each other. She went and jumped into the pool. Koto went back.

The whole night passed. He went home to the village. 'Yemi, there is a girl at my farm.' 'What?' said Yemi. 'When you have gone to the farm and begun to cut the rice, *ŋɛti*,[1] a girl goes and takes the knife. She cuts it all. She thrashes it all. She dries it all. She pounds it all. She cooks it all. She boils all the sauce. She helps it out for you. When you say "Come and eat", she does not accept. When you follow her when she is going, she runs away. You both run against each other for long, she goes and jumps into the pool. I came back.' Yemi said, 'What? We will both go tomorrow.'

The sun rose. He went and wakened Koto. 'Come, let us go to the farm.' They went to the farm. Koto took a knife. When he had made a cut—*tau*—the girl came out. Yemi got up, he looked. 'Koto, is that her? E! Greetings!' The girl took no notice. Yemi went up on to a rock. He sat down. The girl cut all the rice. She thrashed it all. She dried it all. She pounded it all. She cooked, she boiled sauce. She helped it out. The testing time has come![2] She put down the cooked rice. Koto said, 'Yemi, come down, let us eat.' Yemi went and made a handful.[3] 'Here, take this handful.' The girl loosed her head-tie; tightly, she tied it round her waist. She began to run. Yemi followed her. He too began to run. The girl jumped into the pool—*tiriŋ*. Yemi also went and jumped in—*tiraŋ*.[4]

He sank. He went for far. He came to a country like this one here—a fine one. He came to a village, like England,[5] a very fine one. He came on an old woman sitting there. He bathed[6] her completely. The old woman asked, 'What are you coming here for?' 'I am following a girl.' 'Why?' 'She is the one I love.' 'For what?' 'To marry her.' The woman said, 'All right. Sit down here.' Yemi looked all round the place, he had chairs and all put out for him, tables and all. The woman sent to the chief. The chief there was Kanu. But he held one thousand girls there. He had rice brought for him and meat. He cut some off, he gave to the woman.

A dog came. He [Yemi] took rice and meat, he put it down for the dog. While he was still eating, a tsetse-fly pricked him, Yemi, eating his flesh. The woman said, 'Kill the fly on your leg.'[7] 'Ha! I won't kill it; when it is filled, it will go.' The fly was filled, it went. The woman ate, she was filled.

[1] Sound of cutting.

[2] A stock phrase used of any difficult test about to come; used especially to initiands just before they go off to the bush to be operated on.

[3] To give a handful of rice from one's bowl is a mark of love or friendship.

[4] The splash as they dive into the water.

[5] England is often assumed to be a village or town not a country.

[6] Bathing someone is a mark of honour; cf. the new chief being bathed in *The story of Kubasi*.

[7] A common phrase used by one friend to another.

The woman said to Yemi, 'The girl you are following—there are one thousand of them. When they are lined up tomorrow, wherever you see me stand and spin, and take my spindle, she is the one. If you don't pick her out, if you pick another, you will be killed.'

The dog ate, he was filled. 'Why have you come?' 'I love a woman here.' 'Ha! There are many of them, they are one thousand. Well—wherever I go tomorrow, and wag my tail and wag my tail and do this,[1] she is the one.'

The cat ate. She said, 'Why have you come?' 'I love a woman here, the one I followed.' 'Ah, they are many, they are one thousand. The one I rub myself against tomorrow, she is the one.'

The fly came. 'I am filled. The reason you came—there are many, they are one thousand. When they are lined up tomorrow, whoever of them strikes herself *gba*, she is the one.'

The sun rose. He went to greet the chief, Kanu. Kanu said, 'Why have you come?' 'I love a girl here.' 'Do you know her?' 'Yes.' 'What is she like?' 'Beautiful.' 'Ah, they are many, they are one thousand. If you pick her out, you are saved. I will give you money—a million. If you don't pick her out, ha! I will kill you.' Yemi said 'All right.'

They were lined up, as far as from here to Makeni.[2] They put her in the middle, secretly, like at Binkolo. The woman went, she went spinning. The dog went. He wagged his tail, he jumped up on her, he jumped up on her. The cat went. She went and rubbed against her. The fly went. It went and bit her. She struck herself.[3] As soon as she struck herself, Yemi went 'It is she, father.'

'E!' Kanu beat the drum. Kanu went and made money—a million—he took it to the side of the water. He made a machine to sew cloth, a machine to make money.[4] He made everything, very well. He went off. He sent messengers—'Go and tell Yemi: here is the woman. Let him go and open the box, he will get money. Here is a bundle of leaves. Let him untie it, he will see how he is to act.'

As he opened it, he turned into a white man. 'Let him untie this bundle too.' He untied it. There was water in the centre. He saw his brother standing there, Koto. Koto became a clerk—like the well-off Creoles—he became a millionaire. Yemi, he became a white man.

All these things—we can't tell where they came from. Well, we are of one descent with that Koto. It is the doing of Kanu. The woman stood between them. Koto said, 'You are a white man indeed. But I am the

[1] i.e. jump up on her, demonstrated by the teller.

[2] About 20 miles away; Binkolo is a village on the road. Lining up the girls is a common episode in the story, and also occurs as one stage in the final initiation ceremony, the 'coming out'.

[3] To kill the fly.

[4] The power of making money as well as machines is commonly attributed to white men.

owner of the woman.' Yemi said, 'Yes, you own the woman. But I went for her. I did not see Kanu, but he left messengers for me to come and give me these possessions. It is your property.'

Well, do you see how it is? A white man only sits there, a clerk sits, for thirty days. He gives out money, perhaps thirty pounds, paying the clerk. Well, that is it. They are full brothers.

Adamu and Ifu

KARANKE DEMA. *Recorded* 1.2.64

This is Karanke's version of the plot I had briefly narrated some two years before and which he had used several times in story-telling in the meantime. In his narration it was now a characteristically Limba story. Quite apart from the details of style and delivery, the framework as a whole and the treatment of certain episodes are typical. The story purports, as so often, to account for the origin of something, in this case the hostility between snakes and humans and the present hard condition of the Limba—the way a woman is under the authority of her husband and must carry out her function of providing leaves and vegetables for their food as well as weeding the family rice farm; the way the man must pay bridewealth for a wife and woo her for long. All these points closely resemble similar ones made in other stories. Certain other episodes are also familiar—the way in which Kanu from up above put human beings on the earth who then had no food but had to go to Kanu to ask for help (cf. *Kanu gave food*); the woman letting down her husband by favouring her lover (as in *Kanu gives chiefship* and other stories); the way someone called is too fearful to come out from his hiding-place (as in, for example, *The story of Bayo*). The dialogue, the way Kanu called Adamu and Ifu, and the series of parallel episodes in which he addresses the three one after the other are also characteristic.

In spite of its foreign plot, therefore, this story is worth including as one example of Limba literature, and as an interesting instance of the way a 'new' story can arise.

SURI—reply to me. I am going to tell a story, about when the earth came out, how after long we were brought out, we Limba, how after long we came to do work, how we lived. I am going to tell it this evening. You Yenkeni, by your grace. You are to reply to me.

You see—Kanu Masala, he was once up above. In the whole world then there were no people. So Kanu Masala thought; he said, 'I will take people to there.' What he brought out were two human beings

—one man; one woman. What were their names? The man—he was Adamu. The woman—she was Ifu. (Ifu.)[1] Ifu.

When he had brought them out, they came and lived [here]. They spent two days and nights—but they found nothing to eat. So they went to Kanu Masala then—'We have come here to you.' Kanu asked 'Any trouble?' 'No. We—the reason we have come is this: you brought us out, you went and put us on the earth here; but we—hunger! Nothing for us to eat. Will we not die tomorrow?' Then Kanu said, 'I will give you food.' Kanu came down. He came and showed them the trees in fruit. He showed them every tree in fruit for them to eat. 'This is your food.' He showed them one—'Don't eat this one oh!' It was like an orange; when it is in fruit it is red. 'Don't eat this one oh. This is a prohibited one. You are not to eat it.' Adamu said 'All right.'

They lived there for long—they ate from those trees. They did no work. They did nothing except just live there, except that when they were hungry they went and ate.

Then a snake got up there. He came and made love with the woman, Ifu. They travelled far in that love.

Then the snake came near, the *baŋkiboro* snake.[2] He came and said to the woman, Ifu, 'Do you never eat from this tree?' Ifu said, 'No. We do not eat it. We were told before that we should not eat it, it is prohibited.' Then the snake said, 'Oh you! That tree—eat from it.' Ifu said, 'We do not eat it.' 'Eat it! Would I lie to you? We share in love you and I. Just eat it. There is nothing wrong about it.'[3] Ifu said, 'We do not eat it. If we eat it we are doing something wrong.' The snake said, 'Not at all. Just eat.' Ifu said, 'All right.' He picked it, he the snake. He went and gave it to Ifu. Ifu said, 'You eat first.' He the snake—he ate. Ifu took it. She ate one. The other one she kept for Adamu.

When Adamu came, she came and gave it to him. Adamu said, 'I will not eat this oh! We were told before that we should not eat it.' Ifu said, 'Not at all. Just eat it. There is nothing wrong about it.' Adamu refused. She begged him there. Adamu took the fruit, he ate the fruit.

Now Kanu Masala—he saw this. He knew. 'Those people have broken the prohibition I gave them.' When they had eaten it, Adamu—his heart trembled. 'When Kanu Masala comes here tomorrow, this means we have done something wrong.'

When Kanu Masala came down, Adamu was hiding now when he saw Kanu coming. He hid himself. Both of them were by now hiding themselves (seeing Kanu Masala).[4] When Kanu arrived he came and called, calling the man. 'Adamu! Adamu!' Now Adamu was afraid to reply—for he had eaten from the tree. He called him again. 'Adamu! Adamu!'

[1] Suri, one of the listeners, repeats the name.

[2] A very long, red, and spotted fatal snake.

[3] Lit. 'there is no trouble (obstacle)'.

[4] Another interjection by Suri.

He was just a bit afraid to reply. He [Kanu] called 'Ifu! Ifu!' Both of them were afraid to reply.

He called Adamu again. Adamu replied. Adamu came. He came and asked him—'Adamu.' 'Yes?' 'What made you eat from that tree really? I told you you were not to eat it. You took, you ate it just the same. What made you eat it?' Then Adamu said, 'Ah, my father. It was not me. It was the woman. She came and gave it to me—Ifu. I said, "I do not eat this." She said, "Just eat it." She has brought me into trouble.'

Then Kanu called Ifu. 'Ifu! Ifu!' Ifu replied, 'Yes?' 'Come here.' Ifu came near. He asked her, 'What made you give him from that tree for him to eat?' Then Ifu said, 'It was not me, my father; it was the serpent who came and gave me from the tree. He said "Eat it. It is food." I refused for long oh! He said "Just eat it. There is nothing wrong about it." I ate it. What I left I came and gave to Adamu.'

He called the serpent, the *baŋkiboro* snake. The *baŋkiboro* snake came. When he had come, he asked him. 'What made you give those people from that tree for them to eat?' The *baŋkiboro* snake said, 'I gave it to them, yes; there was nothing wrong about it at all.'

Then Kanu said, 'For you, you have not done well. I told them they were not to eat from this tree. You came and gave it to them. You do not want them to prosper.[1] It looks as if you—you will be parted from them. You will go into the bush once and for all. You will never again come out [to live] among human beings.[2] When you meet a human, you will be killed. For you have not done well.' Since the *baŋkiboro* snake went off into the bush—if you see a *baŋkiboro* snake now with human beings, whenever they see each other, they kill him. That is why they hate each other.

When the *baŋkiboro* snake had gone into the bush, then Kanu Masala said, 'Ifu.' 'Yes?' 'You, because you were lied to today and agreed to it, and I told you before that you were not to have suffering but you did not agree to this—now you, you will have suffering. You will now stay behind Adamu. All you women now, when you are married to a man, you will live in his power. That is what I say. When you give birth, when you do that, you will have suffering. That is what I say. When you work now, after the man has cleared and hoed, you will weed. The rain will beat on you there. The sun will burn you there—as you think about your husband's sauce.[3] For that is what you chose. That is what you will do.'

Then he said, 'Adamu.' 'Yes?' 'Because you were lied to by the woman and you agreed to it, you will begin to work. You will work now. When you want to get a wife you will have to woo her. Every man will have to give wealth for long to get her. When you have married

[1] Lit. 'do not like their life'.

[2] Or Limba.

[3] A wife often has the particular responsibility for growing or gathering the vegetables for the 'sauce'

several [wives] you will look for a house—you must build, you the man. You will have to get a farm for them to go to. That is what I give you. For you refused to live in the good fortune you had.'

If you see now—we Limba we live now to work; the sun burns us; the rain soaks us; ha! we endure that suffering; if you want to get something to eat you have to struggle for long—that began from the serpent, the *baŋkiboro* snake. If you see that we hate each other, him and us—that is the only reason. Now the *baŋkiboro* snake, when he sees a human, says, 'That man is coming to kill me'; and if you do not strengthen yourself, you the human, he will catch you, biting you. For he was driven out from among us. If you see how we live, we Limba, working—that was where it began.

That is it, it is finished.

The dog and the wheel

SURI KAMARA. *Recorded* 8.12.61

A story which explains how the animals got their various characteristics, how white men got wisdom, how lorries were first made, and why dogs bark at lorries even at the risk of being crushed to death. In spite of modern references the story is in many ways typically Limba—the attribution of origins, the opening with Kanu, and the style of delivery.

It was told by a driver who said he had heard it from others but had spent some time thinking about it himself before telling it. He added that he himself had 'killed many dogs with his lorries'.

I AM Suri Kamara, I am a driver. I am coming to tell Yenkeni a story this evening, about the animals, who long ago did not know what work there was for them in this world.

All of them had then no ideas. One day, the dogs went and saw Kanu, with the other animals. They asked Kanu, 'Kanu! Now what is in our hearts is to destroy things. But we have no power to destroy those things. Now, we beg you, help us, so you may give us instruments we can destroy things with.' Then Kanu said, 'Well, wait!'

He took a nail, he put it onto the cat's paw. He took a wheel, he gave it to the dog. He took a voice and fastened it to the goat. He took the power to chew for itself,[1] he fastened it to the goat. Kanu said good-bye to them.[2] 'Well, go. When you are going, each of you—don't let anyone touch your own property.' 'All right.'

[1] The goat's way of chewing is often thought specially amusing.

[2] Said a formal good-bye, indicating that he had now finished giving them their gifts.

But, well, there were great crowds of them. They too—their smells were a little bit strong, where they were rubbing against each other! As they began to go along the road, then they said, 'Now, friend, we have come to a spring. Let us bathe.' They all stopped. They undressed. Each of them—what he had been given by Kanu, he went and laid it on one side when he had finished undressing. They all threw themselves into the water.

At that time, there was no black man here in the world. Only the Europeans. These Europeans too, they went to Kanu. Kanu told them, 'Well, you, I will not be able to give you anything at all, but I will attach wisdom[1] to you.' He looked at the centre of the head, there he poured the water of wisdom. That wisdom remains now on a human's head. That is why when a human gets old, when he is old you will see all the hair go from his head.[2] It is the hot water of wisdom that went in there.

Well, when he came and saw all the animals having all gone into the water, into the water to bathe, there he stood up, there he went, very cautiously, he went and took the wheel. He hid. He did not wait once, he did not wait twice since he knew that the animals are a thing that is in the bush.[3] He ran away in secret, he went off to the down country part, he threw himself into the water. After a long time he came out at England.

Well he stayed there with this wheel, he did not know what he should do with it. There he lay down to sleep. There he thought to make a lorry. That lorry, he finished making it, completely. Well, that machine, when it is turned it hums like an animal—*hmmmmmmmŋ*. Ah! Kanu! This animal had come now into being, but they did not know what they should do with it.

Then said the European who had taken the dog's wheel, then he said, 'Wait. I too, I have taken a thing from the animals, it is like a wheel. That wheel, now let us fasten it underneath, on the bottom of the machine.' They took the wheel, they made ones like it, like the one taken from the dog. They fastened it, there one, there one, at the back one and one. It came to four wheels. They took a large bit of iron, they tied it on, bit by bit, on the bottom. E! and did that machine not go humming again? Stop fooling![4] They took a piece of wood, that is what they went and put in the middle. They took that wood, they went and joined it to those bits of iron. Now comes the speeding! They sped along for far.

[1] The 'wisdom' (*funuŋ*) often attributed to Europeans because of their power to invent and control machinery.

[2] This joke about baldness was thought (and intended) to be very funny.

[3] i.e. that he had better take advantage of the animals while he could.

[4] i.e. of course it did.

But the dogs—when they heard the humming, well, they did not know what it was that was bringing the humming. Well, they, the dogs, they were always getting up going to search, going to smell out where the wheel had been taken. But they found no trace.

One day, they saw something coming *fuuu!* As they looked underneath—that minute they saw the wheel that they had lost! It was the young ones, they were the first to see the wheels. Then they stood there calling out—'Here, here, here—*wo wo wo*; come here. Here here here—*wo wo wo. Ŋ ŋ ŋ. Wo wo.*' (I am imitating the humming.)[1] Others there were overcome by anger; others first went and put their heads down when that lorry was passing. That is why they jump on the wheel, to go and pull it off, in anger, trying to take it. But oh! the power the Europeans had been given! What came and happened—the dog was killed.

Since I heard that, I had to tell it to you. It is finished.

The jealous mothers

SURIBA (NEVERTIRE) KONTEH. *Recorded* 28.2.61

A story with the concluding comment that quarrelling is only to be expected when a man marries several wives. As usual in a Limba context the main sphere of jealousy is their children.

The plot is rather confusing at the beginning. Its main interest for the listeners was the brilliant way in which it was told, with particularly vivid characterization of the two women as enacted by the teller. He made full use of the techniques of pausing, varying speed, tone, and volume, and exaggeratedly indicating surprise, horror, or despair.

I AM going to tell you a story, I Suriba Nevertire—about a man who married two wives, and had children by each of them. These wives, they were jealous. They did not like to see their co-wife [each other]. They did not like to see their co-wife's child.

At that time, of the children that of one co-wife was big now. The other did not like that.

One day she looked for a rope, she went and cut a small hole in the wall where her companion's child lay. Well, she wanted to kill him. Her own child was always sickly—she wanted him alone to be left. There where they went to sleep with the husband[2]—now she said to her

[1] An interpolation by the narrator.

[2] Husband and wife usually sleep in a side room in the house, the other women and children in the large central room. The wife bores a hole through the wall between the rooms.

child,[1] an elder one, so big, 'Please when your brother has slept a little, take this rope, and put it round his neck. Do you understand?' 'Yes.'[2] At the time, behold the mother of the child that was intended to be killed, she heard them. She twisted a rope. She bored a hole. She put the rope in, she went and placed it. 'When the time comes, you are to take this rope and hang it on the child of my co-wife, round his neck.'[3]

She went and lay down in the house, with her husband. When she had gone and lain down there, the children went and lay down, the two of them. Well, this woman, it was her child that was to be killed that day. [The third child said] 'Well, we will play a game today.' He took the rope. He went and hung it on her child, who was lying over there. He did not hang it on the other's child. She asked, 'Have you hung the rope?' 'Yes.' She pulled the rope tightly—*thiriŋ*.[4] The child was strangled there. The child died. Well, her heart was joyful where she was lying. She thought she had killed her companion's child. Behold, it was her own she had killed.

When the sun rose, she got up in the morning, she said, 'Oh! the children—why are they sleeping so long today? They refuse to wake up.'[5]

When she went and touched the child—the child was dead![6] It was her own. Oh! She loosed the rope, loosed the rope.[7] She took her companion's child, the one who had not died, she put him on her back.[8] She said, 'This is my child.' She began to walk around.

When her companion came, she found the child dead. She wept. She wept. She said, 'Ha! This child, he is not mine. Ee! It is yours that has died.'[9] 'That is not my child. See, here is my child on my back; he has not died.' 'Oh? Your child has not died?' 'No.' 'What are we to do?' 'You know what we will do?—let us go to Kanu, let us be judged [by him].'

They went. 'Look at this child.[10] It was I who bore him, her child

[1] This is a third child.

[2] The quiet shy reply enacted by the teller is typical of the way a young Limba child often assents to an order.

[3] She also tells the third child what to do.

[4] The sound of the rope being pulled tight and, apparently, of the helpless way the child was caught and strangled; the teller pronounced it as a brief high squeak.

[5] This episode about sleeping late recurs in other stories e.g. *The man killed for a spinach leaf.*

[6] This scene was depicted slowly and quietly to indicate the wordless horror and shock of the woman finding her own child dead.

[7] She is still thunderstruck, the narrator conveys, but suddenly begins to make haste so as to injure the other woman.

[8] The usual way of carrying one's child.

[9] The woman is at first horror-struck, then puzzled, then suspicious.

[10] The mother of the living child is speaking. At first she is rather shy and

died, she left her child, the dead one, she took mine and put him on her back.'

Then he [Kanu] said, 'Do you want me to decide between you?' 'Yes.' 'You want me to decide between you?' 'Yes.' He sharpened his sword. 'Well, you, stand [to be judged]. The child that remains—well, since one has died, let me kill the one that is left, so you may be equal. Neither of you will have a child.' One of them thought—the child was hers, she had borne it, it was her first child, *gbiŋ!*[1]—if she allowed it to be killed, ha! her heart would be broken. She said, 'Kanu, even if you don't kill him and even if she says she was the one who bore him, well I will be willing to look at him as her child. I will be left with the one who has died.' Then Kanu said, 'What about you, what do you say?' 'Kill him![2] kill him! let us stay equal.' Then Kanu said, 'No. You, you are telling lies. It is not you who owns the child. This woman is the one who owns the child who is left. That one owns the dead one.'

Well—theft—thieving in motherhood, it did not begin today.[3] That was the time theft began. Kanu knew how to make the division. Thus if you hate me, if Kanu loves me, whatever he wants to give me he gives. It is Kanu that divides out things. He divides out everything. If you hate someone and Kanu loves him, he gives him luck. Well that was the time they started to quarrel. If you see wives hating each other, well the reason is that they are married to one man. With the Europeans, a man marries one woman. They will not quarrel. She has no co-wife. But we—marrying ten women, one man. They will not love each other. Hence quarrels.

That is the story I have to tell you, I Suriba Nevertire. Women's quarrels will not end. One wife to one husband—they will not quarrel. But two people, three people—they will not love each other. For having children—when they have children in the marriage, they will disagree. That is the story I have to tell you, I, Suriba Nevertire.

Kanu above and Kanu below

KABI KANU. *Dictated* 9.2.61

A story (rather like that of *The girl taken by Kanu*) about how various animals co-operated to bring back the girl who had been taken. Limba do not generally speak of *Kanu below*, but occasionally this term is used

nervous, then gets confidence and the words of complaint come pouring out in a voluble rush.

[1] The term emphasizes that it was really and truly her first child, one loved as first children are.

[2] She is now hoarse with anger and excitement.

[3] i.e. but long ago.

(specially in Kamabai, I think) to cover all the spiritual agencies other than Kanu (above)—i.e. spirits, the dead and, specially, witches. This terminology may possibly be an effect of mission teaching.

The story concludes with the expression of thanks.

KANU above gave Kanu below a child to bring up.[1] When he had given him the girl to bring up, she grew up, her breasts were full. Kanu above came to get the girl. He took her up above. Kanu below came and called. He could not see the girl. He began to cry.

The cane rat came. The ant-eater came. The cockroach came. The spider came. The woodpecker came. They said to Kanu below, 'Your part is finished.'[2]

They travelled for far. They came to the cane grass. The cane rat said, 'Your part is finished.' He cut a road through. He took the road to a river.

The cockroach said, 'Your part is finished.' He spread his wings. They went up on to his wings, he carried them across the river. They went. They came to the place where they had to go up.

The spider said, 'Your part is finished.' He took up his web shining to the sky. He let it down below. He said they were to climb up it. Now they had reached there. They said, 'Well, who will get us inside the sky?'

The woodpecker said, 'Your part is finished.' He knocked it. They went in. They greeted Kanu. Kanu said, 'What have you come here for?' (?) They said, 'The only reason we came—you gave a child to Kanu below to be brought up. The child is now full grown. We have come to take her. That is the only reason we came.' 'All right, sit down.' They sat. They were given food. They ate.

The one they had come for, she had been taken into the *Bondo* society. They came to be brought out and beautified.[3] They were lined up. Kanu said, 'Well if you know the one, take her.' The fly said,[4] 'The one I bite, that is she.' The cat said, 'The one I rub against, and who takes and throws me off, that is she.' They watched. They did not know her. The fly came and bit her; she jumped. They said in their hearts, 'It is she.' The cat came and rubbed against her. It was taken and thrown off. They said, 'It is she.' They went and took her 'It is she.' Kanu said, 'Oh, is it she?' They said 'Yes.'

They said good-bye. They got ready to go. They came a long way.

[1] Children are sometimes brought up in their mother's parents' home. When they are full grown they return to their father's home for initiation.

[2] i.e. the rest is for us to perform.

[3] The girls are brought out of the bush in the final ceremony of the *Bondo* initiation, dressed in fine clothes, put in a line, and admired for their beauty.

[4] The fly and cat have not been mentioned before; perhaps they were omitted from the earlier list, or perhaps, as in *Koto and Yemi*, they had been encountered for the first time in the new land.

They came again to the sky, it was shut. The woodpecker knocked a hole again in the sky. The spider stretched out his web. He let it down below. He carried it up above again. 'Well, let us go down.' They went down. They came again to the river. The cockroach spread his wings. They crossed over. They said 'We have come again to the cane grass.' The cane rat cut a road through, he cut the road to a clear place. They went. They found Kanu. They said 'Is it she?' He said 'Yes, it is she. I thank you, I thank you.'

The girl taken by Kanu

NIAKA DEMA. *Dictated* 11.10.61

A story of co-operation between various animals, each taking his 'own part' in order to bring back the girl taken off by Kanu. The plot is very similar to *Kanu above and Kanu below*, but here only one Kanu occurs, the action is much more elaborately narrated, and the story ends with an implied dilemma about who deserved the girl as his wife, and a blessing. The theme of seeking a girl in another world and having to choose her from among many others drawn up in a long line occurs in several stories e.g. *Koto and Yemi*, *Two twins*.

A GIRL was once born. She was brought up very well. She was full grown, her breasts were full. When she was sent by her people to go for water, the rain came. It was Kanu now who loved the girl. The rain came, the thunder went and clapped. Behold, Kanu loved the girl. He came to take the girl. He took her up above to the sky.

Then the chief said, 'Ah! Ah alas! My child—she has been taken by Kanu Masala up above'—It was as if it was here, here with Alimami Salifu,[1] here: as if his child now had come to be taken away by Kanu.

He wept and wept. But it happened that Kanu came to help him. A spider came, coming to stretch his web on the veranda. When several nights had passed, then the sub-chiefs said, 'E, chief! your man has just come to stretch his web on the veranda! Ha! that is not good.' The chief said, 'It is good. I—men,[2] I love men: for I am chief.' He stayed.

Two nights passed. A fly came, coming to bite people on the veranda. Then the sub-chiefs said again, 'E, chief! your young men have just come to bite people!' Then the chief said, 'Let them just stay with me.' Well, the fly stayed.

[1] The local chief. The implication of 'taken by Kanu' would normally be that she had died.

[2] Usually of the young men who work for the chief.

Two more nights passed. A rat came too, coming to steal the kola the chief put down,[1] coming to steal it. Wherever his wives put down anything, he stole it. Then the sub-chiefs said again, 'E, chief! oh, how long are you just keeping thieves?' Then the chief said, 'Let them stay with me.'

Well, an ant-eater came too, coming to tunnel, digging up the ground in the veranda, just digging holes. Then the sub-chiefs said, 'E, chief! you are just keeping diggers of the veranda!' Then the chief said again, 'I love that man too.' It stayed like that.

The chameleon came too. Whatever gown the chief put on, the chameleon put that one on too. When the chief put a hat on his head, the chameleon put that one on too. Then the sub-chiefs said again, 'E, chief! what honour is this, that if ever you put on a gown your man puts it on too?' Then the chief said again, 'Let them stay with me.' It stayed like that.

Then the chief wept, and said, 'Men, all those who have gathered here—my child went with Kanu up above. Kanu went with my child right up. But if the men of mine who have come here to me, if they will remove my shame and go for me for my child—'

Then the spider said, 'I—to go up above to the sky—I am able.' Then the chameleon said, 'I—the way the chief came and treated me, I like that.' He passed the word to the ant-eater; he said, 'I, I like the way the chief treats me.' They finished passing the word to them all. They accepted.

When the sun rose, the spider took up his thread. He stood up. He ran up the thread—*laŋdiooŋ*. He went right to the sky, right up. He went and tied together a ladder. He brought them in. They all finished going into the sky. They found Kanu there up above. He went and greeted them. 'Greetings to you.' Kanu said, 'What! You, you from below, you have come here? Ha! that is hard. We should be afraid of them.' They had mats spread for them.

They were to go to the chief's court. The fly went all round the veranda. Everything they said, he heard, he came and told them of it. They had had a kola tied up for them, a white one.[2] They had put poison in it. But in the red kola, they had not put poison. It was being brought to them. Then the fly went first to the spider. 'The kola that is coming—let no one eat the white one; it has had poison put in it; so that we do not die.' They took the kola. They said, 'We, we do not like white kola in our country: the red one, that is what we are used to.'

When the head wife began to cook, the fly was there again. He heard what was said, all of it. Well, he was their looker. When the rice was

[1] For sacrifice.

[2] White kola is normally preferred to red, and is the usual gift of friendship and welcome to a stranger.

cooked, they put on palm oil and boiled meat. They put it in a bowl, the oil on one chair, the meat on one chair. They took the one with the meat, they put in poison; those who went are to die, oh, who went for the child to the chief Masala! The fly came again. 'It is good for you not to eat the meat; the one with the oil is good, that is what you can eat.'[1]

Then the spider said, 'Thank you, thank you, thank you, you who have brought us food. But food with meat—we are always eating that down below; the one with the oil, that is the food we want to eat.' They took the one with the meat, they went and threw it on the rubbish heap. Then the fly said, 'How is that, men? The rice has been thrown away. If we had really eaten it, we would have died.'

They did that two, three times. They were unable to catch them. Two nights passed. The strangers were asked [their business]. Then the spider said, 'We have come for this. The chief has lost a child below. This is why we have been sent, for us to come and ask of you here, whether she came here.' Then the sub-chiefs said, 'All right. From here until the day after tomorrow, we will search for her.'

The whole night passed, *kudu*. 'Hey, hey! chief!' said the sub-chiefs, 'Let us not give them food.' Then the rat said, 'Wait, men. It is my time of trial that is come now.' They had not eaten now. For six days they had stayed there without anything. Then the rat got up. They were locked in a house, like in this one here. Everywhere the door was locked. The rat went out into the moonlight. He went and stole a pot. Everything that belongs to a woman, everything to add to the rice,[2] he brought it for them now, everything that is eaten by a person. The chief's kolas—he went and bored into them, *puruthɔ!* The huge basket [of rice] was finished! For six days they did not go outside.

Then the sub-chiefs said, 'It is good for us to put them on fire.' Then the ant-eater said, 'My testing time is coming.' He got up; he tunnelled on one side of the house, 'for we have heard that we are being put on fire in the house where they lodged us.' He spent the day tunnelling in the earth below. He tunnelled from here as far as Magba's house.[3] They came and set it on fire. The house burnt. They got up. They went into the hole that the ant-eater had dug. The house was all burnt.

In the morning they got up, they came out of the hole. They came and swept it over on top in the place where they usually spent the night. They took a big dish. They put there a kola.[4] 'This is it, chief. We are here by your grace. We have met no trouble. But something happened

[1] The sauce containing meat would normally be preferred as being much rarer than the everyday sauce of palm oil.

[2] i.e. all the ingredients from which women cook sauce to accompany the rice.

[3] About fifty or so yards away.

[4] A token to accompany their formal announcement to the chief that the house in which they were lodged has been burnt.

here oh! Our house came and was burnt. But we did not know who was the one who did it.' The chief said, 'It is all right.'

They sat down. The chief beat the drum. 'It is good that we, we, strangers, that whatever clothing each wears, that we and you should show each other who is best in clothing.' The chameleon said, 'For this, men, you sit there. For this has come to me now. I will do this work for you.' The chief came out. He went and put on a long gown, all gold; a hat, all gold; trousers, all gold. The spider went there. At the moment he went to the door, the chameleon now was without a chair, he was without a long gown, he was without a hat: but before he had reached there, he found the chameleon sitting on a chair; he found the chameleon now sitting with a chief's long gowns; in a hat of gold, that is how he found the chameleon sitting.

Then the sub-chiefs said, 'We will be unable for the strangers who have come. Everything we use to drive them away, they see it all. It is good that we take the children to bathe. When we take the children to bathe, we will go and dress them, and they are to show us their child. A man will not mistake his own child. His own child, he will not mistake her.' Then the fly said again, 'For this now, men—we are to go to the water where they are dressed.' They went. The stranger child, the one that Kanu went and took from here down below, they refused to dress her well. Then the fly said, 'Whichever one you see jump, she is ours.' Then the spider said, 'Let us sit then.'

Her name was Boi—the girl's. When they went and dressed them, all their beads were many. When they went and were lined up then the sub-chief said, 'Well, spider, by grace of the fly, by grace of the ant-eater, by grace of the rat, by grace of you all, look for your own; for that is why they sent you, for your own. That is the word.' Then the fly said, 'I—our own, we want her. If we say, "Here is ours" you will not make a difficulty?' Then the sub-chiefs said, 'All right.' Then the spider said, 'I will touch her.' The fly said, 'Whichever one you see jump, that is she.' The spider said, 'Yes.' He [fly] went and touched them all. He came to Boi. He bit her behind. The spider now threw his arms round her. 'Here is ours. Is it not she?' 'It is she.'

The chief Kanu said, 'They are wise men. They have been sent to me here.' He brought out four kolas.[1] 'Here they are. When you reach your chief tell him that here is his child.'

The spider got up. He let out his thread again. They went down again on to our land. When they came to the chief, they came and told their news. The chief said, 'Thank you. Well now, sub-chiefs? You were making talk with me, when the men came you were setting out to abuse them. Well now, did they not go for my child for me? Now we will make a sacrifice for them. An ox.' The ox was killed.

[1] He sends them as greeting to the chief below.

But for the girl—the spider said, 'I took you up up above.' Then the fly said, 'If I had not been there, you would have died from the kola that was first laid out for you—that and the rice too.' Then the ant-eater said, 'What about the place we were being burned? I dug a hole for us to go into there. We were saved.' Then the rat said, 'We were kept for six days, we did not eat anything, I stole for you. Since you have come, the wife—I should get her.' The sub-chiefs said, 'For that word—everyone.' The chameleon said, 'This—when the chief brought out his clothing, if we had not been seen in them, would we not have been killed? I am the one for the wife.'

Then the sub-chiefs, 'For all that, you the men, we make you a sacrifice. No one will get her for a wife. This cow is what you may eat.' The tail—the spider got it, he was the leader. The chief blessed them: wherever the child went might she have blessing, might she be at peace, by grace of the spider.

Ninkinanka

NIAKA DEMA. *Dictated* 27.10.61

The story of a great trapper, his son, and the spirit Ninkinanka. It explains light-heartedly the reason for thunder and lightning. The trapper here is pictured as rather like the stock Limba figure of a hunter, with success, special skill, and secret medicine (normally trapping is not regarded as an expert or important skill). Ninkinanka is one of the best-known spirits among the Limba, and is also known as far away as Senegambia ('a fabulous snake of immense size dwelling in the depths of the forest or swamps'—D. P. Gamble, *The Wolof of Senegambia*, London, 1957, p. 72). Among the Limba he seems sometimes to be conceived of as like a snake, living in the forest, sometimes as like the rainbow, an association which fits well with the description in this story of Ninkinanka's great length, extended from heaven to earth.

A STORY for you. A man once came out, a great trapper in the country. When he set his trap, the trap began to kill [animals]. His son—his name was Sara. When he found three animals there, he loosed them, he came and told his father. The father, he came and cut up the three animals. He had a spirit. That spirit, ha! he was amazing! a great trapper. He went and learnt the leaves from another master. Now that master was Sokoro.[1] At the time when he killed an animal, then he went and spat medicine on to the trap, he spat medicine on to the first trap that he had set.

[1] A well-known spirit, usually associated with hunters and hunting.

When the sun rose, three bush cows were killed in the trap. At that the boy said, 'Father. Ha ha! We have killed in the trap.' 'What animals are they?' 'Bush cows, three of them.' Then the man said—he was called Koto, a great trapper—when he went and cut up the bush cows, 'But the bush cows will not be sufficient for the country. I have worked all this year for nothing. My trap has not killed.'

When he went again and spat medicine on to the trap that he had first set, when the sun rose, three hippopotamuses came and were caught. Then the boy stood up. He went and looked at the trap. He found them. 'Father, ha! I have found three animals in the trap. They are big oh!' The man went—he Koto. When he found the animals, he said, 'Huh! Are these the animals then you fetched me for? They are not much.' Then the boy said, 'E! Father! What animals now are bigger than these?' 'Ah! I will beat you! You—these small fowls,[1] of these you came to tell me "Here are big animals"? I do not like that.' They cut up the big hippopotamuses.

Then he got up again, he went again and spat medicine on the trap he had first set. 'E, Kanu! I have not yet got an animal with which I can satisfy the country. All these—I have found no sense from them. But the time when I kill an animal, then the whole country will know.' Then the boy said, 'E! an elephant too, is that a small thing? Ha! it is hard oh!'

He went and spat the medicine. 'I have not killed an animal that can cool my heart.[2] At the time when I kill an animal that can cool my heart, then I will sleep.' He went and spat the medicine on the trap he had first set. Two nights passed.

Ninkinanka came, he came and was killed. Because of the medicine—every animal was killed in the trap. When Ninkinanka came and was killed in the trap, his tail was fastened down below. Ninkinanka flew up above to the sky. He went and caught the sky in his mouth. He stayed there. But his tail was below.

The boy went to look at the trap. He came. He stood, here. He saw, as from here to the bush at the cotton tree;[3] he saw a big animal. But it was the tail that he saw, he was not able to see the meat. He went to his father. 'Father. The animal you always talked about, it is caught today in the trap. I did not see the head, I did not see the leg, that animal is there in the trap.' His father cried a bit. He took a sword. He sharpened it. He began to go. He found the animal. He turned up his eyes, right up.[4]

[1] The trapper speaks contemptuously of the large animals he has caught as a mere 'collection of guinea fowls'.

[2] i.e. satisfy him, stop his heart being angry.

[3] A reference to the cotton tree just outside the village, about a hundred yards distance.

[4] *Kathinthi*—the high tones describe the man looking up and up right into the sky (to try to see the top of the animal).

'E! My son, I told you the thing—that at the time when I killed an animal, that then the whole country would know.'

He gave the boy the sword and the hunter's bag. 'When you come to the head and the neck, cut it off, chopping through the neck. We have come out from (?) shame today, we have killed an animal today.'

The boy began to climb. Now Ninkinanka had scales fastened on him up above, he Ninkinanka. The boy climbed, for long. He went for about one mile. He said 'Ha! Father! I will be unable to get to the head. Will I cut?' His father said, 'E! No! Not until you get to the head and the neck, then kill.'

He climbed. He climbed, climbed, for long, he climbed for a month. When he shouted his words now, his father could now no longer hear what he was saying. The boy was cunning. He took the words[1] he was saying, he cut them off, he hung them below on the path, on the animal. He climbed, climbed, climbed, climbed. 'E! I will be unable to get to the animal.' He shouted words now. He could not hear his father. Then he said, 'Words, say to my father for me "I will be unable to come right to the head".' His father had it passed to him by the words. Then his father said, 'Words, tell my son that until he gets right to the neck, he is not to wait on the way, but go and cut it, so that the animal may not escape us.' The boy had this passed to him.

He climbed, climbed, climbed. He climbed about two hundred miles. He left his words again on the path. He climbed. He was going to be unable to come to the head. 'Words, say to Words for me, that Words are to say to my father for me "Will I cut?"' Then Words told his father. His father said 'Words, tell Words, that Words are to pass it to Words, that Words are to pass it to my son, that if he has not yet got to the head, don't cut! I don't want that meat to escape. That is the animal I had wanted.'

He climbed again. He went, went, went, went. Now the animal had caught the sky in its mouth, for Ninkinanka is the chief of the spirits, he talks with Kanu. When he got to halfway, he said, 'E! I will be unable now oh!' The boy had a knife now, a sword, sharp. He said, 'Words, say to Words for me now, that Words are to say to Words for me, that Words are to pass it on for me to Words, that Words are to pass it on for me to Words, that Words are to pass it on for me to my father—"Will I cut?"' His father said, 'If it is on the path, let Words say to Words for me, that if he has not got to the head, do not cut!' Words passed to Words. Words said, 'If he has not got to the head, do not cut!' Words passed again to Words, 'If he has not got to the head, his father says

[1] As the story progresses the words or voice (*thampa*) of father and son seem to take on a kind of life of their own, and the interchanges between the two are uttered as a kind of alliterative refrain throughout the rest of the story. This portion of the story depends particularly on the mode of delivery.

do not cut!' Words came to the boy, 'If you have not got to the neck, do not cut.'

There was left now about one mile. Now the animal had the sky in its mouth. The boy now, the one who was called Sara, he had a knife, a sharp one. When he got now to about one mile to climb to the head, he shouted words. 'Words, shout words for me now to Words, that Words are to shout words to Words, that Words are to shout words to Words, that Words are to shout words to Words, that Words are to shout words to my father, that now I have got to the edge of the ribs, there is where I have got to, about to come right to the neck.' Then his father said here below, 'Words, say to Words, that Words are to shout words to Words, that Words are to shout words to Words, that Words are to shout words to Words, that Words are to shout words to my son, that if you have got to the neck, cut!'

He raised the sword, he went—*gbede!* [cutting it]. Ninkinanka's head, and the child, and the sword—they went right into the sky! Ninkinanka fell down. The one who cut—they went right into the sky.

The father now wept below here. 'E, my child, whom I brought up, I no longer see him now.' The boy [above] wept for his father below here.

You see, whenever he weeps, his tears, when he sheds them from his eyes, that is the great, great, great rain. You know the thunder. When he takes up the knife to brandish to find a path to cut to see to come here to his father here, that is called the thunder falling. Always if you hear of great rain, the boy is weeping in the sky, weeping for his father. When he does like this[1] with his knife, to brandish it, that is the thunder, when he thrusts down, *sida!* the thunder falls.

Sara and the guinea fowl

KARANKE DEMA. *Dictated* 28.7.61

A story explaining the origin of the various animals that trouble people and eat their rice. They were due to the greed of Sara and his refusal to stop and listen when people remonstrated with him.

I have not heard this or a similar plot elsewhere, but the series of songs or words by something that someone is trying vainly to get rid of occurs in other stories, e.g. *The forbidden forest* and several others not included here. The actual description of the origin did not seem to be taken too seriously.

The singing of the song and chorus was one of the main highlights of the story for the audience and teller. As often, the words are not easy to translate or catch and some have no clear sense. The song was repeated

[1] The narrator demonstrated, striking with an imaginary knife.

several times throughout the whole story, with only a word in the first line changed on each occasion, thus giving a clear structure to the series of successive actions by Sara. On the later occasions only the introductory verse is reproduced here, but the chorus was in fact repeated many times over each time.

SARA once came out on the earth, a great eater of meat.[1] A bird was also coming out, a guinea fowl in the forest. It was not to be eaten. It had a (?) small path at a *kumɛthɛ* tree (?), there it went to eat. Sara always went there too, he went and tapped wine there, there was his road. He always came on the bird's path.

One day, he made a palm leaf rope. He went and put it down, 'I will make a trap for the bird that always comes here.' When he had placed the rope, he went and tapped wine from the palm tree in the morning. He returned. As he came in the evening, he found the guinea fowl caught there. As he was rejoicing, saying 'Fine! I have killed a guinea fowl today', then the guinea fowl said, 'Do not say "Fine!".' Then it sang a song there, when it had been caught, the guinea fowl, calling Sara. 'Sara is coming to loose me, Sara is coming to loose me. Here he found a path, a night passed, here he came and put a rope for me, the guinea fowl, the guinea fowl, *ko de ba ko naligbe*. What is your name? what is your name?'—Answer![2] 'Tambarenke, Tambarenke.' 'What is your name?' 'Tambarenke, Tambarenke.' 'What is your name?' 'Tambarenke, Tambarenke.' 'What is your name?' 'Tambarenke, Tambarenke.'

Sara came. He heard this on his farm. He came. He found the guinea fowl. He came and loosed it. He put it in his bag. He tapped wine from the palm tree.

He began to come home. He was about to enter his farm hut. Now he, he was a great meat eater, he did not want to give anyone the guinea fowl, 'I alone will eat it.' Now the guinea fowl—it was not to be eaten. Then the guinea fowl spoke in the bag where it had been put, 'Sara is coming to pluck me, Sara is coming to pluck me. Here he found a path, a night passed, here he came and put a rope for me, the guinea fowl, the guinea fowl, *ko de ba ko naligbe*. What is your name? What is your name?' 'Tambarenke, Tambarenke.' 'What is your name? What is your name?' 'Tambarenke, Tambarenke.' 'What is your name? What is your name?' 'Tambarenke, Tambarenke.'

He took out the bird. Everyone was surprised 'E! Sara. E! Sara, what is it in your bag? What is it in your bag?'—surprised that the guinea fowl was speaking in the bag. He took it out. He plucked it. When he put it down, the guinea fowl spoke again there, 'Sara is coming to cut me up, Sara is coming to cut me up. . . .'

[1] *Thebede*—a word always thought amusing.

[2] The narrator calls on the audience to sing the chorus.

He took the guinea fowl, he cut it up. He put it down. The guinea fowl spoke again, 'Sara is coming to wash me, Sara is coming to wash me. . . .'

He washed the guinea fowl. When he had washed it, he put it down. The guinea fowl spoke again, 'Sara is coming to pound me, Sara is coming to pound me. . . .'

He took the guinea fowl there, he pounded it.[1] When he had pounded it, the guinea fowl spoke where he had pounded it, 'Sara is coming to take me out, Sara is coming to take me out. . . .'

He came and took out the guinea fowl. He put it down. The guinea fowl spoke again where he had put it down inside the wooden bowl. 'Sara is coming to mould me, Sara is coming to mould me. . . .'

He moulded that guinea fowl into balls. When he had moulded it, he put it down. The guinea fowl spoke again, 'Sara is coming to put me in, Sara is coming to put me in[2]. . . .'

He put the guinea fowl in the pot. The guinea fowl began to boil. It boiled. It became soft. The guinea fowl spoke again, 'Sara is coming to take me out, Sara is coming to take me out. . . .'

He went and took out the guinea fowl. When he had taken it out, he drained off the water. The guinea fowl spoke again, 'Sara is coming to eat me, Sara is coming to eat me. . . .' He took the guinea fowl there.

The people that were there inside the hut, each of them told Sara not to eat the guinea fowl—'Look at the bird—all the time you have been killing it, it has still spoken. You plucked it. It spoke. You cut it up. It spoke. You pounded it. It spoke. You boiled it. It still spoke. For us, we will not eat it!' He said. 'All right. I will eat it.' He gave to everyone. They did not accept. He alone, he ate that guinea fowl.

When he had eaten it, the guinea fowl spoke again in his stomach, 'Sara is going to lie down, Sara is going to lie down. . . .' He went to lie down. When he had lain down, the guinea fowl spoke again, 'Sara is going to lay me down, Sara is going to lay me down. . . .' They went and lay down to sleep.

When they lay down to sleep—at that time now there were no animals on the earth, except it alone only, the guinea fowl alone was on the earth. When he went and lay down to sleep, the guinea fowl spoke again, 'Sara is going to excrete me, Sara is going to excrete me. . . .'

When he got up, he Sara, as he was getting up, his bowels opened. He went and defecated—baboons, hens, monkeys, bush cows, cattle, every animal on the earth, the snakes and all—they came out from his bowels, they came out from his bowels. He got up from defecating them, and at that time he went and died, he Sara.

[1] Any kind of meat is often pounded in a mortar and then moulded into balls before cooking.

[2] *Thiki*—i.e. put it into the pot in bits, one piece at a time.

Now you see, at that time, the people there said, 'Well Sara, we told you something today, not to eat the bird. You said, "I will eat it." It was your greed for meat there, it did not recognize a prohibited animal. Well, you have seen for yourself.'

If you see now, all the animals that trouble people, that eat the rice—the pigs, the cane rats, the *kuyele* birds, the *libo* birds, the palm birds, the *ndɔpɛ* birds, the rats—all the animals that trouble people in the rice, the cattle that people are troubled to rear, the goats, the hens—Sara caused that excretion, from the bird that he ate then, from his greed for meat. He was told 'Cease![1] Do not eat.' He ate it. That is why there are animals that people are troubled by.

Yenkeni, since you said that I should tell you that story, the story of Sara, I tell you it. Since you have heard me, me Karanke, and they answered me, I (?) sang the words (?), you endured hearing me; I sang, they answered; that story, I had to tell it to Yenkeni. Since I have finished, Yenkeni—it is finished.

Kanu and the star

BUBU DEMA. *Dictated* 15.10.61

A comment on the powerlessness of man to struggle against Kanu's will, or to predict what will happen. As the teller expanded to me later, if Kanu says that someone is fortunate, then even if many people who see him say bad things about him or envy him—the more they do that, the more Kanu helps him.

See remarks on this story pp. 43 and 94.

A STORY. A star up above was once laughing. When the chief Kanu Masala asked it, 'What are you laughing at?'—'The people I always laugh at—[they are] if Kanu makes a thing so, to say they will fix it—it is those people I am laughing at.'

Well then, [a star] down below [lower down] also got up. It laughed. Chief Masala asked, 'What are you laughing at?' 'The people I always laugh at—when I have straightened a thing, the one who would undo it.'

When you see someone like that who would straighten something, then we Limba say he is a fool. Even if you help him with something, whatever it is—Kanu has said once and for all that he is not good.

[1] The persuasive term that, it is continually insisted, every man should listen to—Sara did not, and died.

'Those are the people I always laugh at, who would straighten something I have spoiled, I Kanu.' So the one up above says, 'Those are the ones I am laughing at—well, in that when I have fixed a thing, I Kanu, the one who would undo it—it is those Limba I am laughing at.'

For thus we live here, every one of us. Kanu has made something; they try to disfigure [swell] it. You will not be able. What Kanu has made bad—if it is your wife, if it is your child, even if you sew them a fine dress, if Kanu just makes them bad—well, they will not know how to speak. Kanu makes a person so.

The sun and the moon

NIAKA DEMA. *Dictated* 17.10.61

A story which explains the natures of the sun and the moon. The sun respected his mother-in-law, so now is strong and people fear his heat (or anger); the moon showed disrespect, so now has no power to frighten even a child. The conclusion draws the moral that you should show respect to all women, in case one day one of them may turn out to be your mother-in-law.

THE moon and the sun, they went to woo a wife. The sun came first about the girl. He went and was accepted. The night passed. When the sun rose, the moon came. 'I love the girl.' The girl—the moon went and was accepted.

When they had been accepted there, they began to come. The mother-in-law went on first to a well. She came and went in to bathe.[1] When the moon arrived there, he did not say 'Excuse me!'[2] He went on. The sun came in the distance there. When he was standing like from here to Pa Kanda's house,[3] he saw his mother-in-law. Then he shouted, 'My mother-in-law, excuse me!' His mother-in-law put on her skirt.

When the sun came near her here, she said 'My child, for the respect you have given me, through Kanu, when you shine,[4] everyone will know that it is a man that is shining. That is the blessing I give you.' He said, 'It is all right.' He went on.

When the moon said, 'I want to meet you again', then his mother-in-law said, 'For me, I will not agree. When you found me bathing, you

[1] The women go daily to wash at one of the nearby sources of water, and at certain times the men know to approach with care for this reason.

[2] The men should shout out 'Excuse me!' to warn the women and give them time to dress.

[3] Thirty or forty yards.

[4] *Bɛndi*—shine, be hot, be angry.

did not say to me "Excuse me!" Through Kanu, a child will not fear you. Everyone, whenever you talk, everyone will not hold you in power.' That is the blessing the mother-in-law, Kanu, pronounced. For the sun now, whenever he is shining, ha! that is no play! Even if he talks only a little, he will be answered,[1] there where he is in the sky. All the earth below, it is all burnt. Even if they say a leaf is cut off in the morning, when the sun has come up to the middle, it will be dry. That is the blessing he was given then by his mother-in-law. But the moon—when he shines up above, even a child will be able to sit there. He will not do anything at all to him, except to go at night. That is the blessing the mother-in-law gave him then.

You see—if a woman, even one that you play with, if you come on her bathing, you are to say 'Excuse me!' and pass on. If you pass on and you do not say 'Excuse me!', perhaps sometime she will bear a daughter, perhaps you will go to her to say, 'I love your daughter', she will say, 'You came on me bathing, you did not say "Excuse me!", now you come saying you love my daughter, I will not agree.' That is it.

Contest in strength

FANKA KONTEH. *Dictated* 1.12.61

A story illustrating the skill of humans against animals—mainly owing to their possession of guns. The story is in some ways similar to that of *Bayo*. It accounts, implicitly, for the separation of men and animals and comments on their natures.

For the listeners one of the main attractions of the tale was through their acquaintance with the animals and their recognition of the acts described.

THE elephant once called together the animals of the bush: 'Let us go and discuss something.' They went. They went and sat, all the animals. They went and sat. The elephant said, 'It is I who have called you. The reason I called you is that we may come and have a contest for strength.[2] That is why I called you.' All the animals said, 'Good. What day?' 'On Wednesday.' 'All right.'

They parted. The time came—Wednesday. They began to come. The monkey came. He sat down. The baboon came. He sat down. The chimpanzee came. He sat down. The antelope came. He sat down. The

[1] i.e. obeyed, noticed.

[2] *Hukaiba*—literally 'maleness', here of strength and skill.

leopard came. He sat down. The bush cow came. He sat down. The elephant arrived. He sat down. The human came. He sat down.

The elephant said, 'What! human! what a long time it is since we arrived. Are we to sit here just waiting for you? You have only just arrived now. You are the one we have been waiting for. You were the last to arrive. That is what I want to say.' The human said, 'Now I have come. Now I have come today.' As the human had been coming, he had brought a gun. He had gone and hidden it in a bush. He came. They said, 'Well, all right. The competition we said we would have for strength—that is the word for today.' All the animals said 'Good.'

They said, 'Well now; the monkey is first.' The monkey got up, he jumped on to a tree, he bent over. He jumped over to another tree. He came and stood at the bottom. He said, 'Well, is that not strength?' They all said, 'It is strength, strength; strength, strength. Well, sit down.'

'Well now, baboon: get up, show us strength.' The baboon got up. He went to the farms. He went and broke down the corn. He came to the village. He went and broke down the maize. He caught the hens. He came at a run. He came and put them down. He said, 'Well? Is that not strength?' They all said, 'It is strength, strength; strength, strength. Sit down.' He sat down.

'Well now, chimpanzee: show us strength.' The chimpanzee got up. He went and twisted a tree, he tied it in a knot; he dropped it. He came down. He said, 'Is that not strength?' They all said, 'It is strength, strength; strength, strength. Sit down.'

'Well, leopard: show us strength.' The leopard scratched on the ground—*ruki ruki ruki ruki*. They all jumped, afraid. He said, 'Well? Is that not strength?' 'Ha! It is strength, strength; strength, strength. Well, sit down.' He sat down.

'Well now, antelope: show us strength.' The antelope ran—he ran three miles. He came and stood. 'Well? Is that not strength?' They said, 'It is strength, strength; strength, strength. Sit down.' The antelope sat down.

They said, 'Well, bush cow: show us strength.' The bush cow got up. The cane grass was growing thickly. The bush cow cut a path through it —*raaaa*. The cane grass that was flattened down was like a road for a lorry. He came. 'Well? Is that not strength?' They all said, 'It is strength, strength; strength, strength, for the cane grass the bush cow cut through. Sit down.'

'Well now, elephant: show us strength.' The elephant got up. He leaned against the trees that stood there, all of them—*fɛndɛlɛŋ!* they all fell down, the trees the elephant leaned against. The elephant said, 'Well? Is that not strength?' They all said, 'Ah? it is strength, strength; strength, strength.'

'Well now, human: show us strength.'

The human got up. He whirled over and over, he whirled round. He whirled over and over again.[1] He came and stood. He said, 'Well? Is that not strength?' 'What? No. That is not strength. If that is all —there is no strength there. Show us strength.' The human went, he went and took hold of a tree, he climbed up above.[2] He came down. 'Well? Is that not strength?' 'No. If that is all, it is not strength. Show us strength.' The human went, to where he had hidden his gun in the bush. He went and sat down behind the bush. He took the gun. He looked at the elephant intently—*tiiŋ*. He fired—*loŋkaŋ!* the elephant fell.

Before he could come to say, 'Is that not strength?'—the animals had all run off. And now they were saying, 'Ha! that man is far above us in strength—strength which can kill someone'—saying this as they ran now! Everyone now was amazed, because the elephant was killed by the human. Well? was that not strength?

[1] This recalls the *gbondokale* dance by the young boys the night of their initiation to show off their strength; it is full of cartwheels, handsprings, and whirling round.

[2] Climbing a tree (sc. a palm tree) is typical of Limba humanity.

3 · STORIES ABOUT ANIMALS

The spider and his wife Kayi

FANKA KONTEH. *Dictated* 13.11.61

One of the many stories in which the spider tries to trick his wife Kayi, who is always in the end cleverer than he. The spider is, as often, depicted as acting in every way that is wrong in marriage—he refuses to give his wife some of the food when asked but eats it greedily in her presence; he tries to steal hers when she is asleep; and he ends by 'abusing' or insulting her.

Like other spider stories, it is thought very funny; the spider's simultaneous greed, hunger, and stupidity are constant topics for amusement.

THE spider and Kayi. It was announced that the chief had to be worked for the next day. The sun rose. The spider got up, he and Kayi. They went. The spider saw in one place much smoke going up.[1] He saw on the other side only a little smoke. The spider said, 'Kayi, I am going to where much smoke is going up.' Kayi said, 'I will go where there is little.' 'All right.'

The spider went. He went and found yams[2] being boiled there. He stayed there. Kayi went to the other place, she went and found much rice, very much, being cooked there. She stayed there. They finished cooking completely. She was given a very big basinful. Where the spider went he was given a big basinful—of yams!

They began to return, in the evening, to come home to their house. They came and met each other—face to face, *bis!* The spider said, 'I went and found good fortune. I was given a big bowlful of yams. Here they are. But I won't give you any.' He sat down and ate. He ate and ate for long—until he could eat no more, he the spider. Then Kayi called her child, 'Bring here the big bowl.' The child brought the bowl. Kayi came and helped out the rice that was in the bowl, and the meat too, much of it. The spider said, 'Ee!' He was surprised, 'Ee!' His heart went out to the rice. But he had no chance to eat Kayi's rice! Kayi ate with her children. They were full. She took it, she Kayi, she put it up on the shelf in the middle; for she and the children had been unable to finish the rice.

[1] As is usual the chief is cooking food for those who have come to work for him.

[2] Yams are thought very poor food compared to rice.

Well, they lay down. Before Kayi lay down, she took and stuck a [white] cowry on one eye; she stuck another on the other eye. She lay down, she Kayi. The spider lay there for long; he got up, he went and peeped where Kayi was. He saw the whiteness—*pooŋ*—he thought, 'Kayi is not asleep.' Behold, Kayi was asleep! When he went and looked at where Kayi was lying, 'Alas, is it because of the rice you are not asleep yet?' Kayi took no notice. She was asleep! The spider went back and lay down again. After a long, long time again, he went again and peeped. He said 'Alas; is it for the rice you are not asleep yet? is it for the rice?' Kayi took no notice. She was asleep!

Thus he spent the night; all, all night, he did not sleep, he spent the night peeping in at Kayi.

The sun rose. Kayi got up. She took out the cowries. She washed her face. She sat down to eat with her children. The spider said, 'Kayi. Won't you give me a handful?' Kayi took no notice. Kayi finished eating it all. The spider sat there abusing Kayi, because Kayi did not give him any rice, that is why he abused her.

The spider tries to cheat his wife

FANKA KONTEH. *Dictated* 13.11.61

A story about the spider in which he acts in a typically anti-social, greedy, and, as it turns out, stupid way, for his wife Kayi gets the better of him. The story is mainly centred on food (rice). The spider begins by trying to harvest without his wife, which is known to be wrong for this is the climax of their long year's work. Then the long list of the spider's activities undertaken so that he can eat in comfort and plenty ends time after time in his hunger while others eat. Each new stage is begun by 'in the morning', as the spider prepares yet again to eat. The final stage is when they at last go out to make the preparations together, and the spider is able to eat.

THE spider and Kayi were living there. The spider said, 'Kayi. Away, let us go to work, to clear the farm.' Kayi said, 'All right.'

They went and began clearing. They finished clearing. They put in fire. It burnt. They started reburning. They finished reburning. They began to gather sticks from the farm. They finished gathering the sticks. They sat down to chase the birds from the seed. They chased them from the sown seed. It grew safely. They went back again, they weeded. They finished weeding. The rice was in seed. They sat down to chase the birds from the seeding rice. They chased, for one month.

When the rice was ripe, the spider said, 'Kayi will not eat the rice.' He went and scraped off the bark of the *kuthuru* tree. The juice[1] he put into a cup. He came and hid it. When Kayi lay down to sleep, he took one splinter from a broom, he smeared it all over Kayi, all over Kayi's body. He lay down.

In the morning he got up; he said, 'Kayi, get up. You know how to sleep![2] Get up there from your sleeping, let us go and harvest so we may eat today.' When Kayi had got up from sleeping, she came out, she Kayi. The spider said then, 'Hey, hey, Kayi! You have got the red disease.[3] I don't want you here. Go to your people.' Kayi said, 'Oh?' 'Yes', said the spider.

Kayi got up, she went off. Kayi went and stayed there, she said to her people, to her mother and her father, 'The spider has driven me out, saying I have the red disease.' Her people looked at her. They saw that it was not the red disease that Kayi had. They saw the juice of the *kuthuru* tree. They took soap. They went and washed Kayi, all over.[4] It all came off, the stuff he had smeared on Kayi. Kayi said, 'No; it is all right, I don't care!'[5]

She went to the finch [diviner]. 'Finch, the spider has driven me away; the rice we struggled for in the farm is ripe, we were to eat it today; in the morning he said I had got the red disease.' The finch looked '*Se se se se*,[6] put good, put bad—don't you know what to do? Go and take an antelope's horn. Take it to a moriman, get him to fix it well for you. When you reach the cooking-place[7] in the middle, lift up one stone, dig a hole, and put the horn there and bury it. Go over to your people. You will see what will happen.'

He [the spider] was now harvesting the rice, what he was going to eat that day. He finished harvesting, he the spider. He came and thrashed it. He pounded it. He took a fowl, he killed it—for sauce. He boiled it. He put it down. He put on a pot with water to cook the rice. As soon as he finished cooking it, when he was just coming to help it out,[8] the pot

[1] Used for red dye.

[2] i.e. how lazy you are.

[3] Some kind of skin disease, probably leprosy. Wives often go home if they are ill, but it is bad for a husband to suggest or insist on this.

[4] The parents' care for her is in contrast to the spider's deceit.

[5] Normal phrase used when someone is angry but pretending not to want to make a fuss.

[6] The sound made by throwing the stones used in divining. The whole sentence is delivered by the finch in a special sing-song tone.

[7] i.e. the three stones on which women cook. In the story the spider tries to cook himself but the horn buried in the place prevents him from benefiting from his cooking.

[8] The length and detail of his preparations are insisted on here and later—even after all that, and the hunger that must have accompanied it, he got no food in the end.

with the sauce and the one with the rice—oh! they began to run, going off to Kayi! He the spider followed behind, running unwillingly—*tupɛ tupɛ tupɛ.*[1] He said, 'Well now: I have harvested the rice today, and finished cooking it; now I have brought it here for you. Help it out, let us eat.'[2] Kayi helped out the rice. She ate with her people, she did not give to the spider. He said, 'Well, all right!' He took the pots. He crossed over. He went and spent the whole night hungry.

In the morning, he went early to harvest, he the spider. He finished harvesting, he came and stood. He thrashed it. He dried it. He pounded it. He caught a fowl, he killed it, he boiled it for sauce. He put it down. He put on a pot of water for the rice. He cooked it. It was dry [ready]. As he took the spoon to help it out, the pot with the sauce here and the one with the rice there, they both began running, to go off to Kayi across the water! The spider followed behind. He went and said, 'Well now: I have brought the rice, I have finished cooking it. Come and help it out, let us eat.' Kayi helped it out. She ate, with her mother and father, all of it. They did not give to the spider. He took the pots, he went across the river, he went back home and lay hungry the whole night.

In the morning, he got up, and went to harvest. He went and harvested. He came and thrashed. He dried it. He pounded it. He took another hen, he killed it, he cooked it as sauce. He put it down. He put on a pot to cook the rice. He went for creepers, he came and tied down the pot, he tied it to a tree; he tied it to one tree on this side, he tied it to another tree over there on the other side; so that the rice would not go to Kayi. The rice was dry. At once the creepers broke, both of them. The rice and the sauce began to run to Kayi. Again the spider followed it. The rice arrived. It stopped. The spider arrived. He said, 'Well now: I have brought the rice again; for you to help it out so we can eat.' Kayi stood up and helped it out. They ate it again—she and her mother and her father, all of it. They did not give to the spider. The spider said, 'Alas for me! what will I do? Well, all right.' He took the pots, he crossed over to his side. He came and spent the night.

In the morning he got up again. He went to harvest. He came and harvested. He came and thrashed. He dried it. He pounded it. He went for creepers, he came and put them down. He caught a goat; he killed it for sauce. 'This that I have now Kayi will not eat *it* today.' As he put the pot for the rice on the fire, he took the creepers, he tied them to a tree—he tied one to a tree on one side, he tied one on the other too. He took a third creeper, he tied it round his waist. He sat down. He finished cooking it all. The rice was dry. As he was taking hold of the spoon to help it out, this creeper broke on the one tree, that creeper broke on the

[1] Represents his unwilling steps, not prepared to give up the rice.

[2] He speaks in a would-be plausible and winning tone, pretending he has come on purpose.

other tree; the pot pulled him along, he made wide steps [trying not to go], the pot pulled him for far, far until he fell, then it started to drag him along as it went to Kayi.[1] The rice arrived. He said, 'Kayi! Ha! I have brought the rice. Come and help it out, let us eat.' Kayi said, 'Why is this creeper round your waist?'[2] 'A spirit was coming to take the rice today; *that* is why I tied the creeper round my waist so that the spirit would not take the rice away; so that I could bring it to you. Well now, help it out, let us eat.' Kayi helped it out. They took the rice and ate it—she and her mother and her father, the whole of it, they did not give to the spider. The spider said, 'Alas for me!' He crossed over, he came and sat. He spent the whole night in hunger.

In the morning the spider said, 'This misfortune I have got—I will go for Kayi.' He took a kola nut.[3] He tied it in a bundle. Twenty kolas. He went. He went and called Kayi's mother and Kayi's father. He said, 'Well, father, I have come; I have come for Kayi. For to come here whenever I bring the rice is very far! That is why I have come for Kayi.'[4] Her people said, 'No. Kayi is not well yet.' He begged. They said, 'All right; Kayi, go.'

They got up, he came home with Kayi. They came and spent the night.

In the morning, he went and harvested. They went and harvested, and thrashed. They dried it. They pounded it. They caught a big goat, he killed it for sauce. They finished boiling it for sauce. They cooked the rice. It was dry. Kayi lifted it down. She helped it out. They sat there and they ate.

The spider said, 'Yes. I have eaten the rice you worked for.' Kayi said, 'Spider, ha! You! You have a big belly. Ha! It was the horn that prevented you; that was what I buried in the cooking-place, that was why you could never eat the rice.'

The spider, Kayi, and the bush fowl

FANKA KONTEH. *Recorded* 7.1.64

Another story about the spider's attempt to cheat his wife. The framework is that of a kind of competition between the two, in which the wife wins; the spider is hoist with his own petard, and the way Kayi tells him

[1] This description was given in an excited fast tone, obviously found very effective by the listeners.

[2] The apparently innocent question followed by the spider's plausible but obvious lie caused great amusement.

[3] The usual token gift to ask for his wife's return.

[4] His pretended reason does not deceive the parents, who in their turn pretend that she is not yet better from the disease they in fact know she never had.

that the bush fowl has not only eaten the millet but run right off was regarded as a very good joke.

THE spider and Kayi—they lived in a hut. The spider went and trapped a bush fowl.[1] The bush fowl was killed. He brought it. 'Kayi, here is [food for] sauce. Lay it down.' She laid it down. Kayi got up. She pounded millet. She put it down. She took a bowl, she went to the water. When she had gone to the water, the spider got up. He ate the millet, all of it. When his wife came back, she came and put down the water, she went and looked at the millet. 'E! Spider.' 'Yes?' 'Who ate the millet?' 'The bush fowl ate the millet.' 'What?' 'Yes.' 'Well, all right.'

Later the spider got up, he went to tap his palm tree. When he had gone to tap his palm tree, Kayi got up. She prepared the bush fowl. She boiled it. She cooked the millet. She finished eating it *all*! She sat down. The spider came back. 'Kayi, have you kept anything for me?'[2] 'No.' 'What about the millet?' 'E! Well, the bush fowl ate up all the millet!' 'What about the bush fowl?' 'The bush fowl has gone, gone off to the bush.'

The spider the lover of meat

KARANKE DEMA. *Recorded* 1.2.64

The spider is again frustrated in his attempt to get much meat for himself. The tale ends with the common attribution of origin about why the spider is always to be found on the walls of houses (many different explanations of this are given in different stories). As often, one of the highlights was the vivid representation of the way the spider was beaten.

A STORY for you, Suri; a story for you, Yenkeni. You will reply, Suri won't you?

A spider once came out—a great lover of meat. Of all meat-lovers, he was the 'Commissioner'.[3] Wherever anyone killed, he used to go there.

When the chief fixed a time for people to go and hoe his farm, he made a sacrifice, providing an ox for all the workers who went. The spider was the herald in the village. When he had announced this in the evening, and at night, when all the people were gathered, he announced it. When he had finished announcing it they spent the whole night—*kudu!*

[1] Regarded as a delicacy. [2] A common question on return home.
[3] The English word was used and caused some amusement.

In the morning, then the chief said, 'Here is a cooking pot[1] standing here'—now the pot was very large—'Whoever can carry it, he will get the ox's head.' That pleased the spider, to be given the head, for him alone to eat! That pleased him. He congratulated himself, 'Ha! Kayi! Today we are eating the head now, today we are eating the head now.[2] I am carrying the pot.' He got up. He went and told the chief, 'I am carrying the pot, I am able.' The chief said, 'Are you able?' 'Yes.' 'Are you able?' 'Yes.' 'What if you are not able?' 'You can thrash me.' The chief said, 'All right.'

The servants put the pot up on his head. When they had put it up, he set out to go. When he was going, the pot weighed him down very much. When they came to a rock—the rock was slippery. Just as he went to tread on it—he slipped, *thalabasa—fuuu, puuuŋ!*[3] (on to the rock)[4]—on to the rock. The pot broke. Now the servants were following him. They had heard that, 'If I am unable, they can thrash me.' He was seized there. The chief came. 'The spider has broken the pot oh!' 'Oh? Thrash him!' They lifted him up there, and crashed him down on to the rock, *baŋ!* They—*thrashed* him there.

You see now, the spider is always small, he dwindled. That is why he ran off quickly, *kare kare*, saying, 'I, I will go and cling on to the chief's walls.' You see now, the spider likes the wall where people build—he goes in there, he goes and clings on to the wall. It was his love of meat that caused him to dwindle to the size he is. You see now, whoever treads in the place where the spider was thrashed, they are the people who are great lovers of meat—like vultures. Wherever meat is killed, they have to go there.

Well, since I heard that story, and Yenkeni said that she wanted it, that is that story. Suri, it is finished.

The spider and the needle

KARANKE DEMA. *Recorded* 2.2.64

Again the spider is depicted as greedy and stupid; his great excitement and anticipation over the meat he is confident of getting is frustrated twice over. The spider's excitement and disappointment were found very amusing, particularly the point where he hears he will have to use his needle to eat and the ludicrous way in which he can scarcely get even one grain to stick to his needle; usually people eat great handfuls of rice after a morning's work.

[1] i.e. the large and very heavy iron pot which would be used to cook the ox killed for the workers.

[2] As often the spider starts rejoicing too soon.

[3] The sound of the spider slipping, the pot falling, and both crashing on to the rock.

[4] An interjection by Suri, one of the listeners.

SURI, by your grace, by grace of Fode. You will reply to me won't you? I am going to tell Yenkeni a story about the spider. His craftiness is great. His wisdom is great, ha! very great.

The spider was the herald—as if it was in our village. The chief spoke; he fixed a time when his farm was to be cleared.[1] 'Spider, you are to announce the time—on Sunday, that is the time for the clearing.' He said 'All right.' He announced [it], twice; the third time he announced it at night.[2] Now the chief told all the people that he had brought an ox, 'That is what those who clear will eat.'

When they set out for the clearing—you know the spider! [He said] 'Today I will leave the work to the [other] men.' He did not get any hoe at all; he fastened a needle on to a handle! When he had fastened on the needle—'This is what I am going to clear with.' Now the chief, he did not speak a word. He saw the 'hoe', he did not speak a word. 'Today, I and the spider—because of what he has done, he will not eat today!'

When they went out to clear, the ox was killed. They went and began clearing. The spider stood at the end where he would not work.[3] When he touched the grass, *gbuŋ*, with his hoe, when he went *yokore* with the needle, when he went *yokore* with the needle at the grass—it would not be cut! The chief said, 'All right.' When they were congratulated, 'Oh men! Oh men! Oh men! today we are clearing the grass, today we are clearing the grass'—behold he was not clearing it, he the spider!

When he had done that for a long time, the rice was all cooked. The ox was all boiled. He was called by the chief. He was given some tobacco and told, 'Call the people to eat.' He [the spider] divided out all the tobacco. His heart now, it was happy, 'Today we will eat meat, today, meat, much much meat today, today we will be filled.' When he had finished calling all the people they came. They came and washed, all of them.

Then the chief said, 'Spider, you are to announce oh! that for the work I am doing today there is a special "sacrifice"—that everyone is to eat with the tool he worked with.' *Haaa!* The spider's heart leapt, *haa!* it was bad. When the spider looked at the size of the needle with which he was to take [his food]—the needle was sharp, *sogbeŋ!* He stood there, he thought. The spider was brooding to himself on one side, his heart was sore—'Alas my father!' When they sat down to eat, the spider went and sat down. They all washed their hoes. The spider washed his needle, his sharp needle. The meat was all put on top of the rice and put out. When they sat there to eat, the spider took his needle.

[1] Everyone is being called to help the chief to clear the grass away before sowing the seed; this is done with metal hoes fixed on to a wooden handle.

[2] A herald is asked to make an announcement round the village, usually in the evening; sometimes he is given a small gift, for example of tobacco, as a reward for his services.

[3] The men are working in a long line, encouraging each other.

Whenever he went *sogbeŋ*[1]—perhaps [he got] one grain! The spider [tried to] put it in his mouth. Whenever he went *sogbeŋ*, perhaps he pierced it—but the gravy would not let the grain come! He was just left with the needle—he licked it. But those with the hoes—whenever one of them went *pɛbɔ* [with the hoe], whenever another just went *pɛbɔ*—they ate! But the spider—when he tried to pierce the meat—nothing! (The meat would not come.)[2] The meat would not come. There the spider thought then—but he could do nothing. [The chief said] 'If you put in your hands you will get the ox I brought.'(?) Ha! That hurt the spider, that hurt him. He said, 'All right. Ha! Look at all of us who came to the farm, behold all of them have come to the farm—and no food.'

When a time was fixed again for coming to the farm, he announced it to them all. At that time do you know what he did? He fixed a huge hoe head[3] on to a handle, a big one. 'Ha! I went and spent the day hungry there then—today, today I will go and eat, today, truly truly today, I will be filled, today I will get the biggest share over all the [other] men, the ones who ate before.' Behold, this time—there was no food! When he had fastened on the huge hoe, he set out for the farm.

When they went to hoe, he could not see any cooking pot, he could not see any smoke rising. He called out now, 'Ho ho, ha ha, nothing in my mouth.[4] Chief, is there no food today then? Ha ha!' Then the chief said, 'Just wait. The food is coming just now.' Behold, there was no food! Behold, he was deceiving the spider! When they had hoed for long, he yawned—'Ho ho, ha ha; chief, are we just to spend the day like this then?' 'The food is coming just now.' Behold he was deceiving [him]. The farm was finished. The spider got up. 'Ah! I the spider—my craftiness is always bringing me into trouble.' It was because of what he had done before—clearing with a needle. Behold, the chief was crafty too.

Well, since I heard that story and Yenkeni said she wanted to hear it today, that is the story. Fode, you replied to me, by grace of Suri, by grace of Yenkeni, that is the story. It is finished.

The spider, the whip, and the pot

FANKA KONTEH. *Recorded* 7.1.64

The plot of this story is not in itself very elaborate but because of its vivid narration the story as told was most striking—the way, for example, the mat was portrayed as slowly unrolling itself, then the quick, violent, and

1 The attempt to prick the rice with the sharp needle.

2 An interpolation by one of the listeners.

3 A huge and very heavy hoe, used, I was told, by the Fula to dig potatoes.

4 A rhythmic and amusing phrase in Limba.

unexpected whipping that followed; the way in which the spider's wife Kayi (earlier called Sira) busily went round filling up all the dishes and basins, and then ended up ('just like a woman' commented the narrator) in cleaning and scraping out the pot and so breaking its prohibition; the spider's character, brought out by his obsequious manner to the pot, his overbearing tone to Kayi, and his stupid and unthinking confidence, frustrated each time in turn as he makes his approach to the pot.

The plot is a relatively common one. In another version I heard the two main episodes were reversed so that the spider instead of being triumphant ended up at his wife's mercy, with nothing to eat.

THE spider once lived there with Sira—in very great hunger. When Kayi boiled food, she gave to the spider, he ate.

One day, he made a fish-fence.[1] He went. He went and found a pot there in the fish-fence when he cleared it. He said, 'E! I have caught [killed] a pot.' The pot said, 'A! don't say to me "pot", say "Fill up".' 'Fill up.' The pot filled with [cooked] rice—completely, *pɛ!* He ate. He was filled.

He brought the pot back to the village. He came and sat down. He put it away in a box. When Kayi boiled him a little bit of rice, when she brought it out to the spider saying, 'Here is a little bit of rice' for him and the children, 'Ah! You eat now, this is for you and the children.' While they were still eating, he went inside. 'E!' He got out the pot. 'Pot, fill up.' The pot filled with rice completely, *pɛ!* E! He was filled. Always he did that. When Kayi cooked now, he would not eat.

One day he had just gone off to his palm tree. Kayi got up. 'Hey! I must know the spider's magic, all of it.' She went in, she entered the room. She went and looked in the boxes. She found the pot. She went and took out the pot. 'E! Spider! The spider is a rascal, see he has hidden it in the pot.' Then the pot said, 'Don't say to me "Pot", say now "Fill up".' 'Fill up.' The pot filled up with rice, completely—*pɛ!* She ate. She took it out. She brought out all her dishes—very, very many. 'Pot, fill up.' It filled. She helped out, the children ate. 'Pot, fill up.' The pot filled. The children ate. She took the rice, she put it out [into many dishes]. Then she said, 'Pot, fill up.' She put it out into all the basins. She hid them. She took the pot, she scraped it. Now that was the pot's prohibition. It should not have its scrapings scraped out. Kayi scraped it all! She washed it, she went and put the pot away there.

When he [spider] came to the village, he came and sat down. Kayi got out a little bit of rice. She came and sat down with her children. They ate. When they ate, they did not give to the spider. The spider went inside. He went and sat down. He got out the pot. 'Pot, fill up.' The pot—nothing! It did not fill up. 'Pot, fill up.' Nothing. 'E, master,

[1] A wicker fence sometimes made in rivers to catch fish.

it is me, me the spider.[1] Don't tantalize me. Fill up.' Nothing. 'Oh, it is because I have not taken off my cap, that's it. I have taken off my cap now, master! Fill up.' Nothing. 'Oh, I will take off. . . .' He took off his gown. 'Fill up.' Nothing. He looked. 'It is because I have not taken off my trousers, that's it.' He took off his trousers. 'Fill up.' Nothing. He looked inside—he saw that the scrapings had been scraped out. Then he said 'Well—all right. What Kayi has done to me—that ill fortune—all right.'[2]

He came and sat down. When he had sat down, Kayi brought out one basin. They sat down to eat, she and her children. They finished eating it *all*! They did not give to the spider.

Hunger oppressed the spider![3] He got up. He got up in anger. He went off. He went and found—as soon as he had undone all the fish-fence again, a [rolled-up] mat came out. 'E! a mat! E!' The mat said, 'Don't say to me "Mat", say "Whip!".' 'Whip!' The mat opened itself out there[4]—*fuŋ!* It *beat* him. He wept there. He let it go. He implored it. He let the mat go. It rolled itself up there. He rolled it, he carried it on his head, he brought it to the village. He came and spread it in his room.

When he had spread it, he went off to his palm tree. As soon as he had gone, Kayi went in. 'Iyo! He has brought something else too. For there is a mat lying now.' The mat said, 'Don't say to me "Mat", say "Whip!".' 'Whip!' The mat came out from there, *fuŋ!* It beat her, her and her children. She let go. She wept there.

The spider found them weeping. He stopped the mat. They said, 'E spider, have you brought something troublesome?' 'Yes; because of what you did to me over the pot, that is why.' The spider rolled up the mat. He went and threw it into the water. 'The ill-fortune you caused to me, that is what I have returned to you. That is it.'

The spider, the elephant, and the hippopotamus

BUBU DEMA. *Dictated* 11.10.61

The spider tricks two animals much bigger and stronger than himself. However, this turned out badly in the end for the spider; he had told lies secretly (*yaŋfa*) and as a result had to run to human protection against

[1] The spider is made to speak very plaintively and appealingly.

[2] He speaks with exaggerated and righteous self-control.

[3] The high tones give exaggerated emphasis to the spider's great suffering.

[4] The words were spoken in a slow sinister tone to express the frightening way in which the mat gradually unrolled of itself.

those he had deceived. The narrator, in his usual manner, drew a long analogical moral at the end, almost as long as the narration of the events of the tale. The actual action ends, as so often, with an explanation for and comment on the present distribution of animals, in this case spiders. An explanation of why there are spiders on the walls of houses occurs, in different forms, in several Limba stories.

The struggle between the two animals was in a way the climax of the story as performed; it was depicted in high, vehement, and fast tones. The heavy struggle of the two huge animals is contrasted to the carefree light-hearted way in which the spider so happily went and lay down, his tiny body almost soundless (*kɛlɛthɛ*). The contrast was represented by the change in the narrator's tone from loud vehemence to airy softness.

LONG ago a spider lived on earth who was very full of fight. He went to the elephant and said, 'I want to fight with you.' The elephant said, 'Your power is not for me.'[1] The spider cut a rope and said, 'Hold this; when you feel it shaking *yigbɛ yigbɛ*,[2] it is me; the fight is coming.' He went.

When he had gone a long way, he met a hippopotamus. 'Hippopotamus, I want to fight with you.' The hippopotamus said, 'Huh! your power is not for me.' 'Well, hold this rope.' The hippopotamus took hold of it. The spider went away saying. 'When you feel it shaking *yigbɛ yigbɛ*, it is me, me.' You see, he had first said the same thing to the elephant.

Well, when the spider had gone off, the elephant came up not far from the hippopotamus. When he saw a shake, *yigbɛ*, he said, 'Aha! look now! I can feel where the spider is whom I am fighting with.' The hippopotamus tugged where he was. The whole of that day they spent struggling. But the spider went and lay down lightly—*kɛlɛthɛ!* When they had spent the whole long day there, then the hippopotamus let go the rope: 'Let me go and look if it is really true that all that long time I was tugging it was really the spider.' Well, the elephant was approaching too. When they met, they asked, 'Where were you today?' 'Where were you today?' 'The spider gave me a rope today, saying we would fight.' The hippopotamus answered, 'That is right; it was to me that he gave the rope, he said, "Let us fight".' They greeted each other there saying, 'The spider has tricked us. See, here is the one we were fighting. So for that, my brother, wherever we see the spider, let us kill him.'

The spider did not want to be killed. That is why he ran away to the wall of our houses here.

It is the same with two people. You go into a house and make a quarrel. You, you have nothing yourself, you go and make a quarrel between better people. You make the better ones fight because of you,

[1] i.e. not comparable to mine, much less.

[2] The quiver at the end of the rope when it is pulled from the other end.

you who have nothing. You made them fight; but they did not see each other. So you see, someone who is good at trouble-making injures people. Because he had not great strength himself, he set a fight between those who were great. So too with a Limba man who has nothing in the village himself—he makes two people fight. 'At that time,[1] if we had known about it, we would not have fought; it was the spider that made us fight, we had not seen each other. That is why we said that it was good that wherever we see him [the spider] we should kill him.' Since he heard that in the bush there, that is why he ran away to the humans. If you see us Limba making two people fight when we have nothing—we are not good. They did not fight each other for no reason when they did not see each other.[2] You see then—long ago people were afraid to make trouble against each other, and that is why; that is why people are always afraid to make trouble against each other. This began with the spider.

Since I had heard that story, I told it to Yenkeni. That is it. It is finished.

The python, the antelope, and the spider

KARANKE DEMA. *Recorded* 24.1.64

In this story it is the spider who is clever and the antelope (usually represented as the cleverer) who is gullible. As often the story ends with an explanation for the present relationships between animals.

Karanke was stimulated to tell the story by hearing a recording of Dauda's tale about *Kanu and the python*; the opening of this story is somewhat similar. The phrase about 'good turning out as bad' also occurred in another story I heard (not given here) about a python trying to harm someone who had helped him (in that case a hunter).

A STORY for you. You see—an antelope once went to collect indigo in the cane grass on a great hill. There he went; he met a python there. Now the python was hungry, very, very, very hungry. He had spent two days and found nothing. He could no longer get up from where he was lying.

When the antelope met him there, then he said—the antelope—'E! python; why are you lying here?' 'Ha! ha! my father, I, I cannot go anywhere now, I am light [with hunger].' Then the antelope said, 'What is to be done now? Well, fire is coming along the great, great hill.[3]

[1] This is supposed to be said by the elephant and the hippopotamus.

[2] i.e. they would not have fought if they had known the truth behind the spider's lies.

[3] Fires are lit at certain times of the year by both farmers and Fula herders and these sometimes get out of control.

When the fire reaches you here will the fire not burn you?' He said, 'What am I to do now?' Well, then, at that time the antelope said, 'If I say I will save you and take you with me when I go, perhaps when I have gone and put you down you will say that I am tired (?) and you will eat me.' Then the python said, 'I will not do that. If someone comes and saves your life, and it is saved through that act, will you turn on him and destroy his life? I will not do that.' Then the deer told him to go into the bag he had brought with him—a big, big one—to put the indigo into. (He had not gathered the indigo, he was saving the python's life.) When he had gone in there, he the python, the antelope tied it up. He put him on his head there, he took him to his home. He came and put him down in the compound.

When he had put him down, and as he unloosed him, then the python said, 'Antelope.' 'Yes?' 'Thank you. Thank you. What you have done pleases me. But good, that ends up as bad.' Then the antelope said, 'E! Since I came out in the world I have never seen that, I have never heard that.' Then the python said, 'Go now to the hole.'[1]

When the antelope went to the hole, he went and asked, 'Hole oh!' 'Yes?' 'Please, does good end up as bad?' Then the hole said, 'Yes. Yes indeed. Look at me now. They said they would build a house. They came to me for earth. When they had finished making it all, they went and said, "For you—whatever rubbish is swept out of the house that I made, take it to the hole." Now they bring all the bad stuff to the hole! Has good not ended up as bad?' The antelope said, 'Yes. It has ended up as bad.' He went back. He came and was asked by the python. He said, 'Yes. Good ends up as bad.' 'Go now to the banana also.'

When the antelope went out, he went to the banana. He went and asked. 'Banana oh!' 'Yes?' 'Please, I have come here to ask, please does good ever end up as bad?' Then the banana said, 'Yes. Look at me now. I was given birth, I was brought up for long, I grew. Just when I was about to bear children and had brought up my child completely, my child had survived, and they say they are coming for my child, they come and kill me, me the mother, they carry off my child with them! Has good not ended up as bad?' The antelope said, 'Yes.' He went back. The python came and asked [him]. He said 'Yes. Good ends up as bad.'

Then the python rose up to swallow the antelope.

Now there was a spider standing there watching. Then the spider ran, he came and greeted them, 'Greetings to you.' The python was like that [about to swallow him]—the spider came and greeted him. The spider asked, 'What is happening here?' Then the antelope said, 'Ha! What is hard here oh!—the python is going to swallow me. For I found him in the middle of the cane grass that would have been burnt in the fire, I brought

[1] The hole dug in the ground to take out earth for house-building; it is then later used as a rubbish dump.

him with me, he came and said that "Good ends up as bad", that is why he is going to swallow me.' Then the spider thought—about how to save the antelope's life, coming to help the antelope. For he did not want them all to perish—for what the antelope had done was not bad but the python had come and said something to deceive him. Then the spider said, 'I will not allow it. Now we today—for his life, where he wants to take the antelope, we will take *him* there.'[1]

Then the spider said, 'E! Antelope. E! You are a liar. Look now how big the python is where he is lying—you say "I was able to carry him here"? It is a lie.' Then the antelope said, 'It is not a lie.' 'It is a lie. Take the bag now and let me see whether it is true.' Behold, what he was intending was to kill the python. Well the antelope took the bag. He came and opened up the mouth. The python slithered in. He [the spider] said, 'Well, go for ropes, let us come and tie it up well, all that is left is for you to put it on your head (?).' The antelope went for the rope. They came and tied him up—tightly.

Then the spider said, 'E! Antelope. You are a fool. You knew that you had saved someone, he just said that he would swallow you, and you just agreed! Where he wanted to take you, let us take him there. Go for long sticks so that we can come and kill him.' The python shouted out from where he lay. He tried to cry out there, 'Spider, don't do it.' The spider said, 'I will do it. Well, antelope, let us hit him.' They killed the python there. When the python leapt up now there was nowhere he could go, he was not able to get out of the bag. When they had killed him there they went and threw him away there.

Well you see now how the python is always left with this by the antelope—when they see each other and they meet, he will not now stop and ask [the antelope], but as soon as he finds him he swallows him, because he once killed the python, because of him. That is why there is always hostility now.

The spider and the bat

ALI SISAY. *Recorded* 26.5.61

A story about the mutual tricking of bat and spider, in which the bat in the end gets the better. The whole narrative was found amusing—the topics of greed, over-eating, excretion, and stupidity outwitted are considered funny in themselves.

Several words were used directly taken from English, and pauses for thought were filled throughout by the English exclamation 'All right' which I have not reproduced in every case.

[1] They will kill the python instead of his killing the antelope.

A STORY for you. A spider once went on a journey with a bat. The journey that they were setting out on—it was going to greet his [spider's] friend.[1] They arrived at the village, like at Kamabai.[2] He said to the bat, 'You are called "Greetings stranger"'—the spider speaking—'I am called "Take it stranger".'[3]

When they arrived they went and gave them lodging in a room. Then all the people got up, saying 'Greetings strangers.' Then the spider said, 'E, bat! That is your name. You are called "Greetings stranger".' Then the bat said, 'Yes, greetings.' 'What of the one sitting there?' 'I am called "Take it stranger".' 'Oh.'

He sent to his friend, he the spider, in the place where they had gone to visit. He sent a child saying, 'You have a guest. Come and greet him.' She came, his friend, she came to greet him. She got up, she went and killed a fowl, a cock. Rice was cooked. It was brought. 'Take it strangers.' Then the spider got up. 'E! that is my name. I am called "Take it stranger." You now, you are called "Greetings stranger", you the bat.' The spider sat—he *ate*!

When he had eaten, then he got up, he said, 'I am going to defecate.' Then the bat said, 'Hey! Master. People do not defecate here! I heard the people of the village saying that they do not defecate here at night.' He said, 'Ah! Get out of my way. You are trying to stop me from eating the rice. Look at it now where it is standing—the fowl, it has been fried, with rice, good rice. I am going to eat it, for I am called "Take it stranger".' Then the bat said, 'All right. It is all right. I will sit.' He had brought tobacco with him, he had a little pipe. He sat there. He cut up the tobacco. He sat there smoking, as if sitting in that hammock.[4] He started smoking. Now the spider, he was sitting, he was eating inside [the house]. He [bat] smoked the tobacco for long. He lay down. He slept a little. The spider was eating!

When he had eaten for long, he went out into the night. It was like yesterday night, much rain. He said, 'Master, I am going out to defecate'—speaking to the bat. Then the bat said, 'They do not defecate here. . . .' 'Ah! master, get out of the way there.' He got up. He went. Just as he had gone and loosed his trousers, then the bat got up, and went round [behind], he went with thorns, sharp ones, he went and beat the spider's bottom. The spider got up. He ran. He came to the house. 'E! master! What you said was true! They cannot defecate here at night. Look at this, I went and was beaten.' 'But when I told you that', said the bat, 'when I told you that, you would not agree to it. Well, you will see

[1] A woman.

[2] About 30 miles away.

[3] He suggests the names to trick his companion, so that when the crucial moment of being given food arrives, only he, the spider, will answer the offer.

[4] i.e. the bat is amusingly pictured as acting like an old man sitting swinging a little in his hammock, smoking his pipe—a common sight in a Limba village.

for yourself.' He got up again, he went. As he went and crouched down the bat got up, he went round there, he went and beat him. He *beat* him, he touched him behind on his bottom. A thorn stuck there, a sharp thorn. He came and said 'E! master! I will not go out again.' 'Well, what I told you today you would not agree to.' He came back to the house, he came and sat down there.

Well, where they had been given lodging in the room, there were two earth beds there. They lay down now to sleep. The spider got up, he defecated on to his trousers, he put them on to the beaten earth by the bed. Well, the bat smelt the smell of it. But he did not say anything.

When the sun rose, a child was sent to sweep[1] the place where they had been lodged, in the room. She said, 'Greetings strangers.' Then the bat replied, 'Yes, greetings.' She went and swept at the bat's place, saying, 'Excuse me, stranger, let me sweep.' 'All right.' He [the bat] went out on to the veranda. She swept the place where the bat had slept. She went to the spider's place. 'Spider, let me sweep your place here.' 'Ah! Sweep as far as this point. When I get up in a little, *I* will sweep.' 'Oh! My mother said that I was to sweep it all.' 'That is what children are like! They are prying! I said sweep as far as that—when I get up in a little, *I* will sweep.'[2] Then the child said, 'Well, all right. I will go.' She went back to her mother. That was where the spider's friend was. The spider now, he was ashamed. He thought, 'The child will go and say that the strangers in the room have defecated there.' The spider was worrying about it. He got up, he went as far away as the water by the paths, at the road. He ran away. The bat was left on the veranda. The bat sat there, smoking his tobacco. He [the spider] got up, he went and washed his trousers. He put them on quickly, he came. Now the spider felt ashamed before the bat. He peeped [at him].

When he peeped, well, the spider—the meat that he had not been able for, that he had been eating, he had put that into his bag. He had gone and stored it in his bag for his children, to bring home for Kayi, his wife, when he went home. The bat got up, and went inside the bag. He had been sitting there all that time without eating—*hunger!* Only tobacco. He went into the spider's bag. He ate all the meat, completely! Then the spider got up [and took the bag]. He went, he went, he went. He came on a squirrel lying on the road. He had a stick. He struck [the squirrel] with the stick saying, 'Get out of my way here. Look at this. When the meat is weighing me down in my bag, I don't know what I will do with a squirrel.[3] I am bringing [meat] for Kayi.'

[1] It is normal for a young girl to be sent by her mother to sweep out the hut where guests are lodged.

[2] The spider is represented as speaking very angrily.

[3] Usually the spider would have been glad to find a dead squirrel on the way and would have taken it to eat; this time he complains he already has, as he thinks, a heavy bag of meat.

He arrived. He went and called, 'Kayi oh Kayi! Kayi oh Kayi! The smoke I see in that hut, the smoke I see in that hut—it is from the leaves[1] you are about to eat with your children—go and throw them out. I have brought meat.' Then Kayi said, 'E! I will not throw them out, I don't know what you have brought.' 'I told you to throw them out, to throw them out.' Kayi got up, she put them into a bowl, she went and threw them behind the house. The spider came. His children got up then saying, 'Papa oh papa! papa oh papa!' He lowered the bag [from his head]. He hung it on one of the hut supports. When he had hung it up, the bat came out from there, *puku puku*,[2] from the bag. He went and perched on the eldest child's head. He opened the bag. There was no meat there at all! He [spider] said, 'E, master. Now, believe me, what you have done to me—if *your* life does not end, my life will end! I will kill you.' He sharpened his sword. He hit at his eldest child.[3] The child fell down, he died. He crossed over to another child. He hit at him. He fell down, he died. He hit at the other. He fell down, he died—all three children.

Now the spider had a palm tree there. This palm tree was a strong one. The bat got up again from there, he went to the palm tree. He went and pierced a hole in the gourd. He drank the wine. The spider got up. Kayi was now weeping, the spider was weeping—it was hunger now oh! He got up, 'Well, I am going to the palm tree I left there, so that we can come and drink so we may find a way to live.' He got up. He went. He went and climbed the palm tree. When he had climbed it, he found the bat there. 'E, bat. If your life does not end, mine will end. For now, here, I will kill you.' He shook the gourd. The gourd-cord broke, it [the gourd] fell on to the rock. It broke. Then the bat got up, he went round to the [spider's] climbing strap. As he went round the climbing strap, and as he cut at the strap, the spider's strap, it broke. He fell on to the rock. His head was broken. There he fell, he died.

Well, when he had died, the bat got up, he came here to Kayi. 'I was able for your husband. Now I will marry you. For when we went together, he brought me suffering. Well, that is why I killed him, that is why I killed him.'

[1] Leaves of the *ficus capensis* sometimes eaten for sauce in the wet season when food is short, but not considered very appetizing.

[2] The sound made by the bat's wings on the bag.

[3] Trying to kill the bat on the child's head.

The spider and the bearded cave

FANKA KONTEH. *Dictated* 28.11.61

Another story of how the spider's greed was in the end unsuccessful, for he was caught out by his own stupidity and haste. As so often, the antelope is represented as small, shy, charming, curious, and clever, its character portrayed by tone of voice, expression, and, to a certain extent, gesture. Other versions of the same plot include other animals in the earlier stages.

The meaning of 'a cave with a beard' is not clear, and I could get no further explanation. It may well be intended to be obscure or strange, as is its power of killing anyone who mentions its name, and allowing them to be revived later.

A SPIDER went to clear a palm tree [for palm wine]. He went and found a cave there that had a beard. That cave, it must not have its name called as having a beard. If you call its name, you die and spend the whole day dead; in the evening if you are sprinkled with *mafɔi* medicine, you get up.

Well, the spider called the cave's name, the beard. He fell. He spent the whole day thus; in the evening he was sprinkled with *mafɔi* medicine, he got up. He went to the village. 'Thank you Kanu; I have found here a way to eat my comrades.'

Well, in the evening he went for the giant rat. He spoke, he told the rat, 'I have cleared a palm tree. Tomorrow morning we will go and drink the wine.'[1] They spent the night.

In the morning—'Friend, let us go to the palm tree.' 'All right.' They started to go. When they were about to arrive, 'Friend, go and wait for me in front.' He hid in a tree, he the spider hid. The rat arrived at the cave. He shouted out, 'Spider oo spider.[2] I have come on an amazing thing.' The spider said, 'What is that?' 'I had never before seen a cave with a beard.' He fell. The spider went and took him. He carried him to the village. He went and skinned him. He gave him to Kayi. Kayi boiled him.

He went for one of his comrades. He said, 'Let us go and eat meat.'[3] 'All right.' It was the deer. They went. They sat down to eat the meat. He said '*Gbɛgbɛlɛ gbɛgbɛlɛ*',[4] sucking the bone, 'it is sweet, your comrade's bone; this time tomorrow yours will be sucked *gbɛgbɛlɛ*.' At that the deer asked, 'What's that, spider?' 'No nothing. I was saying that

[1] Early morning is a common time to go to a prepared palm tree to collect the wine. A friend would be delighted to be asked for his company on such an occasion.

[2] The call, long-drawn out and resonant, recurs several times and was half-intoned by the narrator.

[3] A very acceptable invitation by Limba standards, for meat is relatively hard to get and associated mainly with occasional feasts.

[4] Again a kind of refrain, said quickly and pointedly, with intentional effect.

Kayi knows how to cook, but there is not enough salt.'[1] 'Oh.' They lay down.

In the morning he took the deer. 'Deer, let us go to the palm tree.' 'All right.' They went. When they were about to arrive, he hid, he the spider. 'Go and wait for me at the cave.' The deer went. He went and found the cave with a beard. He said, 'Hey! Hey! Spider oo spider.' The spider answered, 'Yes? what is it?' 'I had never before seen a cave with a beard.' He fell. The spider went and took him. He carried him to the village. He went and skinned him.

He went for the bush cow. 'Bush cow; let us go and eat meat.' The bush cow said, 'All right.' They went. They arrived at the spider's house. The meat was brought out. They sat down to eat. They ate for long. He said, he the spider, '*Gbɛgbɛle, gbɛgbɛlɛ*', sucking the bone, 'it is sweet, *gbɛgbɛlɛ gbɛgbɛlɛ*', sucking the bone. 'This time tomorrow yours will be sucked *gbɛgbɛlɛ*.' At that the bush cow asked, 'What's that, spider?' 'No nothing. I was saying that Kayi knows how to cook, but there is not enough salt.' 'Oh.'

Well, they got up in the morning. They went to the palm tree. When they were about to arrive, 'Friend, go and wait for me in front.' He hid, he the spider. The bush cow arrived. He went and found the cave, the one with a beard. He said, 'Hey! Hey! spider.' The spider said, 'What is it?' 'I had never before seen a cave with a beard.' The bush cow fell. He died. The spider went and took him. He carried him to the village. He went and skinned him. He gave him to Kayi.

As Kayi was cooking, he went for the red deer. 'Red deer.' 'Yes?' 'Let us go and eat meat.' 'All right.' They went, he and the red deer. The meat was brought out. They sat down to eat. Then the spider said, '*Gbɛgbɛlɛ gbɛgbɛlɛ*', sucking the bone, 'your comrade's bone; this time tomorrow yours will be sucked *gbɛgbɛlɛ*.' He said, 'What's that, spider?' 'No, nothing. I was saying that Kayi knows how to cook, but there is not enough salt.' 'Oh.' They finished eating.

In the morning, 'Let us go to the palm tree.' They went. When they were about to arrive, the spider hid. 'Red deer, go and wait in front.' The red deer went. He went and found the cave with a beard. He said, 'Spider oo spider.' 'Yes?' 'I had never before seen this—a cave with a beard.' The red deer fell. He went and took him, he the spider, he brought him to the village. He went and skinned him. He gave him to Kayi.

While Kayi was still cooking, he went for the antelope to come and eat the red deer. They sat down to eat. He said, he the spider, '*Gbɛgbɛlɛ gbɛgbɛlɛ*', sucking the bone, 'it is sweet, your comrade's bone. This time tomorrow yours will be sucked *gbɛgbɛlɛ*.' At that the antelope asked,

[1] The spider replies in a plausible airy tone to the quick suspicious question of the other.

'What 's that, spider?' 'No, nothing. I was saying that Kayi's cooking is sweet, but there is not enough salt.' 'Oh.' They lay down.

In the morning 'Friend, let us go to the palm tree.' 'All right.' They went. When they were about to arrive—'Antelope, go and wait for me in front. I am going to the bush.' He hid, he, the spider.

The antelope arrived at the cave. He went and stood, he stood and looked.[1] He looked for long. The spider said, 'E, friend antelope, have you not reached the cave yet?' The antelope said 'I have reached it.' 'What have you found?' 'I don't know.' 'Don't you see what you have found there?' 'No.' 'Oh, you, you are half-witted. Don't you see it?' 'No.' The spider came out. He said, 'Don't you see that thing standing there?' 'No.' He came near. 'What is that?' The antelope said, 'I don't know.' 'Say "the cavern here has a—" —say that now.' The antelope said, 'The cavern here has a—.' He stopped. Then the spider said, 'Just say that the cavern has a beard.' The spider fell! The antelope fell! They spent the whole day there.

In the evening, the spider was the first to be sprinkled with *mafɔi* medicine. He got up. As he was getting up quickly to go and fall on the antelope, the antelope was sprinkled with *mafɔi* medicine. The antelope saw him as he was bringing out his knife to kill the antelope. The antelope said, 'What are you doing?' 'I am coming to help you up.' The antelope said, 'Just stop it!' The antelope got up. The antelope said, 'Did you think that I was half-witted?'

The spider and the chimpanzee

FANKA KONTEH. *Dictated* 30.11.61

The spider, stupidly over-confident and boastful, is not only beaten by the chimpanzee but outdone in courage and strength by his wife Kayi, even by his own children. His lack of forethought not only leads him to challenge the chimpanzee—whose strength is well known—but twice to betray his own hiding place to his enemy. One of the attractions of the story to Limba listeners was the ridiculous and utterly unmanly way in which the spider, the husband, behaves; he puts on his wife's skirt, is weaker than she, cries, runs away—all normally expected characteristics of a woman not a man. The dramatic description and enactment of the fight itself was the main attraction and point of the story as told, rather than the details of the rather sketchy, and well-known, plot.

[1] The antelope is portrayed as acting with an innocent, even simple air which infuriates—and misleads—the spider.

A CHIMPANZEE once reared a goat. 'I will sell it for a fight.' He began to take the goat round the people. Everyone that saw it asked him, 'Is the goat for sale?' The chimpanzee said, 'Yes.' 'For what?' 'For a fight.' 'Go on; I am not able to fight.'

He went on, he the chimpanzee. He went on again forward. Another one asked him, 'Chimpanzee, is the goat for sale?' 'Yes.' 'For what?' 'Sale for a fight.' 'I, I am not strong, go on.'

He went on for far, he went and met another one again. 'Oh, chimpanzee, is the goat for sale?' 'Yes.' 'Sale for what?' 'Sale for a fight.' 'Oh, I am not strong, go on.'

He went for far, he went and met a spider. The spider said, 'Oh, friend chimpanzee, is the goat for sale?' 'Yes.' 'Sale for what?' 'Sale for a fight.' 'I am able to fight.' 'All right, come here.' The chimpanzee gave him the goat. 'All right, come tomorrow morning.' The chimpanzee went off. The spider took the goat, he killed it, he singed it, he skinned it. They cooked it, he and Kayi, plenty of it. They spent the night eating the meat, the whole night.[1]

In the morning the chimpanzee came. 'Greetings to you.' The spider said, 'Yes, greetings.' 'I have come.' 'All right.' 'Well now.' They went and took hold of each other for the fight, the spider and the chimpanzee. First of all he threw down the chimpanzee. Then the spider said, 'Friend, leave him to be beaten (?). See, he is not strong'—because the first thing was that he threw him down. They got up. The chimpanzee lifted the spider, he—*dashed*[2] him down. He got up, 'Come!' They took hold of each other again. He—*dashed* the spider down again. They got up. The chimpanzee said, 'Come!' 'Oh, it is enough.' 'All right, till tomorrow then.' The chimpanzee said, 'All right, no matter.' The chimpanzee went off.

The night passed. In the morning the chimpanzee came. 'Greetings spider.' 'Oh, greetings chimpanzee.'[3] 'All right, I have come.' The spider got up. They went and came together. He—*dashed* the spider down again. He got up. They came together again. He—*dashed* the spider down again. He got up. He said 'Come!' 'Oh, enough. Wait till tomorrow again.' The chimpanzee said, 'All right. I am coming again early in the morning.' The chimpanzee went off.

The spider said, 'Kayi, please, I beg you, help me tomorrow in the fight.' Well Kayi now, she is stronger than the spider. She is the female. Kayi said, 'All right; when the sun rises.'

[1] As so often, the description of their act of eating is in itself amusing as told in a Limba context.

[2] The pause before the word 'dashed' (*lɔpitande*) gives an extra effect of the great strength with which the chimpanzee knocked the spider down suddenly and completely, very hard.

[3] The scene and mood of the two opponents is set by the way in which they exchange greetings.

The sun rose. The spider took his trousers, he gave them to Kayi, the woman. He took her skirt, he the spider, he tied it round him. He sat down to dry the rice.[1] The chimpanzee came. 'Greetings to you, spider.' 'Yes.' 'Well, I have come.' He got up. Kayi went and they came together, she and the chimpanzee. She lifted up the chimpanzee, she—*dashed* him down. He got up. 'Come!' She went and lifted up the chimpanzee again, she—*dashed* him down. Then the spider said—where he was drying the rice—'Go on Kayi; that's the one who is always dashing me down; go on, avenge me now today, beat him today, the scoundrel.'[2] The chimpanzee said, 'Oho! Behold it is not the spider.' He struck Kayi once only, Kayi fell. He went and seized the spider where he was drying the rice. He thumped him, he thumped him again; the spider cried and cried! 'Well, I am going.' 'Ee.'[3] 'I am coming tomorrow'—he the chimpanzee.

As soon as the chimpanzee had gone, 'Kayi, let us go away from here, let us run, the chimpanzee will kill us here if we stay here.' They got up, they ran to the banana trees below there, they went and hid.

In the morning the chimpanzee came. He did not find anyone there. He looked, he saw no one. He went to the finch. 'Finch, come here and divine for me. The spider took a goat from my hand for a fight. That spider, he has now hidden. I can't see him now.' Then the finch said, '*Se se, se se seŋ*; put good, put bad; go and collect stones to the number of the spider's children, three stones; that for his wife Kayi—one big one; that for the spider, the rascal, well a big one, a huge one. You go and stand there above on the hill, then you will hear where they ran away to.'

The chimpanzee came and collected the stones. He went and stood on the hill. He took a small stone, he threw it towards the banana trees—*gbi!*[4] The child was just going to cry, but the spider said, 'No no no. Suck a bone, suck', so that the child would not cry for the chimpanzee to hear. He took another stone. He threw it there again. The child was just going to cry, but the spider said, 'No no no no. Suck a bone, suck a bone.' The child began to suck the bone. The chimpanzee took still another stone. He threw it there again. The child was again just going to cry, he said, 'Suck a bone, suck a bone.' He took the stone for Kayi, he threw it at Kayi. Then the spider said, 'Well, for you, you who remain, who are old, let me say suck a bone—suck a little, suck a little.' He took the stone for the spider, he threw it at the spider! The spider cried and cried. He cried and cried '*Woi, woi.*' The child had not cried, his wife Kayi had

[1] A woman's task.

[2] A very rude word of abuse. The spider's excitement and over-vindictiveness leads him to betray his disguise.

[3] The faint weak cry of the spider illustrates again his complete incapacity to make good his original offer to fight.

[4] He hits one child, then, later, the others.

not cried—but the spider, he cried because he had been hit.[1] The chimpanzee went off.

When the chimpanzee came again when the sun rose, he did not find the spider there. The spider had gone off in the night, he had run secretly away.

The spider woos a wife

NABENI DEMA. *Dictated* 8.10.61

The spider, as often, is shown acting in a ridiculously stupid way: to go through all the trials of winning a wife and then—the extreme of folly—to refuse her when won! Secondly to use insulting words to a mother-in-law, as he does at the end, is not only wrong, but blatantly stupid.

The story is told briefly, and the potentially long account of the various animals who tried to win the girl is referred to only by one sentence.

YOU see—someone once bore a child. She planted a pumpkin. It grew, it reached right up to the sky. She said, 'This has grown up, up to the sky.'

Now the girl—her name was Sira—she said, 'Whoever picks the pumpkin up in the sky, you are the one will marry me as a wife.'

Every animal came, and was unable.

The spider came. 'I have come, about the woman. I want to marry her.' The mother-in-law said, 'Whoever is able to pick the pumpkin up above in the sky, you are the one will marry her as a wife.' The spider said, 'All right.' He began to climb. He said, 'Is it this one my mother-in-law?' The mother-in-law said, 'Not that, the higher one;[2] not that.' He set off again. He said, 'Is it this one my mother-in-law?' She said again, 'Not that, the higher one; not that.' He set off again. 'Is it this one my mother-in-law?' 'Not that, the higher one; not that.' He went up above right into the sky. He said, 'This one mother-in-law?' She said, 'Yes, that one. Don't drop it on the ground. Clutch it in your hands if you want to marry the woman.' The spider clutched[3] the pumpkin. He came down. He said, 'Is this not the one?' The mother-in-law said, 'That is the one. Here is your wife.'

[1] The contrast between the spider's weakness and the endurance of the others was brought out very clearly by the tone.

[2] This repeated phrase by the mother-in-law was half chanted, and in a fuller telling might well have been a proper song.

[3] i.e. he had to come down the tree again clutching the pumpkin to his stomach—a comic picture.

The spider said, '*Kiŋkɛde, kiŋkɛde!* stop bothering me![1] what you did to me because of your daughter!'

That is it, it is finished.

The elephants and the spider

FANKA KONTEH. *Recorded* 6.1.64

A story in which the spider turns out the winner, with the help of his wife (in this version called Sira). The point of the story is in the cleverness of the spider's trick and the ludicrous way in which the dead elephant gets up in its alarm and runs off.

THE elephants were going round about their dead chief, saying that whoever would dig for that elephant who was ill, dig him a grave in the rock, that he would eat the goat.

They went to one hut. They found people there. 'E! Greetings to you.' 'Yes. Where are you going with the goat?' 'Ha! You see—the chief is ill; well, when he dies, whoever can dig him a grave in the rock, for us to bury the chief, he will eat the goat.' They said. 'We don't know how to dig a grave in the rock. Go on.'

For a long time they went. The went and found the spider. The spider welcomed them. 'E! Father, greetings to you. Why are you travelling?' 'We have come to find something for our chief who is ill. When he dies, whoever can dig a grave in the rock, he will eat the goat.' The spider said, 'I know how to dig a grave in the rock.' They said, 'All right. Here is the goat. Eat it.' They took it. The spider took the goat. As for the elephants, they went off.

Then Sira said, 'Ha! Spider, you will get into trouble.' 'Ah! you, get out of the way there. They [the elephants] are stupid.' As soon as the elephants had gone, he killed the goat behind them. They boiled it. They spent all night eating, all all all night.

In the morning the elephants came to the rock. The very, very biggest of them, the chief, he lay down; he died. They called the spider. 'Spider oh!' 'Yes?' 'Come here. The chief has died.' The spider went. As he went, he told his wife, 'When I go, just after I have gone, when a little time has passed, call me quickly quickly quickly. I will come. When I have come, I will know what I am to say.'

When he arrived—'All right. Dig the grave in the rock at once. We will bury the chief, we will go and mourn for him.' 'All right.' He looked for a stick. He measured the length of the grave.[2] He measured

[1] The spider's rude rejection of his mother-in-law's offer caused horrified and appreciative laughter.

[2] A stick is commonly used as a measure for the size of a grave.

it. He cut [the stick]. He went and laid it down on the rock. He raised his hoe; he struck the rock—*gboŋke!* 'Ha! It is hard!' Then one elephant said, 'You—hurry up. We are going to bury our chief, then we will go, we will leave here.' As he turned round there his wife called him quickly quickly quickly, 'Spider oh spider, come here oh come here.'[1] He went. When he went, he went and said, 'Why have you called me?' He stayed there a little. He came back. When he came back the elephants sitting there went and asked him, 'You, just why were you called?—for you came here to bury the chief quickly.' 'Ha! I—it was nothing else I was called for, I was called to say that hunters have come from over there to look for elephant tracks, last year's or this year's.' Then the dead one got up, he lifted his head, 'You, what did you say now when you were asked?'[2] 'I said now, I spoke and said that the elephants were across the stream at the rock.' They got up, running *digi digi digi digi digi*,[3] they ran off.

The spider ate the goat, all of it. The elephants did not come back. The spider did not bury the chief. The dead one and all ran off. The spider was cleverer than they.

The spider and the leopard

FANKA KONTEH. *Dictated* 6.11.61

A story of the spider's cleverness in tricking the leopard who is constantly trying to catch and eat him. His successive wiles, and the characterization of the various animals, were thought very amusing. (I heard several other versions of much the same plot in Kakarima, all opening with the episode about the fire-fly.)

THE spider said, 'Fire-fly, let us go fishing.' The fire-fly said, 'All right.' They went. The spider said, 'Fire-fly, if you get the *seluselu* fishes, well, those are the crabs. Well, if you catch one which puts up its claws—those are the fish.'[4] The fire-fly agreed. They went and sat down to fish. Whenever the fire-fly pulled out a fish, the spider said, 'Ha! that is a crab.' Whenever the fire-fly caught a crab, he said 'Well, those are fishes.' The fire-fly put them in his bag. He sat down again. Whenever the fire-fly caught a fish, he said, 'Oh! those are the crabs.' Whenever he caught a crab, he said, 'Oh! well, those are fishes.'

The spider said, 'E, friend. You are better at fishing than I am. Those

[1] The wife's voice is made to seem very high and far-off.

[2] He gabbles the words very fast in his anxiety.

[3] The words represent their swift running.

[4] The spider is trying deceitfully to get all the fishes for himself, leaving his companion with only the crabs.

fishes of yours, they are many now.' The fire-fly said, 'Spider, let us go home now.' The spider said, 'All right.' After a long time, the fire-fly called again, 'Let us go home now.' Now the spider, he did not reply. The fire-fly began to go home. After a long time, the spider called, 'Friend fire-fly oh!' Then the spider said, 'Oh friend, are you refusing to answer me? oh!' He set out, he the spider. When he had gone for far, he saw that the fire-fly had defecated fire. When the spider reached there, he touched it, he said, 'E! The fire-fly has defecated here.' He went again for far, he again came to fire from the fire-fly. He called the fire-fly, 'Fire-fly!' He said, 'Are you refusing to answer me fire-fly?' He went again and touched it. He said, 'Oh! The fire-fly has defecated here.'

He went for far, he came to a cave. He went there and found a leopard[1] who had borne three children. He said, 'E! For a long time now I have been looking for you, I heard that you had given birth, I came and travelled round for long, it is only now that I have found you.' The leopard said, 'Yes. Greetings. Greetings, stranger.' The spider said, 'Here are fishes I have brought your children.' The leopard said, 'Good. All right, hang them over the fire.' The spider hung them up. The night came. The spider said, 'All right, I will lie down now with the children.' The leopard said, 'All right.' They lay down. The spider had just pinched the leopard's child—the child sobbed, *ta ta ta ta*. The leopard got up to seize the spider, to eat him. The spider said, 'It was for the fish that the child was crying.' 'All right, take one down.' He took one down, he put it on the fire. He took it, he pulled off the fish's head. He ate the fish. He took the fish's head, he put it in the child's mouth.[2] That is what he spent the whole night doing, all all all all night.

In the morning the leopard got up to seize the spider, to eat him. The spider saw that. Then the spider said, 'Leopard, leopard, your cave is going to fall on you and your children. Come and hold it up.' The leopard got up. He took hold of the cave. Then the spider said, 'Is there no axe here?' Then the leopard said, 'There is one over there.' 'Let me go and cut supports to come and put in the cave so that it will not fall.' The spider got up with the axe, he went and cut a tree. He said, 'It is dead.'[3] He went again and cut another; he said, 'It is dead.' The spider went off!

The leopard was left there holding up the cave. The leopard held it

[1] The spider had not expected to meet the leopard, and the whole point of the next episode is the quick recovery he makes to avoid this danger, using the fishes he has taken from the fire-fly as his excuse.

[2] To choke the child.

[3] I am not sure if this refers to the tree (not strong enough to use for a support) or the axe (its edge too blunt to cut a support). In any case it was understood as merely a clever excuse by the spider to go off.

for very, very long. He became thin there. Then a lizard came. 'E! leopard. What is the matter?' 'Ha! The spider said then that the cave was going to fall, hold it! He went off then to cut supports. I haven't seen him since. He has not come back.' Then the lizard said, 'Leopard—since you are aggressive—if I saved you from the cave, as soon as I saved you, as soon as I had done it, you would seize and eat me.' The leopard said, 'I will not do that.' 'All right.' The lizard went round the cave, he went round six times. 'Well, let go.' The leopard let go. The lizard said, 'Well, good-bye.' 'Don't go, sit down for a little.' The lizard sat down. The leopard seized the lizard, he ate him.

The leopard went off, going to look for the spider. He went for far. He went and found the spider up a palm tree. He said, 'Ha! Spider, you will suffer[1] today.' The spider said, 'Don't make me suffer. Do you know what I am eating today?' 'No.' 'Well then, all right, open your mouth wide.' He took a palm kernel, he prepared it well, he smeared salt on to it, he put it into the leopard's mouth. The leopard chewed it up. He said, 'E! spider, it is sweet.' 'Well, open your mouth, a big one is coming.' The leopard stretched wide. He cut off the bunch of palm fruit[2] with its prickles, he put it into the mouth of the leopard—right inside, *rɔ!* The spider came down. He came and thumped him. 'You are a fool.' He went off.

The leopard lay there for long. A giant rat came. 'What is the matter, leopard?' 'The spider said that it was a palm kernel, that I was to open my mouth wide, that a big kernel was coming. Behold it was the bunch of palm fruit that he put into my mouth.' The giant rat said, 'All right, I will take the kernels out.' The rat took them out. The rat went off. The leopard was left there.[3]

Ants came. 'E! Leopard, what is the matter?' 'Ha! the spider put a bunch of palm fruit in my mouth.' 'But—hm! Since you are aggressive—if we eat the bunch, you will stand up and lick us up.' The leopard said, 'I won't do that.' 'All right.' The ants began, they ate the bunch in the mouth of the leopard, all of it. They finished. They said 'All right, good-bye.' 'Don't go.' They stayed. The leopard stood up. He ate all the ants.

The leopard got up, going to look for the spider. He went for far. He went and met the spider. 'Ha! Spider, ha! today you will suffer.' The spider said, 'Ah! Let me go, let me go, let me go, let me go! A great wind is coming, carrying people off. So I am going to tie down my wife's people,[4] so that the wind will not carry them all away.' The leopard

[1] Lit. defecate [from pain].

[2] A big and very heavy cluster.

[3] The point of this episode is not very clear, as it seems from the following paragraph that the leopard still has the bunch in his mouth.

[4] Lit. mothers-in-law, i.e. his wife's mother and her other older female relations.

said, 'First *I* am to be tied down.' The spider stood, he tied him down completely. He fastened him to a tree. The spider thumped him. 'Huh! you are a fool.' The spider went off.

He was there for long, ants came again to where he was tied. 'Please, ants, come and free me.' The ants said, 'We will not do it. Before we went and released you, we took out the palm bunch from your mouth, you stood up, you ate us all. Today we will not do it.' 'Please, I beg you, I will not do that today now.' The ants stood, they ate the ropes, completely. They said, 'All right, we have finished. Well, good-bye.' 'Don't go.' He seized the ants again, he ate them all again.

He set out looking for the spider. He found the spider chasing birds. 'Aha! Spider, today you will suffer.' 'Ah, ah, ah, ah![1] Let me tell you—the chief's farm, a leopard must not tread there. If you tread there you must gather up your tracks.'[2] The leopard set out. Wherever he trod in the farm, he turned round and gathered there. When he gathered there, he trod there again. He turned round again, he trod, he gathered. He turned round again, he trod, he gathered. Wherever he trod, he gathered again there. There he spent the day, the whole day. He was not able to reach the middle of the farm! The sun went. The spider went back to the village. He was saved again from the leopard.

The elephant and the rice

NIAKA DEMA. *Dictated* 17.10.61

The story is mainly about the elephant and the old women, but it starts with a reference to the spider and it is therefore not surprising that the tone of the whole is humorous, indecent, and far-fetched.

THE wet season once came on. The rain fell all day; it fell all night. Now the spider had no wood. But they had rice. He said, 'Kayi, we have no wood. It is good to take the mortar that we pound the rice in.' They took the mortar, they broke it up.[3] She cooked the rice.

When the sun rose, they heated the rice. It became dry. When they had spread it in the sun, then they went round the people.[4] They

[1] Exclamation of fear, well mimed by the teller.

[2] i.e. conceal his tracks by covering them over again. This of course the leopard cannot do as each time he turns round to cover them up he makes new tracks.

[3] They short-sightedly decide to use their rice mortar, instead of going to fetch firewood to cook the rice.

[4] Asking to borrow another mortar, essential for the preparation of rice.

refused to give them [spider and wife] a mortar. After they had heated the rice again, there was ten baskets of it. But they had not found a mortar. As they sat there, hunger took hold of them.[1] There was no food now.

An elephant got up there. He came travelling. He said, 'I am the spider's guest.' 'Ah! We here—we have no mortar here for us to pound rice here; we have nothing that we could give you as a welcome-present.' Then the elephant said, 'I have a mortar.' Then the spider said, 'Ah my father, we wish you to come here. We will beat these five basketfuls.'[2] Kayi and he took up the pestles; they stood holding them. The elephant stood bent over, he put his head on the ground. He opened up his anus. They put all the rice in there, into his anus! He said, 'Put in the pestles.' They stood. They beat the ten basketfuls. He stood up. 'Spread out a big mat.'[3] He poured out the rice on to it. They fanned the rice. They put it into his anus again. They pounded the rice again. 'Spread out a mat.'[3] They fanned the rice again. They put in the clean rice. When they had put it in twice, the third time, when they had shut up his anus, the elephant went off! He left them the chaff. He took off the rice! He went off.

When he came and found an old woman with no husband,[4] he said 'Mother; I want to defecate for you.' The old woman said, 'No! I don't want you to defecate for me! I will not be able to clear up all the dung there.' 'Well, I'm going away.'

The elephant went on. He went. It was a heavy wet season—like now. There was much hunger. The farm settlements were not far away from each other. He came to another old woman. 'Mother; I want to defecate for you.' The old woman said, 'What, father! I have never yet been defecated for by anyone! I have no child to defecate for me. Well, now I would like you to defecate for me.' The elephant said, 'I accept. Get a mat, and spread it out in the compound.' The old woman went and brought out a mat. He took the stopper, he pulled it out from his tail. The rice began to come out from his anus. It piled up, five basketfuls, the amount that had been pounded by the spider. He had brought it here for the old woman. The old woman thanked him many times. 'Oh, my father, what a thing you have done for me this wet season[5]—you have treated me well.'

She took and cooked a little. She gave a bit to the woman who had refused to let the elephant defecate for her. She asked, 'Wherever did

[1] A ridiculous situation—to be short of food through their own stupidity with all that rice around them.

[2] This amount is either a slip by the narrator, or, just possibly, an intentional deceit by the spider, saying five instead of ten.

[3] This follows the regular procedure of pounding the rice several times.

[4] i.e. she was hungry with no one to help her get rice.

[5] i.e. time of hunger.

you find this rice?' The old woman said, 'I—it was the elephant that came and defecated it for me.' Then the other old woman said, 'Oh! I was afraid before. Behold it was the rice that he had in his stomach.' She said, 'I want to make a chance for that elephant to come and defecate.' She was thinking that it had come and defecated rice for the [other] old woman. 'I want him to come and defecate for *me*.' The old woman said, 'It is good; elephant, come here.'

The elephant came. 'I, I want you to come and defecate for me.' The elephant said, 'I refuse. At the beginning I went and said to you that I would defecate for you. You refused. I went on to someone else.' 'No, my father; this hunger is too much for me. That is why I ask.' 'I accept.'

He went—every leaf he found, he ate; every animal he found, he swallowed. His stomach became larger. For six days, he defecated nothing. He said, 'Old woman, I am coming on Tuesday. That is the time I am coming for what we spoke of.' When the time came near, he came. His stomach was bigger than her house! He came to the bush nearby. He said, 'Mother, I have come.' The woman said, 'I accept.' 'Bring out mats.' She brought out mats. 'Have you finished spreading the mats?' She said, 'Yes.'

Then the elephant came. He said, 'Stand on the upper one.' The elephant stood on the lower one. He defecated, he defecated! When he defecated, it was more than the farm hut! Then the old woman said, 'Behold, that is what you have brought for me! I had thought it would be what you defecated before. Behold, what you have brought me is to defecate the leaves!' She had hardly finished speaking, when the dung covered her up! Before her relations could reach her, she was dead, from the dung the elephant had defecated.

Since I heard that story—so now if someone comes and says something to you, accept at the beginning. But for what she did at the beginning she would have got the rice then. But she disliked the elephant's excretion, saying, 'It is too much.' Since I heard that story—it is finished.

The monkey and the chameleon

MUSU KONTEH. *Recorded* 13.1.61

A tale with a somewhat similar framework to *The monkey and the catfish*, *The spider and the bat*, and other stories based on the idea of competition.

A MONKEY and a chameleon went travelling. When they went, they came to someone's palm tree. The monkey drank the palm wine. When they were caught, the monkey said, 'Anyone who drinks palm wine is not hard to know. His eyes turn round.'[1] They looked at the chameleon. They saw his eyes turning round. They took hold of the chameleon. They beat him. The chameleon bore the trouble.

They arrived in the village. Rice was being cooked for them. It was carried to them. When they had eaten, the chameleon smeared [poisonous black] medicine on the pot. When the child went for the pot, when he touched it, he fell down. When they saw that, they said, 'The strangers rubbed medicine on the pot.' The chameleon said, 'If anyone rubs medicine, he is not hard to know.' They looked at the monkey's hands. They were black. They beat him, till his tail fell out. The monkey ran to the bush.[2]

The story is finished.

The monkey and the catfish

NABENI DEMA. *Dictated* 7.10.61

Another story about competition, marking the ingenuity of the two opponents who, ostensibly in all innocence, deprive the other of his expected food.

An English-speaking Limba said that the correct translation should be 'catfish', but I do not know what kind of fish this is.

The narrator 'heard the story from the old people'.

A MONKEY and a catfish formed a company.[3]

The company's turn came to the monkey. The monkey brought out a chair. When they had hoed, they finished; their food was brought. The monkey said, 'Catfish, if you are not able to sit on the chair,[4] you will not eat the rice.' Now the catfish, he has no bottom. When he tried to sit on the chair—it was slippery! As soon as he had sat down, he fell off into the sauce they were eating with the rice. The catfish failed. The monkey ate the rice there.

When the sun rose, it was at the catfish's farm. When they had hoed, they finished; their food was brought. The catfish said, 'What you did

[1] Refers both to the turning round of the chameleon's eyes, and to the sense in which a drunk man's eyes 'turn round'.

[2] This probably implies, or could have been expanded to, 'thus monkeys now live in the bush'.

[3] *Kunɛ*—means both an agricultural company for hoeing in which the participants work and eat in turn on each other's farms, and also an exchange of ill deeds and revenge. Both senses are implied here.

[4] This could be taken as ostensibly a compliment, as chiefs and honoured visitors are given chairs.

to me yesterday I am going to return today.' He told the monkey, 'If you can clean your hand,[1] you may eat the rice.' The monkey scrubbed his hand—it did not come clean, the blood came out. The catfish said, 'Well then, you will not eat the rice.' The catfish ate it. He did not give to the monkey.

When the company was finished, the catfish went into the water, the monkey went up above on to a tree. The catfish jumped. The monkey saw him. Then the monkey said, 'Catfish in the water, stop your half-dying (*matukutu*).' The catfish answered, 'You too, monkey, stop your jerking (*makiribe*).'[2]

Since you said I was to bring you a story, that is it; it is finished.

The dog and the tortoise

MASE KARGBO. *Recorded* 5.8.61

A story about a race for the chiefship between the fast-running dog and the clever tortoise who finally wins by placing his children all along the path, including the goal (the chief's chair); the children in turn take up the tortoise's song so that it seems as if only one tortoise is competing. The conclusion includes both the triumph of the tortoise and also an explanation for the dog's bark and his air of surprise (for which cf. also *The dog and the rice*).

One of the main interests of the story for the audience was Mase's singing, the chorus taken up and repeated by several children who sang away in a disciplined and ordered way as they sat in a tight row on a long bench. The songs were sometimes repeated as many as ten or fifteen times and took about as long as the narrative parts of the story, or longer. Mase's acting of the dog's contempt for the slower tortoise, added to his later weakness and surprise, also contributed to the effect of the whole. There were a number of hesitations and slips by the teller, filled in by such words as 'something', 'someone' (*wanini*): the emphasis was very much on the *singing* rather than the narration.

The story was told by the wife of the Paramount Chief of the Wara Wara Yagala chiefdom, Alimami Gbawuru II. He had been elected a few weeks before after a hard struggle against other competitors, and had been greatly supported and helped by his vigorous senior wife Mase who, like him, had spent many years down country, and spoke English and several other languages in addition to Limba. This story was told immediately

[1] Again this sounds quite polite, as it is usual for anyone to wash his hands, or at least his right hand, before eating. The monkey's black hand will not come clean.

[2] The words are for some reason considered funny in themselves, and were enough to start people laughing at once.

after they had heard a recording describing the election of another Limba chief, and the particular setting and topic of the story were probably stimulated by the current interest in elections to chiefship—this at any rate made it specially effective in the situation in which it was told.

EXCUSE me, you chiefs. . . .[1] I have come, I Mase, Mrs. Gbawuru II.

A dog once competed with a tortoise. They said they were seeking the chiefship. Then the tortoise said—the dog said, 'Let us go to Freetown to seek the chiefship.' When they went to Freetown, they went and did—they went and said, 'All right.' They set a date, saying that at that time, at that time they were to come about the chiefship.

When they went, the dog, the dog said, 'Let us go and get ready.' As they came to get ready, then the dog said, 'Oh! Look at the one who is thinking he is to beat me for the chiefship— [going] *kɔkɔrɔ kɔkɔrɔ kɔkɔrɔ kɔkɔrɔ*.'[2]

Behold, cleverness is more than anything in the world. The tortoise had many children. He took them; all the way from here to Freetown, he came and placed them on the roads.

Now the dog, he trusted to his ability to run. When the dog came and stood ready, he said, 'Now I, the time has come—let us go. You go first. You are not able to go [fast].' The tortoise said, 'All right. I accept. Well, all right, I will go first.'

When he set out, then he said,[3] '*Kombo kɔmbɔ o kɔkɔrɔ tɔ, mba kɔkɔrɔ tɔ. Kombo kɔmbɔ o kɔkɔrɔ tɔ, mba kɔkɔrɔ tɔ. Kombo kɔmbɔ o kɔkɔrɔ tɔ, mba kɔkɔrɔ tɔ. . . .*' Then he did—he sat down to rest.

Then the dog got up. '*Walaahi*,[4] I and the tortoise we are competing. *Walaahi*, I and the tortoise are competing. See the one who is beating me for the chiefship, the one who goes *kɔkɔrɔ kɔkɔrɔ* as he walks. Ha!'

Then he got up. '*Pampaŋ kanthapande*,[5] *pampaŋ kanthapande, saŋsaŋ nuwɛke pande ni wo. Pampaŋ kanthapande, pampaŋ kanthapande, saŋsaŋ nuwɛke pande ni wo. Pampaŋ kanthapande, pampaŋ kanthapande, saŋdsaŋ nuwɛke pande ni wo. . . .*'

Then the tortoise sang '*Kombo kɔmbɔ o kɔkɔrɔ tɔ, mba kɔkɔrɔ tɔ. . . .*' Then he went and he rested.

Then the dog got up. '*Hŋ! Walaahi*, see the *kɔkɔrɔ kɔkɔrɔ* who is

[1] She asks the chief and elders for silence so that she can begin.

[2] The dog is referring contemptuously to the tortoise's gait.

[3] The song represents the way the tortoise walks, and Mase sang it in a rather slow but sharply rhythmic way to make this more vivid. The chorus on each occasion sang *mba kɔkɔrɔ tɔ*. The whole was, here and later, repeated many times over.

[4] An exclamation of surprise or determination, here also representing the sound made by dogs.

[5] The song of the dog's running, sung more quickly than the tortoise's song, the succession of quick short syllables showing his speed.

beating me for the chiefship! *I* will go and sit on the [chief's] hammock. Just wait!' He urinated. '*Pampaŋ kanthapande, pampaŋ kanthapande, saŋsaŋ nuwɛke pande ni wo. . . .*'

The tortoise—wherever he rested, there another [tortoise] answered him in the distance. A [tortoise] child answered there again, '*Kombo kɔmbɔ o kɔkɔrɔ tɔ, mba kɔkɔrɔ tɔ. . . .*' He sat down and rested.

Then the dog said '*Walaahi*, see the tortoise, the *kɔkɔrɔ kɔkɔrɔ* he is beating me, we are competing for it now. Just wait! *Walaahi, pampaŋ kanthapande, pampaŋ kanthapande, saŋsaŋ nuwɛke pande ni wo. . . .*'[1]

Well, when they reached there now, they came now right to here, the tortoise was now here in this house! The tortoise answered now from where he was sitting in the chair. '*Hŋ, kombo kɔmbɔ o kɔkɔrɔ tɔ, mba kɔkɔrɔ tɔ. . . .*'

The tortoise took the chiefship. If you see now that he has the property—the dog failed. If you see now that the dog always goes '*Walaahi*' —if you see the dog sitting, ha! it is the surprise he had when he competed with the tortoise. Behold, the tortoise was now sitting in power (?). The tortoise was now sitting there, doing—saying 'I am here now, see!'

Since I heard that, and Yenkeni came, I had to tell it to her. It is finished.

The goat, the leopard, and the lion

FANKA KONTEH. *Dictated* 1.12.61

The plausible goat tricks the lion with the help of the lion's wife. The moral is that *yaŋfa* (here passing on gossip against another) is bad and ends up to the disadvantage of the doer of it. One of the main attractions of the story was the characterization conveyed through the verbal exchanges between the actors portrayed by the teller—the deceitful and selfish leopard, the clever and apparently innocent goat, and the wife's acting as she at first pretends to be very faint, then gets stronger, playing on her husband's concern.

I have heard a rather similar story about a jackal, lion, and leopard, in which the wife does not appear, but the sick lion is persuaded that pieces of the leopard, mixed with sweet honey, are doing him good.

This story is a good example of the danger in arguing simple-mindedly from one text to a people's actions or beliefs. The conclusion with the moral that the *informer* suffered (a stock ending, it is clear, in Limba stories) might make it appear that the Limba did not also feel strongly about the wrongness of adultery and the rights of the husband—but this

[1] The dog's song is now very breathless and weak. The teller does not need to describe his exhaustion, showing it instead by the way the dog sings.

in fact is a subject on which all married men (including, most definitely, the teller of the story) are quite clearly and explicitly agreed.

A GOAT was once the lover of the lion's wife. Now the leopard knew about this love. The leopard went to the lion, her husband, he went and said, 'Lion. Ha! I have come to tell you about something.' The lion said 'About what?' 'The goat is making love to your wife. That is what I have come to tell you. But I will make a chance to bring you the goat, for you to eat him. For he is your wife's lover.' 'When?' 'The day after tomorrow.' 'Yes; good.'

The lion's wife met her lover, the goat. 'Goat.' 'Yes?' 'The leopard has uttered slander, he said that we are making love. He said he would take you to the lion, to my husband, for him to eat you. For we are lovers. That is what he went and said to my husband. But don't be afraid. Come anyway, and when you are setting out to come, bring with you honey in a pot.'

The time came. The leopard went. He said, 'Goat, the time has come, let us go. What will we take with us?' 'Let us take her honey.' 'All right; good.' They took the honey. They went, and arrived. 'Visitors have come to you, lion', they said. The lion said, 'Good. Sit down.' The lion sat. The leopard sat. The goat sat. The lion's wife sat opposite.

They began to talk. The lion's wife was watching her husband so that he would not catch the goat. When she saw her husband about to spring on the goat, the wife fell down on to the ground. She cried and moaned to herself. 'Oooh.' Her husband said, 'Oh, my wife is going to die. Leopard, don't you know of any medicine?' The leopard said, 'No, I don't know of any medicine.' 'What about you goat? Do you know of any medicine?' The goat said, 'Yes.' 'What is the medicine?' 'The skin of someone spotted.' The lion looked round, he did not see anyone spotted except for the leopard. He said to the leopard, he, the lion, her husband, 'Leopard, lend me some of your spotted skin, so my wife may have the medicine and get well.' 'All right; cut some off.' The lion, the male lion, he cut off one of the leopard's legs. He gave it to the goat. The goat put it in the honey, then he gave it to the woman. The woman ate it. She said, 'Ah, ah.' She turned over.

The lion said, 'Well? Should I give her more?' 'All right.' He cut some more. He gave it to the goat. The goat put it in the honey, he gave it to the lion's wife. She ate it. She opened her eyes.

Her husband asked again, 'Well? Should I give her more of the medicine?' The wife said, 'Yes, give me more.' The male, he the male lion, he asked the goat, 'Well goat?' The goat said, 'I don't want any trouble.[1] I only know that it's a skin, the skin of someone spotted.' The lion, the male lion, said again, 'I beg you, leopard, lend me some.' The

[1] He is disclaiming all responsibility himself, he says innocently.

leopard said, 'All right.' The lion cut again. He gave it to the goat; the goat put it in the honey, he gave it to the lion's wife. She ate it. She got up and sat.

The lion, the male lion, said, 'Well? is it better now?' 'Yes. But not quite better. If a little more could be got, fine.' The lion said, 'Well? goat?' The goat said, 'I don't want any trouble. I only know that it's a skin, the skin of someone spotted.' 'Leopard, lend me some more still.' The leopard said, 'All right.' The lion cut again. He gave it to the goat; the goat put it in the honey, he gave it to the lion's wife. She ate it. She got up and sat on a chair.

She said, 'Aha, if I could get some more of that, it would be fine, so I could be completely better.' The lion said, 'Well, what now goat?' The goat said, 'I want no trouble. I only know that it's a skin, the skin of someone spotted.' 'Leopard, lend me some more.' 'All right.' He cut. He gave it to the goat; the goat put it in the honey, he gave it to the lion's wife. The wife ate it. She said 'Aha!'

Her husband asked, 'Shall I give you more still?' 'Yes.' 'Well, goat?' 'Oh, *I* don't want trouble. I only know that it's a skin, the skin of someone spotted.'

The lion was just about to say, 'Leopard, lend me some more'—before he had spoken, the leopard had run off. The lion, the male lion, followed him. They ran thus for far, but he was not able to catch the leopard.

Then the wife said, 'Well, goat; escape!' When the lion failed to catch the leopard, he said, he the lion, the male, 'Since I have failed to catch the leopard, I have still got the goat, I will go and cut from him. So my wife may be well and not die.' He went home. When he got there, he did not find the goat there. 'What about the goat?' The wife said, 'The goat has run away too.' 'Then he is saved from trouble, for I came here to catch *him*. But since he has run away, all right.'

You see now how it is to tell on someone, to slander them. Well, the leopard uttered slander about the goat, but this slander ended up against himself. Thus slander is bad.

The goat and the leopard

NABENI DEMA. *Dictated* 14.10.61

The goat, in spite of his weakness and small size compared with other animals, beats them in the contest, and kills the leopard. That is why the animals in the bush now fear the sound of a gun, thinking it is the goat coming; why the domestic animals are now with man; and why the goat and the leopard are enemies.

Episodes in the story recall some of those in *Bayo*, and *A contest in strength*.

YOU see—the animals said, 'We are living here foolishly now. We are not fighting.' They fixed a date. They made a place for them to fight. They made it. When they had made it, they fixed the date, 'On Friday, everyone who knows what he knows (?)—let no one forget.'

The day began to draw near. The leopard was the enemy of the goat. The goat began to sit sadly.[1] 'We have fixed a date to fight, but I have nothing to fight with.' He began to go round. He came to where a spirit had spread out his things to dry. The rain came. The spirit was a hunter. He had gone to his hunting. He spread out his things. There was no one there [to watch them]. The rain came. The goat was there when the rain came. The rain fell. The goat took the spirit's things, he took them into the spirit's house. He hid. He thought that if the spirit found him, he would eat him. Behold, he had done good to the spirit.

The spirit, when the rain came, he thought about the things he had spread out in the sun. He began to come. Before he had arrived, the things had been taken up by the goat. He [spirit] said, 'Please, the one who took up my things, if he is near, let him come out, I will not do anything to him. Please, I implore you.' The goat went *bɛɛ*. He said, 'Please, goat, you did good to me today; the things I forgot, you came and took them up, so that they would not be touched by the rain.' The goat came. 'Was it you took up the things?' The goat said, 'Yes.' 'What did you come here for today?' The goat said, 'The animals have said that every animal in the country is to fight. I have nothing for fighting with.' The spirit said, 'Take heart. Sit down. Let yourself be cooked for.' He was cooked for. He ate. He [spirit] took a gun. He loaded it. He gave it to the goat. 'Look now at the tree. Look now at the tree standing there. So that [you may know that] I do not tell lies.' The goat put in the fire.[2] He looked at the tree. He shot. The tree fell. He said, 'Is this not a way of fighting?' The goat said, 'It is a way of fighting, this.' The goat thanked him much there. He began to come back.

The date came near. They gathered. They came. The dog got up there. He came and bit the tree. He said, 'Is that not a way to fight?' They said, 'It is a way to fight.' The cat got up there too. She went and scratched the tree, it peeled off. She said, 'Is that not a way to fight?' They said, 'It is a way to fight, a way to fight.' The leopard got up there. He climbed the tree. He scratched. It peeled off. He said, 'Is that not a way to fight?' They said, 'It is a way to fight.' The elephant got up there. He came and pushed down the tree. He said, 'Is that not a way to fight?' They said, 'It is a way to fight.' The lion got up. A tree was

[1] The posture of one in despair or anxiety, usually with head or chin in hands.

[2] He fires it by putting a match to it.

standing there. He struck it with his hand. The tree split. He said, 'Is that not a way to fight?' They said, 'It is a way to fight.' The leopard got up. 'Goat, you now. If you do not show a great way of fighting, I will eat you.' The goat got up. He went *repe!* he butted the tree. The leopard said, 'Huh! Is that the way you fight? If you do not show a great way of fighting, we will eat you.' The goat said, 'Oh?' 'Yes.' He told them to go like this,[1] stretching out their arms. The leopard did like that. He shot there at the leopard. The leopard died. 'Is that not a way to fight?'

The elephant ran off to the bush. The hens, the cat, the dog, the cow, the sheep, the horse, the donkey, they ran off to us humans here. The other animals ran off to the bush. When they hear *gbu!*[2] they think, 'It is the goat's way of fighting, it is the goat's way of fighting.'

If you ever hear that the goat and the leopard are enemies, there it began then.

The elephant and the goat compete in eating

KUMARU DEMA. *Dictated* 14.10.61

A story told for its amusing plot. The goat is again represented as able to trick an animal immensely bigger than himself.

YOU see, the goat went to eat grass.[3] The elephant came on him there. He said, 'That thing standing there, what will he be able to do?' The goat said, 'I am able to do something.' The elephant said, 'Tomorrow we will meet, we will compete in eating.' The goat said, 'I accept.'

When the sun rose, the goat set out. The elephant came. They went and met. 'E! Have we come together for eating?' The goat said, 'I came because you said yesterday that I was unable to do it. That is why I came —for us to compete in eating.'

They stood, they ate for long, the two. The sun began to set. When the sun had set, they said, 'Where will we sleep?' 'On the rocks.' They went there. They went and lay down. Now the elephant—in the daytime, he chews properly, he swallows. But the goat chews slightly. He does not sleep. He sends it down to his stomach. When they lay there, the goat was bringing it up where he lay in a hollow. He began to chew. Then the elephant asked, 'What are you chewing now?' 'I am chewing something. When I have finished here, I will go over to something big.'[4]

[1] The narrator demonstrated.
[2] The sound of a gun.
[3] Eating with its head on one side, in a way the elephant finds ridiculous.
[4] Implying that when he has finished his present mouthful (which the elephant takes to be the rock) he will go on to the elephant.

Now the elephant, he went and looked. He said, 'E! I will not stay here.' He saw the hollow. When he came to the hollow in the rock where the goat was lying, the elephant said, 'E! I will not stay here.' He rushed off into the bush. The goat was left there.

Now whenever the elephant hears the goat say *bɛɛ* he runs away, thinking, 'The goat has come again for us to compete in eating.' Well, he runs away. That is why the goat is not liked by the elephant. He runs away from the goat.[1]

Well, that is it, it is finished.

The lion and the donkey

FANKA KONTEH. *Dictated* 5.11.61

A story of the misunderstanding of lion and donkey, ending with a kind of competition between the two in which, in this case, *both* lose. The story is enacted in the framework of the various operations needed for building a native thatched hut from wood and earth, a series of operations well known to every Limba, and normally taking several months. Here they seem to be completed in a few days by the two animals in a series of parallel episodes. The animals first end each stage by going home singly, later together, and finally both leaving the house completely.

THE donkey and the lion. The donkey got up, he went to look for a place to build a house. The lion too, he got up to look for a place to build a house. Where the donkey had gone and seen a place there the lion too went and saw the place.

Well. The donkey got up, he went and cleared the place, with his children. They returned.

The lion got up, he went. 'Oh! I had said before that I was coming here to build a house; now today I find it cleared. This country here is good oh! Well, children, this is what we will do—cut poles and small sticks and bush ropes, and pile them up. That then is what we will do today.' They cut the poles. They cut the small sticks and bush ropes. They piled them up. They returned, they came home to the village.

The donkey got up, he went. He went and found the poles and the small sticks and the bush ropes. He said, 'Oh! This country here it is good oh! It makes me glad. For we spent the day yesterday clearing the place, we went home to the village; now, today, we find poles. Well, what then we will do—we will stand them all up, we will bind them. We will go home to the village.' They stood them all up. They bound[2] the house. They went home.

[1] I was told that elephants do always run away when they hear the sound of a goat (or a fowl).

[2] Made the frame of sticks later to be filled in with earth formed into balls.

The lion came, 'Oh! this country is good; we cut poles, we piled them up, when we come today we find that the house is now bound. Well, let us prepare earth, let us put earth balls into the house.' They soaked the earth. They put in balls for the whole house. 'Well, let us go home to the village.' They went home.

The donkey came. 'Oh! We came and stood up all the poles for the house, we bound it. Today when we come we find it balled. Let us splash on earth.' They splashed the house. 'Well, let us go home to the village.' They went home.

The lion came. 'Oh! We only put balls, now we find the house splashed. Let us smooth it out.' They smoothed it. 'Well, let us go home to the village.' They went home.

The donkey came. 'Oh! We only came and splashed the house, now today we find it smoothed out. Let us cut the rafters and the ropes. Let us go home.' They cut the wood and the ropes. They piled them up. They went home to the village.

The donkey[1] came again. 'Oh! This country here is good! Today we find rafters and ropes. Let us roof the house; let us finish putting all the sticks[2] up on it. Let us go home.' They took up and put on the sticks. They bound it all down. They went home to the village.

The lion came. He found the house with the sticks on it. 'Oh! this country is good! Well, we have found the house with the sticks up, well let us gather thatch.' They gathered the thatch. They gathered the thatch and brought it to the village; they came and put it all on. 'Well, let us go home.' They went home.

The donkey came. 'Well, this country is good, isn't it? We left, we put the sticks on the house, we went home; today now we find thatch. Well, let us put the thatch on the house.' They thatched it. They finished thatching it all. They went home.

The lion got up, the lion came. 'Oh! We only gathered the thatch, now we find the house thatched. Well, tomorrow, let us come into the house tomorrow, let us come and sleep in the house with all our things tomorrow.'

The sun rose, the lion came. Well, at the time when the lion came in the evening, the donkey also came in the evening with his family, at the same time. At that time they entered the house. Neither of them knew that the other was doing the work. One came, he entered on one side. The other came, he entered on the other side. They sat down. They did not know about the other.

They began to talk. These ones talked, those ones talked. Then the lion said his children should be quiet—'Be quiet now.' The donkey said

[1] The narrator seems to have made a slip here in the alternation between lion and donkey.

[2] Putting the small sticks across the larger rafters.

over there, 'Be quiet, people are talking.' The donkey got up here, the lion got up there, they came and met in the middle of the house—the middle exactly! Then they said, 'Oh, friend, greetings.' 'Yes, greetings.' 'Oh, behold, we were working here together with you, we did not know about each other! Oh, greetings.' 'Yes.' The lion said, 'My family is large. I, I know how to hunt. Tomorrow let us go to see, since we have come to live with our families.'

The sun rose. They got up, the donkey and the lion. They went to the bush. The lion went and saw the animals, the bush cows. He looked intently—*tiiŋ!* They fell. He looked again at one intently—*tiiŋ!* It fell. It died. He asked the donkey 'Are you able to carry the two animals?' The donkey said, 'If you add to it by killing one more, good.' The lion looked again. Two more fell. 'Will you be able to carry the four, all of them?' The donkey said, 'It is not enough for me yet.' 'What?' 'Add more; kill others.' The lion looked again intently—*tiiŋ!* Two more fell. 'Yes; that is about sufficient.' The donkey went and stood. 'Well hang one here at my side, hang the other one here; well, put these ones on the middle of my back.' He put them on. The lion bound them firmly on the donkey. 'Well, let us go home.'

They started coming. The donkey said, 'If I fart, don't laugh.' After long, they arrived. The donkey shook himself, shaking *yigiyigi*. The animals all fell off. The lion took three, he put them down. He took three, he put them down. 'Well donkey, take those ones so that your children may eat them. I am taking these ones.' They took them. The donkey skinned one, they went to boil it. The lion skinned one, he went to boil it. They finished boiling it all, they sat down to eat. Then the donkey said, 'Ha! my children, that man!—all those animals, he did not fire a gun, he only looked at them intently—*tiiŋ!* they fell. Ha! I am not able to bear this man. Tomorrow if we should have a quarrel, tomorrow he will kill us all, by looking.' As he was finishing speaking, the lion was saying, 'My children, ha! That man, he has power. All these animals I killed today, he said that the load was not much. If we live in the house, if we quarrel here tomorrow with him, tomorrow he will put us all on his back and take us off. I, I will not live in the house, I will leave.' They all went away. The lion went away, the donkey went away, again at the same time. They left the house. They went off. Neither of them knew that his companion had gone off on that same day. They left the house.

The clever cat

KIRINKOMA KONTEH. *Recorded* 15.1.64

A story one of whose points is the paradoxical situation. The rats enter the women's Bondo society with all the usual formalities, and line up behind their revered leader (in this case a cat!) singing as she tells them. The rats' names and, particularly, that of their country were also found very amusing. One of the main attractions was also the catchy song, repeated many times.

A STORY for you. Kirinkoma is to bring you a story which Yenkeni wishes to hear.

Clever ones had not yet begun, foolish ones had not yet begun on the earth here—the cat was a very clever one. She saw that all the people on earth here were foolish, that she could trick them—they were the rats.

The rats then called their country *Katiŋkiritaŋkarakatarina.* That was their country. There they came out. They wanted to know what was meant by the Bondo. In the Bondo, the leader was none other than the cat! The cat told them that she was willing to take them to the Bondo as they wished. The time came. The time was that called the great Monday. On that day she was to begin the Bondo for the rats, for those who came from *Dugutharuma.*

When the great Monday came, she lined them all up. The rats who were in the bush, they had their own names. Each one had a name—Mabela, Barongko, Bakingking, Bapopo; they all came to be put into the Bondo by the cat. On the great Monday the cat told them that they were to line themselves up. But, she said, in her Bondo, everyone she put into the Bondo, whoever was put in—was not to look behind her, only to look forward and to go forward. She took the broom.[1] She said, 'Line up!' They all lined up, the rats. Mabela was in front; she was the clever one among the rats. She [the cat] sang the song. 'The song I sing—when I sing you are to reply to me the same way'—meaning the rats. They said they agreed.

Then she sang, 'When we go, let no one look behind oh, when the cat is free *fo feŋ*.' 'When we go, let no one look behind oh, when the cat is free *fo feŋ*. . . .'[2]

The reason for the cat doing this—behold it was to find a way to catch the rats one by one and to eat them.

[1] One of the symbols of the Bondo leader's authority.

[2] The song is repeated many times over by the narrator then the audience in turn.

When she caught those who were at the back, she finished eating them all. She sang the whole song. Mabela, the one in front, noticed that the song was coming near her now, she recognized the cat's voice now. 'When we go, let no one look behind oh, when the cat is free *fo feŋ*.' 'When we go, let no one look behind oh, when the cat is free *fo feŋ*.'

Mabela now, she turned round behind her to see her sisters now—they had all been eaten up! She saw she was the only one left. *Gbarathi*, she threw herself out of the way! She went off into the bush. She became clever.

Thus are the foolish ones compared to the clever ones. No one will become clever unless someone shows him cleverness. . . . That is it, it is finished.

The finch's loan

FANKA KONTEH. *Dictated* 4.12.61

A story about two birds that are well known in every village—the finch picks away near the cooking place at the food also sought by the hen; and every now and then there are shouts and running to rescue chickens from the hawks that try to swoop down to carry them off.

The moral is the common one about tale-telling (*yaŋfa*) and the story resembles *The sun, the hawk, and the hen*, and, in part, *Kanu and palm wine*.

A FINCH went and borrowed a loan from a hawk. 'But', he said, 'now when I am borrowing this loan, I am only a child. Well now; when I grow big, I will repay you the loan.' The hawk said, 'All right; that is no trouble. When you grow big, you will repay me the loan.' The hawk gave him the loan.

One year passed. The hawk went: 'Finch, I have come for the loan.' The finch came out, from his little house. 'What? Hawk, I have not grown big yet.' The hawk went away.

The hawk went and sat down again, for one year. He went again, he the hawk, going for the loan. He went—'Finch, I have come now today for the loan.' The finch came out again. 'What, hawk? I told you before—when I have grown big I will pay the loan. I have not got big yet. Go away.'[1] The hawk went away again.

A year passed. The hawk got up again, going for the loan. He came. 'Finch, I have come today for the loan. It has now come to two years—even now you have not got big. I have come today for the loan.' The finch came out. 'Hawk, I told you before that when I am big I will pay

[1] As the story proceeds the finch is shown getting angrier and angrier in would-be righteous indignation at the unreasonable demands of the hawk.

you the loan. But I am not big yet. Go away. When I have grown big I will pay you the loan.' The hawk went back. He went and stayed there.

Another year passed. He got up again, he the hawk, to go to the finch for the loan. 'Finch, I have come today for the loan.' 'Hawk, I told you before that when I am big I will pay you the loan. Go away.' The hawk set out home, he began to go back.

There was a hen that he was always passing. The hen took no notice of him. She had asked him no questions. When the hawk began to go back, the hen asked him, 'Hawk, why have you been going along here all these years, always passing me? What is the real reason why you go past here?' The hawk said, 'The finch borrowed a loan from me, he said, "When I grow big I will repay you the loan."' Then the hen said, 'What, the finch? he stays that size. He will not grow big. He is old by now. He will not grow, that is his size. Don't keep going there: you will always find him that size. He will not grow beyond that size.' Then the hawk said, 'Really? Is that the truth?' 'Yes. The finch, I have told you that the finch is that size. Even if you went there after a hundred years the finch would be that size.'

The hawk got up. 'Eee! Behold the finch has tricked me. Behold, he is old already.' The hawk went. 'Finch, I have come for the loan.' The finch said, 'I will not repay you the loan until I am big.' The hawk said, 'It's a lie! You are old already. You have been lying to me the whole time. You are old already. Pay! If you don't pay me the loan, I won't allow it!' The finch said, 'I am not old yet.' The hawk said, 'That is a lie, you are old already. The hen told me you stay that size, that you will not grow big, that even if I kept coming here for a hundred years I would find you the same size. The hen told me.' Then the finch said, 'Ooh! is that what the hen said?' 'Yes.' 'Oh. Well let me tell you: that loan—it was for the hen that I borrowed the loan. Go to the hen, say she is to pay me back the loan. Say that "It was for you the finch borrowed that loan."'

But the hen said, 'It was not for me that he borrowed the loan. He is telling a lie.' The hawk said, 'If you don't pay me the loan, you hen, I won't allow it. I will carry off your children.' The hen said, 'It was not for me he borrowed the loan. Go to him. Let *him* pay you.' The hawk said, 'It was for you.' Before the hen could say, 'It's a lie', he caught the hen's child, he carried it off, he went and ate it. The sun rose again, he [the hawk] came. 'Hen, pay me the loan.' The hen said, 'I am not due to repay you any loan.' The hawk again caught one of her children, he carried it off.

The hen was left with the paying of the loan she had not borrowed. It was because of her tale-telling. Thus tale-telling is bad. If you go tale-telling against someone, it will finish against you. That was what the hen got—repaying the loan she had not borrowed.

The sun, the hawk, and the hen

FANKA KONTEH. *Dictated* 30.11.61

A similar plot to that of *The finch's loan* and also to several other versions I heard where the details differed (one, for example, was about a finch and an eagle, in which the hen was given to the eagle as his slave by the finch). The concluding moral (about 'tale-telling'—*yaŋfa*) is a common one.

THE sun once went and borrowed a loan from a hawk. When he said now that he would go and recover the debt from the sun, when he had flown up for far, he met with the sun—it was hot. He came back. When the sun rose again, as he was trying again to go and recover the debt, he met again with the sun—it was hot. He came back.

One day now, the hen asked him, 'Hawk, where are you always going?' 'I am going to recover my debt from the sun, but we always meet each other when he is hot, and I am not able to go.' Then the hen said, 'Do you not know the time?' 'No.' 'Well, spend the night here with me'—it was the hen speaking—'Well, when I crow in the morning, very early, if you get up just then, you will meet with him just then before he has put on his hot gown. Well, you will meet him.'

The hawk spent the night. In the morning the hen crowed. 'All right. Go. You will meet him today now, he will not have put on his hot gown.' The hawk got up. He flew. The sun was just about to put on his hot gown when the hawk arrived. 'E! Sun! I was always coming, but when we met I was not able to reach you.' Then the sun said, 'Who told you the time?' 'Oh, the hen told me.' 'Ah! Well, go to the hen. Tell him, "The sun says that the loan I came and borrowed for you, you are to pay me now; it was for you the sun borrowed the loan."'

The hawk came to the hen. 'Ha! The sun said that you were to come and pay me the loan, that it was for you that he had borrowed it.' 'He did not borrow a loan for me. He is telling a lie.' The hawk said, 'It was for you.' The hen said, 'It was not for me.' While the hen was still speaking saying, 'It was not for me', he seized a young hen, he carried it off, he ate it.

When the sun rose again, he said, 'I have come for the loan.' While the hen was saying, 'It was not for me' he seized another young hen, he went off. The hen was left to pay the loan that she had not borrowed, for telling tales against someone. Thus tale-telling is bad. That is why the hen got the debt that she had not borrowed, because of tale-telling. It ended up against her.

4 · SHORTER FORMS

1 · 'Proverbs'

The hen is hatched in the grain (*thɛ gbeŋke ka ŋatɛkɛyaŋ*).[1]

Said of someone born in fortune, 'born with a silver spoon in his mouth'. This saying is sometimes used when pleading for someone; the implication is that he should be forgiven since, unlike the hen, he was not born in the grain.

Do not shoot the chimpanzee for his ugliness (*or* Will you pursue the chimpanzee, so that you kill him because of his ugliness?) (*ba haŋ pɛthi na nɛnie wundɛ;* or *e yemine pɛthi na ba na nɛnɔi ndɛ yi kɔŋ ni kɔri?*).

Used to plead, e.g., for a child: however bad he is, one should not go to extremes in scolding or punishing him.

The female hen will not crow (*or* The female hen will not crow in Biriwa; *or* The female hen will not crow, only the cock) (*thɛ wobɔnda sa kokori;* or *thɛ wobɔnda sa kokori ka Biriwa;* or *thɛ wobɔnda sa kokori yɔkɔŋ koki*).

Refers to the fact that the Mandingo strangers will never become chiefs in Biriwa, only the Limba who have the right to authority there through their fathers. (See chapter 2, p. 43.)

You want something big—like an ant-heap getting a felt hat; it did not go to Freetown (*yi thimo bei babuguyɛ, ma hunithi, ba hunithi a nio fɛlɛti; wundɛ kai ta ka Kampi*).

Of someone putting on airs without justification. For explanation see chapter 2, pp. 41–42.

Water will not dry up (*masere sa duthu*).

A reference to the money and goods paid in bridewealth. It will never cease coming because all husbands, even a new husband after a divorce, must pay this bridewealth.

[1] This and several other of these sayings were written for me by Mr. Thomas Kargbo in Tonko Limba (where they are called *thaiŋ*), and the comments in quotations are his.

Walking in a European way with a loin cloth (*or* Do not walk in a European way with a loin cloth) (*a yathi maporotho, kufama;* or *ba yathi maporotho, kufama*).

Of someone putting on airs when he is in fact poor or inexperienced. This is analogous to someone wearing the long flapping loin cloth worn only by small boys yet thinking he can walk with the pride of a European. 'A white man is associated with pomposity, pride, and wealth; and it is ridiculous for anyone without the same amount of wealth to put on the airs of the European.'

Do not give a fool an onion to peel (*ba duŋkune wɔ thɔkɔi huyaba ba kumpa*).

'An onion consists of a series of "skins", and the fool cannot differentiate between the edible portion and the dry skin. In other words, a delicate job should not be left in the hands of an unskilled person.'

An ordinary person does not know a rosary (*pɔmpɔdi kɔta bɔlisa*).

Someone with normal sight (without 'clear' eyes or 'double eyes') cannot recognize the *bɔlisa*, i.e. 'chaplet or rosary of Roman Catholics and other people with supernatural abilities. About the same sense as "casting pearls before swine".'

A stranger will not share out the rice-flour (*thahine sa hani dɛkɛ*).

Just as a stranger does not know the people to whom rice-flour should be shared out after a ritual, so he does not know the details of local affairs and cannot speak wisely about them. Someone may say this if he is asked to speak in public about some case; if he just uses this sentence people will understand that he does not consider himself qualified to speak.

A dog is caught for his own misdeed (*kutheŋ bɔyɔkɔi kasi nama*).

i.e. a dog possesses nothing, he can't pay, he can't speak; so the only thing is for him to be beaten. This may be said to the father when a small child has broken something and been beaten for it. It is also sometimes said by a wife's relations if her husband had beaten her for something and she has gone home to complain; if he has been in the right her relations tell her this, signifying that she has not been beaten for no good reason.

2. Riddles[1]

Gbekeŋ gbakaŋ—The axe comes out of the tree (*gbekeŋ gbakaŋ, kubapi ko kaŋɔi ka nimbo*).

i.e. the sound recalls the noise and reverberating echo made by chopping a tree with an axe.

[1] See the discussion of riddles in chapter 2, p. 41.

Kikiri kɔkɔrɔ—A pregnant woman cannot climb a hill (*kikiri kɔkɔrɔ—bafɔlɛ sa duŋkɔ ka kusɛri*).

i.e. the sound of the first two words suggests the great size of the pregnant woman and the way she is therefore not capable of moving round easily.

Two other versions are: *kikiri kɔkɔrɔ*, do you know that?—A pregnant woman cannot carry another (*kikiri kɔkɔrɔ, e beŋ kɔthɛŋ kiŋ? bafɔlɛ sa ŋgbande*); *kikiri kɔkɔrɔ*—A pregnant woman cannot climb a palm tree (*kikiri kɔkɔrɔ—bafɔyɛ sa duŋkɔ ka hutaa*).

Quiver quiver behind, quiver quiver before—The sticks carried by an old person (*thɔlɛ thɔlɛ kahɛŋ, thɔlɛ thɔlɛ ka kɔtɔkɔi . . .*).

When people come back from the farm they often carry a bundle of long sticks for firewood which project and quiver before and behind them.

Kindiliŋ kandalaŋ kandi kɔndɔlɔŋ, this is my incantation for hunting buffaloes—Can you put a sword in your pocket? (*kindiliŋ kandalaŋ kandi kɔndɔlɔŋ, keriaŋ bɛna ba yenke tatiŋ—e kɔŋ thii silanhi ka gboti?*)

Another acoustic riddle written for me by Mr. Kargbo. He explains it: 'The unwary audience will hardly realize that *kindiliŋ kandalaŋ*, etc., refers to the struggle in attempting to put the sword in the pocket.'

Seŋsekede—You cannot put a needle on a rock (*seŋsekede—yiŋ sa ki masande ka gbore baŋ*).

i.e. a needle cannot be made to stand upright on a rock; the sound seems to suggest the way the needle falls over.

I have tied water in a bundle—Orange (*yuku mandi sondo—hunimpiri*).

Father's trousers were burnt but the belt was not burnt—A path. (*yaŋkira ba papa tɔki kɛrɛ mbumbusu ki tha tɔki—gboŋa*).

i.e. the bush for the farm was burnt, but the path there was not burnt.

The girl Yenken is coming—The dew (*hatibɛthɔ Yeŋken se—mapɔthɛ*).

i.e. of what does the young girl Yenken fresh from initiation remind one? Answer: of the freshness and beauty of the dew.

A story (or riddle—*mbɔrɔ*) for you. The children of my father once went on a journey. They went, two of them. When they were coming back you could not count them—hundreds, hundreds, hundreds, thirty. It is finished—Groundnuts (*mbɔrɔ bena. Mpati be papa bindɛ bi na kaiyɛ nde kubiasi. Bindɛ ke biiye. Bi si nda se ba kɔndi yi sa puŋku. Kɛmɛŋ, kɛmɛŋ, kɛmɛŋ, kɔhi katati. Wung thaŋki—Mandɛrɛ*).

i.e. when you put the two parts of the nut into your mouth and chew, the pieces become very many. A similar riddle is told about palm kernels; they begin as one and become hundreds.

A riddle (*mbɔrɔ*) for you. My father's children once came out, going on a journey. When they were going on the journey they were speaking. When they were coming [back] now, dumb—Gourds (*mbɔrɔ bena. Mpati be papa na huŋɛ nde thɔŋ a ke huthahine, bi si ke huthahine haŋ, be gboŋkoyi. Bi si nda se, boboi—Thatoko*).

i.e. when the gourds are carried out in the morning they rattle because they are empty. In the evening when they have been filled with palm wine they are quiet.

The children of the old man—from the time they killed the goat right up to this day the blood lies there. Who knows that? We do not know. See the spider [i.e. we give up]—Have you not seen the seed? From the time when it was burnt there the grass has not come up. Well, that is it (*mpati be yapa, kabi bindɛ kore bahu haŋ hɛ marɛŋ ŋoleŋ kɛndɛ. Mbɛ wo kɔthɛ kiŋ? Miŋ kɔɔta. Ya wosi. E beŋ kuuta sugbu? Kabi kɛndɛ ŋindo bu, kɛndɛ sa nda fuŋ fande. Awa, wuna*).

A reference apparently to the firing of the bush where rice is later sown and the extra grass weeded away by the women.

The children of the old man—since they were born they have not been plaited. Do you know that?—Have you ever seen a palm tree plaited? (*mpati be yapa kabi bindɛ kio bindɛ ŋɛthɔi ta. E beŋ kɔthɛŋ wuŋ?—e yiŋ kuteŋ hutala ŋɛthɔi?*).

i.e. the foliage of a palm tree stands out rather like a woman's hair just before she plaits it.

Two other versions of basically the same riddle are: The children of the old man are never plaited—The palm tree (*mpati be yapa bindɛ sa ŋɛtha—hutala ha*). My father's daughter, since she combed her hair, thus she remains [i.e. unplaited]—The palm tree (*hati papa na pɛki nde thɔŋ bɔyɛ nama nɛ kɔi ma—taa*).

Many soldiers went to war, but the old people were not able to fight, the tiny babies were able to fight. What is that?—Cane grass (*baloŋgboiŋ bemandi be kai ka kuloŋgbo, kɛrɛ bethanthɛ beŋ puŋke ta degila malethe ma mɛna puŋke degila. Mbɛ mu na muŋ?—huthaka*).

This refers to the way the new shoots of the grass are stronger and sharper than the old ones.

APPENDIX I

TEXTS WITH WORD-FOR-WORD TRANSLATION

I append three short texts with literal translations into English. Two are in the well-known Biriwa dialect, one in the Yaka dialect spoken by those in Kakarima.

The words *a*, which qualifies a verb, and *na* when used to emphasize the preceding word, are left untranslated.

1. *The toad and death* (Biriwa dialect)

Kanu na dɔmɛ nde na na yaŋ leheni mafɔi ba Limbaiŋ
Kanu said long-ago that when I make medicine for Limba

be, na ŋka na kati mafɔi ma ka Limbaiŋ be? Bathuthu dome
the, that who carries medicine the to Limba the? Snake said

na yama kati. Hunopo dome na bathuthu tɛ kati na yama kati.
that I carry. Toad said that snake not carry that I carry.

Hunopo segithe mafɔi ma, wundɛ tutɔkɔi. Wundɛ kube ba
Toad took medicine the, he put-on-head. He set-out for

saa. Na male thɔŋ ndɛ, wundɛ male hɛlɛŋ, wundɛ koŋe
to-come. When jumped just he, he jumped again, he spilt

mafɔi ma. Wundɛ koŋ mafɔi ma, wundɛ tha mɛŋ sisi ka
medicine the. He spilt medicine the, he not it bring to

Limbaiŋ be. Wuna bathuthu iŋ hunopo a thalikande. Na
Limba the. Therefore snake and toad quarrel. When

bathuthu kute hunopo na, a bohi niŋ. Na yina tha nde me
snake sees toad, catch him. That you not long-ago allow

ba kata mafɔi ma. Wuna hunopo iŋ bathuthu a thalikande.
for to-carry medicine the. Therefore toad and snake quarrel.

Wuna dɔmɛ nde nda Limbaiŋ siŋ tuku. Mɛnɛ bathuthu sisi
Therefore said long-ago now Limba are die. If snake bring

nɔŋ nde mafɔi ma, Limbaiŋ sa nɔŋ nde tuku. Kɛrɛ
then long-ago medicine the, Limba will-not then long-ago die. But

hunopo tha me. Wundɛ koŋiti mafɔi ma ka gboŋa. Wuna
toad not allow. He spilt medicine the on road. Therefore

bathuthu iŋ hunopo a thalikande.
snake and toad quarrel.

2. *The toad did not love us* (Yaka dialect)

Kunopo, kunopo tha mina thimo. Kanu Masala ko nde fɔsɔi
Toad, toad not us love. Kanu Masala was long-ago squeeze

mahɔi. Wundɛ hɔsɔi mafɔi maŋ, wundɛ ba na sa bia
medicine. He squeeze medicine the, he for that will-not people

kute hutuka. Na kɔnɔ mahɔi maŋ, na mbɛ wo katiɛ Yumbɛŋ?
see dying. That but medicine the, that what who carry-to Limba?

Bathuthu dome, na ma kati. Wuna dome kunopo na ali. Na ma
Snake said that I carry. Then said toad that no. That I

bindɛ katiɛ. Na mina thuriande. Ndɛ nɛnɛ, ha, wundɛ
them carry-to. That we close-to-each-other. He now, ha, he

tha mina thimo. Wundɛ thimo mina ba kɔrua. Wundɛ domo na
not us love. He loved us for to-kill-all. He was-told that

ba hiŋ nda mahɔi maŋ. Wundɛ thɔ mɛŋ ba thɔŋ tutɔkɔ.
for here now medicine the. He entered it for just carry-on-head.

Wundɛ ŋaye ba kaa. Mamalɛ thɔŋ hanthe ma, na tɔliŋ, na bukute
He rose for to-go. Jumping just once the, that *tɔliŋ*, that fell-off

mafɔi maŋ. Ndɛ koŋe mɛŋ. Hŋ. Ba wuŋ tepo nde na
medicine the. He spilt it. Hng. For it was said long-ago that

mahɔi maŋ na na wa ko kata mɛŋ, na ba koŋ nde.
medicine the that if person will carry it, that do-not spill oh.

Bathuthu wo thimo nde mina woŋ, wundɛ tha me ba wundɛ
Snake who loved long-ago us the, he not allow for he

mɛŋ yisa. Wundɛ thɔŋ wo thambo mina woŋ, ndɛ na katiɛ mɛŋ.
it to-bring. He just who hated us the, he carry-to it.

Ndɛ ke tiŋ mɛŋ koŋ. Awa, yi kuteŋ nde nda e miŋ ko
He went just it spill. Well, you see long-ago now and we are

tuka, kunopo na. Kɔrɔ befufɛ, miŋ do Yumbɛŋ, miŋ sa
dying, toad. But white-people, we are Limba, we will-not

nde ndɛ ko tuku, kɔrɔ kunopo baŋa. Miŋ ndai iŋ kunopo, na
long-ago now are die, but toad refuse. We now and toad, when

miŋ thoi nda, kɛ thimo maŋ tiŋ. Wuna miŋ niŋ kanthi. Awa,
we build now, there love he just. Thus we him chase. Well,

bathuthu wo thimoŋ nde mina woŋ, wundɛ ko yeŋkande niŋ,
snake who love long-ago us the, he will pursue him,

a yeŋkande kunopo na. Kunopo kiti kɛntuŋ do. Awa, wo thimo
pursuing toad. Toad runs to-us here. Well, who love

nde mina woŋ, awa na ndɛ peŋke nda mina, miŋ niŋ a kɔri.
long-ago us the, well, when he find now us, we him kill.

Miŋ sa nda kɔri kunopo na. Awa Kanu kute mina ba wuŋ.
We will-not now kill toad. Well, Kanu sees us for that.

Mɛnɛ yiŋ dome nɛ na yiŋ do thimo ba yuya, awa, hiŋ na
Since you said now that you are want for to-hear, well, here-is that

miŋ niŋ kunopo. Huna, lɔŋthaŋ.
we and toad. That, finished.

3. *Contest in strength* (Biriwa dialect)

Kampa na thuŋkunande nde mamɛŋ be ka feli haŋ. Na ŋkaŋ
Elephant called-together once animals the of bush the. That let-us-go

ka nia magbɔma. Bindɛ kai. Bindɛ kai dɔŋɔ, mamɛŋ be foma.
to make discussion. They went. They went sat, animals the all.

Bindɛ kai dɔŋɔ. Kampa dome na yama yoŋine bena. Na ba
They went sat. Elephant said that I called you. That why

yoŋine yaŋ bena, na ba miŋ se gbuŋkande ba nia hukaiba.
called I you, that for us come compete for to-do strength.

Na huna yoŋine yaŋ bena. Mamaiŋ be foma dome na alɔhɔ.
That that-is-why called I you. Animals the all said that good.

Na mbɛ malɔkɔ? Na ka yaraba. Na awa.
That what time? That on Wednesday. That all-right.

Bindɛ paŋande. Malɔkɔ ma fuŋande ma ka yaraba. Bindɛ
They parted. Time the arrived the on Wednesday. They

thɛrɛŋ ba saa. Bakɔ tɛŋ. Wundɛ dɔŋɔi. Toka tɛŋ.
began for to-come. Monkey came. He sat-down. Baboon came.

Wundɛ dɔŋɔi. Pɛthi tɛŋ. Wundɛ dɔŋɔi. Baloma tɛŋ.
He sat-down. Chimpanzee came. He sat-down. Antelope came.

Wundɛ dɔŋɔi. Thambili tɛŋ. Wundɛ dɔŋɔi. Tati tɛŋ.
He sat-down. Leopard came. He sat-down. Bush-cow came.

Wundɛ dɔŋɔi. Kampa se. Wundɛ dɔŋɔi. Limba mɛti tɛŋ.
He sat-down. Elephant came. He sat-down. Limba human came.

Wundɛ dɔŋɔi.
He sat-down.

Wuna dome kampa na ɛ Limba mɛti. Na te thɔkɔti hɛ
Then said elephant that e Limba human. That how long today

nda miŋ saa te, na dɔŋɔ hɛ nda thuŋ ka sitha yina. Na
now we to-come how, that sit today now just to wait you. That

yɔkɔŋ na yiŋ thɔŋ madɔi saa. Na yina sithe hɛ yi miŋ.
but that you just long to-come. That you wait today you we.

Yina pɛ ba saa. Na huna. Limba mɛti tepe na yaŋ se
You last for to-come. That that-is-it. Limba human said that I come

nda. Na yaŋ se hɛ nda. Limba mɛti nɛnɛ siŋ thɔŋ se,
now. That I come today now. Limba human now while just come,

ndɛ diŋe pinkari baŋ. Wundɛ kai rɔgbi bɛŋ ka huyitha ha. Wundɛ
he brought gun the. He went hid it in bush the. He

se. Bindɛ dome na ŋ ŋ, na awa. Na ba gbuŋkande thuŋ
came. They said that yes, that all-right. That for compete just

ba hukaiba ha ho tepe yeheŋ miŋ haŋ, na huna fɛ.
about strength the which said before we the, that that-is-it today.

Mamaiŋ be foma tepe na alɔhɔ.
Animals the all said that good.

Bindɛ dome na awa, bakɔ leŋke. Bakɔ ŋale. Wundɛ
They said that all-right, monkey first. Monkey rose. He

thalande ka kuyeŋ ka. Wundɛ putɔi. Wundɛ thalande hɛlɛŋ
jumped-across to tree to. He bent. He jumped-across again

ka kuyeŋ. Wundɛ se kɔ kapothi. Wundɛ dome na namɛ? na
to tree. He came stood below. He said that how? that

hukaiba tɛ? Bindɛ foma dome na hukaiba hukaiba, hukaiba
strength not? They all said that strength strength, strength

hukaiba. Na awa dɔŋɔ.
strength. That all-right, sit.

Na awa toka. Na ŋale, na tɔŋina hukaiba. Toka ŋale.
That all-right baboon. That rise, that show strength. Baboon rose.

Wundɛ kai ka duŋgbuiŋ ba. Wundɛ kai theŋki lɔŋgbɔ wo. Wundɛ
He went to farms the. He went broke corn the. He

du ka mɛti ka. Wundɛ kai theŋki thaŋki ba. Wundɛ bohe
came-home to village to. He went broke maize the. He caught

thɛni. Wundɛ se ka nthari. Wundɛ se muŋ dɛŋ. Wundɛ
hens. He came at run. He came it put-down. He

dome na namɛ? na hukaiba tɛ? Bindɛ foma dome na hukaiba
said that how? that strength not? They all said that strength,

hukaiba, hukaiba hukaiba. Na dɔŋɔ. Wundɛ dɔŋɔi.
strength, strength strength. That sit. He sat-down.

Na awa, pɛthi, na tɔŋine hukaiba. Pɛthi ŋale.
That all-right, chimpanzee, that show-us strength. Chimpanzee rose.

Wundɛ kai sikili kuyeŋ ko. Wundɛ luke hugbɔgbɔ. Wundɛ toŋe.
He came twisted tree the. He tied knot. He dropped.

Wundɛ thuhu. Wundɛ dome na namɛ? na hukaiba tɛ? Bindɛ
He came-down. He said that how? that strength not? They

foma dome na hukaiba hukaiba, hukaiba hukaiba. Na dɔŋɔ.
all said that strength strength, strength, strength. That sit.

Na awa, thambili. Na tɔŋina hukaiba. Thambili gboke na
That all-right leopard. That show strength. Leopard scratched that

ruki ruki ruki ruki. Bindɛ foma thunɔkɔi, a palɔi. Wundɛ dome na
ruki ruki ruki ruki. They all started, afraid. He said that

namɛ? na e hukaiba tɛ? Ha, na hukaiba hukaiba, hukaiba
how? that is strength not? Ha, that strength strength, strength

hukaiba. Na awa, na dɔŋɔ. Wundɛ dɔŋɔi.
strength. That all-right, that sit. He sat-down.

Na awa, baloma, na tɔŋine hukaiba. Baloma thare, mailiŋ
That all-right, antelope, that show-us strength. Antelope ran, miles

bitati. Ndɛ teŋkilege. Wundɛ se kɔ. Na namɛ? na e hukaiba
three. He returned. He came stood. That how? that is strength

tɛ?
not?

Bindɛ dome na awa, na tati. Na tɔŋine hukaiba.
They said that all-right, that bush-cow. That show-us strength.

Tati ŋale. Kuboli ko nɛnɛ a bɔi. Tati sayaŋ kɛndɛ
Bush-cow rose. Cane-grass the now much. Bush-cow cut there

gboŋa, na raaa. Wu ŋoleke kɛndɛ yina gboŋa ba ka mantoka.
road, that *raaa*. What lay-down there you road the of lorry.

Wundɛ se. Na namɛ? na e hukaiba tɛ? Bindɛ foma dome na
He came. That how? that is strength not? They all said that

hukaiba hukaiba, hukaiba hukaiba, ba kuboli ko sayaŋ tati
strength strength, strength strength, for cane-grass that cut bush-cow

ko. Na dɔŋɔ.
the. That sit.

Na awa kampa. Na tɔŋine hukaiba. Kampa ŋale. Ndɛ
That all-right elephant. That show-us strength. Elephant rose. He

diŋite ŋayeŋ ŋa kɔi ke foma na fɛndɛlɛŋ. Dɛŋ ŋɔti foma
leaned-on trees that stood there all that *fɛndɛlɛŋ*. They fell all

ŋayeŋ ŋa ka diŋite kampa ka. Kampa dome na namɛ?
trees the where leaned-on elephant where. Elephant said that how?

na e hukaiba tɛ? Bindɛ foma dome na a, na hukaiba hukaiba,
that is strength not? They all said that a, that strength strength,

hukaiba hukaiba.
strength strength.

Na awa Limba mɛti. Na tɔŋina hukaiba.
That all-right Limba human. That show strength.

Limba mɛti ŋale. Wundɛ dapilɔkɔi, wundɛ dapilɔkɔi. Wundɛ
Limba human rose. He whirled, he whirled. He

dapilɔkɔi hɛlɛŋ. Wundɛ se kɔ. Wundɛ dome na namɛ? Na
whirled again. He came stood. He said that how? That

hukaiba tɛ? Na ŋ. Na iŋ na kaiba tɛ thɔŋ nde. Na mɛnɛ
strength not? That no. That no that strength not just oh. That if

huna patɛ, na hukaiba tɛ thɔŋ nde. Na tɔŋine hukaiba.
that is-finished, that strength not just oh. That show-us strength.

Limba mɛti kai, wundɛ kai bohe kuyeŋ ko. Wundɛ duŋkɔi
Limba human went, he went took tree the. He climbed

kabegede, ndɛ thuhu, na namɛ? na hukaiba tɛ? Na ŋ ŋ.
above, he came-down, that how? that strength not? That no.

Na mɛnɛ huna patɛ thɔŋ na hukaiba tɛ. Na tɔŋina hukaiba.
That if that is-finished just that strength not. That show strength.

Limba mɛti kai ka rogbɛ wundɛ piŋkari ba ka huyitha ha.
Limba human went where hid he gun the in bush the.

Wundɛ kai dɔŋɔ mafɛŋ ka huyitha ha. Ndɛ segithe piŋkari ba. Ndɛ
He went sat behind to bush the. He took gun the. He

neke kampa na, na tiiŋ. Wundɛ faŋe na loŋkaŋ. Kampa wo
looked-at elephant, that *tiiŋ*. He shot that *loŋkaŋ*. Elephant the

ŋɔti.
fell.

Wundɛ si se haŋ ba dɔma na e hukaiba tɛ? mamaiŋ be
He while come the for to-say that is strength not? animals the

homa thareke. Bindɛ ka nda dɔŋ ha na woŋ daŋkande hukaiba
all ran-away. They in now say ha that this-one surpass strength

ho kɔrɛ wa haŋ—ka nthare nda. Wumɔ wumɔ nda a ni
which kill someone the—in running now. Everyone now make

kaba ba wu koro kampa woŋ iŋ Limba mɛti. Namɛ,
surprise for that was-killed elephant the by Limba human. How,

hukaiba tɛ?
strength not?

APPENDIX II

LIST OF NARRATORS

I have given the list of narrators in alphabetical order of first names, followed by brief notes. Unfortunately about some of them I have few details; those given refer, unless otherwise indicated, to 1961.

The number of stories by each narrator included in the present volume is given in brackets after each name.

ABU KANU (1). Youngish man from Kamabai. He had worked for some years in Freetown where he had not succeeded in making much money, but had learnt Krio. Rather soft-voiced and slow-moving, he could tell a story with great pathos.

ALI SISAY (1). Biriwa man, probably in early thirties, had been away from home for some years, mainly working as a lorry apprentice, much attracted to the bright lights of the town. He spoke Krio, and used many Krio words in his Limba. He told his story with great vigour with special emphasis on all the humorous episodes.

BANKOLO MANSARAY (5). Middle-aged man in Kamabai, related to one of household heads. He enjoyed telling stories, which he did with calm competence and attention to plot rather than with dramatic vigour.

BIASI LOBA (1). Middle-aged household head in Kamabai.

BOKARI SAIO (i.e. Bokari the son of Saio) (1). Man in Kakarima.

BUBU DEMA (3). One of the elders in Kakarima, related to the local chief. An old man of great dignity and kindliness, very fond of his children, wives, and friends. One of his favourite remarks in story or conversation was to comment on the power and unpredictability of Kanu; he liked to generalize and comment with affectionate detachment on the activities of those around him, and to speak well and persuasively to reconcile or advise people.

BUREMA DEMA (3). Household head in Kakarima, middle-aged and vigorous, but on the verge of becoming accepted as almost one of the elders.

DAUDA KONTEH (6). See chapter 4. Son of one of the leading elders in Kamabai, married with several children. He has been totally blind for the last few years, but is still able to farm, dye cloth, and walk about freely—for which he is very much admired. He told stories in a mainly rather quiet tone, but with occasional flashes of excited drama, and a more expressive face and beauty of gesture than I saw with any other story-teller. By 1963 he had developed still further his own characteristic style (see chapter 5, pp. 94–95).

FANKA KONTEH (21). Middle-aged man in Kamabai, who had joined the army and gone abroad during the war. In 1961 he had no land, thus could not farm, and felt a grievance about this. He was very devoted to his small son, but his wife had left him and gone off down country. He was efficient and responsible and, because of his army training and knowledge of some English, liked working for Europeans. He was employed as my 'watchman' in Kamabai, thus giving an opportunity for him to dictate or record many stories in the evenings. He told the stories in a relatively quiet and straightforward way, without many songs or elaborate imitations, but with a few semi-chants, vehement exaggeration, and, usually, stress on a clearly structured plot. On the whole, he seems to have preferred the animal stories.

FODE KAMARA (1). An oldish man from Bafodea who knew many Sierra Leone languages, including a certain amount of English. He had worked for Europeans as a cook for many years. He had a rather beautiful singing voice which he used with pride and effect in his stories.

GBELU WUTIA (1). A small and not very strong youth in Kakarima; though he was initiated and thus in theory a man, he was plagued by those younger than himself. He also had rather bad eyes, which gave him an unusual appearance. He claimed to be able to divine, and was building up a following among his contemporaries and juniors, who, in this context, did take him seriously. He told his stories rather briefly and haltingly.

GBOSO DEMA (1). Household head in Kakarima with several wives and children. He was Niaka's elder brother, but did not share his artistic accomplishments in either singing or story-telling. In the story he told, the emphasis was rather on the ridiculous and boisterous side of the plot than on, e.g., the meditative side (as Bubu would have done) or on the beauty of language or repetition (as would have been evident in a story of Niaka's).

KABI KANU (2). Boy in Kamabai, lorry apprentice. Though young, he told stories with most expressive face and gestures and took every opportunity to go and hear stories told by older men.

KARANKE DEMA (17). For description see chapter 4. He greatly enjoyed telling stories, and used to derive obvious enjoyment from the flavour of the words themselves. He told stories with very versatile artistry, varying from quiet pathos, emotion or moralizing, to violent drama or excitement, accompanying the narration with the frequent introduction of songs. On the whole he seems to have preferred stories about people, possibly because these gave more opportunities for expansion and elaboration.

KELFA KONTEH (2). A young man from Kamabai, on holiday from his teachers' training college, and thus the most highly educated of the narrators here. He was among the most popular of the story-tellers I encountered, mainly because of his powers of vivid imitation, drama, and exaggerations of tone, pace, and surprise.

KIRINKOMA KONTEH (1). Young man from Kamabai, younger brother of Dauda Konteh. He had spent several years in the diamond area and in 1963–4 was merely making a short visit home for Christmas. Compared with most people in Kamabai he was very well-off and was helping to pay for the building of a family house for his old father Fane Konteh. He took a real interest in national politics and, like the new chief, was a Muslim. He also knew how to charm the older people in the village and used to spend hours sitting listening to the oldest of the women there telling him about her young days. He enjoyed talking and telling stories, and particularly insisted on a good audience and chorus for his singing.

KOLOI DEMA (1). Boy in Kakarima, rather serious and responsible, who depicted his stories with great care.

KUMARU DEMA (1). One of the older sons of the chief at Kakarima, now taking very seriously the need to learn the traditional rituals and speeches. He was ambitious to be counted as no longer among the younger men, and was always rather busy.

LAMINA MANSARAY (1). Connected with the ruling house in Kabala. He had travelled extensively down country. He was greatly excited by the drama and content of his own stories, and told them with a great air of conviction and realism.

MASE KARGBO (1). The senior wife of the Paramount Chief of Wara Wara Yagala, a most vigorous, expansive, and powerful personality. She greatly enjoyed singing, and had the children well organized to reply to her song.

MUSU KONTEH (1). A youngish woman in Kamabai, totally blind; quiet and affectionate and rather popular with everyone. She had been greatly influenced by the local mission, and knew the words of all the mission hymns (Limba) by heart. She told her stories in a rather quiet tone, but with confidence and considerable amusement, often interrupting herself to laugh and laugh.

NABENI DEMA (4). A small boy in Kakarima, very clever and artistic. He used to accompany Karanke Dema on his *ŋkali* drum, and his playing was regarded as rather good. He used to tell stories with tremendous concentration and pleasure, with a quiet voice and pleased smile.

NIAKA DEMA (10). For description see chapter 4. He was particularly proud of the fund of Limba stories that he was able to tell, night after night, and was fond of singing and repetition. He was very ready to adapt tone and representation to the nature of the subject, whether rather quiet and moving, or boisterous and dramatic.

SANGBANG YELEME (2). One of the older boys in Kakarima, not yet initiated in spite of his age; this made his position a rather unhappy one. He had been to school for a short while, but was ill with his stomach for so long that it was decided that 'the dead' did not agree to this, and his younger brother was sent instead. He was ambitious and rather frustrated, with a tremendous imagination which half-convinced himself at times. He was also a great actor, and used this in his story-telling; and he could put on a charm that could entice almost anything out of people.

SELI KONTEH (1). A man in Biriwa who had travelled for some years. He was always smiling, brisk, and neat about his clothes, and a great player of the local form of draughts. By 1963, when his kinsman had become chief, he had been accepted as one of the close circle round the chief with much responsibility in the chiefdom.

SURI DEMA (2). Boy in Kakarima, cousin of Karanke's. In 1963 he had gone to Kabala to try to make money there, but was finding work very difficult to get. Usually rather quiet and more liable to listen than to tell stories, but occasionally coming out with an elaborate and carefully executed one.

SURI KAMARA (2). My assistant in the field. He had spent several years at a mission school, and could speak and write some English. He was partly Temne, and had an affection for that language too, but had been brought up in a Limba area. He regarded himself primarily as a driver, a profession he had followed for many years previously. He had been in the army for some time, and had there acquired a great liking for what he considered European ways, and was efficient and an excellent talker, though sometimes considered rather over-bearing by other Limba. He told stories with great vehemence and drama, always emphasizing the excitement or strength rather than subtle characterization or pathos.

SURIBA KONTEH (3). Related to the ruling house in Bumban where he was living. He had been in the army for some years and had there acquired the nickname of 'Nevertire'. He told stories with particularly vivid characterization and great verve.

YAYA DEMA (1). A hunter in Kakarima, oldest son of the chief. He was known to be a 'traveller' and to refuse to settle, and had gone as far as Conakry to find work. Very artistic, plausible, and charming, but said to be a bit irresponsible.

SELECT BIBLIOGRAPHIES

1. *Oral literature*

W. R. Bascom. 'West Africa and the Complexity of Primitive Cultures', *American Anthropologist*, l, 1948.

——'Folklore and Anthropology', *Journal of American Folklore*, lxvi, 1953.

——'Verbal Art', Ibid., lxviii, 1955.

R. Benedict. *Zuni Mythology*. 2 vols. New York, 1935.

J. Berry. *Spoken Art in West Africa*. London, 1961.

H. M. and N. K. Chadwick. *The Growth of Literature*. 3 vols. Cambridge, 1932–40.

L. Dégh. 'Some Questions of the Social Function of Story-telling', *Acta Ethnographica*, vi, 1958.

J. H. Delargy. 'The Gaelic Story-Teller', *Proceedings of the British Academy*, xxxi, 1945.

R. M. Dorson. 'Oral Styles of American Folk Narrators', In ed. T. A. Sebeok, *Style in language*. New York, 1960.

M. M. Green. 'The Unwritten Literature of the Igbo-speaking Peoples of South-Eastern Nigeria', *Bulletin of the School of Oriental and African Studies*, xii, 1948.

S. W. Koelle. *African Native Literature; or Proverbs, Tales, Fables, and Historical Fragments in the Kanuri or Bornu Language*. London, 1854.

A. B. Lord. *The Singer of Tales*. Cambridge, Mass., 1960.

B. Malinowski. *Myth in Primitive Psychology*. London, 1926.

V. Propp. *Morphology of the Folktale*. Transl. L. Scott. Bloomington, 1958.

P. Radin. *African Folktales and Sculpture*. New York, 1953.

R. S. Rattray. *Akan-Ashanti Folk-tales*. Oxford, 1930.

C. F. Schlenker. *A Collection of Temne Traditions, Fables and Proverbs*. London, 1861.

S. Thompson. *The Folktale*. New York, 1946.

—— *Motif-index of Folk-literature*. Revised ed., 6 vols. Copenhagen, 1955–8.

W. H. Whiteley. *A Selection of African Prose*. 1. Traditional oral texts. Oxford, 1964.

2. *The Limba*

J. Berry. 'Nominal Classes in Hu-Limba', *Sierra Leone Studies*, xi, 1958.

—— 'A Note on Voice and Aspect in Hu-Limba', Ibid., xiii, 1960.

M. L. Clarke. *Limba-English Dictionary*. Freetown, 1929.

R. H. FINNEGAN. 'Limba Religious Vocabulary', *Sierra Leone Language Review*, ii, 1963.

—— 'The Traditional Concept of Chiefship among the Limba', *Sierra Leone Studies*, xvii, 1963.

—— ' "Swears" among the Limba', *Sierra Leone Bulletin of Religion*, vi, 1, 1964.

—— *Survey of the Limba people of Northern Sierra Leone*. H.M.S.O., 1965. (Includes select bibliography on the Limba.)

C. A. KING-HARMAN. *Visits to the Protectorate*. London, 1902.

M. MCCULLOCH. *The Peoples of Sierra Leone Protectorate*. London, 1950.

E. F. SAYERS. Notes on the Native Language Affinities in Sierra Leone, *Sierra Leone Studies* (old series), x, 1927.

D. H. WESTERMANN and M. A. BRYAN. *Languages of West Africa*. London, 1952.

www.ingramcontent.com/pod-product-compliance
Lightning Source LLC
LaVergne TN
LVHW020527100826
845148LV00010B/1372

* 9 7 8 1 5 3 2 6 4 5 0 5 1 *